Chuck
with all my
love Sally

FATHER ELIJAH

An Apocalypse

MICHAEL D. O'BRIEN

FATHER ELIJAH

An Apocalypse

IGNATIUS PRESS   SAN FRANCISCO

Cover art by Michael D. O'Brien
Cover design by Roxanne Mei Lum
David Schäfer's Vision

Awake, and strengthen what remains and is on the point of death. . . .
(Revelation 3:2)

Contents

Acknowledgments

I am indebted to the Polish Canadian poet Christopher Zakrzewski for his translations of *The Crimean Sonnets* by Adam Mickiewicz, for permission to quote from them in *Father Elijah,* and for his editorial assistance. I am also most grateful to Marc Sebanc, translator, essayist, and novelist, for his wise insights and honesty. Above all, I wish to thank my wife, Sheila, whose editorial sense is unsurpassed, and whose patience as I stare glassy-eyed over many a meal will one day be rewarded.

Introduction

An apocalypse is a work of literature dealing with the end of human history. For millennia apocalypses of various sorts have arisen throughout the world in the cultural life of many peoples and religions. They are generated by philosophical speculation, by visions of the future, or by inarticulate longings and apprehensions, and not infrequently by the abiding human passion for what J. R. R. Tolkien called "sub-creation". These poems, epics, fantasies, myths, and prophetic works bear a common witness to man's transient state upon the earth. Man is a stranger and sojourner. His existence is inexpressibly beautiful—and dangerous. It is fraught with mysteries that beg to be deciphered. The Greek word *apokalypsis* means an uncovering, or revealing. Through such revelations man gazes into the panorama of human history in search of the key to his identity, in search of permanence and completion.

Perhaps the worst of the "demythologizing" so endemic to our times is the message that the stories of the Christian Faith are merely our version of universal "myths". It is suggested that many cultures have produced tales about a hero who is killed and then returns to life; many more have imagined a cataclysm that will occur at the end of history. G. K. Chesterton once wrote that the demythologizers' position really adds up to this: since a truth has impressed itself deeply in the imagination of a vast number of ancient peoples, therefore it simply cannot be true. He pointed out that the demythologizer has failed to examine the most important consideration of all: that people of various times and places may have been informed at an intuitive level of actual events that would one day take place in history; that in their inner longings there was a glimmer of light, a presentiment, a yearning forward through the medium of art toward the fullness of Truth that would one day be made flesh in the Incarnation. Saint John's Revelation is an apocalypse of a higher order. It is genuine prophecy in the sense that it is not merely a work of foretelling, but is a communication from the Lord of history Himself. It is an exhortation, an encouragement, a teaching vehicle, and a vision of actual events that will one day occur.

As the drama of our century speeds toward some unknown climax, numerous speculations arise and new attention is given to John's Apocalypse, stimulating a plethora of interpretation. One school of thought has it that the book refers solely to John's own time; another asserts that it is exclusively a meditation on the end of things in some indeterminate future; still another believes that the book is a map of the Church's history, unfolded in seven major epochs. A fourth interpretation, one favored by most of the Church Fathers, holds that it is a theological vision of a vast spiritual landscape, containing descriptions of the situation of the Church in John's own time, and also the events that are to unfold at the end of time. For John, the "end times" *begin* with the Incarnation of Christ into the world, and there remains only a last battle through which the Church must pass.

This, in my view, is the fullest and best interpretation, and it is the one I have followed in *Father Elijah*. The reader will encounter here an apocalypse in the old literary sense, but one that was written in the light of Christian revelation. It is a speculation, a work of fiction. It does not attempt to predict certain details of the final Apocalypse so much as to ask how human personality would respond under conditions of intolerable tension, in a moral climate that grows steadily chillier, in a spiritual state of constantly shifting horizons. The near future holds for us many possible variations on the apocalyptic theme, some more dire than others. I have presented only one scenario. And yet, the central character is plunged into a dilemma that would face him in any apocalypse. He finds himself *within* the events that are unfolding, and thus he is faced with the problem of perception: how to see the hidden structure of his chaotic times, how to step outside it and to view it objectively while remaining within it as a participant, as an agent for the good.

The reader should be forewarned that this book is a novel of ideas. It does not proceed at the addictive pace of a television micro-drama, nor does it offer simplistic resolutions and false piety. It offers the Cross. It bears witness, I hope, to the ultimate victory of light.

I

Carmel

Brother Ass found Father Elijah in the onion garden. The old monk was hoeing, sweating under his straw bonnet, and the young brother felt a moment of pity for him.

"Father Prior wants you."

"Thank you, Brother."

"You're to go right now, he says. Don't worry about washing up. Come right away." His words spilled out all ajumble, as they usually did. He was referred to as Brother Ass because of his simplicity and his preference for any household task that could be accomplished by beasts of burden. Elijah thought of him as *the small one.*

"Hurry, hurry", he nagged. His good eye was laughing; the other was scarred and set in a permanent wink. He was a Christian Palestinian, a gangly, uncomplicated boy who did not mind being insignificant.

He was not held in esteem by most of the fathers and brothers. He was sloppy and forgot the Rule almost every day—although he was always sincerely repentant. Their attitude toward him was usually patient; at its worst, and then only rarely, it was condescending. Elijah liked him very much, and between them there was a sincere, if detached, affection.

"I happen to know, Father, that a big telephone call came from Italy an hour ago. Brother Sylvester told me when we passed in the hall after prayers."

He clapped a hand over his mouth, and his one good eye contorted in shame.

"I'm sure that you and Brother Sylvester didn't mean to break the Silence", said Elijah.

"That's right Father, we didn't mean to break the Silence."

"And I'm sure that tomorrow you will remember to keep the Rule perfectly."

"Yes, tomorrow I will keep the Rule perfectly."

"God sees your heart. He knows that you love Him."

The small one nodded emphatically.

"When you are praying, when you are asking Him to remind you of things, please pray for me so that I may keep the Rule perfectly?"

"I will, Father."

"I am grateful for your prayers."

"Thank you, Father."

They parted in the hallway outside the prior's office. The small one bustled off to the church where he would kneel before the Presence and ask pardon for yet another day in which he had failed to avoid transgression.

Elijah knocked.

The prior said, *Enter.* Elijah did so, and waited. The prior bid him be seated. He was a German. His high, domed forehead, solemn features, and thoughtful gray eyes rightly belonged in the face of a scholastic, perhaps a northern Benedictine. But Elijah had long ago learned not to judge by appearances. This prior in particular was not what he seemed. He stood by the window overlooking the Bay of Haifa, watching the sun fall into the sea.

"It is most irregular, Father Elijah. I do not feel peace about it."

"About what, Father Prior?"

"Your namesake dwelt on this holy mountain three thousand years ago. He came here to listen for the voice of God."

Elijah waited, knowing there would be more forthcoming. The wind rummaged uneasily in the grape arbors.

"He heard it in a gentle breeze, not in rushing about the world looking for *projects*. Our vocation is a call to listening. To adoration of the One who dwells among us. That is why you came here. That is why you were born."

Elijah nodded.

"As prior I have been given a grace of discernment for my spiritual sons. And I am distressed."

"Are you distressed about me?"

"Excuse me, I have been talking without explaining. A telephone message came today. You are being called to Rome."

"Rome? But our house there is full to overflowing. We are practically empty here."

"You are not being called to the house in Rome. It's to the Vatican."

"The Vatican?"

"I spoke with a senior official in the Secretariat of State this afternoon. He sent the necessary documents by fax shortly afterward. The formal letter of instruction and the information for your flight. You are to meet with certain officials at the secretariat as soon as possible."

"Did he explain the purpose of the trip?"

"Very little. You will be informed when you arrive."

"When do I leave?"

"That is the part which surprises me. The man I spoke with expressed a certain urgency. You leave on the next flight from Ben Gurion. Everything has been arranged. Visa, tickets. Rome arranged the details directly with the Israelis."

"Surely he mentioned the purpose."

"Only that it pertains to archeology."

"Archeology?"

"You have a longstanding interest in archeology do you not, Father?"

"An amateur's interest."

"You have published papers on biblical archeology in international journals."

"Yes, but they weren't exceptional essays. Mere speculations. More a spirituality of biblical archeology than the strict science."

"They seem to have drawn the attention of the Vatican."

"There are no conferences on the subject in the near future. I don't understand the urgency."

"Nor do I." The prior stared at his desk.

"How long will I be gone?"

"The official didn't want to say. He would tell me only that there is work which may demand your absence for a considerable length of time. He said that the duration of the mission was uncertain and that it was of the highest importance."

"What of my theology classes? Who will instruct the novices?"

"Father John can take them."

"I was to preach the retreats at Bethlehem next week."

"I can take them."

Father Prior was a gifted preacher and much in demand. The two men sat in silence for some minutes, listening to the evening birds.

"Can you tell me the source of your distress?"

"I'm not sure. I sense that you are going into grave danger."

"In archeology?"

"We have an extraordinary Pope, a man of the spirit, and heart and intellect—a saint. It has been centuries since we have been given such a shepherd. But he is surrounded by enemies. The Church is in crisis to her very foundations."

"Yes, bleeding from many wounds."

"The worst of these wounds have been inflicted by her own children. Rome is a troubled place right now. A place of shifting illusions."

"You spoke of danger?"

"Yes."

"What kind of danger?"

"The spiritual kind. I tell you, I'm not at peace. I send you to Italy under obedience, for what does our life mean without obedience? Still, I know that I'm sending you into some form of peril."

"I'm not afraid of death."

"Death", said the prior, sighing, "could be the least of dangers."

"May I speak plainly, as son to father?"

"Of course you may. Do you think I fail to see the similarities between us? You are a convert from Judaism chosen by God to become a Carmelite priest—a branch pulled from the fire. And I, a refugee from German atheism. Both exiles who have come home. Brothers."

"I revere you as my father."

"Only three votes would have reversed the chairs in which we are sitting."

"The Holy Spirit chose you."

"And I wouldn't be surprised if He chooses you at the next election. I would die in peace if this were so. But now I don't think it will be."

Father Elijah looked at the prior quizzically. "No?"

"Since the telephone call, I have been praying. And I hear a word that tells me you won't return."

"If that is so, then I'm grieved. This is my only home. You are my friend."

"Friend. I treasure this word from you. Not good to have attachments, is it? But even here where we maintain universal charity, it is impossible not to see that certain ones are called to walk the same path."

"I have long walked behind you on this ascent of Mount Carmel. You have taught me everything a father could teach a son."

"If I have taught you to carry the cross and to die on it, then I have taught you everything. Have I taught you this?"

"You have taught it to me from the very moment of my arrival."

"Do you know that when you first came here I thought you wouldn't last. A Jew. A famous survivor of the Holocaust. A man powerful in Israel. How could a person like you accept becoming a hidden man of God? That is why I was so hard on you in the beginning."

"The brothers used to say that there was never a novice master as rigorous as you."

"The Prussian?"

"You heard that? It wasn't a charitable nickname."

"It was accurate. I had much to learn in those days. There were zones in my character where faith had not penetrated. Our century leaves its peculiar wounds in the soul, does it not?"

"I often wondered if you were testing me."

"Yes, I tested you. It was something unresolved in me. I didn't have enough faith to overcome 'impossible cultural barriers'. I simply assumed that the Palestinian brothers would never accept you. I assumed that you were bringing into these poor walls the disease of famous men: pride, the destroyer of souls—and communities. I was wrong."

"You were right."

Father Prior looked at him steadily.

"You were right because no man is exempt from that temptation. Everyone must wrestle with it, whatever form it takes. I wasn't proud because I had been a minister of the government, nor because it was said that I would be prime minister one day. I wasn't proud because of my books. I was proud because a secret gnawing ideal kept whispering within me, a voice that said I could save the world. That I could prevent another holocaust. I thought I was like God. A good, humble god, of course."

"Ah, Elijah," said the prior, waving his hand as if to dismiss the thought, "you weren't pulled from the fire for nothing."

20

"Fire is a test. It purifies or it destroys. It took years for me to throw off the thirst for vengeance disguised as justice. I was full of idealistic hatred — the worst kind."

"Your whole family was annihilated. How could you not hate us?"

"I did for years. I became a cold, dead man. A shell. The mercy of God shattered it when I became a believer."

"But not everything is accomplished at one stroke."

"True. When I came to this house I brought the rage with me. Rage and indignation."

"I often wondered how you controlled your dislike of me?"

"I didn't want to dislike you. But the German accent. The mannerisms. It was too much for me."

"I know. We have never spoken of this, Father. But I remember the month and the year when you forgave everything, totally. Your eyes changed. Until then you had forgiven much, but not everything."

"You taught me this."

"I taught you this?"

"Yes. You see, I knew that you knew my dislike. A lesser man than you would have become more severe or, worse, more kind. But you remained detached, and gradually I came to understand you. It took years to see it, and when I finally saw it, I knew the great act of charity you had made. You had resigned yourself to being forever the Teutonic despot in our eyes."

The prior replied: "Man projects his wounds upon the world, my friend. He judges everything, and in the judging he reveals himself. Some of my family were persecuted by Hitler, a few, a pitiful few. My uncle, a priest, was martyred in Dachau. But most of my relatives were complacent, asleep, or frightened. They collaborated with evil. Several were members of the Party. One of my cousins was in the SS. Quite a mixture, my family."

"A portrait of the human race."

"Yes, the human race. It doesn't change much from people to

people, nation to nation. Only the seasons and the themes of the struggle change. If I had been a little older, I'm not sure whom I would have followed, my martyred uncle or my heroic cousin. Does that shock you?"

"No."

"It shocks me, Elijah."

"You were a boy."

"I was never a boy like you. It is true that I was a youth during the Holocaust. Technically speaking I committed no sins. I console myself with that at certain moments, but it's cold comfort. The Holocaust was a warning to the whole world. The most cultured, religious nation in Europe allowed the unthinkable to arise in its midst. My relatives and neighbors."

They sat in silence for several more minutes until the prior shook himself and stood.

"You had better wash and pack. Brother Sylvester will drive you to the airport in the morning. Don't wear your habit."

"Why may I not wear the habit?"

"There have been incidents in Rome. Priests and nuns spat on and physically attacked. It's growing more frequent."

"What if there is someone on my journey who needs to confess? If he sees a priest he may be moved to ask for help. Can we deny him the opportunity?"

The prior looked at the floor and thought.

"As usual, you are right, Elijah. Wear your habit."

He bowed his head for the prior's blessing. Then the two men embraced without another word, and Elijah went to his cell. There he prayed for several hours and slept fitfully until about four in the morning, when Brother Sylvester woke him.

They drove south on the coastal highway in the predawn. As they went through the northern suburbs of Tel Aviv, he glanced east toward Ramat Gan, where he and Ruth had lived for two years. He wondered, as he had many times, what his life would have become if the bomb had not exploded. Or if she had gone to Jerusalem early, as he had suggested. But she had shrugged off his anxiety.

"I'm a *sabra,* Dovidl. I'm used to terrorist threats. They're just part of the landscape."

She had a class to teach at the university in Jerusalem that afternoon and would not be home until late. She said that she would buy some feta cheese, pears, and smoked cod at the market first and would leave it in the refrigerator for supper. She scolded him fondly. He promised to feed himself properly. *Go,* he said, *go.* If she hurried she would be on time for her class. She kissed him and left. A half-hour later he heard the explosion from the office, and he knew. He could not explain how he knew, because he was not then a believer. At that time he believed only in Israel and in Ruth.

Brother Sylvester passed Ramat Gan at just above the speed limit, and mercifully they slipped through the city before traffic began in earnest. They checked in at Ben Gurion terminal by eight. There were some raised eyebrows at security when they saw his habit, but the name on his passport and a brisk consultation between officials got him through without the usual strip-search—a custom intended more for the purpose of humiliation than for prevention of terrorism.

"You're lucky you have friends in the Knesset", said a guard.

At nine o'clock, Father Elijah was aboard the morning flight to Rome. He had a window seat. It had been many years since he had flown, and he enjoyed each sensation immensely. The jet rose up at a sharp angle over the Mediterranean, which was already a sheet of molten silver.

* * *

His two seatmates barely acknowledged his presence. The middle-aged woman beside him wore yellow plastic jewelry and smelled of gardenias. She was reading a French mystery novel. In the aisle seat, a sunburned man in a blue-flowered sports shirt typed on his lap computer.

23

Elijah drowsed until breakfast.

The stewardess served the meal to his two seatmates, seasoned with smiles and friendly chatter. She served him without a glance and did not respond to his thanks. He dismissed her omission as absentmindedness. But when she took the trays away a half-hour later, repeating the same warmth toward the others, and increasing the chill toward him, he thought it might be deliberate. He said a prayer for her and resisted a mild tug toward paranoia.

The in-flight film portrayed a legal battle between the lawyers of an unnamed Western superpower and a psychotic cult-leader. The idealist young lawyers, male and female, were handsome, witty, brilliant, moralistic (aside from their fornications), and determined to save the world from fanatics. By contrast, the cult leader was nothing short of loathsome. Between acts of sexual violence and brainwashing, he repeatedly barked his fidelity to "my Lord and Savior Jesus Christ". At the film's climax, he led his entire following in an act of communal suicide. Father Elijah wondered if he had missed a few developments since entering the monastery twenty years before.

The stewardess returned and repeated the pattern of selective charm. She offered a choice of periodicals. Elijah took *Jerusalem Daily News* and *Worldview*. He had never heard of the latter. Its masthead informed him that it was a journal of international events, published weekly in English, Italian, Spanish, German, Japanese, and French editions. Worldwide circulation: seven and a half million. The face on the cover was unknown to him. A distinguished-looking man in his early fifties. The caption read in bold letters: *A New President for the Federation of European States.*

The feature article discussed the President's rapid rise, his background, his numerous achievements, honors, degrees. A figure of outstanding human qualities. There was a paragraph about his sociopolitical philosophy. He was first and foremost a humanist, it seemed. He was speaking everywhere about the "forging of a global civilization" and the "rebirth of a fundamental option for mankind".

Addressing the International Court of Human Rights in The Hague the week before, he had said, "Because of the widespread violation of human rights during the past century, we have suffered a loss of confidence in man." He reminded the jurists that the age of nation-states waging war for territorial acquisition was drawing to a close. "As we approach the third millennium of the Common Era, all mankind must turn toward the future and accept a vision of our destiny that embraces everything human, in its totality, including the concept of man as a spiritual being."

Elijah paused.

This indeed was a leader above the usual run of politicians. A philosopher perhaps.

The woman beside him tapped the cover of the magazine.

"C'est beau, ça! Le monde a besoin de cet homme."

Speaking in French, Elijah agreed with her that the President was saying some important things. True things. He might, indeed, do some good for the world.

She looked at him askance.

"*Some* good? But this man is the best thing Europe has produced since the War. He's the one to do it. You watch. He's the one."

Elijah nodded and went back to the article. It said that the President was currently at his villa near Naples, resting from a prolonged speaking tour.

The woman leaned over him and pointed out the window. "Look, over there. It's the heel of the boot. We're going to cross the coast of Italy in a minute."

Elijah offered to trade his seat, and she readily accepted.

The man on the aisle glanced over and said in English, "Going to see the Vatican?"

"Yes, I am."

"Rome's a great place. You been there before?"

"No."

"Israeli?"

"Yes."

The young man did not need to tell Elijah that he was an American.

"Are you returning to the United States?"

"Uh-huh. Shore leave."

"How long have you been away?"

"Three years."

"Are you lonely for America?"

"You bet. Land of the free, home of the brave."

"Ah, yes. Tell me, please, what do Americans think of this new European president?"

"We've got our own new president to worry about. They're all pretty much the same these days, you know."

"In what way?"

"Everybody's a sociologist."

"But not you?"

"Nope. My workshop's the good old dependable human body. Give me an appendix over a psyche any day."

"You are a doctor?"

"Uh-huh. I've been an embassy staffer in the Near East the last couple of years."

"Jerusalem?"

"Several places."

"Are you a military doctor?"

"Navy", he said tonelessly.

Changing the subject, the American flipped open a copy of *Worldview.* It was an older issue of the magazine.

"Hey, this guy's in every one of these. He gets around. Here he is arranging with the World Bank to prop up the Russian economy again. A month ago he stopped a war between two banana republics in Africa. Quite a guy. Looks like a class-act hero."

"So it seems", said Elijah pensively.

"You some kind of monk?"

"Yes. I am some kind of monk."

"I used to be Catholic."

"No longer?"

"Nope. I gave it up for Lent a long time ago."

"Why did you give it up?"

"It didn't work. It never did work too well, did it? Hell, you people are still galloping into the twentieth century on the back of a snail. This ain't the Middle Ages anymore, fellah."

He proceeded to instruct the priest on the several follies of the Church's doctrine.

"I was at the Cairo conference on population, as an observer. You know what they were saying in the halls? They were saying there are two main problems in today's world. The first is, there are three billion people too many on this planet, and they gotta go. The second problem is the Roman Catholic Church. And it's gotta go."

"I have read reports about this conference, and I saw no such remarks."

"It was the kind of thing delegates were saying in the hallways, private conversations, you know. The public speeches were something else. Working papers and all that stuff. You could get the drift of it, but not loud and clear, not what people really felt. Even so, your Pope rejected most of the Cairo statements. He'd better smarten up fast if he wants to keep what remains."

"What do you mean?"

"I mean, your Church is the only thing that stands in the way of making this a healthy planet to live on."

"You are perhaps overlooking the Red Chinese."

"Things are changing there. They're bringing their population problem under tight control. Capitalism's coming on strong, and elections scheduled for two years from now."

"The Chinese can be masters of illusion."

"The bottom line is they've got massive birth control and compulsory abortion now."

"If we destroy three billion people to make this a supposedly healthy place to live, what kind of a place will it be? Would you want to live with the people who remain?"

"Look, it's the age of democracy, and you guys are still trying to run a medieval monarchy over there in Rome. At least the U.S. bishops have got it right. They're trying to decentralize, trying to get power back into regional governments."

"I have heard."

"Not that it matters really, because I don't think you have too many believers left over there."

"Fifty million."

"How many of them listen to the Pope?"

"I don't know."

"Well, there y'go. Take a look around, pal. It's a whole new world shaping up fast."

The American opened his magazine and began to read to himself.

Elijah glanced over at the window and saw mountains below. The Apennines. The jet banked imperceptibly and began its slow descent toward Rome. He saw across the aisle the west coast and a bay that must be Naples.

He opened his copy of *Worldview* and turned to the religion section. Under the title, *World's Theologians Reject Latest Papal Encyclical,* he read the following:

Six decades ago Albert Einstein rejected the idea of an anthropomorphic God and declared his love for beauty, mystery, and contemplation of the "marvelous structure of the universe". Theologians at the time were upset that he bypassed the tradition of Judaism and Christianity, which proclaimed a God who exists beyond and above his creation. But theology has come of age, and the perennial role of theologian as handmaiden to the papacy is gone forever. A new generation of religious thinkers strives to address transcendent realities from a broader perspective.

Meeting last week in Tübingen, Germany, the International Association of Catholic Theologians hammered out a definitive response to the latest papal encyclical. The result is nothing less than a little masterpiece, an articulate manifesto for a religious vision appropriate to the twenty-first century. The co-chairperson of the association, Dr. Felix von Tilman, a former priest and present director of the Gaia Institute for Studies in Religion and Politics, spoke for the 5,000–world membership when he said, "The time has come for the human community to take a quantum leap in its theology of creation. The former distinctions between plant, animal, and human realms have proved disastrous for our planet. No longer can thinking persons accept without question the tragically stunted utterances of hierarchs or bonzes, ayatollahs or gurus."

Although Dr. von Tilman made no accusations against the present Pope or direct association of the religious tyrannies of the past with the papacy in its present form, he emphasized the concern of world theologians that the Pope's encyclical, *On Freedom and the Human Person,* neglected consideration of recent breakthroughs in theology and spirituality — what von Tilman calls "the deep ecumenism". There is a consensus among theologians, he states, that the papal document overemphasizes the concept of absolute truths to the detriment of dialogue between world religions.

Taking the podium, Dr. Mary-Beth Miller, OSVM, of Milwaukee, Wisconsin, past president of the International Council of Superiors of Women Religious, affirmed her organization's support of the IACT's document and called for the Vatican to reassess its positions on moral theology.

Speaking calmly, with conviction, she pointed out to the assembly that "hierarchies tend to degenerate into tyrannies. There are vestiges of the Inquisitional Church still active in the modern church, forces that work against the progress of humanity toward an era of universal harmony. These forces must be confronted at every turn and forced into powerlessness. The empowerment of the people of God has come into its own."

Citing numerous references from the recent encyclical, she demonstrated that the church of Rome clings to a kind of absolute authority over the conscience, which, she argues, negates the concept of personal freedom and contradicts the avowed objectives of the encyclical. The manner in which theologians have been handled by the Vatican, she pointed out, is a prime example of its actual view of freedom. "Enforcement of bad theology by hierarchs is unworthy of the name church and should be called by its true name", she concluded. "Its name is injustice. Its name is sacrilege."

Archbishop Raymond Welland of New York added his voice to the growing chorus of dissent, when he said in a homily at the association's closing mass, "Under this pontificate, the church has displayed a flagrant disregard for the *vox populi*. The voice of the people is, in a profound sense, the voice of God. We have too long ignored this grass roots *magisterium* in favour of an isolated man sitting on a lonely throne in distant Rome, demanding blind obedience."

Elijah shook his head slowly.

The jet's wheels hit the runway at that moment, and the lurch of the craft prevented any return to the article.

He was cleared through customs after considerable difficulty. He just barely passed an interview with the head of airport security, who snapped questions at him and interrupted every one of his answers. He was strip-searched by two guards, one of whom was female. They tore his luggage apart. When he emerged through the customs barrier he was somewhat dazed and unprepared for his reception committee.

II

Rome

It was a committee of one, a short, fat man with a florid face waving to him from the end of the gate at the main terminal lobby.

"Davy!" the man yelled with a show of teeth. "Over here, lad!"

It took a moment for the face and the grin to register, and then Elijah burst out laughing. "I don't believe it! Is that you, Billy?"

"In the flesh!"

"This is a surprise. Are you the one sent to meet me?"

"None other."

"I had no idea you were in Rome."

"I came visiting with the primate of England last year, and the Curia asked if they could keep me for a while. Special missions for various congregations. A glorified 'gofer' is what I am, with a *Monsignore* tacked to the front o' me name and a purple sash and everythin'."

"I don't believe it! You, a monsignor."

"That sounds like a compliment and an insult all in one."

"Same old Billy."

"Yeah, same old Billy."

"Congratulations! That's wonderful news."

He pumped the Englishman's hand.

Billy Stangsby was now over fifty years of age. Despite his rise to the position of curial monsignor, he was as fresh-faced and as childlike as ever. "Billy the Kid", someone had called him at L'École Biblique. Many people thought him a frivolous personality. Elijah had spotted the depths and taken to him instantly. Obviously, someone at the Vatican had too. To look at him you would never guess that he was a master of biblical theology, a civil lawyer, ex–Member of Parliament, and a famous convert from Anglicanism. He was a diocesan priest of Birmingham, England. In his last letter, written from there over a year ago, he had mentioned that he was trying to obtain his doctorate in canon law. He looked like a taxi driver and talked like one. Elijah noted that he was not dressed in blacks and collar. He wore a salmon pink sports shirt, a light cotton jacket, gray flannel slacks, and expensive leather shoes. The wristwatch was gold, the pen in his breastpocket was gold, several of his teeth were gold, but the shock of unruly hair was pure Billy.

"You look more prosperous, Monsignor, than the last time we met."

"And you still look like a rabbi with a bad haircut. Wow, the hair's white, what's left of it."

"Getting old, getting old."

"Looks like they ruffled you up in Customs."

"Do they treat everyone this way?"

"Nope. Special treatment for clerics. I thought for sure my boss told your boss to send you in civvies."

"He did suggest something like that. I argued against it and won. I wish I had lost."

Billy took his suitcase and said, "Let's get out of here. You're getting more hate stares than a sensitive lad like me can stand."

On the way to the main entrance, they passed an illuminated kiosk displaying a poster of a nude man and woman embracing. It was an advertisement for perfume.

"That is astounding", said Elijah, looking away from it.

"Ooh, you're in for some big surprises, Davy. That's nothing. Take a look at the other side."

The reverse side of the kiosk was an advertisement for cognac. Displayed on it were two nude men lying on their backs in bed, arm in arm, gazing into each other's eyes, both sipping through straws from a single brandy glass.

"Am I seeing correctly?"

"You are. You are", grumbled Billy. "Maybe I should blindfold you till we get out to the parking lot."

"It's all right. I'll keep custody of the eyes."

Billy laughed humorlessly.

"Now, there's an antique expression", he said. "You've no idea how refreshing it is to hear that. Most of the clerics I know say we shouldn't be so puritanical; we should be grown-up."

"What do you say?"

"I say it's a damn hard thing to see a naked woman and pretend she's an umbrella stand. Better not let me see a naked woman. That way I keep my vows."

"What's that?" said Elijah pointing at a kiosk near the exit.

"Don't look."

"Has the world gone mad?"

"I'm afraid it has, old lad."

"But why are they displaying this! This is a horrible crime and they advertise it as . . . "

"As entertainment."

"What is it?"

"It's a play. Well, actually it's a sort of *art* happening. The theatre company has rights to the abortuary dumpsters. They're used for the evening show. It's called . . . "

Elijah stared at Billy and walked through the door into the blast of the Italian sun.

"It's the Colosseum all over again", muttered Billy as he unlocked the door of a dark green Jaguar.

"What has happened to the world?"

"It's a long story."

"I have read nothing about this."

"What you been reading? Theology? Spirituality? I hear you still dabble in archeology too. I'll bet that's all you pay attention to."

"We receive a synopsis of the world news. And *L'Osservatore Romano* tells us much about the state of things. But *this,* this is unspeakable."

"I'm afraid the unspeakable has become the ordinary, old boy."

"I can't have been away from the world so long that it has changed this much."

"I don't want to jar your innocent nervous system too soon, but you should be advised that it gets worse."

"What could be worse than this?"

"You'd be amazed."

Elijah shook his head.

"The pace of change is accelerating too. That's one of the ominous parts."

Billy drove the car out onto the highway and turned north toward the city.

"Are we going to the Vatican?"

"We have an appointment there this evening."

"With whom?"

"With my boss. I'm taking you to my apartment first. You can have a shower, and while you're doing that I'd better go out and get you some clothes."

"No, I don't wish to . . . "

"It's camouflage. You're a walking target the way you're dressed."

"If persecution comes, are we to cease to be what we are?" Elijah asked in a quiet voice.

"You're under obedience on this one, Davy. That's the way the Secretary wants it. Sorry."

"But we are priests of Christ!"

"I know. But there's more at stake here than getting spit at or punched up."

"What do you mean?"

"I think I'd better let the boss tell you."

Elijah watched the hills of the city roll over, and when the dome of Saint Peter's came into view his heart gave a jump. He sat forward and stared.

"First time in Rome?"

"Yes."

"You'd be surprised how many people are disappointed by Saint Peter's. It's huge, of course. Biggest church in Christendom. Crammed to the gills with priceless art. Awesome. But it doesn't come near what you feel in the catacombs of Saint Calixtus, outside of town. That's the real foundation of the Church. That and Peter's tomb. I touched his bones, you know?"

"You touched his bones?"

"Uh-huh. They opened the tomb last autumn during some renovations of the shrine under the main altar. You know, it wasn't at all like I expected it would be. I was looking forward to pious passions and ecstasies. There was nothing of the sort."

"Can you describe it?"

"I guess I can try. When I touched the bones there wasn't anything macabre about it. It was so simple, like here was the big fisherman, the guy who ran away. The guy who denied Jesus. The guy who came back again. I felt it, Davy. I felt the timelessness of the Church. As if time didn't exist. There was a stillness like you wouldn't believe. It was beautiful. And peace. Yeah, a peace so odorless, tasteless, and soundless you wouldn't think it was there. But it was there. *Here's the rock,* I said to myself. This man, this rough, humble, big man was just like me. Jesus looked at him and loved him. Peter looked at Jesus and said, Get away from me, I'm a sinful man. A dumb guy from Galilee named Pete. Jesus made him into Bishop of Rome, chief of the apostles, the foundation stone. Christ built a Church on all that weakness. That's what hit me most of all, the weakness. Inside the weakness was a terrific secret."

"That is an extraordinary grace."

"Yeah, it was. You hungry?"

"I'm afraid I lost my appetite at the airport."

"Don't worry. I know a little restaurant where you just walk in the door and start to drool. Pasta. Seafood."

"I'm not very hungry."

"Okay, but what say we go there later for a sip of *vino?* Cool of the evening and all that. It'll relax you for your debut at the big house."

"All right, Billy."

Billy's apartment was a twenty-minute walk from Vatican City, in a street full of parked sports cars. It contained a public garden, a fountain, and a dozen children playing sidewalk games. He lived in an old *palazzo* broken up into private flats. The steps to the third floor were marble, the hallways olive green, the walls sweating and heavily defaced with graffiti.

"Home sweet home", he said, unlocking two door locks and a padlock.

Inside it was cool and modern. The tiled floors were white and the walls were painted a pale blue. Through an open window came children's laughter, radios, someone practicing a cello, and beeping car horns, the entire symphony underscored by the whisper of Lombardy poplars in the park across the street.

"*Viva Roma!*" said Billy.

He went into the kitchen and returned with a bottle of Perrier water and two glasses. It was ice cold and Elijah drank it gratefully.

The living room was lined from floor to ceiling with books. There was a polychromed carving of a Madonna, late Gothic, a French impressionist landscape, an African crucifix, a signed photograph of the Pope, a stereo set. Off to the side, parallel to the kitchen, was a bedroom alcove, containing a single cot, functional, austere. A wooden rosary dangled from a peg by the pillow. A small panda bear, missing one ear and sprouting straw, sat on the headboard.

"My cell."

"It's charming."

"Do you remember Andy?"

"I remember him well."

"Say hello to him."

"Hello, Andy!"

"Andy says hello back at you."

"He has aged."

"He's been through a lot. British Customs buggered him."

"Customs people seem to have become rather unfriendly during the past two decades."

"They have indeed. If they were half as nasty to terrorists as they are to flaming Catholics like you and me, we'd live in a safer world."

"No place is safe for our kind."

"You're right. Thanks for reminding me."

Billy turned the stereo on low—traditional hymns sung in operatic style.

"Placido Domingo", he said. "I prefer him to Pavarotti. How about you?"

"They both sound miraculous."

"Look, Davy, I think I've got a fairly good idea of your sizes. I'm going to go buy you some pants, shirts, sport jackets. You'll need a real suit and tie soon, but we can get that fitted sometime during the next few days. Right now we've got to get you into camouflage."

"Really, my friend, is it as bad as all that?"

"Yup, as bad as all that", said Billy soberly.

He went out, locking up behind.

Elijah sat on the couch and listened to the noises from the street. The tension of his body gradually eased. He gazed around the apartment and saw that Billy was still an eclectic: there was an Australian flag pinned to the ceiling, a Bavarian beer stein on an antique sideboard, a balsawood model of a racing sloop half-completed on the desk, a Texan ten-gallon hat tipsy on the plaster bust of a Roman matron. Billy had retained his boyish enthusiasm, his love of novelty, while time had seasoned Elijah into a slow-moving pedant.

At L'École Biblique, they had become friends and had remained friends. He had often asked himself why he liked Billy so much. There was an intellectual rapport, of course. But more than that, Billy was one of the few people he had met who did not hold his own ego in high esteem. He loved to clown to the point of silliness. He seemed undamaged by tragedy. His zest for life and his lighthearted temperament were a perfect foil for Elijah's own somber, rabbinic cast of mind.

But Billy was not liked by everyone. He was rich and brilliant, which earned him enemies. Over drinks one evening, a group of professors and students had discussed the little Englishman and pronounced him unsuitable for theology.

"That Stangsby!" a Frenchman expostulated. "What an idiot!"

"Charity, charity", said a Dutchman. "Let us say rather that he is an *idiot savant.*"

"Oh, yes, he's smart", said another. "But he's always joking. It palls."

"Billy has a great seriousness inside him", said Elijah.

"He is never serious."

"He is a confused personality", said the Frenchman. "He is always saying *yeah* like the Americans."

Several of the students laughed.

"That's not exactly a damning fault", interjected an overly serious young priest named Smith. He was a convert from Episcopalianism and spoke with a distinctly British accent. He was from Idaho. "Billy's approach to things is Chestertonian", he added.

"But you, Smith," said the Frenchman, "you are a dour Bellocian. Complete with the accent!"

"Thank you."

The ensuing banter strained for joviality, but there were barbs in the commentary.

"Stangsby talks like an American and Smith like a Britisher", said the Frenchman. "Why do English-speaking clerics always want to be something other than themselves?"

"Perhaps we do not assume that our native culture is superior", said Smith coolly.

"That is not very patriotic."

"We are not as blessed with one-dimensionality as certain continental Europeans", Smith added.

"Ah, yes, your famous melting pot. Come to Paris and study next year, Smith. She is the Queen. She will teach you the meaning of culture."

"Your attitude reeks of national chauvinism, Jean", said a German. "I think Berlin merits that crown."

But this remark was greeted by an uncomfortable silence, for the guilt of Germans was a subject that few wished to explore.

An Italian eventually saved the situation by pantomiming himself and saying with a clownish grin, "But there is no debate on this matter! Roma is the undisputed Queen."

"It is a fascinating phenomenon", said the Frenchman, unimpressed, "that the fault-line of the northern Reformation corresponds more or less to the old frontiers of the Roman Empire. Civilization and Catholicism to the south; barbarians, and hence Protestantism, to the north."

"That is facile", said the German. "You are forgetting the Russians."

"Ah, yes, the Russians. Savages entranced by the glitter of Byzantium."

And so it went for a while, until the Frenchman brought it full circle.

"Paris, Paris. Queen of Europe. Smith, abandon your infatuation with the British, who after all are merely displaced Normans."

"I would sound quite silly affecting a French accent, Jean. I much prefer my ancestral roots."

"King George would approve."

"The American Revolution was a long time ago", said the Dutchman. "Billy and Smith are merely seeking their missing parts, like orphans."

At the time Elijah had mused on this last comment and thought there was some truth in it. Billy, an extroverted Englishman who sounded like a bit player in an American film, and Smith, an introverted prairie boy who sounded as if he had graduated from Oxford? Was there indeed something essential missing in the composition of their characters, a fracture in the psyche left by violent revolution? One might live comfortably within such a chasm if there were compensations — power, for example, or wealth, space, and frontiers. But the globe had shrunk drastically since the War. *Rule Brittania* and the brash pragmatism of *Pax Americana* had both been eclipsed. Was that it? But it was not only the Americans and the British who had suffered from the revolutions of the past three hundred years. What of the French themselves? And the Germans? What of the great blow dealt to the consciousness of the West by the Reformation? No, take it farther back to the split between the Church of the East and the Church of the West. Perhaps even farther.

Was there a missing component in all human beings? The rural masses seeking the metropolis; the urban young fleeing to the woods. Women pretending to be men; men becoming more like women; everyone aping divinity in his desperation to escape creaturehood? Western youths seeking the Orient; orientals seeking capitalism? Monks abandoning their monasteries; married men pining for solitude. Liberals seeking to demythologize the Scriptures in an attempt to flee the exigencies of biblical faith; fundamentalists seeking to fill the empty places in their religion by a return to the Old Testament, fleeing the tasks of the baptized intellect. Was the promise always to be found *elsewhere,* always just beyond the next horizon? Why this persistent need for signs, wonders, new pillars of fire, arks of covenant, tablets of stone—anything other than the demands of raw, laborious, darkest faith?

At the time he had asked himself, ruthlessly, if his conversion to Christianity was a variation on the dynamic of escape—a kind of pseudo-transcendence. There was no doubt that he, a child of the Diaspora seeking God in the New Testament, was in flight from the horror of the past. The birth of Israel had not dispersed his abiding sense of victimhood. Terror had merely been replaced by rage, and he knew that both were reverse images of each other. He was still shaken by the events that had brought him to Catholicism—his childhood, Ruth's death, his long wrestling match with the black archon of despair. Eventually he saw that he had been running *to* Christ, and the flight from the past had been one of the means used by God to propel him forward. But when he met Billy in Jerusalem he was still young in the Faith, still largely impelled by fear, still struggling with chronic self-doubt, still questioning everything, even those things that at some other level of his being he believed. He was a fractured man.

"There is a secret smile on the face of God", Billy once told him. It was a thought so alien to Elijah that it had startled him. Life was a grave business. A large majority of the people he had loved had died violently. A secret smile? Really? What sort of smile?

Billy had caught him on the hook of this intriguing idea, had made him doubt his doubt, question his questions, taught him to smile (secretly), and eventually to laugh. Now they were old in the Faith, it seemed. Each had continued the search for his missing part. Elijah had gradually learned to dig deep for the well of joy; and Billy had grown reflective beneath his comedy.

Elijah stretched out on the couch. The CD finished its repertoire and shut itself off. His mind, long accustomed to the gentle routine of prayer and labor, rest, and solitary meditation, was swarming with jagged shards of brutal imagery. He could not shake the poster of the murdered children from his thoughts. It was only midafternoon, six hours since his departure from Ben Gurion, but it felt as if days had passed. He was exhausted. Closing his eyes he slipped past the screen of horror into sleep.

Two hours later he woke in a semi-stupor, staring at the wall. His lips were dry and his eyes ached. He saw a middle-aged man seated at a desk. The man was staring down, reading a file that lay open before him. He was dressed entirely in black clericals. He was lean and ascetic, but in a way that was cold and thoroughly alien. His eyes were intelligent, even dedicated. Elijah could not tell if the visitor was corrupt or an ideologue of some kind. He knew only that he was evil. But the evil was of a quality that was new to Elijah. There were no traces of vice on that proud and guarded face. On the contrary, the man radiated virtue, character, and nobility. But all of these qualities were without charity, and the cumulative effect of so much good turned to some undefined ill was to invoke fear—rather like a dazzling arch that lacked a keystone.

Why was this man in Billy's apartment? Elijah shook himself and sat upright on the couch. At that moment Billy entered the room carrying steaming cups of coffee. He set them on a low table beside the couch and took the armchair opposite.

"Drink", he commanded.

Elijah gestured to the visitor. "Please introduce us", he said.

Billy looked at him strangely.

"Huh?"

Elijah looked to the spot where the visitor had been and was astonished to find no one there.

"You feeling all right, Davy?"

"I must have been dreaming."

"You slept two hours. You must have needed it. We'll go out for supper in a bit."

"My head is spinning. I can't get that face out of my mind."

"Somebody you know?"

"No. A stranger. But I saw him as if he were real, sitting just over there."

"Overheated brain. Drink up, lad."

Elijah rubbed his eyes.

"So many changes; so quickly they have come. Strange how one creates an abstract picture of the world, and yet the smells, the sounds, the heat, and anguish of it escape you. It must be that the senses read some things between the lines."

"What are your senses telling you?"

"It is as if some vast crime has occurred, or is occurring."

"Well, you're right there. None dares call it by name. Only a few will admit that anything's wrong. But something *is* wrong. Terribly wrong."

"I feel it in the air, Billy, like an invisible gas. You have to go away from the world and come back again after a long time, in order to see the change."

"Your instinct matches my feeling exactly. If you read what the Holy Father's been saying, you know he's spotted it too, bang-on. He knows it better than any of us."

"What is it?"

"I'm not sure. Exterior enemies are only part of the problem. There's trouble *inside* the House of God."

"I have seen hints of it creeping into the journals."

"Hints? Lord, what have you been reading! It's everywhere."

"Just how bad is it, do you think?"

"I don't think anyone has an accurate reading on the extent of it. But I'd say it's pretty big. It's going to get worse."

"Why is it happening?"

"A lot of reasons. Spiritual temptation first and foremost. Intellectual pride. The thrill of being revolutionaries. It's the disease of the century. C. S. Lewis called these people Late Western Man. They're educated, affluent, restless, and unfulfilled. They're rational man explaining and theorizing all the way down as he sinks into a totally subjectivized world. What better project for him than the complete demolition and reconstruction of the House of God, right?"

"Is it as conscious as that?"

"Not for most of them. There's a pattern to their assumptions. With few exceptions, their ideas might be roughly summed up this way: 'I am an idealist but a realist; I hope for a collective solution of the human problem; I no longer believe (or never have believed) in a transcendent God and organized religion. I believe in the god in man.' "

"An ancient seduction."

"Yes, and it always works so well."

"This man, von Tilman, what do you think of him?"

"Gag! Now I'm losing *my* appetite. Where did you hear about him?"

"A magazine on the airplane. It reported a theological conference at Tübingen."

"Tübingen!" groaned Billy in disgust. "Von Tilman's diatribes against the universal Church are disgusting. He's one of those passionate types that got a Ph.D. before he learned to think."

"He sounded quite rational in the article."

"They usually do. They're very nice people. They speak in measured tones. They have nothing to lose, you see. They're not on the defensive, like us."

"He seemed quite optimistic about the future of man."

"Oh, yes. He's a utopian. He's a first-class Brave New Worlder for sure. You've probably read that he and some of his buddies condemn the organs of institutional religion as the real monsters of history."

"In the article he is quoted as saying that the world he hopes for is one freed from domination by an all-powerful world régime or world bureaucracy; with no domination in the name of religion; no coercion on behalf of religious juridicism, dogmatism, or moralism."

"What he really means is he can't stand the Church looking over his shoulder, making him accountable for his nutty pronouncements and for warping the minds of a generation of kids. You watch, Davy, he'll be the first to ally himself with some *political* world régime, some tyranny, as long as it superficially looks like a liberator, and as long as it feeds him and lets him play revolutionary."

"It can't possibly be a conscious blindness on his part."

"No. The dear doctor is simply stupid." Billy's face reddened. "Sorry, this conversation is taking a nasty turn. You always knew I had a mean streak?"

"There is a zealot in you, I would say."

"But it's *so* infuriating! He thinks he's saving the Church, and he's actually undermining it, precisely at that moment in history when we need to keep our wits about us."

"It is hard to discuss anything with a man like that. I have met many like him in my life: Marxist zealots, fascist zealots, Zionists, fundamentalists, materialist zealots, atheist zealots, millennialist zealots . . . "

"Chubby English zealots?"

"Yes, them too. But they are the least dangerous."

"Thank you so much."

"Billy, perhaps in von Tilman's world the Pope and an ayatollah are fundamentally the same thing—tyrants."

"Exercising their tyranny most cruelly, no doubt, over the freedom of theologians."

"One wonders if he has examined the problem raised by the specter of a world in which everyone has become his own pope or ayatollah, in which everyone has become infallible—everyone, that is, except the Pope of Rome."

"Good point. I hope I go to my eternal reward before that happens."

"It may already be happening."

Billy sighed again and said, "Maybe so. Well, you almost succeeded in making me lose my appetite. *Almost,* I say. Let's go to Mamma Garibaldi's. They make a lasagna there called *the red shirt.* It's unbeatable."

After Elijah changed clothes, they set off for the restaurant across town. Elijah marveled at the way Billy maneuvered his Jaguar through the hysteria of city traffic. Neither of them spoke until they were past the worst of it.

"Why does a Catholic priest drive a car that costs what this thing costs?" said Billy.

"I don't know. Why does he?"

"Because his mum gave it to him."

"You don't need to justify yourself to me."

"I'm trying to justify myself to myself."

"Are you ashamed of the car?"

"Ashamed and infatuated. It's the third one Mum gave me this year. I auctioned the Mercedes and gave the proceeds to the sisters in Calcutta, and the Maserati for a refugee center in Tanzania. I'm just screwing up my courage to dispose of this one."

"How wealthy is your mother?"

"Very, Davy, very. She wants her little monsignor to be happy. She can't imagine a man being happy without sex—you know what men are like—so she makes sure there are compensations. All boys like toy cars, right?"

Billy looked over at Elijah archly, and both men broke into laughter.

"It's absolutely astounding how few people, I mean even *very* religious people," Billy said, "believe that celibate happiness is possible."

"It's not always easy."

"They don't understand how you can fall in love with Christ."

"I know."

"I had everything in life. I mean everything that you could want. I spent most of my youth enjoying it, and thinking about

46

women. I was crazy in love with several. Then it hit me one day that there was a pattern to my life. I'd be willing to die today for this one, and forget her tomorrow, and ready to die for somebody else the day after, only to forget the whole thing the following morning."

"A passionate heart, Billy."

"A fickle heart."

"An undisciplined heart."

"A greedy heart and that's the truth."

"A zealot's heart."

"Zealous for every sensation life could offer. But not much of a brain, Davy. I was so bloody stupid it boggles my mind. I lived like a drug addict. And like an addict, I couldn't believe there was happiness outside of my addiction. The addiction had become life itself, you see."

"What changed you?"

"A Saint Paul experience. I got knocked off my horse one day. I don't mean literally. I mean I was driving through the Cotswolds on a back road. I wasn't depressed or anything like that. In fact, things were going rather marvelously. But it struck me with some kind of magisterial certainty that my way of life was pointless. It all seemed so meaningless. I stopped the car, got out, and walked up a knoll and sat under a tree and looked at my life. And I saw it. I really saw it. A nice life. I wasn't an evil man. Just incredibly shallow. It was a moment of hard grace."

"Perhaps the real grace was the ability to accept what you had seen."

"Maybe so. But then I heard a voice. A quiet voice. Where it came from I don't know. I never heard it before and I haven't heard it since, at least not like that."

"What did the voice say?"

"It said, *I open a door before you. I ask you to walk through it.* Then I turned around and saw a light in the trees, a piece of sky where a cutting had been made through the forest. It was a deer path running into the woods. I knew that I was supposed to go there. At first I wanted to wipe it out of my mind. But I just kept looking at it. I was frightened and happy all at once. I saw that the biggest thing a fellow like me could do was to scoop the whole thing up in my hands—all of it, the ladies, the degrees, the money, the fame, the seat in Parliament—and just give it away. Crazy eh?"

"Crazy and holy."

"Believe me, I wasn't a holy joe at the time. I wasn't even religious."

"What happened next?"

"I just walked into the woods. I wanted to give it all away on the spot. I wanted to walk forever into those woods and just be empty and poor. It was a great feeling. Like release from prison. I walked over an oak-covered hill. It was autumn, the trees were dropping brown leaves and acorns on me, the wind was so sweet. It was just perfect joy. I came over this rise and what to my wondering eyes did appear?"

"What did appear?"

"A monastery."

"A monastery?"

"That's when I began to suspect that God might have a few tricks up His sleeve. I argued to myself that it was an accident. It could just as easily have been an ashram up there, I said, or a college, or a scientific institute, or just miles of bog. But it was a Catholic monastery and it wouldn't go away. It refused to mutate. So I went up to the door, knocked on it, and asked to speak to the boss.

"The porter told me the abbot was busy.

"I said, that's okay; I'll wait. So I sat on the grass outside the church and I waited. For hours I waited. I've come this far, I said to myself. I'm going all the way. All the way! I was beginning to doubt my sanity at that point, but I didn't care anymore. You see, for the first time in my life I had one little scrap of evidence that there might be something more than my comfortable, well-ordered life. I saw that I'd succeeded at everything so far. Simply everything. I decided I wanted to try being a failure for awhile. I thought it might teach me something useful."

"Has it?"

"It's taught me everything important there is to know. That and meeting Pete under the altar."

"What happened next?"

"Eventually the abbot himself came out. A nice chap. He smiled when I told him who I was and what I wanted to do. He suggested that I go home and think about it some more."

"Which you did."

"Nope. I threw myself on his mercy and asked to stay as a guest. He agreed reluctantly. I was a nominal Anglican with just a scrap of faith that I clung to as if it were life itself. I left eight months later, a Catholic. I wanted to become a saint. I knew I wasn't cut out to be a contemplative. I'm too bloody outgoing for that."

"Where did you go?"

"To L'École Biblique in Jerusalem. That's where we met."

"You seemed such a sensible English Catholic. I had no idea you'd been knocked off a horse."

"A Bentley. I was knocked off a Bentley."

"It sounds to me as if you were chosen."

"Chosen for what, I wonder. I'm just a glorified errand boy."

"Zealots think of themselves as useless unless they are in the thick of battle."

"The battlefront is so ominously quiet, like a dead calm before a storm. The rumble of the von Tilmans is just saber rattling. I keep asking myself when's the real fighting going to start."

"It began in earnest some time ago. The deadliest part of the battle is hidden. Some of it is above our heads in the heavenly realms where the righteous angels battle against the demons. But there is much unseen warfare on earth."

"Please, Davy, I want a sword. Push me out into the Colosseum. Anything other than this ennui that's slowly crushing the life out of the world. I wanted to be a missionary, but they sent me to the Secretariat of State. I wanted to be poor like Saint Francis, live in rags, love God, beg for crusts. No bloody way. I get an apartment and a salary. Tell me why I was knocked off my Bentley only to be popped into a Jaguar?"

"Perhaps you are asked to use your gifts in a less heroic way. The Church needs good administrators."

"It's a perverse form of martyrdom, I suppose. Sports cars and lasagna when you want it. I'd much prefer a concentration camp."

Elijah looked out the passenger window.

"Oh, God," exclaimed Billy, "I forgot. Your parents died in one, didn't they?"

"Yes. Practically everyone I knew died in one."

"Bloody insensitive I am."

"Real suffering is always different from what we imagine", Elijah said quietly.

"I got peas for brains."

"Obedience is the best form of poverty, Billy. I think that is the kind of martyrdom you have been given."

"What! No flags and flashing swords? No glory on the battlefield?"

"No false glory."

III

The Vatican

After supper they drove to the Vatican. Billy parked the car in the Belvedere Courtyard and led Elijah by an indirect route of halls, elevators, and staircases to the offices of the Secretariat of State. He went into a side office off the main corridor and emerged a moment later buttoning up a black soutane with purple piping and a gash of violet across the midriff.

"Camouflage", said Billy.

He walked past a secretary and two Swiss guards into a spacious light-filled reception office, and through another door into a smaller room. A cardinal stood behind a desk with his back to them, looking out a window to the courtyard below.

"Ahem", said Billy.

The cardinal turned. Tall and silver-haired, he came to them with his hand extended, a slight smile on his face. Elijah thought that this face, urbane and composed, princely and Italian, contained the most intelligent eyes he had ever seen.

"William", said the cardinal in heavily accented English. "You have brought us Father Elijah."

After an exchange of greetings and cordialities, the cardinal gestured them toward a cluster of easy chairs.

"Has William told you anything about the purpose of your visit?"

"Nothing, Your Eminence."

"A prodigious feat for William."

"That's His Eminence's subtle way of telling you, Davy, that I'm not to be trusted."

Elijah looked back and forth between the two men, unsure of how to respond. The cardinal and his secretary burst out laughing.

"Don't look so worried. That was your first dose of *romanità.*"

Elijah saw that there was a bond of humor between the two men, and something rarer—mutual trust.

"We will leave it to the Holy Father to explain the situation", said the cardinal. He glanced at his watch. "We meet him ten minutes from now."

"You've never met him before?" said Billy.

"No."

"Nervous?"

"A little."

"You'll like him. He's not imposing."

"Unlike *Stato* and *Dottrina*", said the cardinal.

"Precisely", said Billy with a wink at Elijah.

"The Holy Father has asked me and the Cardinal Prefect of the Congregation for the Doctrine of the Faith to be present at your meeting with him."

"Your Eminence, I'm surprised by the swiftness of this", said Elijah. "Yesterday evening at this time, I was working in the garden at Carmel. I have rarely left the monastery for almost twenty years. There have been no explanations."

"I know how overwhelming this must be for you", said the cardinal. "There are good reasons why there have been no explanations. You'll understand shortly. Now, tell me, how is your good prior? We taught together at Freiburg, you know, many years ago."

"The prior is aging, though his mind is young."

"He has been through much during the past year."

"The murder of two of our brothers by terrorists weighs heavily on him."

"He is grieving."

"Yes."

The cardinal sighed. "No doubt that *angst* of his is compounding his sorrows. He never should have got into Hegel as a young man. And Nietzsche, Feuerbach. Brrrr! They leave an icy spot in the soul."

"Father Prior sends you his fraternal greetings", said Elijah, hoping to change the subject.

"I know your Father Prior very well. He blames himself, of course."

"Unfortunately, it is so. He feels that if he had been more conscious of security it would not have happened."

"Still as hard on himself as ever, I see. I will write to him."

"There have been so many developments lately. The New World cult has its headquarters in Haifa. One can see their temple from our bell tower. There have been riots at our gate. Small affairs staged as media events."

"If I recall correctly, their philosophy is one of universal tolerance, isn't it?"

"It is. However, they say that the Roman Catholic Church is the only remaining bastion of intolerance left on the planet."

"And thus they will not tolerate it."

"I believe they are not a significant enemy. The assault is underway on every level of society. I think the noisiest of the attacks are the least dangerous."

Stato turned and looked significantly at Billy.

"You see, William, why he is the right choice?"

"I always said he was a smart lad."

The cardinal looked at his watch.

"Time to go."

The three men walked through a labyrinth of corridors. Elijah did not attempt to make a mental map of their route, for his attention was distracted every few feet by works of art. The collection seemed inexhaustible, and he felt a longing that was close to physical pain. Mount Carmel was a place of exquisite beauty, but a beauty of architectural restraint, flowers, fruits, and vegetables, orchards basking in the sun, dusk on the ocean, the broad sweep of the mountain as it declined toward the east, eloquent stretches of purple hills in which Christ and the devil had walked. A stark, eternal kind of beauty. Macrocosmic beauty. Here, in these varnished hallways smelling of floor wax and opulence, the beauty was of another order. Here, the imagery expressed the human drama. The interior universe. The microcosm. Raphael, Fra Angelico, Michelangelo, Bramante, Giacomo Manzu. Ancient funerary busts of first-century Roman couples, their faces surprisingly modern, radiating personality. The idealized marble portraits of emperors. Classic gods and goddesses. A Byzantine icon of Mother and Child. A Romanesque crucifix. Frescoes, tapestries, mosaics, Renaissance paintings. Saints, heroes, traitors, princes, popes—the height and breadth of the human soul displayed in myriad incarnate forms. There was mysticism, sanctity, sex, violence, civic stability and instability, the collapse of empires, and the clash of demonic warfare. There were visions of Heaven and Hell, the city of man and the city of God, the New Jerusalem, and the restoration of the entire creation to divine order. There was Fall and there was Redemption. There was Genesis to Apocalypse. It was all here.

Billy grabbed his arm and pulled him along behind the cardinal. Elijah had to remind himself from moment to moment that he was on his way to meet the pontiff of the universal Church.

"One, holy, catholic, apostolic Church", he whispered to himself.

"Are you all right? You look a bit distracted, old boy."

"I'm all right. It's difficult to shut this out."

"Too bloody true", Billy laughed. "But you get used to it. Look neither to the right nor to the left. Concentrate on the busts of the Roman emperors—a nasty-looking crew. They killed our forefathers and foremothers, remember. Focus on that. Into the valley of death rode the six hundred!"

"The valley of death? Six hundred?"

"Old poem. English schoolboy stuff. Doesn't mean a thing. Relax."

Elijah's heart beat hard and he breathed more deeply. He felt a mixture of fear and joy. There was no time to dwell on it because they had arrived at the entrance to the papal apartments. The cardinal spoke with a priest seated at a desk. The priest penned a notation in a book and nodded to the two Swiss guards who stood at the door.

The Pope's private apartment was not what Elijah had expected. It was a modern suite of rooms, carpeted in dove gray. The walls, plastered white, were appointed with one or two discreet works of art and a few furnishings of the simplest design. The lack of embellishment was in marked contrast to the opulence of the outer hallways.

An elderly nun in a white habit came from a dining room to the right. The cardinal exchanged pleasantries with her. She explained that she and a chamberlain were just setting the table for tomorrow's breakfast. The Holy Father was in the chapel. He would be out in a few minutes. The Holy Father would like His Eminence and guests to wait for him in the parlor. The chamberlain would bring them refreshments.

The cardinal and the little nun bowed to each other, and she left through the main entrance.

Billy squeezed Elijah's arm and said, "I'm gone too. See you later in *Stato's* office for a debriefing."

The cardinal and Elijah seated themselves in the parlor. The only image in the room was a Russian icon of the crucifixion, with a red votive light burning beneath it. A cluster of potted trees bloomed beneath a skylight. The couch and four armchairs, upholstered in white, verged on comfort, but studiously avoided luxuriance.

"You are surprised?" said the cardinal.

"Yes."

"The decor is like him", he explained. "Simplicity of form." He gestured to the cross: "And holiness."

At that moment, the Pope walked into the room.

He was not a tall man. Of moderate height, he walked with a slight stoop, almost unnoticeable because of his face. The face drew the attention with a gentle absoluteness. It was a radiant face, kind, grave, and serene, but in no way distant. The wrinkles expressed a lifetime of laughter and sorrow. He had been a slave laborer under the Nazis as a youth, ordained in an underground seminary during the Soviet régime. An outstanding scholar, poet, playwright, a man of vast cultural formation, in no way an isolated academic. Perhaps one of the foremost philosophers of the century, he had accepted with reluctance becoming a bishop. It had proved the making of the man. The ensuing decades of the late twentieth century had thrown him into most of its major moral and sociopolitical conflicts, during which he had learned to function under fire not only as a teacher but as a pastor. He was gifted with a genius for imparting the Gospel message as a reality anyone could live. He made goodness credible. He had impressed upon the world his conviction that Truth and Love were made to work together, were not at war with each other—an insight that had long fallen into disuse. Whether or not the world took it to heart, or even remembered that he had said it, was daily becoming a moot issue. If many had heard, many had rejected.

Elijah fell to his knees and took the pontiff's ring hand in order to kiss it, but the Pope grasped him by the arms and made him rise.

"Father Elijah, welcome to Saint Peter's."

"Thank you, Holy Father."

"Have you made a pleasant journey? You must be tired? Please, come, everyone, let us sit."

The Pope took the center of a grouping of three chairs facing a single chair. *Stato* took the seat to his right, and a slender, white-haired man took the chair to his left. This must be *Dottrina*, the prefect of the Congregation for the Doctrine of the Faith, that secretariat which guarded the purity of the Church's teaching.

They were introduced, and Elijah felt himself assessed by the prefect—his eyes were cool, clear, set in a transparent face.

"I enjoyed your article on biblical spirituality very much", said the prefect. "You write with courage, yet you avoid the vertigo of personal rancor."

"Thank you, Eminence."

"Few exegetes agree with your position. Biblical criticism is dominated by modernist thinking, so there is a vested interest in disproving your hypothesis."

"The recent discoveries at Ephesus and the Dead Sea are objective facts. I believe they will restore many scholars to sanity."

"I hope you are right, Father. They will restore the sincere ones. Those who pursue other agendas will not be moved, not even by this overwhelming evidence offered by the new scrolls."

"It is to be hoped that the codices will at the very least expose the subjectivity of the dissidents to themselves. A moment of grace."

"When a scholar realizes that he has been subjective," interjected *Stato,* "it is a moment of painful awakening. It is the test of a man. If he is intellectually honest, he reexamines his opinions and begins again."

"And, I think, he becomes a better scholar because of his humbling", *Dottrina* added.

"Much good can come from this", said the Pope. "More than the restoration of our Catholic scholars. There is, above all, the evangelical reality. This discovery is within the plans of divine Providence, for the Lord has revealed the scrolls at precisely the moment in history when they are most needed."

The chamberlain wheeled in a trolley on which stood a tea pot, a carafe of coffee, cups and saucers, black bread and butter, cheese, and lemon biscuits. The chamberlain served Elijah first, the priest noted with some discomfort, the cardinals next, and the Pope last of all.

"Father," said the Pope, "you are wondering why we have called you here to Rome under such unusual circumstances."

"Yes, Holy Father."

"The matter before us only superficially concerns archeology. It is a most delicate subject. I ask you to keep the things we are about to discuss in the strictest confidence."

"Of course."

"The destiny of many souls depends on what passes between us this evening."

Elijah waited.

"I will ask the Cardinal Secretary of State to describe a certain situation which now confronts the Church."

"As you know," said the urbane Italian, "we face hostility on several levels. As a city-state, the Vatican is presently embroiled in difficulties with the Italian national government, which for some time has vacillated between a return to neofascism on the one hand and euro-communism on the other. That is a problem on the regional level, and although it is potentially a source of practical difficulties, it offers little threat to the survival of the universal Church. As shepherd of the universal Church, however, the Holy Father now faces a number of challenges on the level of global development, massive shifts in the geopolitical structure of the world. There is spiritual confusion everywhere, deformation of our own faithful through perversion of the communications media, and dissension within because of the influence of false teachers. These are but some of the challenges facing us in the years ahead. In none of these fields is there notable promise of improvement, at least in the near future. Throughout the world we are characterized as the major stumbling block between man and universal prosperity. All social problems are blamed on inadequate global population policy, and, of course, we stand opposed to any policy that demeans the value of a single human person for the sake of 'the people'."

The Pope leaned forward.

58

"Thank you, Cardinal Secretary. Of utmost concern to me is an ominous tendency in the West to remain blind to new forms of totalitarianism. Throughout the world fascist materialism and socialist materialism are almost dead, with the exception of China, but atheistic materialism in its capitalistic form is showing itself every bit as destructive. Tens of millions are dying each year through abortion and euthanasia. This has been a century of violent materialistic ideology, which has left in its wake a civilization almost entirely denuded of its sense of the meaning of life. Man is a creature of heaven *and* earth, but he no longer knows it. He no longer knows himself. He no longer listens. He no longer hears. As a result, we are approaching a crisis of major proportions."

Elijah realized that the Pope and his two most powerful cardinals were setting a stage for something. Something they wanted of him. He could not begin to imagine what that might be. He considered himself an insignificant creature in the drama of the times, so hidden that the thought of himself as a useful servant of the Church was as laughable as it was mystifying. He was in no way afflicted with false humility, for he had a sense of his own qualities. But he considered himself useful to God only to the degree that he had given away his life and to the degree that he had built a life of prayer on the foundation of self-abandonment. He was a monk. He praised God and he interceded to Him for mankind.

Dottrina shifted in his seat and unfolded his arms.

"It may be that we are now facing the final confrontation between the Gospel and the anti-Gospel," he said gravely, "between the Church and the anti-Church."

"You use the word *final,* Eminence. Are you speaking in an apocalyptic sense?"

The three men nodded in assent.

"Do you mean in the sense of the ultimate Apocalypse?"

"The Scriptures tell us that no man knows the hour or the day of the coming of the Son of Man", said the Pope. "Yet each generation is called to vigilance."

"Holy Father, may I ask you to clarify? Do you—you personally—believe that these are the times prophesied by the prophets of the Old Testament, by our Lord Himself, and by Saint Paul and Saint John in the New Testament?"

The Pope looked at the floor, his eyes filled with some vast grief of a kind no other human being could experience.

"Several popes and many of the Church Fathers, in their respective centuries, believed that theirs was the time of the End, and that their flocks were the children of the Last Days. It is a dangerous thing to speculate. It is not always the best thing for the Pope to speak his mind. My intuitions, indeed my convictions, are not *ex cathedra.* However, they are mine. And I suspect that the Holy Spirit put me in this chair for a reason."

"I think the Holy Father would like an assurance from you", said *Dottrina,* "that his personal thoughts on apocalyptic subjects will remain strictly a private exchange between the four of us."

"You have my solemn assurance. If you wish, I will treat it as covered by the sacramental seal of confession."

"That is not necessary, Father. I know that your word is good. To answer your question, my son: Yes. I believe we are living through the culmination of history as we know it. I believe that the return of the Lord is imminent, perhaps within three or four years, possibly a decade."

Elijah's heart contracted. He felt a thrill of fear. Then, a wave of blackness rose up before him. He felt his limbs tremble and was surprised by this reaction. Apocalyptics was a field of biblical studies, academic, abstract, a scenario for the future, detached from the reality of his life—at worst it was a distant thunder.

The wave subsided as he called upon his faith in Christ.

"You are silent. Almost surely you are feeling in your heart what untold millions would feel if I were to speak of this from the Chair of Peter. They would hear it without the benefit of your strong faith. Modern man could not presently endure this knowledge. He suffers from the major disease of our century, a kind of absolute despair. As a result, he would simply ignore the truth or reject it out of hand."

Stato spoke next: "If you have followed the Holy Father's pastoral plan for his pontificate, you will see that he goes everywhere on earth proclaiming Jesus Christ as the Savior of the world, as Lord of History. The Pope is everywhere maligned because he is a sign of contradiction, because men no longer think history is redeemable by ordinary methods. They are turning more and more to radical solutions of a collectivist nature. Marxism and fascism are brutal forms of the same principle. Despair drives modern man to these solutions, but horrified by the brutality of the recent past, he seeks new forms that preserve the *appearances* of democracy. The horror is now hidden."

During this soliloquy, the Pope appeared to be no longer listening. He was staring toward the end of the room where the trees grew. One of them was in flower.

"It is a dark century", said *Dottrina*. "To look into this darkness and see there the victory of Christ is the essence of hope."

The Pope stood up, walked to the end of the room, and stopped at the cluster of trees. He looked at them without speaking.

Stato continued as if the Pope were not present: "The Holy Father goes about the world speaking of Jesus and speaking of hope. He believes that when men have hope they can look into the face of reality and awaken to their danger."

The Pope turned and looked at the two cardinals and the priest.

"Do you recall the passage in Matthew's Gospel where the Lord curses the barren fig tree?" he asked.

They murmured assent.

"Do you know why the Lord did such an amazing thing?"

"As a sign to them", said *Stato*. "The barren tree was a figure of the Pharisees, masters of the Law who would not produce good fruit because of their unbelief."

"That is part of the meaning", said the Pope. "There is more. Father Elijah?"

"Your Holiness, I think the Lord meant it as a warning to the shepherds of his people. A fig tree that is covered with leaves yet bears no fruit has the appearance of life, but does not bear life."

"Yes. Go on."

"It is a warning."

"One of the Lord's hard sayings?"

"Yes."

"My brothers," said the Pope, touching the branch of a tree, looking sternly at the cardinals, "do you know what species of tree this is?"

"A fig", said the cardinals simultaneously.

"And you, Father, do you recognize this other one, this flowering one?"

"An almond. We have many in our garden at Carmel."

"What does it say to us?"

"The local people sometimes call it *the watching tree,* because it is the first to bloom in the spring. It is like a watchman."

"Do you know what the Lord has to say to the watchman who does not keep a watchful eye over his household?"

None of the others knew the answer precisely.

"You will find his admonition in Ezekiel, chapter 3", said the Pope. "And you know what the Lord has to say to shepherds who do not feed and protect their flocks. Ezekiel again, my friends. Chapter 34."

He returned to his seat and looked at Elijah.

"In Matthew 24 are written the Lord's apocalyptic warnings. There, he again speaks of the fig tree. I ask you, is the household of faith bearing the fruit it is called to bear?"

None replied.

"The Lord is close, my brothers. The time is not far off."

"You seem troubled, Father", said *Stato.*

"I am. In my heart is a confirmation of all that you have said.

It is, in a manner of speaking, the unfolding of a blossom that has been budding within me for most of my life. It has opened here in a few short minutes, and suddenly I see the events of my past in an entirely new light."

"Tell me of this new consciousness. What do you see?" said the Pope.

"I am unsure of it, Holy Father."

"This light which has shone upon your life is not new to us. For many years we have known of you and loved you as a son, though you knew nothing of our attention. Your life has been full of suffering. You have been tried in the furnace of affliction in a way that few men endure. You have emerged a man of faith. That is rare."

"There are many like me."

"There are many watching trees blooming in the world. None with those qualifications which bring you to this place at this moment in history."

"Perhaps it is time to speak of that, Holy Father", said *Dottrina.*

"Father Elijah, many wolves are presently circling my flock. I repeatedly call my flock to vigilance, but few of them hear my voice. Many of the lambs are pulled from us and destroyed. Many. Many."

The Pope's eyes filled with grief.

"Certain figures on the world's stage are now moving toward the flock for a definitive attack. They are approaching the moment when they will exert every effort at division and destruction. They are crying *peace, peace,* but there is no peace. Their hearts are full of murder. They hate the flock of God, and yet everywhere they are proclaimed as saviors. This too lies within the plan of divine Providence. This too He permits, for the final confrontation between the Church and the anti-Church must come. It can only be put off from generation to generation. In our time, I believe, it has come."

"How can I help you, Holy Father?"

"A man is rising in global power. I have prayed for this man for many years. Early in my pontificate, his face arose before me while I was at prayer. To all the world he appears as a kind of secular saint. The press lauds him as a man of destiny. His face is on the covers of journals, on the television, in essays and editorials, and his books are selling in the millions. He has reinvigorated a lagging European Parliament. He is being courted by the United Nations as the one man who can moderate a peaceful transition from the era of nation-states to world federation."

Elijah knew the name of the man even before *Stato* spoke it.

"You are familiar with this name?"

"Yes, Eminence. I have heard of little else since leaving the monastery."

"In addition to the presidency of the European Parliament, he is the current director of the Council of Western Nations, consultant to the United Nations, and member of the Club of Rome. He is on the board of directors of several of the world's most prosperous corporations. He has controlling interest in a publishing empire, a Swiss bank, and *Globaltek,* the firm which has revolutionized computer imaging technology. He is also the founder of *Centro Mondiale Commerciale,* possibly the world's most important trade center. There are other accomplishments too numerous to mention."

"There are many who are openly against Christ," said the Pope, "and others who come falsely in the name of Christ. But this one who stands quietly among them is more powerful than them all. His moment in history is approaching."

"Does it disturb you?" asked *Dottrina.*

"I am not so much disturbed as puzzled. What is my role in this?"

"I ask you to be a messenger."

"A messenger, Holy Father?"

"I desire to warn him of his personal spiritual danger. I must warn him that he could drag the world into the abyss."

"Would not a personal meeting between yourself and him be more effective?"

"I have asked him to visit me, but he will not come. There is always some excuse. I understand now that this man is politically astute."

"Why won't he come?"

"He wishes it to be seen in the world's press that he does not come to the Pope; the Pope comes to him. I would gladly go to him and wash his feet if it would move his soul to repentance. But he would see the gesture only as a ripe plum falling into his hands. It would do more evil than good."

"The media would be present", *Stato* interjected. "A photograph of this would be worth to him, in propaganda value, a thousand newspaper articles."

"He wishes to use the Church for as long as he needs her", said the Pope. "But he despises her, because he has never understood her divine nature. He does not understand her strength. He thinks she is only a human institution. The human aspect of the Church is flawed, wavering, internally divided, badly shaken by the events of this century. She is a weak thing in his eyes, a thing to be used and then destroyed when it suits him."

"You find this difficult to believe?" said *Dottrina,* holding Elijah in his gaze.

"It is difficult to believe that any human being could be that callous."

"Is it so difficult? You say this, you who suffered during the Holocaust?"

"A good point, Eminence."

"He is not openly against us, at least not yet", said the Pope. "But he is preparing. There still may be time. There may be hope beyond hope. I do not call any man Antichrist while his soul hangs in the balance, while he is still free to choose the good. But with utmost certainty, I tell you that his ideas move in the realm of Antichrist. Even so, Christ would come for even one man. Christ died for this man."

"You wish to send me to him?"

"Yes."

"I am afraid."

"I would be gravely concerned if you were not afraid."

"I do not have sufficient wits to battle a . . . "

Stato interjected: "The President appears to the entire world to embody the very best in human nature. He counts heavily on that image. Although there is a hidden side to him, we are blessed with a short period during which he preserves the public appearance of goodness. This is the moment when you may speak the truth to him. In a year, two years from now, it may be too late. The loss in human souls would be catastrophic."

"The loss of even one soul is catastrophic", said the Pope. "This is a terrible responsibility, Father. I do not exact obedience from you. I ask it of you. Will you be the bearer of my message to this man?"

Elijah hesitated. He knew that he was free to decline. He could return on tomorrow's flight to Israel, bury himself in Carmel, pray for the endangered souls, pray for the conversion of the false lord of the world, pray for the Pope—yes, and wonder for the rest of his life what might have been had he agreed.

"I ask you to go and bear witness to him while there is still time."

"I will go."

A noticeable exhalation escaped from the three men who sat facing Elijah.

"Thank you", said the Pope.

Stato supplied the details:

"Father Elijah, you are to meet the President in order to present a report of the Pontifical Commission for Biblical Archeology on the new discoveries in caves near Ephesus and by the Dead Sea. The scrolls therein effectively date the writings of the Gospels to the time of the apostles and confirm the accuracy of orthodox translations, thus confounding modernist biblical criticism. The President is a devotee of archeology and classical studies. This report will be delivered as a gesture of personal welcome to the incoming President of the European Parliament and as a first gesture of dialogue between the Vatican City State and the new government. The ostensible purpose of the meeting is an exchange of courtesies. In private conversation with the President, however, you will attempt to discover his covert intentions and relay a message of spiritual exhortation from His Holiness the Pope. You must conduct your side of the exchange in the most cordial manner. You must use the utmost discretion. If the warning cannot be communicated to good effect, either through interference or lack of receptivity on his part, you must then attempt to establish a means of continuing the dialogue."

"Is this clear?" asked *Dottrina.*

"I see that you have suggested the general parameters, yet it leaves room for creativity."

"Certainly. You are not a cipher, Father. We could send a fax or a diplomatic note. Instead, we send him a minister of God. The quality of the messenger is an essential aspect of the message."

"I am still perplexed regarding your choice of messengers."

"Your many outstanding qualities are not the deciding factor", said *Stato.* "Nor is Monsignor Stangsby to be blamed for your predicament. It was not our William who, as it were, pushed you forward."

"Then how do I come to be sitting here?"

"You can blame your prior", said *Stato.* "He and I are old friends. He has observed you closely for many years. He believes that you have a unique insight into men of power."

"Is he aware of the nature of this mission?"

"He knows only that it is urgent, and that you will carry a message from His Holiness to a politically sensitive recipient."

"You were once a man of power", said *Dottrina.* "Why did you give it up?"

"I received a message", Elijah replied slowly.

"A message? Like this one?"

"Different. A world of difference. But it dislodged me from a path that might have led to errors similar to the President's. I was heading toward a future that contained power, the power to do good for mankind. It was an extraordinarily magnetic thing. It took a total effort of the will to throw it off."

"If the objective was good, why did you?"

"Because I saw that we were doing some of the things that had been done to us by the Hitlerites. There were violations of human rights committed by our own people. I had turned a blind eye to it. I had begun to excuse the inexcusable—in the name of a just cause."

The Pope and his two cardinals listened without speaking.

"The foundation of my thinking was wrong", said Elijah. "I hated. I hated those who had destroyed my family. I wanted as much power as possible because I thought if I had it, I could rehabilitate the entire universe. How strange that temptation seems to me now. But then it seemed to be the highest good imaginable, saving mankind."

"You thought yourself a savior?"

"Yes. I dread to think what I might have become, if such *worldpower* had been put into my hands."

"But you chose a different path," said the Pope, "and for that choice I will be eternally grateful. You will be able to discern the interior dynamics of this man in a way that none of us could. You must pray earnestly to the Holy Spirit. Ask Him to give you the words to unlock this man's heart."

"You must pray for me, Holy Father."

"I will. Daily. Hourly. Continuously."

"When does my mission begin?"

"In a week's time, the President will again receive visitors at his estate on the island of Capri. He is presently overseeing the reconstruction of Tiberius' palace. Preliminary agreement has been reached that an emissary from the Vatican will deliver a papal message to him there on Monday of next week. Today is Tuesday. I would like you to spend several days in preparation at the Franciscan convent at Assisi. A friar who lives there is a friend of mine. He will strengthen you."

The Pope stood.

"Please give my apostolic blessing to Don Matteo, and tell him that the Pope asks for his prayers."

He embraced Elijah. The priest closed his eyes and drank from the strength in the old prelate's arms. It was a timeless feeling, as if harmony and hope existed at this one quiet station on a whirling planet.

The Pope traced the sign of the cross on Elijah's forehead, bid each of them good night, and left.

"Well," said *Stato,* "let us go find William. We have many things to tell him."

"How much of this am I free to discuss with him?"

"You can discuss the general nature of the mission. I have already outlined it to him. He is to accompany you to Capri."

Elijah looked at the cardinal thoughtfully.

"I understand your hesitation", said *Stato.* "William is a solid fellow, but his tongue . . . ah, that tongue can be a problem. I have pointed out to him the need for absolute confidentiality."

Elijah nodded.

"He may need reminding", said *Stato.*

* * *

"Onward to Mordor!" shouted Billy, brandishing an invisible sword.

"Mordor? We're going to Capri."

"A figure of speech, Davy. Literary reference, English school-boy stuff."

"I see."

"You never quite understand my peculiar mental aberrations, do you?"

"I take it on faith that you know what you're talking about."

"I always know what I'm talking about. It's the *image* that confuses the other team, you see?"

"I'm not sure that I do see."

"The Billy the Kid routine. You'd be surprised at how useful it is. When people think one is an ambitious fool, they tend to say all sorts of things in front of you, revealing themselves, where they're at, and where they're bound."

"So, you are a kind of Vatican spy."

Billy snorted. "There ain't no such critter. But it pays to know your adversary. And I'd say that some of our worst adversaries are pretty close to home."

"Is it as serious as some think?"

Billy sat back on his couch and looked out his apartment window at the dome of light reflecting off the Roman night. He sighed.

"It only takes one Judas. Only one Judas." He tilted his glass and emptied it in a gulp.

"Do you know if there is a Judas active within the Church presently?"

"Lots of them."

"Close to the Holy Father?"

"I think so. Certainly within the Curia, there are some who've never been happy about the papal election. The Pope put the brakes on their interpretation of Vatican II. You've got a lot of unhappy people there."

"What about the spirit of obedience . . . and humility?"

"Good question."

"Don't they see it? Can't they recognize the temptation?"

"It begins with little things, Davy. Things that look harmless at first. Irritation, grumbling, resentment. Then, gradually, like-minded individuals gravitate toward each other. They reinforce each other's criticisms, grow bolder, gain confidence. They tell each other that *they* have interpreted the Council correctly, and the Pontiff's a throwback, an unfortunate accident, stumbling into the Chair of Peter by a fluke of ecclesial politics. Heady stuff. After a while, they convince themselves that they're *saving* the Church, dragging it against its will into the twentieth century, despite the Pope."

"Don't they see the diabolical pride in such an approach?"

"They are prelates imbued with *romanità*. They have gradually come to think that the politics of manipulation govern the Church."

"Where is the Holy Spirit in all of this?"

"They think the Holy Spirit works through their politics."

"A potent drug."

"It makes them accountable to nothing other than their own opinions and agendas."

"Do you know who these men are?"

Billy's face went expressionless. He looked intensely at Elijah and pointed at the ceiling. He got up and tapped each of the four walls.

"What are you telling me?"

"I think I'd rather not continue this discussion at the moment."

"What is it? What's the trouble?"

"Let's go for a walk."

In the precise center of the park, surrounded by sighing cypresses, Billy said, "There's pretty good evidence that somebody's been running electronic surveillance on high-level Vatican staffers. The Prefect discovered a bugging device in his office last month, and a few other offices have been penetrated. I think we'd better assume that my apartment may be subject to listeners. A lot of sensitive information crosses my desk. And as you may have guessed, I haven't always been discreet in my conversation. I've had to watch my tongue more carefully."

"Is there a possibility that the Holy Father's offices have been penetrated?"

"Security put every papal space through a sweep. We found a bug in his secretary's desk. But the papal apartment's clean."

"I'm glad of that. Our discussion last evening concerned a subject of highest sensitivity."

"He may have asked you to meet him there because it's the safest place of all. Though, heaven knows, if they eavesdropped on the Holy Father they wouldn't get much except edification. They'd be asking for baptism within the week."

"You spoke of a Judas?"

"Judases would be more accurate."

"Do you know their names?"

"I'm not sure. I believe the Holy Father knows who they are. But you have to understand him. He's really a saint, Davy. He accuses no one, he's charitable to everyone, even those he knows are his strongest opponents in the Curia."

"Are the Prefect for Doctrine and the Secretary of State loyal to him?"

"Absolutely. He hand-picked them both. *Stato* and *Dottrina* are two *very* different personalities. Radically different. But both of them love the Church and both of them love the Holy Father."

"A courageous position. *Dottrina* especially is not a popular man."

"You've observed that already? It's true. He's probably the most unpopular man in the world. They call him the Grand Inquisitor behind his back. The press grossly characterizes him as the *Éminence grise,* the sinister force behind the throne. But it's not true. He's a humble man with nerves of steel. He does the job he's supposed to do, calling people to task when they teach falsehood in the name of the Church. He's got his hands full these days. I've never seen him blow his cool. He's amazing. He's a different kind of saint, maybe a tougher kind than the Pope. I think he accepted early on that he'd be despised by anyone who has an axe to grind against the Faith, and he knew he'd be especially reviled by the media."

"I was drawn to him."

"I knew you'd be. He's without guile, as clear as a bell. He hates *romanità* with a passion and never uses it."

"And *Stato?*"

"My boss is the kind of prince of the Church whom everyone admires. Even his detractors respect him. He's something of a genius when it comes to international diplomacy, and he's a master of *romanità*. He doesn't necessarily like it but he maneuvers with it, and often succeeds in getting his way by using it. The Holy Father knew who he was dealing with when he asked him to take over the office of state."

"Do you trust him?"

"Completely. He's a brilliant administrator, frightfully clever. He's not exactly a saint—he's got a temper. But he's a fiercely righteous man."

"Why didn't the Holy Father choose him to communicate with the man on Capri?"

"That's where you're naïve. The new President knows *romanità*. He expects visiting delegations to play games with him. The last thing he expects is a missionary who will try to convert his soul."

Elijah sat in the dark on a park bench.

"It's too much for me, Billy. It's too big."

Billy sat down beside him.

"Of course it's too big. Do you think the Holy Father's so dumb he'd choose someone who thinks he can handle it? No, he knew you'd run into your weakness pretty fast. That's where the real work begins, doesn't it? When we find out it's too big for us."

"I wish I could talk with our friend Peter at this moment, Billy."

"He's praying for you, lad. The Holy Spirit's guiding this thing too. Besides, you got someone else helping you."

"Who?"

"Me!" cried Billy, brandishing his invisible sword.

Elijah did not smile.

"Onward to Mordor!" cried Billy, laughing in the dark.

IV

Assisi

Elijah meditated on the green of Umbria and tried to ignore the screeching tires of the Jaguar. Billy's ability to maneuver the back roads of the hill country was admirable, but tended to stimulate rushes of adrenaline.

"There's Mount Subasio", said Billy as they rounded a curve in the hills. "Halfway up is the town. The first thing you'll see is the walls of the basilica and the convent."

"I see them. Like a fortress."

"It's a bit of a museum piece. But don't let that deceive you. There's a nice thriving modern town behind those walls—houses, restaurants, theatres, convents, tourists, pilgrims, even some ordinary folk. The kind of stock that Francis and Clare were born into."

"I feel as if I am coming into a valley of God."

"Everyone feels something when they see Assisi for the first time. But it's really quite an ordinary place."

"Billy, I feel something I have felt nowhere else."

Billy threw him an analytical look.

"You'd be amazed at how many people have sat in that passenger seat and said those very words."

"What is it about this place?"

"It's beautiful isn't it?"

"Yes. But Mount Carmel is beautiful. Many places can boast of beauty, many of them more beautiful to the eye than this."

"It's the light of Umbria. When it falls on that village perched up there on its rocky spur, add a few larks, the groves, and the river — it's a recipe for medieval romance, old chap. You just got bit by the virus."

"It's something more, but I can't guess what."

"I always expect to bump into Dante and Beatrice here. It's the thrill of plunging back through the centuries and finding that the mythological past was real. It was somebody's present. Francis and Clare walked in those streets and loved it. Their world was more real to them than ours is to us."

"What do you mean?"

"I mean their world was so beautiful and dangerous."

"So is ours."

"Our world's pretty damn ugly, if you ask me. Look what we've done to it. We think we've licked the inconveniences by good old technology. By the way, is the air conditioning too cold for you?"

"Just right, Billy."

"Good old technology."

"I think we live in the most ugly and dangerous time of all."

"It's ugly and haunted by a sense of unreality, but is that dangerous?"

"Isn't the time of false peace the most dangerous?"

"If it *is* false peace. But if it's a time of *real* peace then the lad who runs about shouting *the end is near* needs to see a shrink."

"Then a great deal depends on how well the prophet listens to God, and how well he reads the signs of the times."

"Right. As the well-known prophet Chicken Little once said, *The sky is falling, the sky is falling!*"

"You are teasing me with your unique British sense of humor."

"Just trying to cheer you up, Davy. You're looking altogether too somber for my taste. Assisi's going to be just what the doctor ordered. You'll see."

"I feel it already."

"It's the romance of the past, I expect. For tourists it's historical romance. For religious guys like you 'n' me it's religious romance."

"I must disagree. For myself, it's not a romantic feeling. Do you remember when we spoke of a great crime the other day? An unmentionable crime that none will acknowledge?"

"Yeah?"

"It's as if the antithesis to that crime had occurred here. Some great blessing that came to mankind, but which is now falling into deep forgetfulness."

Billy did not at first respond. Then he said, "Maybe you're right. Maybe I've read too many tourist brochures."

"The presence of Saint Francis is here, not like a fossil memory lingering in the subconscious. Rather, one expects at any moment to look to the side of the road and see a little poor man in sackcloth, holding up his arms to us. He has holes in his hands. He is here. I feel it."

"Well, hold onto your hat, Davy, 'cause we're gonna do some hairpin curves up ahead. If we pass Saint Francis, tell him I can't stop at these speeds. Besides, I never pick up hitchhikers."

"Never?"

Billy's face clouded over.

"Correction. There was one. I'll tell you about it sometime."

He wheeled into the parking lot of the basilica, hopped out, and stretched.

"*Buon giorno,* Assisi!" he said with pleasure, flipping up his sunglasses and rubbing his eyes. His gold silk shirt looked cool and unruffled. Elijah began to perspire heavily in his Carmelite habit.

It was cooler inside the portals of the sacred convent. They introduced themselves to the guestmaster, a wizened little Italian who grinned when Billy handed him a note for the prior, written by the Cardinal Secretary of State.

"We've been expecting you. Come, this way, I'll show you to your rooms."

He bustled ahead of them, guiding them through the complex of the monastery to a secluded wing, which overlooked the plain lying between Perugia and Foligno. A warm breeze came through the open windows of the hallways.

"We're putting you in the annex. It's extra quiet here. Private too. Come and go as you please. You'll want to see the Giotto frescoes, no doubt, and the tomb of the Saint? Everyone does. Monsignor Stangsby shouldn't forget to show you the little Church of San Damiano. That's where the crucifix spoke to Francis. And don't miss the *Portiuncula* inside Santa Maria degli Angeli! That's the little church where Clare made her vows of poverty. Oh dear, there's always so much to see, and it's so busy now. The tourists have started in full flood. If you want some peace and quiet, go after visiting hours. I'll give Monsignor the keys. Just let me know when you're ready. Now here's a private dining room for you. It's not fancy. Even the Pope eats here when he comes. *Don't put on the dog for me, Brother,* he says. *Simple,* he says, *I love simple best of all,* he always says to me. Such a special man, our Holy Father. How is he? How's his health? Good? Glad to hear it! Tell him hello for me."

He led Billy to a guest room beside the dining hall, then dragged Elijah to the one beside it.

"My apologies, Father. What did you say your name was? Now, Monsignor Stangsby gets the Pope's bedroom, because he's a rung up the ladder, but you get the corner room with the view, so I'd say you have the best of the bargain. My apologies, Monsignor. You'll find a refrigerator in the kitchenette. Fruit, coffee, bread. Make yourselves at home. There's the private chapel at the end of the corridor. No one else is staying in this wing. *Pax et bonum.* Goodbye. Ring for me if you need assistance. *Pax et bonum.*"

The friar backed down the hall, smiling and blessing them verbally, bowing repeatedly and retreating until he parted the double doors, leaving the two visitors standing in a ringing silence.

Then the song of larks came in on the breeze. Elijah felt indescribably happy.

"I'm going to catch a snooze", said Billy. "Come in for half a mo' and see the pontifical suite."

Elijah peeked into Billy's room, a small cell with cot, desk, and chair. A private bathroom contained a shower, sink, and toilet. The only decoration was a single icon above the bed—a copy of the cross of San Damiano that had spoken to Saint Francis.

"Palatial, isn't it?" sighed Billy.

"Full of romance", said Elijah.

"You think you can tease me with Israeli humor, don't you! No such luck! Begone!"

"Have a good rest, Billy."

"Thanks. You too."

"Good night, Andy."

Billy shook his luggage. "Good night, Father", said a wee voice from inside the suitcase.

Elijah went back to his own room and lay down on the cot. He realized suddenly how very tired he was, a fatigue that reached into his bones. He fell asleep and did not wake until a bell rang for supper.

The meal porter, a massive young friar in a frayed robe, pushed a trolly into the dining room and placed a tray beside the setting for one.

Elijah introduced himself.

"I am Jakov", the brother replied.

After some pleasantries, he dug out of Jakov that he was a Croatian Franciscan, a refugee from the Balkan wars.

"Is perfect joy", he said with an enigmatic look.

"Perfect joy?" said Elijah, straining to understand what was being communicated.

"Perfect joy", the friar repeated, bobbing his head up and down. He was alone in the world, he explained, his family had been massacred.

He pointed to the sky and said, "Brother Francis is my family, no?"

"Your brother and your father", suggested Elijah.

The friar stood motionless, staring into middle space, reliving an experience.

"Is Monsignor Stangsby not eating?" said Elijah.

"Oh, I forget it too much. He leaves a letter for you, Father. He is gone for make visiting with the friends at San Crispin's. He talk you tomorrow."

The brother removed a letter that had suffered considerably in his apron pocket. He attempted to unfold and unstain it, putting it on the table by the plate. Elijah thanked him and the brother departed.

Dear Davy,
Have gone to see some people at S. Crispin's on Agnes Street. We're going out to dinner at a real restaurant. Sorry to abandon you, but you know it's good for your soul. The Pope's friend, Father Matteo, will track you down after seven o'clock or thereabouts. Relax. There's no such thing as time in Assisi. Pax et Bonum!
Yours,
B.

Elijah consumed a meal of sliced eggs, cheese, celery, crusty white rolls, downed a miniature carafe of the driest red wine, and finished with a basket of green grapes.

When he went out of the dining room the sun was low, bursting through the window at the end of the corridor. He went to the chapel and knelt there before the Presence. The peace he felt was different from that of Carmel or Rome. It was saturated in the charism of this extraordinary shrine, a sense that could not be described without resort to crudely rendered metaphors. It was an incense that hung in the air. Like childhood restored after a long corruption. Like a maiden singing in the dusk. It was like an ode to beauty that was beauty itself, incarnating beauty while it tried to avoid the folly of talking *about* beauty. Assisi was *like* something, but like what? Like something one had always known, but never seen. Something perceived from afar, like a wind from the promised land that greeted the stranger and sojourner coming up out of bondage from Egypt.

It was joy, no doubt about that. But a joy unlike any other joy he had ever experienced. Unexpected joy in a dark time. Curious joy. There was no other word that approximated it. A taste of sweetness like the fecundity of grape arbors in the terraces below, sweetness on the tongue and a promise of scent on the night air. It was sensual in the best meaning of that word, saturating every sense at once, so that the flesh was known, finally, as a thing of such goodness that man blessed his Creator from morning to night for having made him. Here in this medieval town where once an extraordinary little fellow had burst forth with songs to God, as a passionate lover speaks to his bride, here the restoration of man to his own true home was no longer the dream of saints. It was the wedding feast. It was a word made flesh.

He closed his eyes and prayed a thanksgiving. When he opened them again the chapel was dark and night had fallen. Only the sanctuary lamp illuminated the interior of the room. He became aware that another person was there also, a friar, motionless in the back pew.

He thought it must be the guestmaster or the young Croatian, but as he passed the kneeling figure on the way out, the other friar looked up. Elijah saw that he was a man of advanced age.

The friar stood and followed him into the corridor. "Father Elijah?" he said in a frail voice.

"Yes?"

"I am Don Matteo."

The friar bowed to him and did not appear to notice Elijah's hand extended in greeting.

Elijah returned the bow.

"Don Matteo, the Holy Father sends you his embrace and apostolic blessing. He asks for your prayers for an urgent intention."

"I will pray", said the friar. He was an unimpressive figure, pale, sickly, his hands hidden in folds of dark brown cloth. His habit was patched and looked several sizes too large for him.

Elijah waited silently, at a loss for words. It now struck him that his purpose in coming to the convent at Assisi had not been described in precise terms.

He will strengthen you, the Pope had said.

"The Holy Father wishes you to rest here", said Don Matteo.

"Did the Holy Father communicate to you the nature of my mission?"

"I know the nature of your mission."

"He said that you would strengthen me."

"The Lord will strengthen you. Spend much time before Him in the Blessed Sacrament. Bask in the radiance of the tabernacle. Tomorrow before breakfast we will say Mass in the chapel, hidden from the eyes of the curious."

"Is there anything else I should do?"

"Fast a little, if you like. Remember that obedience is the great fast. Practice interior mortifications frequently throughout the days that you are with us. It is better than giving up a chocolate bar." Father Matteo smiled gently.

"Should I read?"

"Read Matthew 24, and anything else in Scripture the Holy Spirit prompts you to read. I suggest that you keep your mind free. Be still. Wait for God."

"I crave silence, Father. It has been three days of continuous noise since I left Israel. My mind is reeling."

"The world is a noisy place. Yes, keep silence. Then, when you are rested, visit the tomb of Francis and pray before his crucifix."

"It would be a great joy for me if you would accompany me to these places."

"We'll go together. But I see that you are very tired. Tonight and tomorrow you must rest. Pray and rest."

With that, the old friar bade him a good night and limped off through the doors to the enclosure.

Elijah fell asleep listening to the choir of insects and night birds praising outside the screened window of his room.

*　　*　　*

Don Matteo returned before dawn. No amount of knocking on Billy's door was able to rouse him from sleep, and thus Elijah concelebrated Mass alone with the friar. In his many years as a priest he had never attended a Mass offered with such rapt attention. The friar lingered over each word. At the Consecration, Elijah wondered if he had lost the other priest to unconsciousness, for the friar stood without moving, holding the host aloft for several minutes. As the folds of his habit fell back from his wrists, his hands were exposed. Elijah saw that he wore black woollen gloves from which the finger sections had been removed. His exposed fingers were long, white, extremely fragile, yet the palms hidden beneath the gloves appeared to be thick, as if swollen.

The sun rose at the moment of the elevation and burst through the stained glass window, throwing burning colors across the room. Father Matteo's eyes were closed; he did not seem to notice the epiphany of light. Time itself was suspended above the world, held within his hands, transfixed by the rapture of his upturned face. The broken fragments of color had begun to cross the tiles of the central aisle when he lowered his arms and continued with the words of the canon.

During their prayer of silent thanksgiving after Mass, Elijah noticed again that the friar slipped into what appeared to be perfect composure of body, a stillness that approached languid immobility. The eyes were closed, the attention fixed within. The friar remained kneeling for so long that Elijah could not persevere in that position. His joints were aching. He left the chapel briefly to go to the bathroom, and when he returned the friar was gone.

The remainder of the day was spent in silence, with periods of reading and sleep alternating with hours of stillness before the Blessed Sacrament. He felt the tension of the preceding days melting away.

Before supper he accomplished a slow meditative reading of Matthew 24 and was struck especially by the warning of Christ: *In the days before the flood people were eating and drinking, marrying and being married, right up until the day Noah entered the Ark. They were totally unconcerned until the flood came and destroyed them. So it will be at the coming of the Son of Man.*

Elijah sat in his room gazing out over the peaceful Umbrian countryside until the bell rang for supper. The Croatian brought in a tray loaded with blue cheese, sliced ham, crusty Italian rolls, olives, grapes, and a bowl of chocolate pudding. A jug of iced tea sweated beside a glass into which a quarter of a lemon had been dropped.

Jakov seemed unusually solemn.

Elijah saw that the Croatian's eyes were troubled. To his amazement, Jakov sat down in the chair beside him, laid his head on his arms, and burst into sobs.

"What is it, my brother?" Elijah said, touching the man's shoulder.

"I sorry, Father. I no want to make cry. I want finish serve supper, go pray, and cry nobody see me."

"Tell me, what is it?"

"This day is feast of my family killed in Croatia."

"How long ago?"

"Four years this day."

"I am sorry, Jakov. You carry a heavy suffering. I will pray for their souls at Mass."

"I pray. I forgive killers. But again I am want to kill them in my heart. I hate them!" he said through gritted teeth.

"I know this feeling. My own family . . ."

"Nobody know what I feel. They put us inside church. I see my mother shooted. I see my father shooted, my little brothers shooted. They rape my sister, many, many soldiers rape my sister and then they shoot her. They do all this in front of God. They shoot Jesus on altar. It too bad I cannot speak it."

"How did you escape?"

"Soldiers hit me with hammer all over. They cut me, burn me. They shoot priest, but they keep me for torture. Our army attack next day and bomb in that house. I almost die. The bad soldiers run away. I spend long time in hospital."

"God will deal with those men, Jakov. Don't let the hatred poison you."

"I forgive. Then I hate, then I forgive. Hate, forgive, hate, forgive."

"Your family is in Paradise."

"I hope this."

"They are happy now. They smile on you. They love you. They see you so unhappy and want you to be consoled."

"Father, but I ask one thing you tell me?"

"What is it, Jakov?"

"Where God?" he said in a small voice.

"He suffered in them. They suffered on the Cross with Him. Their reward will be great in heaven."

"I want this be true. But today it be too hard. Today it hard believe this be true. Tomorrow maybe better."

"I will pray that you know it's true."

"I sorry, Father. I talk too much, you no eat supper."

"Tonight I fast for you and your family. Please take the meal away."

Brother Jakov looked horrified.

"I make it you no hungry!"

"I am hungry. But I am happy to fast. I fast for you."

"I no like it", he cried. "You eat. Get strong."

"If I don't eat tonight I will be stronger than if I had eaten."

"No, no. I bad. I do this to you."

"You are not bad. You did not do this to me. You are a messenger, a good messenger."

Elijah loaded everything back onto the tray while Jakov dried his eyes on his sleeve. He took the brother by the arm and guided him through the refectory door to the kitchen. He put the food away in the refrigerator.

"You see. It's here if I get very hungry."

"Promise, Father, eat if get weak."

"I promise. Come here, Jakov."

Jakov took a step closer.

"I wish to pray for you. May I pray for you?"

"Yes."

The giant bent his head. Elijah placed both hands on the crown of the friar's head and invoked healing upon his tormented memory. He felt a current of warmth begin to glow in his hands. He appealed to the mercy of Christ who once had been nailed in agony. He implored divine healing to come upon this anguished heart.

Jakov began to sigh deeply, and groans came from his mouth. Tears streamed from his eyes, but they were no longer noisy sobs. Peace gradually enveloped the two men, and presently Elijah felt the current of warmth subside. Jakov's sighs died away, and he wiped his eyes.

"Jesus suffers in us, my brother. He heals in us too."

"I know it. Don Matteo, he sometime put his hands on my head. I feel warm in my head and it go down to my heart. His hands got hole in it, and God comes through this holes. Just like you. He help me."

Elijah nodded, although he did not quite grasp the meaning of the last comment. Yes, perhaps the hands of a healer were like that, he mused, an instrument, a channel or a hole through which the power of heaven poured into the broken heart.

Jakov reached down and took Elijah's hands in his. The giant bent and kissed them. Then, embarrassed, he backed through the door, after eliciting yet another promise that Father would eat if he became weak.

He sat in the chapel without thoughts, without words. He turned out the lights before nine, but tossed and turned for some time before a fitful sleep overtook him.

*   *   *

The next morning Elijah celebrated Mass by himself in the empty chapel. Shortly afterward, Jakov delivered breakfast to the dining room. His face was composed, neither happy nor unhappy.

"How are you today, my friend?"

"I good, Father. Monsignor say he come back for supper. He go to Spoleto with friends."

"Thank you, Jakov."

Don Matteo came by after breakfast and asked if Elijah would like to see the image that "spoke" to Saint Francis. A short walk brought them to the stone building Francis and his companions had restored after the saint heard the words of Christ.

A rose window above the central arch illuminated the interior with a faint light. The gray walls of the nave created the impression of a cave. Suspended above the altar was the famous cross. It was primitive, Byzantine, painted on wood during the twelfth century.

"Francis fell in love with God", said Don Matteo. "He saw the heart of God radiating from the beauty in all creation. One day he was riding on the plain of Assisi. He met a leper whose sores were so loathsome that Francis was struck with horror and desired strongly to flee. But this spoiled young man, the son of a wealthy cloth merchant, had gradually come to understand that spiritual warfare for Christ begins with victory over one's self. He dismounted, and as the leper stretched forth his hands, begging for alms, Francis embraced him and kissed him. His revulsion was overcome by love welling up within his heart.

"Some traditions have it that when Francis remounted and turned back to the leper to say good-bye, the poor man had disappeared. The leper was Christ in disguise, you see. It is sometimes said that this last detail may be a pious embellishment. Nevertheless, it is theologically insightful."

"Father Matteo, do you think he was Christ in disguise?"

"I am certain of it."

"Why are you certain?"

"Because I have seen more wondrous things than that with my own eyes. And because it is so much in the character of our Lord to hide Himself, that men may learn to love with *the eye that hath not seen.*"

"A love that springs from an interior seeing?"

"*Sì.* That encounter was only the beginning for Francis. One day he stopped to pray in this very church. It was in a tumble-down state, uncared for. Francis knelt before the cross, probably right here where we're standing. As he prayed, he heard a voice speak to him from the image. It said to him three times, *Francis, go and repair my church, which is falling into ruins.*

"Francis was overwhelmed. But he resolved to do what the voice had asked of him. He thought the Lord meant that this building must be repaired. He returned to his home and took a horseload of cloth from his father's warehouse and sold it, along with the horse, to raise funds for the repairs. He took the money to the poor priest of San Damiano's and asked if he could be allowed to stay with him. His father, hearing what the boy had done, came in a fury, dragged him home and locked him up until he was restored to his senses. Francis ran away again. The bishop intervened in favor of the father and declared that the Church could not profit from stolen goods. Francis returned the money, then stripped himself of his fine clothes, naked, and handed them to his father.

"He went forth from that place dressed only in the rags of a laborer. He became a beggar and a pilgrim. Considered mad by all who had known the rich young man, he was everywhere reviled as a scandal and treated with contempt as a son who had brought shame upon his father's house. He returned to San Damiano and began to repair it with his bare hands, stone by stone. He next did the same for another old church, then for a little chapel called the Portiuncula, which was also in ruinous condition. The boy grew in holiness. One by one, other young men came and joined in his work. They lived on scraps of food that the townsfolk threw to them. Francis was given the gift of prophecy and miracles. A man in Spoleto was afflicted with a cancer that had disfigured him quite hideously. He heard about the holy young man and came to see him in the hope of obtaining prayers. He met Francis and was about to throw himself at his feet, when Francis prevented him and kissed his diseased face, which was instantly healed."

"Father, is this detail an embellishment?"

"Ah, you mean is it romantic hagiography?"

"Do you think it happened just like that?"

"I do", the friar said simply.

"Because you have seen wondrous things with your own eyes?"

"Once again I tell you, I have seen more wondrous things than that. But I will add what Saint Bonaventure once wrote about this incident. He said, 'I know not which I ought to wonder at, such a cure or such a kiss.'"

Elijah nodded. Bonaventure's insight was the concise summation of the whole problem. Which was the greater miracle, the suspension of natural law for the sake of physical healing, or the conversion of the human heart by absolute love?

The friar said no more. They returned to the convent in silence. At the New Gate, Don Matteo paused and took Elijah's arm in his gloved hand.

"There is another thing Francis would show you."

"What is that?"

"In the beginning, he thought that he was called to repair the physical ruins of a few little churches in the Umbrian hill country. He did not see that the universal Church was falling headlong into ruin through the sins of her members, especially the clergy of the time. As his band of followers grew, he began to understand that the restoration of the House of God to grace was to be his work. His order spread rapidly throughout Italy and beyond. There were five thousand professed brothers when Francis was only in his thirties. They preached everywhere in Europe, lived a life of radical poverty, and almost singlehandedly restored Christendom to the Faith."

"You said that you think Francis is showing me something in this?"

"He is showing you a simple thing, but one so often missed by those who pursue holiness. God frequently leads the soul to a rather insignificant chore. If the soul is faithful to it, he leads him on to other tasks. He begins with the particular and consummates the work in the universal."

"I can see that. But, I confess, I don't see how it applies to my life."

"Do you not?" said the friar with his small smile. He patted Elijah's arm then shuffled away to his enclosure.

V

Ruth

For the remainder of that day he could not shake a memory from his thoughts:

Jerusalem in winter. Morning light. Snow fell on the city that year, as it did once every six years or so. A cold wind. Arab children singing Christmas carols. Slate-colored clouds wandering across the yellow sky. The Shrine of the Book, the museum of the Dead Sea Scrolls, was practically deserted. A tall woman in her late twenties came up beside him and gazed into a glass case where the scroll of Isaiah was displayed. David happened to be looking at a passage of the same scroll. The woman was squinting, trying to read it. He found himself staring at her face reflected in the glass. A confident intelligence shone from her eyes. She was attractive. But there was something else—a mixture of sweetness and strength—none of the stridency that was customary with many young Israelis.

"*Look to Abraham your father, and to Sarah who gave you birth*", she said without looking at him, as if they had always known each other. "*When he was but alone I called him, I blessed him and made him many.*"

He cleared his throat.

"I think the prophet intends that passage to read, *When he was but one I called him, I blessed him and made him many.*"

Then she turned and looked at him.

"You are correct. I was mistaken."

"You were very close."

"I have been studying these scrolls carefully. They repudiate those scholars who say the Scriptures have changed since their original composition. The scrolls prove that they have survived perfectly, without perversion."

"Are you a scholar, Miss?"

"Not of Scripture. I teach at the university, but not this. This is my avocation."

"What do you teach?"

"Modern European literature."

"Postwar?"

"Prewar and postwar."

He ran quickly out of questions and began to panic over his blank mind. He did not want the conversation to end.

"And you. Are you a Scripture scholar?"

"I'm a lawyer", he said with an apologetic dip of the head.

"You know the text very well."

"I studied it as a child."

"You're Polish, aren't you?"

He had never thought of himself as Polish.

"I came from Poland after the war."

"Were you one of those child prodigies the Hasidim produced?"

"I was."

"Where are your *payos?*"

"The Nazis cut them off. Later, when I reached Israel I had become something else. I cut them off myself."

She did not respond and he sensed disapproval.

"You don't wear a *kipah,* a *yarmulke.* Why not?"

"I'm no longer a believer."

"Oh", she said sadly. "Like so many postwar writers."

"Do you have faith?"

"A kind of faith."

"The *Shoah* burnt faith out of us."

"The *Shoah* made the faith of some grow stronger. In others it grew weaker, and in some it disappeared altogether."

"Why is that?"

"It wouldn't be fair of me to conjecture. I didn't suffer as so many did. My family has been here in Israel since the eighteen-hundreds. We came from Germany and were involved with the first agricultural settlements."

"Yet you have strong opinions. I can hear them beneath your polite words."

"You are indeed a lawyer", she said.

"My first love is Scripture. But it has become a literary interest. When I was a boy I thought the world was founded upon the Torah."

"You think it isn't?"

He was surprised by her surprise. To meet an intellectual who radiated at least the minimal symptoms of biblical faith was an oddity. He did not know what to make of her.

"Many were burned in the body and died", she said. "Others were burned in the soul and lived. Are you one of those?"

He shrugged. "I must be one of those."

"I think you are. And I think you need a drink of wine. You need to dance and to laugh. I wager that you don't laugh overmuch."

He was being analyzed with discomfiting accuracy. He did not like it.

"I have experienced very little in my life that is amusing."

"I'm sorry", she said, chastened. "I have been intrusive. Please forgive me?"

"What is your name? How can I forgive you if I don't know your name?"

"My name is Ruth Sonnenberg."

"I forgive you, Ruth."

"What is your name?"

He did not immediately answer because he had a number of

names. There was the name of the boy who had lived on Zamenhofa in Warsaw. There was the name he gave to the British, hoping they would believe he was a Jewish Palestinian accidentally fallen on the wrong side of the border, needing repatriation. They spotted that nonsense instantly and put him in a detention camp on Cyprus. Then there was the name that the Haganah gave to him when he became an agent, before the declaration of Independence. He had kept that name. It was his public persona in the new Israel and had been for the past twelve years.

He realized suddenly that her head was cocked sideways, waiting for him to answer.

"Don't you have a name, *payos* boy?"

"I have a name."

"You don't want to tell me?"

"It's David . . . " For his last name he used the one the Haganah had given him.

"David. King David." She laughed. He loved her laugh because it revealed who she was. It was a gentle, joy-bearing sound. It contained delight. He fell in love with that laugh, and asked her to come with him for a glass of tea, so that she would bring that sound along with her. They passed several hours together in a café and chatted about inconsequential things. He merely sat, planning nothing, hoping for nothing, simply overcome by her presence. It was not her large black eyes or her physical grace that gripped him. It was not her intelligence, though she had been amply endowed with that.

He liked the sweetness, but he puzzled over the strength. The combination was unnerving. He told himself that this was a passing diversion. That he would never see her again. That it was merely interesting to look through a warp in existence and observe a person who lived on a different planet.

Then he admitted to himself that he was lying. He knew that he would have to be physically evicted from the café before he would willingly part from her presence. They would have to bludgeon him to stop him being with her. Yet he could not tell her that. Despite the fact that he was a master of words—legal words—he could barely speak coherently. He began sentences and did not complete them. He stammered. His mind was an empty chamber waiting to be filled. She sensed this and did most of the talking, leaving him plenty of room for interjections. They stayed together until closing time. He kept clearing his throat, preparing things to say that he did not, in the end, say. She kept looking at him with a disturbing blend of curiosity and affection, in which was mixed a thread of sympathy for his unnamed sufferings. She talked of many things: books and political figures, the ever-looming threat of war, flowers, the ocean. She loved the ocean. She loved all water. She loved floating in the Dead Sea, she told him. She asked him if he had seen Masada. No, he had not. Some day they must go there together, she said. Yes, they should, he agreed. Together, he said.

Three months later they stood under the canopy and smashed the glass. Then he learned again to dance. He danced and the dancing made him weep at his own wedding. No one commented on this because they knew he was a survivor.

A spring evening. The pink house in Ramat Gan. The western sky running with iridescent colors. A breeze from the sea. Bread baking somewhere in the neighborhood. Children's cries spilling down the street. Jewish children shouting in Hebrew as if it were not a reinvented language.

He was stretched out on a deck chair in the shade of the almond tree. Ruth came across the terrace carrying two lime-green glasses, frosted, tinkling with ice. He lifted an arm and waved at her. It had been a bleak day at the office. The Eichmann trial was pending, and he was an assistant prosecutor weighted with the task of assembling the case. He was in charge of photographic evidence.

She walked toward him, the antithesis of the horror photos,

those heaps of motionless faces, limbs, torsos, tangled, locked in a cat's cradle of glossy 8 × 10, black-and-white death. She was brown, her lips full, her eyes tender and humorous on him, her skirt and her blouse the color of cream conch shells. She put a glass into his hands. He lay back on the deck chair and closed his eyes. She stroked the hair away from his forehead, undid his tie, and took off his shoes. She undid the spots of jade at her ear lobes.

"Supper's almost ready."

"What is it?"

"Fish. Latke. Melon. Miriam sent Brazilian coffee. It came in the mail today, just in time for my tired man."

"Just in time."

"What's he like, this Eichmann?"

"He's the most normal person you can imagine."

"Doesn't he froth at the mouth?"

"A reflective sort. He speaks in measured tones."

"You've spoken with him?"

"I met him today for the first time. We had to verify certain photos the Americans took at Wobbelin. The British have supplied more photos from Bergen-Belsen. He confirmed them all."

"Did you have to look at any from Treblinka?"

"Yes."

"Oh David", she said, stroking his arm.

"Treblinka and Oświęcim and Belzec, and the others. The list is so long. Some new German archive photos were found in a warehouse by U.S. Army Intelligence. They were forwarded to us by the embassy. Boxes of them. The SS delighted in keeping scrapbooks apparently."

"The Treblinka pictures. Did you . . . recognize any of the victims?"

"My mother? My father? My brothers? My sisters? No. The faces were strangers. It was unbelievable, Ruth. The faces all looked the same, drained of personality. Human masks in life and in death."

"That's terrible."

"I felt nothing. How strange to look at that and feel nothing. It becomes impossible to think about evil on that scale. The mind switches off after certain boundaries have been crossed. In a way the Nazis have won. They have turned the victims into statistics even for us."

"Don't say that. It's not true."

"Intellectually, I agree with you. It's not true. And philosophically, I maintain my outrage. But you can't sustain it for long before it starts eating you up from the inside out."

"Maybe you should hand this over to someone else. There are lots of jobs for a lawyer of your caliber. I've heard rumors about you." She wagged her finger at him, teasing.

"What rumors?"

"You're being groomed for higher things. My department head, who's a friend of the wife of the Minister of Justice, says she heard that you're cabinet material within a decade."

"I want to stay with the trial, Ruth. I want to see this bastard hung. If God died at Oświęcim, Eichmann will follow him on the gallows in Jerusalem."

"Shhh!" she said, putting her finger across his lips. She was of that genre of *sabra* who believed in God in a distracted way, but who thought that Zionism was the form divine action must take in this century. Nevertheless, she retained a certain vestige of reverence, an inheritance from her Sephardic ancestors.

Their bedroom in the night was a tropical garden. Consolations of the flesh. Union of the flesh. Joy of the flesh. No more hungers of the flesh. No more pits full of dead flesh.

He woke up yelling, gasping for air in the hot little bedroom in Ramat Gan.

"Shhhh, shhhhh", she said to him.

"They won, Ruth."

"They lost. We beat them. God beat them."

"Where is God?"

She took his hand and pulled it across her belly.

"The Lord God planted a garden in Eden, in the east", she whispered. "And he placed there the man whom he had formed. The Lord God cast a deep sleep on the man, and while he was asleep, he took one of his ribs from his side and closed up his side with flesh. Then the Lord God formed the woman from the flesh of the man. He woke the man and gave her to him, and he to her."

The breezes sighed through the room, bearing the scent of the sea, and lemon blossoms.

"We are a *zivig*", she said. "We are chosen, a heaven-blessed couple. Let us bring a child into this world, you and me. Together."

Though they had been long married, seasoned lovers, comfortable in their familiar flesh, on that night he kissed her with a kiss that was the first kiss ever created in the world. Then the man and the woman became one flesh with a passion that transcended all previous passions. They clung to each other and were naked and knew no shame.

A month later she took his hand again and pressed it to her abdomen.

"In here is God's answer to you, David. A child lives in here. We made this one together from your flesh and my flesh."

He held her and knew that it was good. Joy of the flesh. Joy of the heart. Joy of the soul. He had them all at Ramat Gan.

"We have won", she said.

A few weeks later the terrorist bomb exploded in the marketplace, and the empty years began in earnest.

Elijah shook himself.

Too much time had passed. The sweetest memories—and those that were bitter unto death—each in its turn had sunk beneath the waves of healing that had come with faith. But the healing had not effaced that abiding sense of loss, the gap left by an amputated marriage, the awareness that the entire world was aching with the pain of abandonment. Faith had tamed the tyranny of his emotions. It had defused their power to cast him into despair. But the grief remained.

In the Assisian night, that human loneliness now cut deep with a sharpness he had not felt for many years. He got out of bed and went to the window. There were a few stars scattered here and there across the sky. The breeze was warm and scented with crops. Sprinklers hissed in the vineyards. The loneliness bit into his soul like a cry in the darkness. He searched within himself for a word that might answer this cry, and found himself empty. He stared into the night, as if to penetrate its riddle by the force of his will. Did the absence of light contain answers? Only insofar as it pointed to the missing light, bearing mute witness to what would return with the dawn. Perhaps he merely wished to state his rejection of illusion. As if to say, *I will outstare you.*

"You have not won", he said finally, aloud, and went back to bed.

* * *

That night she came to him in a dream. She did not speak. She looked at him and love came to him from her eyes. She was happy. She stood in a shallow river. Its water was blue, effervescent. In the background, there were loaded fig trees, almond trees, lemon trees, limes, oranges, grapefruit, pomegranates.

She placed both hands on her belly and cupped them. She offered the cup of her palms to him, and he saw within it a small child curled, asleep.

"This is our daughter", she said in words that were soundless.

"I don't know her", he said anxiously.

"You know her. She sleeps but her heart is awake."

"Where is my mother?" he cried.

"Your mother and your father are asleep, but their hearts are awake. They will rise on the last day."

"Where is she, my mother?"

Ruth looked to her right and upward. His eyes searched for the place to which her glance was directed.

"There is your mother", said Ruth. "Your new mother. She is given to you this day for the work that is before you."

He looked up and saw a woman clothed with the sun, with the moon under her feet and on her head a crown of twelve stars. Because she was with child she cried aloud in pain as she labored to give birth.

Then another sign appeared in the sky: it was a huge dragon, flaming red, with seven heads and ten horns; on his heads were seven crowns. His tail swept a third of the stars from the sky and hurled them down to earth. Then the dragon stood before the woman about to give birth, ready to devour her child when it should be born.

She gave birth to a son—a boy destined to shepherd all the nations. Her child was caught up to God and to His throne. The woman herself fled into the desert where a special place had been prepared for her by God; there she was taken care of for twelve hundred and sixty days.

Then war broke out in Heaven; Michael and his angels battled against the dragon. Although the dragon and his angels fought back, they were overpowered and lost their place in heaven. The huge dragon, the ancient serpent known as the devil or Satan, the seducer of the whole world, was driven out; he was hurled down to earth and his minions with him.

Then he heard a voice in Heaven say:

> Now have salvation and power come,
> the reign of our God and the authority of His Anointed
>   One.
> For the accuser of our brothers is cast out,
> who night and day accused them before our God.
> They defeated him by the blood of the Lamb
> and by their testimony;
> love for life did not deter them from death.

So rejoice you heavens, and you that dwell therein!
But woe to you, earth and sea,
for the devil has come down upon you!
His fury knows no limits
for his time is short.

Elijah looked at the face of the woman clothed with the sun and was no longer afraid.

"All Heaven is waiting to be filled with her martyrs", she said.

Then the seasons changed and the clouds raced like maddened horses, leaves fell from the trees, and the fruit of it fell too, and the sea raged.

After that he remembered nothing.

* * *

Elijah woke with the first light.

When Don Matteo did not appear at the time they had agreed upon, he went in search of the guestmaster.

"Where is Don Matteo?"

"Oh," said the wizened Italian friar, "he's been wrestling with the devil again."

"The devil?"

"The prior has given Don Matteo an obedience. He must stay in bed until his bruises are healed."

"Bruises? Has he fallen?"

"No, no", said the friar irritably. "The bruises the devil gave him last night!"

Thoroughly puzzled, Elijah found the prior's office and knocked on the door. A voice said *Ammesso!* He entered and found himself face to face with a pleasant-looking individual in his fifties, staring at him through thick glasses.

"*Buon giorno,* Father. You are the guest from the Vatican?"

"I am."

"How can I help you?"

"I am worried about Don Matteo. We had agreed to say Mass together this morning and he hasn't arrived as planned. The porter tells me that he is . . . "

"He is unwell. It is not possible for anyone to see him for several days."

"But I leave this morning. May I not at least say good-bye to him?"

"I regret . . . "

"It is of utmost importance that I speak with him. Last night he said our meeting this morning would be essential to my mission."

"He didn't explain?"

"Nothing."

"I am truly sorry, Father, but it is impossible."

"Is he near death?"

"No."

"Then I must see him. It concerns a papal mission."

The prior stiffened and light glanced off his glasses.

"I have an entire community to deal with. This house cannot be permitted to collapse into disorder because of a single friar, even one who is singularly blessed by God. He has his work for God and I have my work for God. Please accept this. I can explain no further."

Elijah left the office more perplexed than ever. After saying Mass alone in the chapel, he went to the refectory.

Jakov brought him breakfast.

"You go today?"

"We are leaving after breakfast."

Jakov thrust out his hand and Elijah shook it.

"Good-bye, Father. I thank you pray me. I better. I think it my family in heaven."

"I am glad you feel better. Let us keep praying for each other."

The giant bobbed his head up and down, but he made no signs to leave.

"Jakov, do you know what has happened to Don Matteo?"

"I hear it he got hurt. He got sores on him. Doctor come. Don Matteo in bed."

"I would like to see him."

"Nobody can see him."

"Why not?"

"Prior say no."

"Where is Don Matteo's cell?"

"Far away", said the brother looking at him curiously.

"I know that you can't break obedience. But I too am under obedience. The Pope told me to see Don Matteo."

"This is good", said Jakov uneasily.

"Do you remember what you felt when I put my hands on your head and we prayed?"

"I never forget it."

"My soul needs Don Matteo like that. I need his hands on my head."

Jakov considered this development.

"Holy Father tell you?"

"I believe the Holy Father wants this."

"It is difficulty. I have holy obedience. You have holy obedience. But these two bump."

"They bump into each other only if they drive toward each other head on. If my obedience steers around your obedience then there is no crash."

"I think on this, Father."

He went away in the direction of the chapel. He was back within five minutes and said gravely, "I take it you his cell."

Elijah had to trot to keep up with the stride of the young friar, who passed nervously through a maze of hallways and wings. They did not meet a soul. Finally, they came to a full stop in a side corridor near the back of the complex. It smelled of age and desertion.

"You stay here by this door. I go. That way, no crash."

"No crash, Jakov. Thank you and bless you."

"Perfect joy, Father!"

He rapped gently on the door. A feeble word came from the interior and he entered.

He was shocked by what he saw. It was a tiny cell containing only a washstand, a prie-dieu, a recessed wall shrine in which stood a statue of the Blessed Virgin, and a crucifix. Behind the door there was a hospital bed, painted white, peeling badly. On the bed lay a body with arms stretched out at its sides. When the face turned to him he gasped.

The face was covered in livid purple splotches from the brow to the chin. The arms that protruded from the sleeves of a hospital gown were also bruised. The hands were bandaged across the palms and brown stains showed through the material.

"My angel told me that Jakov would bring you."

"Don Matteo! What has happened to you?!"

"It's nothing, nothing."

"It doesn't look like nothing."

He pulled a chair beside the bed.

"It's the usual. I should have known it was coming."

"I don't understand."

"It's a good sign. Don't look so worried, my son."

"Father, I repeat, what has happened to you? You have had an accident. Did you fall down?"

"Yes. I fell down."

"I detect a mental reservation behind that answer. Tell me."

"We needn't speak of it. It's enough that God has brought you here. All is well."

"Did someone hurt you?"

"Someone hurt me. But it's over now."

"Who was it? A madman? Has the culprit been punished?"

"The culprit will be punished on the Last Day."

Elijah sat staring, breathing heavily, indignant.

He looked at the face of the old priest and saw ages upon ages of wisdom in it. He looked at the ancient hands with their bleeding bandages. He looked at the feet. They too were bandaged and stained.

Then he understood.

"Why don't you speak, my son?"

Elijah could not answer.

"Are you afraid?"

"Yes."

"Are you afraid of the work the Lord has given you to do?"

"Yes."

"You are afraid you will be deceived?"

"Yes."

"You are afraid you might be seduced into serving the enemy?"

"Yes."

The friar asked several such questions, which informed Elijah that he had read his soul.

"You have no strength for this mission?" concluded the priest.

"I have no strength. Rome has made a mistake. This mission needs a saint."

"Rome hasn't made a mistake."

"I am weakness itself. I have lost confidence. Exteriorly, I will do what I can, but I have no certainty that I can accomplish anything. Quite the reverse. I fear that I may do more damage."

"Why do you fear such a thing?"

"I don't know."

"You have been a priest these many years and you don't know?"

"Sincerely, Father, I do not understand what has been occurring in my soul during these last few days. I feel less prepared than ever."

"It's good you feel your weakness."

"Strength is needed for this task."

"No. Weakness is needed."

"What do you mean? I'm confused."

"This is what Francis wished to show you. Weakness is your strength."

Again, Elijah could not answer.

"You are a man who has borne many afflictions. From your childhood you have suffered at the hands of evil men. In my mind is a picture of a little boy in a black suit. He is dancing for God. He is full of joy. The fire tries to eat him. But he runs away and a man saves him. Then he runs across the world. But he forgets to dance. He loses joy."

"You have described my youth accurately."

"Then he is dealt a severe blow. He loves a woman. This is the one great love of his life. She is life itself to him. He no longer believes in God. He believes only in this woman. She is good, but her knowledge of the truth is limited. She loves him. There is a child within her womb they have conceived together, man and wife."

"Now you have described my early manhood."

"The woman dies. The child dies within her. They are taken to a place of joy, but the young husband and father feels the darkness of the world go deeper into his soul. He is angry with God. He thinks he hates this God whom he proclaims doesn't exist. He fills his life with brave actions. He rises to power in a nation of the East. At the very moment when he is offered a pathway into total power, he is given a message."

"What was that message?"

"A word of love from his past. A word of sacrificial love. It is something wholly unexpected. It jars him, it shakes his confidence in his own judgment. He leaves the paths of power. He wanders aimless and alone. He is an empty shell. Eventually he comes to the mountain of Elijah, and there he wishes to throw himself from a height over a precipice. On the height he sees a building like a solitary fortress, the last refuge in a sea of adversity and meaninglessness. For no reason he suddenly remembers the little boy that he once was. He feels for an instant—oh, such a very short instant—a burst of joy. He remembers his dance before the throne of God.

"He decides to give the absent God a last chance. He knocks on the door of the building and finds a place where men live together in peace. Men of all kinds, poor, rich, brave, cowardly, smart, dumb, saints, sinners. They work the soil and pray. They plant and they harvest. They listen for the voice of God. They listen in the dark. They are the ones who believe beyond the point of all believing, when it is no longer possible to believe.

"They invite him in. He stays a day, two days, a week, a month. He no longer wishes to throw himself over a precipice. He asks new questions. He learns that until now he has seen only a part of creation. For many years he has stared into the darkness and lost all hope of dawn. Now he is given glimpses of the love that is all love. At first he is not given great amounts. He is too fragile for that. Yet he accepts that there is much, much more to existence than he had supposed. He argues, he doubts, he thinks, and he wrestles with God."

"Father. Say no more. I know it is me you speak of."

The friar nodded and Elijah felt a wave of love come to him from the old man.

"The little dancing boy in the black suit and the fur hat," the friar continued, "he is a chosen one of God. He is a brand pulled from the burning. He is a soul who from his earliest years has hungered for Truth. Because of this hunger, he has borne many wounds for God and did not know it."

"I know it now."

"You will bear many more wounds for Him."

"There is no strength in me."

"That is how it must be."

"Last night, I felt a flood of anguish that I had not experienced for years. I saw clearly everything I had lost. My family. My wife, my child. I felt as if I were falling into a bottomless pool of grief."

"Above us, there is an ocean of joy. You will see it. You will go up to it, and it will come down to meet you. Didn't the woman clothed with the sun speak to you of this? I saw her come to you in a dream."

"She did", he choked.

"Why are you afraid? She is with you. Her mission is like yours, to crush the head of the serpent that coils itself around the world. You are an instrument to confound the serpent as he prepares to ensnare the very House of God. Yet no man can resist him without divine assistance. The Lord has given to the woman a role for the Last Days that no other human could accomplish, not even our saintly Pope. She sustains him just as she sustains you, by graces given to her from the hands of her Son. She will intercede for you and protect you. She too is a servant, but the greatest of servants, for she bore the Lamb within her own womb."

"The enemy killed the Lamb."

"You know the rest of it."

"And the Lamb overcame death."

"Yes. But first He had to die."

"Why did He have to die? Why did my wife die? Why are you covered with bruises?"

"Because we are in a real war."

"It is not right!"

"You a priest for so many years and you say that? Of course it's not right. The Cross isn't right. But our Lord took it and turned it into the great sign that the devil hates above all other signs. Each time we accept to bear that cross and be nailed to it, believing against all believing—when it's impossible any longer to believe because of our pain—that's when we defeat him. By the blood of the Lamb!"

"What are these bruises?"

"You don't need to know, my brother."

"I think you bore them for me. Tell me the truth."

The old friar sighed.

"You were exhausted when you came here. The enemy knows of you, and he sees you approaching, though he doesn't grasp the mind of Christ in your mission. He sees only a threat to his plans, though he can't guess what it is. He never learns."

"You took these blows in my place."

"I asked a favor of the Lord. I asked that some of the attack intended for you would be deflected onto me."

"But to strike you in the flesh! What purpose does that serve?"

"The enemy rages. He tries to frighten. He would like to frighten you. Ordinarily, he is not permitted to frighten souls by material appearances. His work is largely silent. He is most effective when he is unseen. On occasion, God permits that the devil should be allowed to use crude weapons, and thereby reveal himself for what he is. He grabs the opportunity, even though he knows he is losing ground by revealing himself. But his malice is so great he can't resist."

"I ask you to pray for me", Elijah said in a broken voice. "I am afraid."

"Do you see these wounds? These bruises?"

"Yes."

"They are my joy."

"Pain is your joy?"

"The pain in itself is not joy. It is simply pain. But the *meaning* of the pain, that is joy."

Elijah lay his head on the bed beside the friar's hand.

"Please pray for me."

With much effort Don Matteo turned on his side and put his hands on Elijah's head. He prayed, and Elijah felt a warm current flow through him.

"You are going into the lion's mouth", said the old man. "You must not be afraid. Be at peace and trust in God. Trust in the Father, in Jesus, and in the Holy Spirit."

They remained without moving for some time. Then, Don Matteo pointed to the wall shrine.

"Get me the relic. Over there by our Lady. It's in the brass thing."

He found a reliquary at the foot of the statue. A plain round container, the size of a pillbox.

"Bring it here."

Elijah did so.

"Open it."

Inside was a dark brown chip of wood.

"This is a relic of the true Cross. I give it to you. It's now yours."

"This is too great a gift!"

"That's true", said the friar sadly. "It's so great a gift that we bear it badly. Even so, carry it, my son."

"I will carry it next to my heart. I thank you, Father."

"Do you know that the scoffers say if all the supposed relics of the Cross were gathered together, it would compose ten crosses?"

"I have heard."

"Did you know that's a lie? If all the relics of the true Cross that are known today were to be collected, they would not come near to making a single cross. You see, the scoffers hate the Cross. The Cross is scandalous. They can't understand it. And so they can only believe it's a superstition of gullible Catholics."

"Who are the gullible?"

"Indeed. Now, my son, I must tell you that this splinter of wood was soaked in the blood of the Lamb. I know it. I have placed this relic on the incurable, and they have been healed. Demons screech and flee when they see it."

"Father, why didn't this relic of the Lord's Cross protect you from the evil one?"

"Ordinarily, he loathes the sign of the cross, and most of all he hates those pieces that come from the true Cross. But he is not an ordinary demon, easily driven away with a word. Furthermore, the Lord permitted that I should feel some of the blows that fell on Him."

At that moment the hall door squealed open and a friar entered. He wore a stethoscope around his neck, and he carried a tray of medicine. A shocked expression crossed his face.

"It is not permitted", he said. "He must have rest! Don Matteo, the prior expressly forbid . . . "

Don Matteo made the sign of the cross on Elijah's forehead and observed with some amusement as the brother physician conducted Elijah from the room without any pretense of diplomacy.

"Go to the cathedral at Orvieto!" called Don Matteo. "And write to me, my son."

VI

Naples

He knocked repeatedly on Billy's door before he heard a mumbled reply.

"Billy not happy. Billy got sore bloody head. Billy no feel good. Billy drink lots o' coffee, feel better. Meet nice Father at parking lot by nine."

Elijah left a goodbye note for Don Matteo. He left another for the giant.

> Dear Brother Jakov,
> This gift was carved by a member of my community. He gave it to me on the day of my ordination. He is a Christian Arab. He lost his family in the bombing of a Palestinian camp by the Israeli army. Those who have lost everything belong to a fellowship of the spirit. To survive is a suffering that only another survivor can know. I too lost my family. They were massacred in Poland during the war. None was saved. Only me. I am a Christian Jew. All my life I have asked, why did God save me and not them? It is the hardest question of all. But God will answer it. Trust in this. God will answer it. I believe that our pain, united to the pain of Jesus on the Cross, may help in the saving of souls. I pray for you. Please pray for me.
> In Christ, true Savior of the World,
> Father Elijah.

Into the envelope he put a wooden crucifix. Though it lacked art, Brother Ass had carved it with love. He was the first of the Palestinian brothers who had accepted him.

"Father, see this cross I made for you. It's from a tree that grows in Bethlehem. I cut a piece from it myself. Ooh, you wouldn't believe what I had to pay that rich olive merchant who said he owned the tree. How can anyone own a tree of the Lord, I ask you? This tree is a seed of the seed of the tree that grew beside the stable of Bethlehem. Baby Jesus blessed this tree on the night when he was a running away from Herod. It was watered by the blood of the babies who were slaughtered. It's holy wood!"

The small brother's faith, as strong as an ass, and as unpredictable, could not be dislodged from certain embellishments on doctrine. Was the mystique of this crucifix merely a superstition? A pious fiction? Or was it a literary device of the illiterate, formed over centuries of suffering by simple people who had no other way to hold hope on high when the soldiers of Herod left their bloody litter throughout history? Nevertheless, the carving was an icon of redemption, sitting in the palm of his hand like a solid compression of a million words, a summation of the entire Gospel. This crude image was his greatest earthly treasure. He placed it into an envelope, printed the Croatian brother's name on it, and left it at the porter's desk.

Billy arrived at the parking lot looking miserable.

"Good morning, Monsignor."

"Don't call me that."

"You look ill. Do you have a fever, a chill?"

"Grappa", grunted Billy.

"Grappa?"

"These friends of mine. They asked me back to their place last night after Frankie's bar closed. They served home-made grappa. Like a fool, I drank it."

"And so, you pay the price today."

"Don't look at me with that pitying smile. If you had a skull like this, you wouldn't think it quite so funny."

"Would you like me to drive? It's a long way to Naples."

"Right. You drive", he groaned, holding his head.

Elijah drove the Jaguar sedately out of the town and turned south.

"I wasn't drunk, you understand. I only had a shot glass or two, but it kicked like a rhino."

"Your head hurts?"

"Yes."

"What happened?"

"This couple and me got to talking at Frankie's. We took a liking to each other. The mum's a Brit married to an Italian. They have a villa around the mountain. We were having such a good time, but they had to get back to their kids. Babysitter had to be home by midnight or the carriage would turn into a pumpkin."

Elijah's brow furrowed. He did not always understand Billy's ideas.

"So they asked me back to the villa for a nightcap. While the mum's driving the babysitter home, the dad cranks open a bottle of this stuff that looks like pure kero. *Have a sip of this, Monsignor,* he says as innocent as a lamb. The blighter!"

"What is grappa?"

"It's an unbelievable liquor that only the bloody Romans could have invented. This lad takes me down to the cellar and shows me his private still. He has a crock of green wine down there. Sticking out of it are two bare wires, the remains of an electric lamp. He plugs it in and sparks go zapping inside the glass. Steam starts bubbling up the top, coiling through a bunch of copper tubes and before you know it, he's got distilled alcohol dripping out the end."

"Amazing."

"Aaaar! So resourceful these people. It looked like Doctor Frankenstein's workshop down there. The stuff tasted like it too."

"You perhaps sipped more of it than you had intended?"

"That's very charitable of you. The answer to that question is yes."

"I'm sorry you feel unwell."

"I feel properly chastened by my head. Every sin has its consequences, doesn't it?"

They drove on without further conversation until Elijah turned west toward Orvieto.

"Where you going? Naples is the other way."

"Don Matteo suggested we make a detour to the cathedral at Orvieto."

"What for? There are a dozen cathedrals on the way south, most of them just as impressive."

"Have you seen inside?"

"No. I've passed it once or twice. Did he say why you're supposed to go there?"

"He wants me to see something. But I didn't have time to find out what it is."

They reached Orvieto by midmorning. Spatters of rain had begun to hit the pavement outside the cathedral. The air was cooler than the day before, but humidity was high, and there was rumbling above the gray blanket of sky.

It took a moment for their eyes to adjust to the darkness of the interior. It smelled of incense and beeswax. The apse echoed faintly with hushed whispers. A few old women were praying their beads and making the Stations.

Elijah and Billy genuflected toward the tabernacle and then stood gazing about them.

The interior was beautiful but did not differ notably from the numerous other cathedrals that dotted Italy.

"Well, where's the big secret?"

"It's here. Whatever it is, Don Matteo thought it important enough for us to make a detour to find it."

They entered a side chapel.

Four monumental frescoes, representing the end of the world, had been painted on the walls in vivid colors, in a style of epic grandeur that must have been innovative at the time of its execution.

"1499 to 1500", said Billy reading a bronze plaque. "These frescoes are by Luca Signorelli."

"Who was he?"

"A disciple of the painter Piero della Francesco. Michelangelo admired his work."

"He has made an apocalypse."

"And a jolly unattractive one it is! This mural here is *The Damned Cast into Hell.* Ugh! I hate crowds. That lot isn't bound for a soccer match. Gor, I wouldn't trade my mind for this man's imagination, not for a million pounds. It's horrible."

"Yes. I think that must be what he wanted to teach us. The horror of damnation."

"Looks like all the deadly sins are here. Let's see, I'm going to try to find drunkenness. Sure enough, there it is, right beside lust. Let me look into the drunkard's face. I knew it! I knew it! He looks just like me."

Billy's attempt at humor did nothing to relieve the pall of tragedy hanging over the scene.

"They look too damned human for my taste. And so do the devils."

Elijah went over to another mural.

His eyes were drawn to the central figure of the image, a figure of Christ. *How strange,* he thought, *to see a representation of the Lord with the figure of Satan whispering in His ear, and his arm penetrating His robes. Is that Christ's hand or the devil's that emerges from the folds of cloth?*

It was not a literal depiction of a scriptural scene, he concluded; although it might be the artist's imaginative rendering of the temptation in the desert? But there was something out of character in the way Christ leaned into Satan's embrace and listened with such attention.

He stared at it for a long time. Suddenly, the meaning of the mural became clear, like a scene viewed through lenses revolving into focus. The blurred shapes of reality drew together into a sharp, piercing landscape of moral disaster.

The figure held in the devil's embrace was not Christ but Antichrist.

Elijah understood why Don Matteo had wanted him to see it. Now he knew why the old friar would not tell him the reason for his request. Matteo had wanted Elijah to discover the secret of the mural for himself, and in the process, to observe the mechanics of perception.

"What you staring at?" said Billy.

"The Antichrist."

"That's not the Antichrist. It's the Lord."

"Look at it carefully. Pray as you look."

Billy obeyed and a few moments later he shuddered.

"I see what you mean."

"The painting seems to operate at a number of levels", said Elijah. "On the surface, it tells a dramatic tale, a narrative. On another level, it is a moral lecture about sin and betrayal. On still another level, the artist is reaching for the deepest organs of perception in the soul. The artist wants us to hear a soundless cry, an alarm, a warning."

"That might be stretching it. Were those fifteenth-century painters such sophisticated theologians?"

"Some of them were. Some were mystics as well. In those days, the civilized world was Catholic. Life was short, eternity was always just a breath away. Salvation and damnation saturated the normal atmosphere of life. Even so, the painter was compelled to attempt a most urgent warning. I think he's saying that if we can be so easily deceived by a few strokes of the brush, by art, which of its very nature is a medium of illusion, how vulnerable are we to the power of the senses? Couldn't a flesh-and-blood Antichrist far more effectively create the *appearance* of goodness, while hiding his attachment to evil?"

"Theoretically. But he'd have to be quite a conjurer."

"This Antichrist resembles our traditional images of Christ. What if he should also imitate Christ in his public actions?"

"Granted, it's possible. But I can't believe a man who's that evil would be able to fool the whole world for long."

"What if the world desired to be fooled?"

"You'd still have hundreds of millions of believers on guard. They'd spot him."

"Do you think so? We are presently in the midst of a massive apostasy. Never in the history of the Church has there been such widespread loss of faith. In a few years, will there be any faith left on the earth?"

"You're rather pessimistic today, Davy."

"Scripture says that unless the days be shortened even the elect would be deceived."

"Well, I suppose the eye could be deceived, but what about the mind? Any Christian worth his salt could tell when your hypothetical Antichrist was preaching false doctrine. Couldn't he?"

"But what if for a generation or two before his appearance, the formation of Catholics were to fall into confusion? What if a generation of religious illiterates had been formed, unable to distinguish between religious truth and religious sentiment?"

"All right. It could happen. And I get your not-so-subtle point. You think we're that generation."

"I do. But there is another important message at work in this masterpiece."

"Hold on, half a mo'! The soul has powers. It can detect things the eye and the mind can't see, don't you think? I mean, even if an Antichrist were to fool our eyes by appearances, and also deceive our minds by plausible lies, wouldn't there be something deep down inside of us that was uneasy? A faint warning bell that rang and rang until we answered?"

"I agree. But you know as well as I do that this warning system can be deactivated. Sin can cover it with layer after layer until eventually we hear nothing. We forget it ever existed."

Billy sighed heavily.

"I need a cup of coffee", he declared with solemnity.

He went out, leaving Elijah alone with the mural.

* * *

With Billy at the wheel, the Jaguar was cruising at one hundred and twenty kilometers per hour on the superhighway between Rome and Naples. Elijah tried not to pay attention to the speedometer. He buried himself in his breviary and prayed the office.

When he was finished, he closed the book.

"Napoli in half an hour!" said Billy with false cheeriness.

They drove on without further exchange.

When they passed Capua, Billy said, "Something's wrong."

"With the car?"

"No. With the Monsignor."

"What's wrong, Billy?"

"Something's crazy here, Davy. I wasn't myself at Assisi. No, I don't mean that exactly. What I mean is, I was my *old* self. My bad old self."

"I could see you were struggling with something."

"I wasn't my real self. It scares me."

"Was it a time of temptation?"

"Yeah. But different from the usual stuff. Usually, it's like a tennis match. Ho-hum. Today I batted away ten urges to overeat, five invitations to impure thoughts, and one impulse to gossip about an enemy. Yesterday, today, tomorrow, it's business as usual. Some days are better than others, but I work hard at being faithful. Really, I do."

"You are a good priest, Billy. I know it."

"The Holy Father's a good priest. *Stato, Dottrina,* they're good priests. You're a good priest. But I know what I am."

"Are you feeling depressed?"

"Yes, dammit, I'm depressed. But that's not the problem. I'm a fat, spoiled, middle-aged man who didn't grow up. I try to be good. Mostly, I am good. But I'm not the stuff that martyrs are made of."

"No one is."

"Don't give me that! I know myself. I'm a weak man."

"Tell me why you think you are a weak man."

"I went to Assisi all geared up to do penance, pray for hours every day, get close to you, encourage you. I said to myself, Davy's got a big load on his shoulders, and he needs a pal to help him carry it when it gets heavy. Time to shape up, Billy, I said to myself. Do you know how long that lasted?"

"How long?"

"About as long as it took me to get into some cool duds and think of a drink. I've been to Frankie's before, you know. It's got atmosphere. People there are good folks. You don't go there for sin. You go in for a scotch on the rocks and conviviality with comfy Catholics. All in moderation of course. Assisi's sanctified territory. You know what I mean? You go there to have a rousing good chat with rich, devout Americans, exchange stories, get the latest on apparitions and on the regional churches—always loads of bad news in that department—you know what I mean? I wasn't looking for a lady friend or to get drunk or to pretend I wasn't a cleric. I wanted some good Catholic fun. I wanted music and a belly laugh."

"Is that so wrong?"

"Not really. I'm a great fan of Chesterton, you know. He once said that he became a Catholic because we're the only religion that sees no contradiction between a pint, a pipe, and a cross."

Elijah smiled.

"It was a joke, but it had some truth in it. Old G. K. knew when to fast and when to down a good ale. It's the timing. It's all in the timing."

"There is Christmas and there is Lent."

"Bang on! So what bothers me about these past few days is that something inside of me said, dammit, I want it to be Christmas and I don't care if it is Lent."

"It is Ordinary Time."

"Listen, I'm serious here. I know it's Ordinary Time. I'm speaking metaphorically. We went to Assisi for a retreat, didn't we? A mini-Lent. We went there to get strong, because something pretty bloody serious is brewing. But when we were driving up the mountain and talking about the spirit of Saint Francis and all that—I don't know why, but it irritated me. Which is really out of character, because I love Saint Francis."

"You were as fatigued as I was."

"I know, I know. And we've been under a lot of stress lately. The office is smothered in paperwork; we're understaffed; the diplomatic service is a bloody minefield. But it was something more than stress."

"I suspect it was temptation of a kind."

"Yeah, of a kind. When I hopped out of the car all I wanted to do was get to Frankie's, get mellow, bee-bop on the dance floor, and hold court to admiring tourists until the wee small hours. I wanted to slay them with laughs. I succeeded. I didn't commit a single confessable sin, technically speaking. But the long and short of it is, I just wasn't around much. I wasn't there for you, Davy. And I feel sick about it."

"God may have permitted it for a reason."

"What reason?"

"There were things I had to learn about myself which might not have been possible with you there."

"Thanks a lot!"

"I mean, if the laughing swordsman had been at my right hand, I might have been seduced into false confidence."

"Hmm, now there's a thought."

"So you see, I think you are being a little hard on yourself."

"Wrong. It's about time I started being hard on myself. All my life I've been nothing but nice to myself. Since I got religion, the niceness takes a legitimate form, but it's still pampering. No more adultery, no more drunkenness, no daydreaming about embezzling the Bank of England. But try denying me a third helping of lasagna and an old dusty bottle of dry red."

Elijah chuckled.

"Go ahead, laugh. Laugh if you like. But I've got to live inside this weak character, this body, so visibly round, so eminently unadmirable. It's mine, all mine. It's me, and I don't like it."

"Billy, Billy," said Elijah, "you can't convince me you are such a cad. I have met mass murderers."

"You have?" said Billy. "Like who?"

"I talked with Adolf Eichmann on a few occasions."

"Are you serious?"

"I am serious. Let me tell you about him. He was a disciplined man. He didn't drink or eat immoderately. He was intelligent, quiet-spoken, modest, and, some say, charming. He liked Mozart and roses. He engineered the death of several million people. He had character."

"So, what you're really getting at is that character can serve good or it can serve evil. Right?"

"Most human qualities can be misused."

"Where does that leave me? I don't have the quality to do either."

Elijah looked at him and said with a hint of severity, "That is untrue."

Billy kept his mouth closed for several minutes. When eventually he spoke, his eyes were full of tears: "I hate being a weak, fat man."

"We are all weak men. I am weak in ways that you are not. You are weak in a way that I am not. These are the thorns in the flesh that keep us both from becoming puffed up."

"You needed a saint on this trip", Billy said bitterly.

"I have a friend with me. You were the one chosen. Do you think Rome made an error in judgment?"

"Rome made a big mistake."

"Rome did not make a mistake."

Billy shook his head and looked glum.

"You don't realize it, but you are surely a messenger from God. You have affirmed many things He showed me during this week."

"How nice. I suppose I'm to remind you of what *not* to be. Yes, they knew I'd be instructive at some point."

"You misunderstand."

"Explain it to me."

"You want to be a saint, Billy. But you want to be a saint on your own terms. You want glorious victories with your sword; most of all, you want victories over your personal weaknesses and faults."

"What's wrong with that?"

"It is a good desire, but it can also be a kind of idealism masking pride."

"That's too complicated for me."

"Who is the saint? The one who obeys God in his weakness, or the one who demands to have every admirable quality before he sets forth on his quest?"

"Put that way, it's obvious."

"You accused me of romanticism a few days ago. Aren't all of us romantics who want our armor to shine and our swords to flash and our *bella figura* to draw many admiring glances as we make battle for God?"

"You can be nasty, old lad."

"What I say is true. I know it is true because I am describing myself."

"Oh", said Billy in a small voice.

"Also, among your many outstanding gifts you have the gift

of humor. You make me laugh. I'm a serious person, you may have noticed."

"I noticed that. You're not exactly a funny guy, Davy."

"You see, you can't help yourself. You always say amusing things. That is a gift from the Lord. It lifts the heart."

"I used to make the cardinal primate of England laugh too. Court jester I was. He was sad to lose me to the Vatican, but he knew they needed a good laugh over there at State."

"You mustn't demean yourself. The Cardinal Secretary chose you because of your intelligence and honesty. He knows that you love Christ and His Church. He trusts you. Do you think anyone trusts a buffoon?"

"Maybe you're right", said Billy pensively.

"I think you were hit with more than one kind of temptation during this past week. First of all, you let yourself be drawn away from prayer. You weren't distracted by evil things, for the enemy knows that you have been converted from them. He drew you away by legitimate pleasures."

"Legitimate but untimely, and immoderate."

"Correct. That was weakness, simple human weakness."

"Say it. I should have known better."

"My friend, we should have seen it coming. But we didn't. And so, we lost a minor skirmish. But we have learned a valuable lesson. And just in time, for a major battle lies before us."

"Well spoken. Now, my other temptations?"

"The second temptation is of a more sinister nature. The temptation to hate yourself because you have not lived up to your ideal. That is pride, and it is very dangerous. It opens the door to much worse things."

"All right, I repent of the lot in dust and ashes. What do you suggest by way of penance?"

"I suggest that we stop at that restaurant over there. We will each consume a single serving of lasagna and a single glass of ale."

"Sheer torture. But I deserve it."

When they were seated at their table, Elijah rubbed his eyes and yawned.

"You're tired, aren't you?" said Billy.

"It was a long night."

"Temptations?"

"Yes, my own kind."

"What were they?"

"The past. Old lamentations."

"Tell me about them."

"I would like to tell you about them some day. But they are too close to the surface now, and this is not the best place for it."

"To be continued?"

"To be continued."

The window by their table overlooked the Gulf of Salerno. The sea was black and tossing, the sky lowering quickly.

"How far is it to the marina, Billy? Will we be on time for the President's boat?"

"Lots of time. We're almost there. We passed Naples while you were giving me therapy."

"I didn't notice."

"Didn't notice Napoli! You *are* tired."

"What is this city?"

"Salerno. The big man's private marina is just around that bend. They're expecting us at the dock by seven. Ordinarily, we could make the crossing in under an hour, but by the looks of that water it might take longer. We're probably going nowhere tonight."

They ate their meal making small talk. By six-thirty the sea was raging, and rain was coming down in torrents. It was obvious that a crossing would be impossible. Billy used the pay phone to call Capri.

"I got ahold of the appointment secretary. He says that the

boat's too small to risk it. He wants us to stay here tonight and see how the water looks in the morning."

"Is there an inexpensive hotel nearby?"

"All kinds of them. But he said we should stay at the boathouse. A place the President owns, about five minute's drive from here. I got directions; it's on a side road above the marina. There's no one there except some employees. He's phoning ahead so they'll be expecting us."

The Jaguar crept slowly through the downpour until the headlights picked up a gate sign that read: *No Admittance! Property of Centro Mondiale Commerciale.* To their surprise, the electronic gate opened automatically as they approached. They drove through and went uphill on a driveway lined with thrashing pines and recessed lights.

The house stood at the crest of a grassy terrace. It was larger than they had expected, ultramodern, constructed largely of stone and glass, designed along lines borrowed from the American architect Frank Lloyd Wright. The exterior was lit by hidden flood lights.

"Take a look at the boathouse", Billy whistled.

The front door opened as they pulled to a stop, and a man stepped out onto the covered veranda. He was thin, silver-haired, and greeted them with relaxed elegance.

"Signore Stangsby? Signore Schäfer? Please, enter. The weather is atrocious!"

"And you are . . . ?"

"I am Roberto, the guestmaster. The President asks me to offer you his regret for the inconvenience. He hopes to meet you tomorrow on Capri."

"Thank you so much."

"I know that you have eaten," said Roberto, "but may I bring you a cup of coffee in the drawing room? We also have English tea? Cognac? A glass of milk?"

"Nothing for me, thank you", said Elijah.

"But I am dismayed!" Roberto said in a tone of mock dis-approval.

"I'm afraid we've had rather a long day of it", explained Billy. "We'll turn in early if that's all right."

"But of course. I will show you to your rooms, and then, if you wish you may select from a number of entertainments. There is a swimming pool and sauna, if the gentlemen so desire. A whirlpool? No? The films from the Cannes festival on video?"

"Nothing, thanks."

"My master will be disappointed in me. My reputation for entertaining guests will decline. No, I cannot convince you? Well, so be it", he concluded with a charming smile.

"Look, Roberto," said Billy, squeezing his arm, and exercising a tone of voice that Elijah recognised as *romanità*, "I'd hate for you to lose your job. Why don't you bring me some cognac and cake if you have any?"

"We have cake, we have biscuits, we have chocolates, we have . . ."

"Wonderful. Anything at all, Roberto, just a nightcap to keep our tummies from rumbling unpleasantly. There's the fellow."

The guestmaster went out and returned shortly, looking well pleased, carrying a covered tray. He led them up a circular staircase to a wing of bedrooms that opened to a private parlor overlooking the sea. The roaring of wind in the pines could be heard through the thick panes of the floor-to-ceiling windows. A fire blazed in the hearth of each bedroom.

"It's magnificent, Roberto. I should hope to be inconvenienced like this quite often!"

"Signore Stangsby, how you say it, pulls my leg, no?"

"That's right. We're terrific leg-pullers where I come from. It's a rotten habit!"

The guestmaster laughed outright.

"There is your room. And Signore Schäfer sleeps across the hall, here. Also, my master would scold me if he thought I had neglected to invite you to see his art collection. There are many significant works scattered throughout the house. Please, be at home; wander at your leisure. My wife and I are the only staff here, and I am leaving in a moment or two. We live across the garden in that cottage over there. Ring on the house phone if you need anything. I bid you a restful evening and shall return in the morning. My wife will come to make a breakfast for you."

"Thank you so much", said Billy, reaching out his hand for a shake. "You've been delightful. I'll put in a good word for you on Capri."

Roberto laughed again.

"You English. Always, how do you say it, joshing! *Buona notte,* gentlemen. Please, use this house as if it were your own. *A domani!*"

They wished him good night and he left.

"Gee, Davy, a mansion all to ourselves."

"Aren't you accustomed to big buildings, Billy?"

"The Vatican's smaller than you think, especially when you're an old hand. Familiarity breeds contempt and all that. Oh, I like this! First class."

"First class."

"Do you think his master spends much time here?"

"I suspect not. As beautiful as it is, it seems rather sterile, as if no one ever really lives here. This is a transit house between Capri and Brussels."

"If this is the boathouse, I can hardly wait to see the boat!"

"Do you feel uneasy?"

"No."

"I do."

"Any idea why?"

"Not really. A feeling."

"That Roberto chap seemed quite friendly. More like a faithful family retainer than a hired hand. I suppose when you live at this level even the servants inspire reverence."

"I wouldn't have chosen that word."

"You're tired and that always colors how you feel. You need a good night's sleep, lad."

"Let's sit up and talk. I feel suddenly very alone. There is a strange chill in this building."

"It's quite toasty as a matter of fact. A lovely place. Whoever designed it has superb taste. Look, there's an early Picasso on that wall, and here's a Modigliani! A Giacometti bronze by the fireplace. I bet when we check out the bedrooms we'll find that somebody put up religious stuff just for us."

"Look, there at the end of the corridor—that marble statue. Is it a religious piece? I think it's a Saint Sebastian."

"Whoever he is, he's stuck full of arrows like a pincushion. Now, tell me the truth, is that a look of death agony on the lad's face, or an orgasm?"

"The collector's tastes are eclectic", said Elijah, looking distractedly here and there.

"Davy! Keep your eyes off those Aphrodites!"

His mind had grown vulnerable to the power of imagery. The monastery had strengthened him for certain battles, and lowered his defenses for others—especially the visual. Monasticism was built on the assumption that one went away forever into the silence of God. The monastery walls were designed to protect the eye and the heart, to shut a few of the many doors through which temptation came. One did not look back. There was no television set at Carmel, and the journals that reached them contained few photographs. Women became an image in the mind.

"The Aphrodites are somewhat disturbing," he explained to Billy, "but they are not a serious threat."

"Are you made of sterner stuff than I am? Eyes to the right, lad. Just you ignore those ladies without no clothes on."

"I'm doing just that."

"Our invisible host must be quite a fellow. What does all this exquisite taste tell you about him?"

128

"I'm not sure. On the surface, it's a beautiful place. One couldn't ask for a more comfortable, more welcoming environment. Yet I feel quite odd. What has occurred in these rooms, I wonder?"

"If it will make you feel better, let's pray for spiritual protection."

Billy took a purple stole from his jacket pocket, unrolled it, and put it around his neck.

Slowly, as if fighting some overpowering reluctance, Elijah did the same.

The two priests raised their arms in supplication, invoked the blessing of Christ and the protection of the holy angels upon each other, and prayed the words of exorcism against the oppressing spirit of this house.

"There, feel better?"

"I do."

"It's only eight o'clock. Want to take in a film? This year's Cannes festival? Look at the size of that telly."

"I would rather visit with you. Billy, I feel . . . "

"Not again! What do you feel?"

"As if we are standing on the edge of a cliff."

"Well, we are on the edge of a cliff. The architect designed it that way. And if Vesuvius—which lurks only a few miles back yonder—decides to blow tonight, we'll slide right into the Tyrrhenian Sea. We're in terrible danger at this very moment. Let that be a consolation to you."

Elijah smiled.

"Perhaps you are right. I'm overtired and imagining things."

"You need some *divertimento*. I'll bet a monk like you doesn't get too much fun in his life, do you?"

"Billy, you are irrepressible. Much of what you consider fun is not fun for me. However, I do have an idea."

"Go ahead, amaze me."

"I suggest that we get into our pajamas and bathrobes, and each of us tell the other a story."

"That's a fabulous suggestion", shouted Billy, slapping his hands together. "Oh dear, how I wish I'd brought Andy along. He would have loved this! Well, never mind. I can tell it to him when I get home."

When Billy had tucked himself into the bed in his suite, he lay back on a mountain of pillows, sipping cognac and nibbling fruit cake.

Elijah came in wearing an old bathrobe. He seated himself in a chair at the foot of the bed. The fireplace to his right cast a soft light across the room. Billy looked as if he would at any given moment whisk a panda bear from under the covers.

"Did you find any Rembrandts in your room?" asked Billy.

"Only a landscape by Watteau. And you?"

"Something frightfully avante garde by a Rumanian. Surrealist. Look at it."

"It looks like a Madonna and Child from here. Why do you say it's surrealist?"

"Look closely."

Elijah went up to the painting, stopped, and took three steps backward.

"See what he's done? Fiendish, isn't it?"

"He has composed the portrait of our Lady and the Christ Child with miniatures of every sin known to man. This is diabolical."

"The product of a deranged id. Now, go across the room and look at it from a distance."

Elijah followed Billy's instructions. He looked back toward the image and a scowl crossed his face.

"You see it?"

"I see it. He has once again produced an optical illusion. Here is a third level of the image, using shadows and light. Now it is the face of a huge demon opening its jaws to swallow the Christ Child and the Mother."

"Whoever painted this thing is Not a Nice Man, I'd say", said Billy.

Elijah took the painting off the wall and left the room.

"Where did you go? What did you do?" said Billy when he returned.

"I found a closet down the hall. It can stay in there for the night."

Elijah sat down on the chair by the fire and stared into the flames.

"Now come on, Davy, tell me a story."

"Give me a few moments to collect myself."

"Don't tell me that painting gave you the willies. It's just paint on canvas."

"It's a word. It speaks a message from the realm of darkness."

"Come on now, you're just giving into that mood you had when we first got here. Shake it off!"

Elijah looked away from the flames. He rubbed his face.

"You are probably right."

"Your nerves are really on edge, old boy. Why don't you tell me a story, then we'll both feel better."

"You are right, Billy."

"Come on! Out with it. And make it a fairy tale while you're at it. How about a Polish one!"

"I do have a fairy story. A friend told it to me many years ago. Do you promise you won't be frightened?"

"I promise."

"Do you promise not to interrupt?"

"I'll try."

"It is about a dragon and a prince and a princess."

"Oh, lovely! Does it end happily?"

"Happily for the humans. Not so well for the dragon."

"Just as it should be. Commence."

And thus, Elijah recounted the story Pawel Tarnowski first told him on a bitterly cold winter's eve in 1943, in Warsaw, when they were starving.

"There was a boy", said Elijah. "He was the prince of a

kingdom on the mountains. His father the King went away when the child was young, barely able to walk, for the Queen had died and the man could not bear to enter the house of his first and only love."

"Go on. Go on", urged Billy in a soft voice. His eyes were large. He drew up his knees under the covers.

Elijah cleared his throat and continued the tale of the prince who lost his heart, and the lark *zabawa* who gave it back to him, and the dragon *smok,* which the prince slew by the castle of the dead lands.

When it was completed Elijah stared into the fire and remembered Warsaw. He saw the face of Pawel shaking with fever. He saw the stone that sat on Pawel's heart.

"That's quite good", said Billy.

"Now. You tell me yours."

"Well, now that it comes down to it, I don't have any stories. Just a head full of gossip and English Lit exams."

"I don't believe you. Make one up."

Billy looked genuinely at a loss.

"I don't think I could. I've never tried."

"But you told me you had a story."

"I never."

"Last week, you said that you would tell me about a hitchhiker."

"Oh, that! It's not a proper story, really."

"It will be good enough."

"It's not a made up one. It really happened."

"So much the better. Now commence!"

"Do you promise not to be frightened?"

"I do."

"Do you promise not to interrupt?"

"I will try."

"No, I won't tell it. You'd never believe me."

"I will. I promise I will. If you promise that it is a true story, I will believe it."

He saw that Billy was not joking.

"It *is* true", he said in a low voice. "It happened to me, and I swear it happened exactly the way I'm going to tell it."

"Go ahead."

"Eight months ago I was driving north on M40 to Birmingham. I wanted to see some people I know up there who are faithful to the Magisterium. They run a catechetical institute that spreads the Church's teaching. They publish a lot of stuff that's true-blue, mostly for kids. I was praying the Rosary at a hundred and forty klicks on the dial, when I heard a voice.

"I was alone in the car. The radio was off. So where did the voice come from? Who knows? Now don't look so worried. I'm not the kind of lad who hears voices, if you know what I mean."

"I am not worried."

"My cousin Winnie hears voices too, but she's in the schizo ward at Netherne. Now, you and I know I'm not a schizo or a mystic, so don't ask me to explain what I'm going to tell you. I'm just saying I *heard* a voice."

"With your own ears?"

"That's the part that's hard to describe. It was someone or something speaking *to* me. But it wasn't exactly exterior. It wasn't sound waves hitting the ear drum. I heard it inside of me, but it came from outside."

"What did the voice say?"

"It said—you'll laugh, I know you'll laugh—it said that I should stop and pick up the next hitchhiker I see on the road. At first I shook it off. No bloody way, I said. That's crazy. I never pick up hitchhikers. Not only is it dangerous in these times, I'm always going too fast. I chalked it up to imagination. So I kept saying my beads like the good lad I am, and the voice came a second time.

" 'You must stop and pick up the next hitchhiker', it said.

"I was starting to get nervous, wondering what I'd eaten for breakfast, asking myself if I'd been having enough fun lately, the usual checklist for neurosis. Then the voice came a third time, just as I was going over a rise in the road, and there at the bottom, half a mile ahead, was a fellow with his thumb out.

"So I said, all right, but I gave that voice a big groan!

"I pulled over to the curb and this nice-looking lad jumped in. Nothing unusual about him except he had a really decent face.

"We made small talk for about thirty seconds, and I was tearing up to 140 again when he turned to me and said, *The first trumpet has sounded.*

"Oh-oh, I said to myself, I've picked up a loony.

"I eased back on the accelerator and looked for an exit from the motorway that might have a copper station at the end of it. I was down to eighty klicks when he said it again: *The first trumpet has sounded.*

" 'What's this about a trumpet? You're a musician, are you?' I said.

"He just repeated for the third time, *The first trumpet has sounded.*

" 'Who are you?' I asked him.

" 'My name is Gabriel', he answered.

"By this point I was really scared. I just stared straight ahead at the pavement, and we kept going at eighty. Then it dawned on me that he must be putting me on. He had to be."

Billy's voice trembled and he looked Elijah full in the eyes.

"What's the matter, Billy? What happened?"

"I looked over to the passenger side and he wasn't there."

"Not there?"

"He was there. And then he wasn't there."

"Are you serious?"

"I couldn't be more serious."

"Was he perhaps a spiritual meditation in your mind?"

"It wasn't like that. He was real. You could have reached out and touched his arm. His jacket rustled. You could hear him breathe. His voice hit my ear drums the way the first voice didn't. It was solid."

"What did you do next?"

"I was so shaken my hands weren't controlling the wheel too well. I slowed the car and pulled over onto the shoulder. I just sat there. I couldn't think. I couldn't do anything. I just sat there playing it and replaying it in my mind. My hands wouldn't stop shaking. Then a constable pulled in behind me and walked up to the window.

" 'Having trouble?' he said.

" 'Nope', I said.

"But you know coppers; they can read minds. He said, 'Are you sure, sir? You look like you've had a spot of trouble.'

" 'Constable,' I said, 'if I told you, you wouldn't believe me.'

" 'Why don't you try me?' he said. So I told him what happened."

"What did he say to that?"

"He just pushed back his cap and scratched his head. Then he said, 'Sir, if you'd told me this yesterday, I would have thought you were mad as a hatter, but you're the fourth person to tell me that very story this morning.' "

"Astounding."

"Believe me, Davy. I've made nothing of this up."

"I do believe you."

"I've not exaggerated any of it either."

"I believe you. How many people have you told?"

"How badly do you think I want to lose credibility? Think of it, in my position."

"Have you told anyone?"

"I told *Stato*. He's got eyes like a hawk. He dug it out of me. He believes me. I think he told the Holy Father, but what he makes of it I couldn't begin to guess."

"This is very meaningful."

"It is? Why?"

"My life seems to be haunted by the Book of Revelation lately. Your experience is of a piece with some things that have been happening."

"Can you tell me about it?"

"I will tell you in the morning. If we get started on this subject we'll never stop. We both need a good night's sleep if we're going to put our heads in the lion's mouth tomorrow. Agreed?"

"Agreed. God bless you, Davy."

"God bless you, Billy."

"Good night."

VII

Isola di Capri

He tossed and turned in fitful half-sleep for several hours. Occasionally, he heard muttering and sporadic groans from Billy's room. Obviously, the Monsignor was dreaming. In the middle of the night, the groans became yelps and then, suddenly, a loud cry for help.

"Oh, Lord! My gut!"

Elijah went into the other room and found Billy sitting up in bed with a look of terror on his face. He was holding his belly and rocking back and forth. In a contortion of physical agony, he threw himself onto the pillows, rolled around, and then tried to get out of bed.

"Quick! The bathroom!" said Billy and ran for it. He staggered out again about twenty minutes later.

"Something's really wrong. I've been retching and retching, and it just won't stop, even though my stomach's empty. Nasty bouts of diarrhea too. It's something more than indigestion. I've never had cramps like this in my life."

He began groaning again and tears of pain sprang to his eyes.

"It sounds like something serious", said Elijah. "I'm taking you to a hospital."

He rang Roberto on the house phone and asked for directions to the closest one. Fifteen minutes later they were staggering into the emergency ward at Salerno. Billy was still retching.

In heavily accented Italian, Billy described his symptoms to an intern.

The young doctor asked what they had eaten the evening before, and when they both replied, simultaneously, *lasagna,* he asked if Billy had eaten anything different from Elijah.

"Christmas cake and cognac", said Billy making a clown face. The doctor was unamused.

"You aren't in shock," he said somberly, "so there is no immediate danger of death."

"Thank you for that reassurance", Billy said in English.

"It is possible you have eaten something that makes a neurotoxin. Did you eat canned peas yesterday?"

Billy shook his head.

"Fish, chicken, mayonnaise?"

"No. No. No."

"You have picked up something. You may have a staphylococcus or salmonella — ordinary food poisoning. I want to keep you here until morning. It could be something worse. We will keep an eye on you and do some tests."

"His bedside manner leaves something to be desired", said Billy. "But he's a bright lad and just might pull me through!" He attempted a wry look, but a spasm of torment crossed his face. He begged for directions to the nearest toilet and dashed for it.

The doctor turned to Elijah and said, "He will be dehydrated. I will put an intravenous into him and place him under observation."

"Do you have any idea what may have caused it?"

"I don't know. Cognac wouldn't do this, and I don't think the cake is guilty."

"Then what could have done this to him?"

"It's a mystery. Life is full of mystery."

"Is it possible he will be better by morning? We are scheduled to attend an important meeting in a few hours from now."

"It would be unwise for him to leave that soon. Although his symptoms are not life-threatening, they are severe. Salmonella can last several days and is debilitating. I wouldn't want to discharge him after a few hours, especially if he is dehydrated."

Billy wobbled out of the bathroom. A nurse ordered him into a wheelchair. Elijah walked along with them to the ward.

When the patient was bundled into bed, and they were alone, Elijah said: "You are here for a few days. I will look in on you when I get back from Capri this afternoon."

"Damn! That's foolish. You can't go by yourself."

"I can."

"Into Mordor without Billy? Think twice, lad!"

"I don't want to go alone, my friend. I am sorely afraid of it. But Christ will be with me."

"You'll be needing a legion of angels with you too, not to mention a suit of asbestos armor!"

"You must pray for me."

"I'll pray for you, but I don't like it. I think you should wait."

"There may not be another opportunity. This is the moment that divine Providence has arranged."

"Maybe. But I think there's something fishy about this, if you'll pardon the salmonella pun. Maybe the enemy wants you to go alone into the lion's mouth."

"I won't be alone."

"That's very edifying of you; how can I argue with that!"

The pain took over again, followed by more retching. They did not discuss the matter further. A nurse arrived with bottles and tubes. An intravenous needle was planted in Billy's arm. He turned away while she was inserting it.

"No martyr me. Billy hate pain."

"You'll feel better soon", said the nurse.

"Did you get much sleep?" asked Billy with a frown.

"Almost none."

"I thought so. You look like I feel. Why don't you go back to the boathouse and try to catch a few hours? It's five o'clock now.

You could easily get three more hours before they take you to the marina. Those three hours might change the future of the world. Ow, ow, ow, Billy hurt! Billy wanna go home!"

"I can't leave you like this."

"You bloody well can. I outrank you. I'm a Monsignor and you're a lowly monk. Holy obedience, remember? Now git!"

Elijah obeyed, but on his return to the boathouse he did not sleep. He lay in bed staring at the ceiling until the birds began their dawn chorus. He got up and prayed his morning office, but it was dry. The prayer of faith, with no spiritual consolations. He wondered over this. Did the Lord wish him to go into the mouth of the lion with a sense of emptiness, and perhaps with his confidence shaken? Or did He want him to go forward in sheer faith, conscious only of his weakness?

"My Savior," he whispered, "Jesus, true Lord of the world, I do not ask for human strength. But I ask for the grace to speak to him only those words that you desire to be spoken. Give me a right heart. Gird me with truth. Armor me with faith. Protect my soul from the principalities and powers that rule this man, even those that are unknown to himself. Grant me the sword of the Spirit, that the words of my mouth might move the thoughts of his heart, that this enemy of Yours might no longer walk with the foe, but be restored unto righteousness. For the glory of the Lamb!"

Stillness filled him. The peace of the poor men. The consolation of the chosen ones. He knelt by the end of the bed and held the chip of wood in his hand as if it were the first and final anchor in a spinning cosmos. In that position, unmoving, he waited for the dawn.

At first light, he telephoned the hospital. The doctor on morning duty informed him that Billy's condition was stable, and that the patient was sleeping. There was some danger yet, he said, but it was not critical. It was a matter of waiting. He suggested that Elijah call again in the evening. The patient could receive visitors then.

He asked the doctor to tell Billy that he had gone on to Capri, and unless something unforeseen occurred, he would return to the mainland by late afternoon. He would come by the hospital in the early evening.

Roberto's wife made him an ample breakfast of sausages and scrambled eggs. Over her protests, he rejected the grand dining room and ate instead at the breakfast nook in the kitchen. As she poured more coffee into his cup, she murmured her sympathies regarding "poor Signore Stangsby". She beat her breast and hoped aloud that it was not the Christmas cake that had done it. She asked where they had eaten supper the night before, and when he told her, she threw up her hands, and said, "*Ecco!* Those little restaurants, they don't keep an eye on the heat! Two tourists died last year from shellfish. Now this!"

"We both ate from the same dish", Elijah said. "Lasagna."

She shrugged, "Maybe you have a strong stomach."

"If anyone has a strong stomach it's Signore Stangsby."

"*Allora!*" she shrugged again, sighing and muttering to her pots.

Roberto put his head in to say that the marina was expecting him within the hour. The appointment secretary had phoned from Capri to say that the President hoped to meet him sometime between nine and ten o'clock.

Elijah steered the Jaguar down the winding driveway to the highway, following Roberto, who manipulated a yellow Land Rover as if he were in the Grand Prix. Five minutes later, they turned onto a private lane leading to the waterside. There, he saw a solitary cabin cruiser rising and falling in the swell beside the dock.

Roberto waved, honked, and roared back up the lane.

The boat's crew came forward across the parking lot as Elijah locked the car. The captain, an older man with dyed red hair, greeted him politely but impersonally, and introduced the second mate, a man of about thirty years, who looked as if he would be more suitably employed at a family enterprise in Sicily.

"My son-in-law", explained the captain.

Neither of the men looked at him for more than a second. Their eyes turned back to the boat and immediately they set to the task of departure. Elijah climbed aboard, the engine rumbled, and within seconds the boat was skimming across the blue waters of the gulf. Running alongside the Sorrento Peninsula, they moved at astonishing speed toward the west.

Elijah sat in the stern seat, in the open air, relishing the exhilaration of wind and spray. The cruiser turned slightly to the right, entering the Gulf of Naples, where a massive cliff rose out of the sea before them. The captain came back and pointed to it.

"Isola di Capri", he yelled into Elijah's ear. "We stop at the marina soon. Up there on top, that is Monte Tiberio. The white building is the President's *palazzo.* Beside it is Tiberius' palace, the Villa Jovis. The old emperor, he used to throw people off that cliff there if they made him mad."

The captain roared laughing, went back to the pilot house, and took over the helm. The younger man stood to the side and stared at Elijah without expression. Shortly after, the boat slid up beside a wharf. The son-in-law jumped over the gunwales, moored the boat, and waved Elijah out.

"You come this way."

He led him onto the shore and through a gate to a concrete pad where a long, sleek, red helicopter sat warming its engines.

The son-in-law opened the passenger door and nodded to the pilot. Elijah climbed in and fastened his seatbelt. The motors began to hum at high pitch. The machine rose straight up, as smooth as an elevator, banked without a tremor, and flew straight for the height of Monte Tiberio. Within a minute, Elijah was standing on a white landing pad, so bright that he had to shield his eyes from the reflection. He heard the helicopter take off again, leaving him blinking, dazzled, and disoriented.

"Professor Schäfer, welcome", said a disembodied voice.

A hand shook his, took him by the elbow, and led him off the pad to a building that closely resembled the beach house at Salerno. The voice at the end of the hand introduced itself as the appointment secretary, and then materialized as a man in his sixties. He was dressed fastidiously but comfortably, and looked as if he should be managing a transnational corporation. The expression, like Roberto's, was poised, cordial, quick to smile, and exquisitely polite.

"Please come into the reception building, sir", he said. "It's so much cooler in there. You can wash up if you like, and I'll have someone bring you tea. I understand you prefer tea to coffee. Yes? And you take lemon, no sugar, I believe."

"That's correct", said Elijah. "How did you know?"

The secretary smiled knowingly and conducted him along a glass corridor into a window-lined semicircular room overlooking the Gulf of Naples to the north and the Gulf of Salerno to the east. The back wall was paneled in rosewood. Far below, speedboats made white trails, moving at a snail's pace across the sea.

"The President is not available until 9:30, when he will be very pleased to receive you in the *studiolo*, a private library in his residence. He has an outstanding collection of ancient documents. You would find many of them unique. The Cordova Codex, for example, is the only existing copy of a manuscript of Aristotle that was long considered lost in the great fire of Alexandria. As you are an archeologist, I'm sure you realize the significance of this discovery."

"This is astounding news", said Elijah, excited. "Which of the lost books has been found?"

"I will let the President answer that question. Archeology is one of his great loves, and one of his pleasures is to share personally the discoveries his antiquities foundation makes possible."

"Very good", said Elijah.

"Please make yourself comfortable until I return. Then we will go directly to his residence."

He was left alone to meditate on the sea, to sink into the Scandinavian furniture, to run his feet (he had temporarily removed his shoes) back and forth over a pale amethyst carpet. The mahogany coffee table invited him to notice the reflection of his face. Wild roses brushed against the window pane. Swallows darted across the sky. A blue bronze horse begged the hand to stroke its arched back. Elijah did so. He sipped from the cup of tea and delighted in the room.

Every now and then he felt a pang in his heart when he recalled the man with whom he would soon be speaking. Potentially the most skilled adversary the Church had ever faced. The sensation was one of mild fear mingled with curiosity, and even—to Elijah's surprise—anticipation. When he recognized this impulse he immediately recollected his thoughts and began to pray. He wondered at himself. How easily he had forgotten to pray! What had happened to his sense of vigilance? Had he been anesthetized by the accumulation of fatigue, his distraction over Billy's health, and the pleasure of these surroundings?

He admonished himself. Vigilance gathered strength within him. The spirit of prayer pushed back a sensation of lurking shadows. He rested in this state for some minutes until the secretary strode into the room and announced: "He is ready. Please, come, Professor Schäfer."

He was led through a glass-encased causeway over a tumble of rocks and ornamental gardens to a larger building, designed to match the visitor's pavilion. They went through two security stations and entered a hall that opened onto a vaulted living room. This room was almost a full circle, fully 300 degrees of which was floor-to-ceiling glass. The air was cool, scented with jasmine. Elijah had no time to look at the artwork, for the secretary turned and walked backward, extending one arm wide, guiding him to another annex, smiling broadly all the while. He entered a large room and announced, "Elijah Schäfer, sir."

A tall, silver-haired man got up from his armchair and came

forward with an extended hand. He wore a white cardigan over a turquoise polo shirt, gray slacks, and burgundy oxfords. His face was handsome, well-complexioned, grave, and kindly; it radiated openness. His grip was warm and firm.

"Father Schäfer, a very great pleasure." His voice was deep, modulated with that hint of age which denotes dignity rather than decline.

"Mr. President, I bring greetings from His Holiness, and his best wishes for your health."

"Please convey my thanks to His Holiness, and in return, my wishes for his health."

"He has asked me to convey to you his personal gratitude for your efforts in the cause of world peace, and to assure you of his prayers for you."

"That is most kind. Please convey to His Holiness my gratitude and esteem."

He removed his reading glasses, looked into Elijah's eyes, and smiled.

"Now that we have completed the formalities, why don't we relax?"

He took Elijah by the arm and led him to a large leather chair facing the sea. The President sat opposite him, crossed his legs, and surveyed Elijah's attire.

"I note that you have not traveled in clerical clothing."

"At the request of the Holy See. The Holy See would appreciate a certain informality, and discretion, to mark the style of our meeting."

"Ah, yes", said the President. "I know your Cardinal Secretary of State quite well, though only by reputation. He is, I understand, an astute judge of political implications."

"I am sure that he is among those who applaud your efforts in the cause of peace between nations. But, regrettably, in the present world there is much confusion. The Church is very old. She has seen civilizations rise and fall. She must exercise caution."

"Understandably so. We too must exercise caution about governments and movements. Not all men in this world are committed to the ideals for which we both strive."

"I am happy that you do not take any offense at our approach."

"We are at the preliminary stage of discussions, which I hope will grow into friendship between our government and yours. Your caution only increases my respect for your Pope and the Church."

The secretary entered at that moment, preventing a reply. He asked to speak privately with the President. The President apologized and left the room. During the interim, Elijah noted that the walls were lined with thousands of volumes of books. Inbuilt display cases contained ancient coins, amphoras, pottery, and Roman bronzes.

The President returned.

"I see you are admiring my collection. These artifacts were unearthed during the reconstruction of the Villa Jovis. They date from the first century, almost certainly the years when Tiberius ruled the empire from this very place."

"This site resonates with history."

"Indeed, an embarrassing glut of history."

"If I recall my lessons correctly, wasn't he regarded as one of Rome's most bloody tyrants?"

"That is a myth which grew up around his memory. Recent studies indicate that he may have been maligned by the early Church in its zeal to posit Religion against the State. During the last sixty years he has been more fairly judged. The prevailing opinion among scholars is that Tiberius was a ruler faithful to his duties, prudent, just, and self-contained. Did you know he didn't leave Capriae during the last ten years of his life?"

"I can understand why. It is a beautiful island."

"That, and the fact that Rome was a sewer of intrigue."

"This home and these gardens must give you great pleasure."

"They are an island of calm in a sea of trouble. The world hasn't changed much since Tiberius' time."

"I agree, sir. Human nature changes little from age to age."

"That is because man has not had the ability to remove the causes of his anxiety. War, greed, fear, hatred—do they not stem from the inequalities of life? How can a man be at peace when he can barely feed himself, while his neighbor lives like . . ."

"Like a Roman emperor?"

"Exactly", said the President. He looked about the room. "All people should be able to live like this. And some day they will. In the meantime, a few are given the privilege of developing the pattern. We lead the way. A paradigm, a model of the man of the new age."

"Sir, man hardly seems to be entering a new era. The crimes of this century are unprecedented. Unless there is a change of heart in many nations, we can expect more horrible crimes."

"Correct. Unless there is a change of heart. But we are working toward the development of this consciousness. We are approaching an omega point in history. During this period, all that is deformed in human nature threatens to erupt and to drag civilization into the abyss. This threat arises at the very moment when all that is best in man is poised for a quantum leap forward. The atavistic instincts in man cannot be permitted to stop this breakthrough into the next stage of evolution."

The secretary entered the room carrying a case bound in green leather. He placed it on the coffee table in front of the President. The President opened it and removed an ocher, broadmouthed clay jar.

"Please, Father Schäfer. I have a gift to send to His Holiness. Would you accept it in his name?"

"I would be honored, sir."

"Come, look at it. It is a treasure of inestimable worth. I give this unique heritage of the human community into the safekeeping of the Church."

He withdrew a parchment roll from the jar.

"It is Aristotle's lost dialogue, *On Justice.*"

Elijah's heart quickened.

"Mr. President, this is extraordinary!"

"I hope that the Church will accept this gift as a sign of our good will."

"In the name of the Church, I thank you, sir. I know that it will become a major treasure in the Vatican Library."

"It is a priceless cultural artifact. But it is of even greater value academically — a keystone in the history of human thought. It was long believed that this lost book was a work similar to Plato's *Republic. The Republic,* too, discusses justice, and indeed its alternative title is *On Justice.*"

"You mean to say that this document may be one of the Great Books of Western man — but an unknown one?"

"It will soon be well known indeed. It is all that we could hope for, and more. In some aspects it surpasses Plato for the splendor of its vision."

"This is overwhelming. How can we thank you?"

"There is no need for thanks. It is a token of my commitment to our common values."

The two men seated themselves as before.

"May I ask how it was discovered?"

"Perhaps you are aware that I am a lover of antiquities — strictly an amateur, mind you. My Foundation for the Development of Archeology perceived early on that many of the major lost books of the world might be sequestered in unexamined caches of ancient documents, guarded by the ignorant, unknown by all save a few jealous bibliophiles clinging to outmoded philosophies. It was my theory that by tracing the historical spoor left by falling civilizations we might obtain a narrowing of probabilities.

"Take this Codex, for example. I knew that Córdoba in the twelfth century was the great seat of Arab learning, and that Arab learning had included the study of Aristotelian treatises, and especially those works which examined psychology, physics, and metaphysics. I discovered, in addition, that the tradition of Aristotle had survived among the Syrians, and I conjectured that the Arabs might have obtained the book when they conquered Syria in the seventh century. This pointed back to an important presupposition: that the lost books had not burned in the Great Fire but had been rescued at the time or at an earlier period. Their subsequent eclipse was due to the necessity of hiding them from fundamentalists, both Islamic and Christian.

"I next realized that the great Aristotelian commentators, especially Ibn Rushd, known as Averroës, who died in Arabic Spain in 1198, were possessed of an insight into their master that the Latin West did not have. Their exegesis must surely have come from Arabic versions of Aristotle's books, which in turn derived from Syrian versions of the original texts. The rest was simple detective work. I found a hidden cache of codices in a sealed crypt of a monastery, now abandoned, which had once been a Moorish mosque. It's clear that the monks, not the Arabs, hid these precious works from Church authorities, for the interpretations of Aristotle's thought advanced by the Averroësts was considered a dangerous corruption. Among those codices lay the lost book, in addition to a number of previously unknown works by ancient philosophers. The Arabs had brought the lost books to the mountainous deserts of Spain, on an ark of culture, as it were. For some reason buried in the secrets of history, the collection fell into the hands of the Christian monastics, who in turn allowed the knowledge of this treasure to pass out of human memory."

"Mr. President, in my limited study of Aristotle, I learned that the works known in the West came by way of Constantinople."

"That is correct", said the President tilting his head reflectively. "But the translations that came from the Greek through Western scholars took on interpretations that were distinctively Latin. At the very least, this altered Aristotle's intent. The discoveries in

Moorish Spain, I believe, will be a healthy counterbalance to the excessive rationalism of the West. These new books breathe with the very soul of the mystical East, but they breathe through a mind that transcends both West and East. This discovery will be a milestone in the history of ideas."

"Its importance cannot be exaggerated. I know that the Vatican will be overwhelmed by your generosity."

"Then I am content."

"Sir," said Elijah, opening his briefcase, "I too bring a gift. His Holiness is well aware of your love of archeology and history. He has asked me to present to you the report of the Pontifical Commission for Biblical Archeology on the findings at Ephesus and at the new caves by the Dead Sea."

"Ah, yes, I have read about the latest discoveries. I have also read your articles on the subject. Most impressive."

The President took the brief, fanned through the pages, and placed it carefully on the table beside him.

"Father Schäfer, you must personally thank His Holiness for me, and tell him that I appreciate this gesture of courtesy. I see it as a first step toward an open dialogue."

"His Holiness very much wants this dialogue. Furthermore, he extends to you his warmest personal invitation to meet with him at the earliest mutual convenience. He asks that you advise him regarding the most appropriate site for this meeting. He suggests as his first choices the Vatican City or his summer residence, Castel Gandolfo."

The President's eyes clouded, and he looked out the window. He seemed lost in thought for a moment, then inhaled sharply, and sat straighter in his chair.

"This is a welcome invitation. The dialogue must certainly continue. However, I am sure His Holiness appreciates the immense burdens of responsibility that I am presently bearing. The Europarliament is in disarray, the economy of the world is radically destabilized. I am being asked by the United Nations to go here and there to negotiate between warring tribes of various kinds. Only this morning, for example, the Japanese requested that I mediate in their trade war with the Americans. It is difficult at this stage to arrange even half a day during which to pursue personal interests. I believe that is what His Holiness is suggesting— a personal, not a state visit."

"Precisely."

"Then I am doubly grieved. I regret, it is not possible at this time."

"Sir, I am sure he will anticipate the day when it does become possible."

The President smiled suddenly. "You have a saying: the Pope is the prisoner of the Vatican. Please tell him that I too am a prisoner—the prisoner of civilization."

Elijah floundered in his thoughts, searching for a response, a way to retrieve the conversation, and to direct it toward the development of a continuing dialogue.

"There is an alternative", said the President.

"Sir?"

"I would be honored if the Holy Father would consider an invitation to Capri. If he accepts, I would dispatch my helicopter to the Vatican, bring him here for an informal meeting, and return him safely to Saint Peter's, all within a few hours. I have an uncommitted hour on my schedule next week. One of those rare luncheons which no guest has yet claimed."

The President observed Elijah with an expectant gaze.

"I regret that is not possible, considering his upcoming visit to the Far East. He will be in Japan and Korea next week."

"But of course! I had forgotten. Forgive me, my mind is spilling over with far too much information. Perhaps at some point in the future, then, at a place and time that is mutually convenient . . . "

"I'm sure His Holiness looks forward to that."

"Very good. We will be in touch."

The President rose and extended his hand.

"Father Elijah, I have enjoyed our little chat very much. Perhaps we will meet again."

"I hope so, sir."

"You may be surprised to know that I have followed your career for some years now."

This was indeed a surprise.

"Come, let's walk together to the helicopter. We can talk on the way."

"You say you have followed my career? You must be thinking of someone else. My career is that of every monk at Carmel, to be buried in the hidden life. Careers are the last thing in the world pursued by people such as myself."

The President smiled to himself and took Elijah's arm. The security personnel stood and bowed slightly as the two men passed through the checkpoints.

"I would be shocked if it were otherwise", said the President. "Yet your life before conversion to Catholicism was not without notoriety. Your political career was at one time marked by every sign of destiny. It has not escaped my notice that, had you chosen a different path for your life, you might be standing where I am now standing, in the position of maximum influence. In the *parlement des nations* what good might you have accomplished for mankind!"

A sadness clouded the President's face.

"Life is mysterious, and full of strange turns", said Elijah.

"What great good!" the President repeated to himself.

"God alone sees everything. I believe He is bringing a different good through my life as a monk."

"But, still, what a loss; what a pity."

"I think you exaggerate my importance, sir."

"No", the President said soberly, shaking his head, "No, I do not. You are an extraordinarily gifted man. You were a *zaddik* at the age of twelve."

"No," said Elijah in horror, "I was never a *zaddik*."

"No? Then for the sake of your modesty, we will say that you weren't a holy man, but a wise child. Is that acceptable?"

"It is inaccurate."

"Then let us at least agree that you were a talmudic prodigy at the age of thirteen. You were engaged in scholarly correspondence with the great Dabrova Rev when the Nazis invaded Poland. Admit it", said the President, amused. "Vestiges of that gift shine through your articles."

"How do you know all this?"

The President did not reply. He merely looked into Elijah's eyes with warmth and respect. For an instant Elijah's mind blurred. He felt at once confused and exalted by the praise. It pleased and frightened him, though he could not have explained this curious mixture of emotions.

"I have also read about your work with the government of Israel. Your dossiers on Eichmann were prescient. Your later career as a prosecutor of war criminals was brilliant, to say the least. Your rise in the party. Your speeches at international conventions. These were a foundation on which a great work might have been built."

"I was a shell filled with idealistic passions; I pursued them only to fill my emptiness."

"You were much admired."

"And much hated."

"That too. Yes, that is part of the burden of destiny. Those who make history, small or great, must accept being misunderstood by their contemporaries."

"I have found something much greater. The greatest thing in the world . . ."

But at that moment the President's attention was distracted by a commotion on the helicopter pad. A second aircraft was landing, a dark blue, two-seat minicopter. A security guard rushed out and yelled something to the pilot.

Fragments of sentences, faint but intelligible, broke through the glass paneling.

"You're an hour early! This is irregular!"

"Sorry! But he said it was top priority", yelled the pilot pointing to his passenger.

A man dressed in a black suit, white shirt, and black tie stepped out of the vehicle and strode toward the entrance. The guard caught up to him and bowed to him, speaking rapidly. The man in the black suit ignored him and walked through into the foyer. He stopped short when he saw the President.

"My apologies. I realize that I'm early, but it's most urgent . . . " He looked Elijah up and down with unfriendly curiosity.

"Let's discuss this in my study", said the President with an air of calm authority.

The visitor nodded assent in a mood of cold restraint. He gripped a valise under his arm.

"And now, I must say good-bye to you, my friend", the President said, turning to Elijah. "I hope that we shall meet again soon."

Once again they shook hands. Then, without another word, the President and his visitor walked back down the hall toward the residence.

Elijah stared after them, haunted by the certainty that he had seen that face somewhere before. Then it came to him that this was the man in his dream, the face he had seen in Billy's apartment.

* * *

"Well, how was Mister Big?" said Billy sitting up in bed with a grin.

A nurse reminded Elijah that Monsignor Stangsby was not yet out of danger and needed rest.

"You have five minutes with him", she warned. "Five minutes and no more."

Billy looked ghostly pale. His eyes were haggard, but the comic light was still in them, as if he had joked with the angel of death and tricked him.

"Mister Big, as you call him, was not so big that he was overwhelming. Yet I was . . . impressed by him."

"Impressed? Why does that make me nervous?"

"It needn't. I knew there was danger there too. The spiritual opposition was subtle but very powerful. I felt something unseen trying to bend my mind at certain points. He flatters, but in such a way as to make one feel truly complimented. He exudes sincerity."

"Now I *am* nervous. What did he say?"

"He expressed the hope that we could work together for world peace. He was open to a continuing dialogue with the Vatican. It was a preliminary exchange of protocol."

"Nothing exciting?"

"He gave us a gift that I think is very exciting. He is donating an original manuscript to the Vatican. One of Aristotle's lost books, *On Justice.*"

"Too intellectual for me. Sorry if I don't get worked up over it. Now tell me the gory details. Did he have a black cape, and weren't his incisors just ever so slightly longer than normal?"

"I'm sorry to tell you that he appeared to be a normal human being."

"That's disappointing. If I'd been there with my little Sting, my trusty orc-killer in hand, oooh, just you believe it, I would have flushed out the demons."

"They were there in force, but were quiet."

"Weren't you frightened?"

"Yes, a little, in the beginning. But it wasn't like the frightful feeling one has when a possessed person is delivered of an evil spirit or when you narrowly escape some kind of physical danger. It was like a slowly growing pressure, an awareness of black clouds gathering silently, not yet ready to unleash a storm. The man was surrounded by this cloud."

"Now you're getting spooky. The real stuff! More, tell me more!"

"The cloud was invisible. The coming storm was invisible too, yet it was there all the time on the edge of consciousness."

"So he's a sinister figure after all."

"No. He wasn't personally sinister. At least nothing in his character or temperament gave off the tell-tale signs of evil. He emanates a rather admirable stability, a kindly but firm authority. It was difficult to direct the conversation where the Holy Father hoped it would go—to the subject of conversion. He was definitely in charge of everything that happened this morning, but he controlled it without any of the ordinary apparatus of control. It was most interesting. I will be a long time trying to understand how he did it."

"Mesmerism?"

"Nothing of the sort."

"Did he drug your drink?" said Billy eagerly.

"My single cup of tea was delicious and had no aftereffects."

"Then you're not making sense, old boy. I detect a hesitation in your voice, as if something happened, but didn't happen. Something that made you nervous, but it was so insignificant that you dismissed it."

"Yes, it was like that."

"Your conscious perceptions are telling you one thing, but I'll bet your spirit picked something up on another level. What was it—that's the question."

"Perhaps it was that I felt myself *handled* by a master of public relations, a man so talented that he puts you at ease and dispels the suspicion that you are being handled. You sense genuine rapport, intimacy, equality."

"And that was the master of the world?"

Elijah nodded. "It was a surprise. But I should have known it would be that way. The apocalypse is not melodrama. If it were, most people would wake up and see the danger they are in. That is our real peril. Our own times, no matter how troubled they may be, are our *idea* of what is real. It is almost impossible to step outside of it in order to see it for what it is."

"I see what you mean. It's *our* world. Other times and places can only be conceived in the intellect or imagination."

"Exactly. The living apocalypse radiates a sense of normality. We are *inside* it."

Billy stared down at his hands, the open palms lying on his lap like fallen leaves.

"Where's my little sword?" he said in a faint voice. "Where's my Sting?"

"Sting?"

"Fairy story. Hobbit. Literary."

"Are you all right?"

"Fine, fine", Billy muttered, still staring down at his empty hands.

"What is it? What are you thinking?"

"I'm thinking I should have been there with you, Davy. I'm thinking it's a dangerous thing to go alone into Mordor. Your head could get bent."

"I don't understand."

"You don't need to. Tell me some more. What was this guy really like?"

"I sensed a sort of personal greatness. The word *destiny* comes to mind. Yet there was nothing pretentious or pompous about him. Instead, I found him to be noble, even spiritual."

"I'll bet he was even . . . humble", said Billy, peering at Elijah with a sharp eye.

"Yes. That's the word. A unique sort of humility. I was impressed."

"You said that before."

"Did I?"

"You'd think a chap like him would be an egomaniac. I read that people who meet him for the first time, and don't know who he is, think he's a modestly well-known but not outstanding professor at a small college in the Midlands. You'd never suspect he's a polymath, speaks all those languages, has about seven degrees, and is probably going to get the Nobel Prize for Peace this year. Leave aside the question of all that power he's got. Start adding it up and straightaway it gets amazing. Now, tell me, how does a lad like that keep from getting a swelled head?"

"It's said that he is a humble person."

"Yeah, I've read that too. Maybe it's true and maybe it isn't. Do you believe everything the press feeds us?"

"No, of course not."

Billy looked at him strangely, then looked down at his hands again. Elijah wondered why he was doing that. He felt mildly irritated.

Billy went on: "Apparently, in his talks on spirituality he often refers to humility as one of the great virtues."

"Which it is. The fundamental one."

"I always feel uneasy about great men who talk overmuch about humility."

"Why is that?"

"They remind me ever so slightly of Uriah Heep."

"What a comical name! You English! Who is Uriah Heep?"

"A character in a novel by Dickens. He was always 'umble, so very, very 'umble. But he turned out to be rather sinister in the end."

They were forced to terminate their conversation on that note because a tyrannical head nurse entered the room and commanded Elijah to leave.

"Don't worry about me, Davy. I'll catch the train to Rome in a few days from now, when I've served my sentence. Tell the boss I'm sorry about fumbling the ball. I'll be back on duty early next week. And look ... I'm really sorry about letting you down again."

"You didn't let me down, Billy. You didn't choose to be ill."

"Maybe. But this was one time I really should have been there."

"The mission is launched. No harm was done."

"I hope you're right. Well, God bless and good-bye! Away with you now, there's a good lad! Back home to the Shire!"

Elijah went out shaking his head.

VIII

Rome

On returning to the city, Elijah telephoned the Secretariat of State. After he passed an interrogation by an officious clerk, his call was transferred through to the cardinal himself. *Stato* did not want to hear the details of the journey to Capri over the telephone, asking Elijah to come to the Vatican early the next day. He would arrange a meeting with the Holy Father for ten in the morning.

Elijah approached the papal offices with a mixture of elation and apprehension, aggravated by the fact that he would have to report that his mission had failed. The Pope's private secretary opened a high oak door and Elijah entered.

"Father Schäfer, Your Holiness."

The old man rose from his desk and approached with his right hand extended. The secretary withdrew, and Elijah bent a knee to kiss the pontiff's ring. Once again he was not permitted to do so, as the Pope embraced him with both arms and made him rise.

He looked deeply into the priest's eyes, then stepped back. A worried look crossed his face. He continued to grip Elijah by the shoulders.

"Do you bear some wounds from the encounter?"

"Not that I am aware of."

"Perhaps they are hidden even from yourself, my son."

The Pope drew Elijah to the window overlooking Saint Peter's

Square. They stood side by side silently, until at last the Pope said, "He has captured the admiration of many of my brothers in the episcopate. Has he harmed you as well?"

"Holy Father, permit me, but I don't feel harmed in any way. Of course, I am troubled by the meeting, but he has not shaken my faith."

Crowds of pilgrims were streaming across the pavement.

"Father Elijah, our adversary is subtle. He buries his arrows deep in men's hearts. So deep that they are almost invisible."

"What is the nature of these arrows?"

"They strike where one's humanity is most weak. I cannot read souls as well as Don Matteo does, but I see that in your past you have suffered from that great wound which afflicts modern man."

"Which is . . . ?"

"The temptation to absolute despair."

"It is true that in the past I was much afflicted by this, but I no longer feel it."

"Not even when the consolations of God are absent? Not even during the times of dryness? When you are exhausted, when all your sacrifices seem to have produced little or no fruit?"

"Not even then. But there are moments when I grieve for my wife and my child, and for my murdered family."

"You grieve with the heart of a husband and father. I too grieve."

"You, Holy Father?"

"I grieve over the state of mankind. A father's heart grieves. Love suffers, does it not?"

"At times I suffer, I admit. But nothing that would drive me into our adversary's sphere of influence."

"I believe what you say is true. But I must warn you, as I warn myself daily and have repeatedly warned our shepherds: no man knows his own soul so well that he is invincible to the tactics of the enemy. No man."

The Pope spoke with firmness, even as he stared out at the square. The crowds were filling the thousands of chairs arrayed before an outdoor altar on the steps of Saint Peter's. The cordoned sections for tens of thousands of others who would stand behind were also beginning to swell.

"They come early today", said the Pope. "This afternoon when I celebrate the canonization of the new African martyrs, I will speak on the question of vigilance. The press is saying that this is a political canonization. It is not. Those who died as victims of tribalism are not the same as these who died bearing witness to the Name. They were offered a means of escape and rejected it. They refused to apostatize. Priests, bishops, nuns, and the lay faithful—all those who were crucified under the hot African sun—they had spent a life of sacrifice. They were ready when the moment of choice came for them."

"There were children among them. Did those little ones choose?"

"Have you ever seen a child crucified, Father?"

"I have seen children beaten to death. In the ghetto, when I was a boy."

"It is beyond belief. The mind recoils. We say to ourselves, such things cannot happen. And yet they happen. In this very city, not so many centuries ago, our brothers and sisters were offered the same choice: sacrifice to the emperor or die. A single grain of incense, that's all. Just a grain and you are free. No death. No dismemberment. Go home and live. Be a good citizen. But they refused. Did you know, Father, there are records of Christian children who walked to the cross or to the Colosseum, ignoring the pleading of their parents? So young, but they had learned the only thing one must know. They knew something that we, who wrestle endlessly with our prodigious intellects and our complicated emotions, can rarely know. You ask me if they chose? I believe they did. They had clarity. They had the eye of childhood."

162

"I have often sensed, Holy Father, that the people of our generation move as if in a thick, but invisible, cloud. Every faculty of perception is clogged."

"The atmosphere infects us all, my son. That is why I ask, has the adversary infected you?"

Elijah did not respond immediately. After some thought he said: "If the enemy has penetrated me, he could do so only at a level beyond my own self-awareness. But if he has done so, I ask God to root it out of me, whatever it may be."

"You are not offended by my question?"

"No, I understand it."

"Good. You realize what temptation can do to even the strongest virtue?"

"Yes. I have seen noble men descend to the level of beasts. I have seen stars fall from the heavens, and the pillars of the firmament shaken."

"You quote ably. So you understand that we have entered the end-phase of history."

"Yes, we have spoken of this."

"At our last meeting, we spoke of the general parameters of an apocalypse. Apocalypses contain real men and women, and children—no less the final Apocalypse. Do you understand that in those days every human being will be put to the test? Each will be asked to render an account of himself? Do you realize how universal this trial will be? How dreadful will be the cost of faithfulness?"

"I sensed the immensity of it when I spoke to the President. There was nothing overtly ominous in his words or his manner, and yet behind him I felt a storm brewing, as if the whole sky were engorging slowly with darkness and thunderous wrath. When that storm is unleashed, there will be no holding it back. Nor will anyone fail to feel its breath."

"Then you have seen rightly, my son."

"Holy Father, I must confess that I feel a sense of failure about my mission. Despite good intentions to open a dialogue of a spiritual nature, despite all effort to find opportunities to bring the truth to bear upon this man's soul, I was not able to do so."

The Pope nodded. "You will have another opportunity. He comes to Rome next month for the assembly of The Club of Rome. I am certain he will ask for a meeting with you."

"You think so?"

"Yes. He believes he can win you over to himself."

"Why do you think that?" Elijah asked in a barely audible voice.

"He knows that anyone can fall. Consider the apostles. Their performance was not outstanding on the night of Christ's arrest. Are we made of different material than our predecessors?"

"Isn't there a crucial difference, Holy Father? We have the benefit of two thousand years of hindsight. Most important, we are the children of God who come *after* the descent of the Holy Spirit."

"A good point, my son. But it underlines the fact that those who do not live in the power of the Holy Spirit are most vulnerable. Even believers can reduce the Faith to a philosophical system. They can retain the exterior forms of religion and lose its heart."

"Do you think this of me?"

"No. However, as your spiritual father, I am compelled to remind you to be as awake as the watchman. Guard your heart in everything. We are all in danger in times such as these. In your case, our adversary knows that with your history and your personal gifts you would be a great prize. You would greatly aid his efforts to usher in the new era."

"If the danger is such, then it is unwise for me to expose myself to him."

"And yet, you, more than almost any other man in my flock, have eyes to discern the deception. You have experiences few others can equal. Indeed, once, long ago, you approached the position of *worldpower* he has attained. It was offered to you, and you rejected it. I suspect that it was a kind of inoculation. You must ask yourself why you refused."

"I'm not entirely sure of the motivations of my heart during that period of my life. My mind was no less confused than it had been before my decision to abandon power. I think it was something quite deep in the soul. It may have been a brief parting of the curtain that covers the meaning of things. Perhaps it was a word of pure love, a life sacrificed for me, that shattered an illusion. I can make no more sense of it than that."

"You have answered well. There is more, but I will leave it to the Lord Himself to reveal it to you. You are not far from seeing it."

"I understand less and less, Holiness."

"Yes, yes," the old man smiled, "that is how it should be."

"It leaves me uncertain of the landscape, and the parameters of my own soul. What if I should be deceived?"

"I do not think you would be easily deceived, though of course you must not let down your guard for a moment. I think, Father, you have endured many fearful things in your life. There is still a great uncertainty in your heart."

"I thought it had gone forever. Those feelings gradually faded as I grew in faith. I thought I would never again be afraid."

"But you are afraid?"

"I am afraid."

"Why do you feel so?"

"Lately, I have felt very much alone. As if I were thrown back upon my own feeble strength, returned to the darkness of my youth when I was forced to depend only upon myself. I was betrayed. I was a hunted thing. It does something to a child's heart to know that powerful men wish to kill him. I believed for a very long time that no human being could be trusted. None . . . except one. The one who had saved me. And he is dead."

"Was God not with you?"

"I know now that He was. I see His hand upon all of my life during that period. Yet at the time I felt absolutely abandoned. I felt rage. The rage came from a kind of total fear, a cosmic terror that grew and grew. Eventually, it grew into hatred."

"Long ago."

"Yes. So long ago that I thought it was gone forever."

"And now you are afraid of your own fear, once again, is it not so?"

"Yes."

"Do not be afraid. The enemy has not harmed you mortally."

"But Holy Father, there have been some grave doubts in my mind. I have recently wondered about grace. I felt nothing of divine intervention during my meeting with the President."

"Surely you must know that the most powerful graces cannot be *felt* in the senses or the affections."

"I forgot this truth when I was in his presence. Strange, how I forgot a number of important things. I have failed. I was manipulated in so subtle a manner that the very words which might have altered the storm refused to take shape on my tongue. In that atmosphere, in that cordial and reasonable atmosphere, words of warning would have seemed inappropriate. For a moment, despite my years of study, despite the riches of the Catholic intellectual life, I felt myself to be . . . a defender of the irrational."

"You felt perhaps that you were the ambassador of a myth?"

"Yes, something like that. The champion of a pathetic legend."

"That was to be expected. It is in the nature of his cosmology to perceive all religions as the same, each a culturally conditioned complex of symbols, each in its own limited way a path to the divine principle."

"Yes, he hinted as much. In one of his books, he says that all religions are merely misunderstood mythologies. That is why he can send you presents, as if there is no contradiction between his beliefs and ours."

"Yesterday, the codex arrived at the Vatican Library by special courier."

"It is really a display of overwhelming generosity on his part."

"Oh, yes, it is a magnificent gift", said the Pope, musing. "Yet it is flawed. He does nothing without calculation. The gift is intended to lull us into easing our vigilance. At the same time, it speeds the subjectivization of scholarly life. It is a treasure, but this treasure, curiously, will further weaken the rational mind of the West."

"But it is by Aristotle!"

"It is an interpretation of Aristotle—*Iustitia* adapted by the oriental mind."

"You do not think it authentic?"

"It is undoubtedly authentic. It is what the President says it is, an Averroëst copy of a Syrian translation of the lost book. As such, it is an invaluable cultural artifact. But in this version, the shape of reality itself is bent. The warp will be discernible to scholars who know Aristotle to the core and who know the history of ideas in its height and breadth. The ordinary scholar, the young especially, will be swayed by a concept of state and cosmos that is cultic. This manuscript breathes a spirit far from that wisdom which, in Aristotle and other pre-Christian philosophers, we might call 'natural theology'."

"I am straining to understand. I have a hunger to read it."

"Many will hunger when they hear of it."

"Is there such great danger in this manuscript?"

"I have spent an entire night reading it. The book is not a danger such as we faced when fascism and Marxism swept across the West. Those voracious beasts revealed their appetites openly. Nor is it like postcommunist materialism, that dark and sly thing which coils about the vital organs of the world, killing it slowly. The danger in this book is that it is *spiritual.* It reintroduces the concept of the divine into the civic order, precisely at the moment of history when the mass of men have lost their bearings, have abandoned all hope that there is anything beyond this material world. More and more, they long for systemic solutions to 'the problem of man'. They want totalitarianism without brutality. This book is a gentle, oh, so very subtle, but powerful, nudge toward that world system, mixed with intoxications of the pagan East. Although there is no evidence in the text, its gnostic origins are obvious. As if Aristotle's great intellect were to be mixed with that of a necromancer, or a shaman! It may provide the philosophical motivation for the New Age the President hopes to usher in."

"Through Aristotle?"

"Not Aristotle as we have known him. Aristotle stolen and pressed through a filter. Aristotle lined up beside alluring distortions of spirituality without the absolute demands of the one true God, and beside the President's own pseudomystical social writings. Drawing upon Averroës and other non-Christian mystics, he believes that religion and reason can be in conflict with each other and yet both be right."

"In other words, the concept that all divisions, and all distinctions, are ultimately illusions."

"Correct. And thus is formed a philosophy that posits unity above truth."

"Yet we too believe in unity."

"Ah, yes, but unity can be authentic only if it is founded upon truth. We cannot pretend that there are two conflicting truths, both of which are right. This is madness. It destroys the interior unity of the human person and the meaning of personhood."

"Holy Father, may I ask, is there such grave danger in the codex? Would it not simply remain an object of academic discussion, among philosophers?"

"Philosophers have students, and students who love their teachers spread their ideas into every realm of human endeavor. Abstract academic discussions have a way of leaving their mark on entire civilizations, as the events of this century have proved all too well. In another age this codex might have been relatively harmless, especially if we were to be blessed with the original Greek text, against which it could be measured. But the true text eludes us, and thus we must now contend with a chimera that has come back from the dead and that uses Aristotle's great name as a charm and a passkey into men's minds."

Still, Elijah wondered if the Pope were not making more of the danger than was warranted.

"I hear your silent reservations, Father Elijah. But you must understand that the arrival of this document is no accident. It can be understood only within the larger context of this present struggle. *Iustitia* is not, in the end, about justice. Its purpose is to reconcile men to an ultimate bondage, but it does so — oh, bitterest of ironies — it does so in the name of freedom."

"And so, you are faced with a dilemma?"

"Indeed. Should the manuscript be quietly placed in the archives, awaiting a better time in history? Or should we open it to the world and bear the burden of knowing that some souls may be misled by it?"

"Have you decided?"

"I have. The manuscript will be open for study by all serious scholars. Translations will be made and published in various languages, in editions that carry an explanation of its background, its shortcomings, and the danger of misinterpretations."

"If I may be frank, Your Holiness, I think your decision is wise. The modern age has styled us as anti-intellectual."

"Modern man ignores the fact that the Church, virtually alone, preserved the intellectual heritage of the West throughout the Dark Ages."

"Enemies of the Church would achieve far more propaganda value from a decision to keep the manuscript discreetly in the archives."

"Their terminology would not be as charitable as yours. They would call it hiding. They would call it cheating."

"It could be called prudence."

The Pope sighed.

"We are living at the end of a civilization, one heavily loaded with ideology. There are hundreds of thousands of books published each year, most of them far from the mind of Christ. It would be useless to keep one flawed volume from a people that does not understand what it is reading, and refuses to learn to think. However, there are some who will benefit. It is always in the interests of Truth to make available a piece of cultural heritage that may enrich man's understanding of his past. The publication of *On Justice* must be seen in that light."

"The fundamentalists will accuse us of liberalism."

"Yes, and the liberals will accuse us of fundamentalism when they read the cautionary introduction. They will interpret it only as a sour note, one more critical utterance by a decaying institution, muttering in its dotage, a stumbling block to the evolution of human thought."

"We have been called worse things, Holy Father."

The Pope smiled.

He turned to face the room and took Elijah by the arm.

"Come, my son, let us sit, and I will hear what you have to say. Tell me of your meeting with this President. Omit nothing."

* * *

A light rain spattered the crowd. In a few moments the Mass of canonization would begin. Eighteen thousand people prayed, talked, and sang contrapuntally as they awaited the Pope. The cardinals and bishops sat around the papal altar, protected under a canopy. Seated with them were several dozen dignitaries from various African nations. In the crowd were many thousands of black faces.

Elijah found a place halfway down the square, in the standing-room-only section, beside a flock of nuns from Zaire. Each carried a little flag of her nation and a Vatican City flag, clutched together in a symbolic unity that was more idealized than actual.

Two elegant European matrons were standing in front of the nuns, discussing the day's event in loud voices.

"This is a mistake", said one. "The process has been too fast. I mean, did anyone investigate the manner of life of the *beati?* Did the so-called *martyrs* really understand the *realpolitik* of the African social struggle?"

"Would it have made any difference?" said her companion. "This Pope is so insecure he would rush into sainthood anyone who shares his opinion on ecclesiastical affairs."

"He's getting old. His hands shake. I saw it on television last night. I think, my dear, before too long we'll see a new pope, one who understands the twentieth century."

Elijah resisted a feeling of resentment. He wished to bend over and say, "The Holy Spirit has given you a pope who understands this century better than anyone." But he sealed his lips, making an interior mortification, and he prayed for them.

It was not easy to ignore their pontification.

"It doesn't sit well with me", continued one of the matrons in an irritable voice.

"Nor with me", said the other. "I heard Professor ———, the famous theologian, say that the faith in Africa is like a river that's a mile wide and an inch deep."

Elijah moved away from them and turned toward the black sisters. He wondered if they had overheard the matrons' conversation and hoped they had not. He asked them if they had known any of the blessed who were being canonized today. The sisters nodded emphatically. Their mouths opened in large, beautiful smiles, and their eyes spilled over with tears.

Their superior, a tall woman with a badly scarred face, said, "Our mother—the mother before me—she was killed. They kill her with axe. But she is call on Jesus to the last minute. She smile. I watch her die. I see dove fly up to heaven from her blood. She forgive soldiers as she die."

At which all of the sisters burst into sobs and began to explain things to Elijah in their native tongue. He was shaking his head, stunned, when two hands clamped down on his shoulders from behind.

"Davy. I thought I spied your silvery head bobbing out here in the crowd."

"Billy!"

"Myself. And fit as a fiddle. Come up higher, lad. I've got some seats roped off in the very first row, right by the altar, for friends of the secretariat."

"I would rather stay here, thanks. Among these ladies. They are the best, Billy. They lost a mother superior in the massacres."

Billy looked sober and said, "Hmm."

"Hmm?"

"Billy got idea."

"Idea?"

"Yep. Come with me."

He went over to the black nuns and spoke in rapid-fire Billy-talk. They seemed surprised, glanced at each other, and looked inquiringly at their mother superior, who nodded assent.

Billy took her by the arm and dragged her off into a sea of people. He looked back and beckoned Elijah to follow. The monsignor led the little flock of nuns and the priest through the crowd, past security checkpoints, up the steps of Saint Peter's to the highest platform, and stopped by a section to the right of the altar, in the first row.

"Best seats in the house, ladies."

The nuns thanked Billy profusely. He smiled, waving away their gracious compliments.

When they went to take their seats, there were two short. Elijah and the mother superior remained standing. Billy looked flustered and went hot in the face.

Two very old men dressed in scarlet came over to them and said in Italian, "Excuse us, Monsignor, but we couldn't help overhearing. We would be honored if the mother superior and this priest would have our seats. We will sit back there."

After diplomatic protests and complicated negotiations, exercised with masterful *romanità,* Billy accepted and placed the mother and Elijah in the front row, beside the other sisters. He took his seat between Elijah and the Cardinal Secretary of State.

The mother superior turned her black, scarred face to Elijah, and he saw there a pool of experience that was as old and as wise as humanity. He saw holiness. The woman took a rosary from the pocket of her habit. It was made of white seeds. It was tinted irregularly with brown stains.

"It is true, the Faith in Africa is sometime like a shallow river", said the woman. "But you should see our Africa rivers in flood. They are strong and run very fast. They turn over trees. They move hills and big stones. This river", and here she pointed to the rosary in the pink palm of her hand, "is the biggest river in Africa. It is the river of blood, run fast and deep for Jesus now. This spots here and here, they are my mother sister's blood. I give it to you."

He looked down at the relic and said nothing. She took his hand and pressed the rosary into it. Then patted his hand closed.

Why is this given to me? he wondered, *Why not to Billy? He engineered this, so why doesn't she give it to him?*

"My mother she speak in my heart when I see you in crowd down below. She say to me, give my relic to that priest. I don't know why."

Still Elijah could say nothing, but he looked into her eyes and she knew his gratitude.

The woman turned away from him then, opened a breviary and began to pray silently.

Elijah remained without movement or thought for several minutes. At his left, Billy began to pour out a stream of whispered chatter, but Elijah could hear none of it.

His eyes wandered over the rows of prelates and dignitaries seated across from him on the far side of the altar. The African cardinals and bishops were there. He knew some of their faces from articles about them, or by them. He noted the presence of high curial cardinals, especially the Prefect for the Doctrine of the Faith—*Dottrina,* Billy called him. Then his eyes wandered aimlessly in the rows behind, and eventually stopped at one figure.

The face of this cardinal arrested his attention, though he could not have explained the reason for it. A balding man in his late fifties. The remaining hair still dark. He was looking down, reading, but every so often he would glance up and sweep the crowd with his eyes. The face was sensitive, intelligent, lined, but still young. It was an excessively serious face, with deep-set, grave eyes and a thin mouth that seemed poised on the edge of indifference, hinting at a frown.

"Billy, who is that cardinal?"

"Which one? There are rather a lot of them over there."

"The young one, two rows behind and three seats to the left of the cardinal archbishop of Vienna."

"Where's Vienna? There, I see him beside Nairobi and Paris. Okay, now two rows back and three seats to the left. Right, I've spotted him. Oh, that's Cardinal Vettore. He's one of the Curia boys."

"Can you tell me about him?"

"There's not much to tell. He's a smart lad. On the rise. The gossip mill say he's in the running for *Stato's* job, when the boss retires someday."

"Do you think he would be suitable for the job?"

Billy pondered a moment.

"He'd be good all right. Important connections to euro-politics and the former Soviet states. He's doing a bang-on job over in the Pontifical Council for Dialogue with Non-Christian Religions. He works with a number of Vatican offices as some kind of networker. He's not exactly my cup of tea, though. Cold intellectual type. Makes you feel silly if you ask him anything direct."

"Is he one of the modernist bishops?"

"No. He's not in their camp. He's the quiet sort. You'd never be able to tell by talking with him, or by reading his published stuff, whether he's liberal or conservative. As a result, he's considered a moderate. But you could say he's in a class by himself."

"How would you describe that class?"

Billy's brow furrowed.

"I'm not sure how to describe it. There are a few guys like him around the place. Definitely a subculture. Tremendously gifted men, excellent administrators, clever at dealing with all kinds of personalities. But they never show their cards, you see. They're clean, spotless. But they're sort of heartless too."

"Heartless?"

"Oh, I don't mean cruel or anything like that. It's just, well, I feel a wave of chill whenever they pass in the hall. They're always perfectly polite. They ask about one's health. But you get the sense that there's something else going on, far in the background. My barometer always quivers, and I haven't deciphered what it means."

Billy lowered his voice: "Now, take the boss here, to my left. Second most powerful man in the Church. He deals with political pirates from morning till night. He's got *romanità* coming out of his ears, but he's also got heart. He gives away most of his salary to the poor, lives in an apartment that's shoddier than mine, drives a twenty-year-old Volkswagen, and needs to be reminded to buy himself new shoes from time to time. He prays when nobody's watching—I've caught him at it a few times— and that says a great deal about a man. He told me once he wanted to be nothing more than a Carthusian monk, but as you can see God had other ideas. He likes nineteenth-century Italian novels and sweet wine—yuck! He weeps at the sad parts in opera and gets really down when he reads about a bishop spouting off to the press on 'the present pope's Inquisitional Church'. He laughs heartily at a good joke, but I think he hurts a lot inside.

He's smart and noble and a faithful priest, and of course he's got his faults, especially that temper. But he loves the Lord and the Church with a devotion that's quite childlike. You can read him like a book. He is what he is, if you know what I mean."

"He is what he appears to be?"

"Precisely. I could run you through a few more profiles of the lads scattered here and there around this altar. The Pope's band of merry men, goofs and saints galore. But the guys like Vettore are something else entirely. A real puzzle to me."

"Are there many like him?"

"No."

Elijah looked down at the blood-stained rosary in his hand and began to pray silently for the Church.

"Why the sudden interest in Vettore?" said Billy.

"Do you remember the afternoon I first arrived in Rome?"

"Yeah."

"Do you remember that I fell asleep, and when I woke up the dream continued for a few seconds and became . . . I shouldn't want to call it a vision. I can only say that I was awake and I saw a face. It frightened me. I told you about it."

"I vaguely remember."

"That cardinal bears an uncanny resemblance to the man of my dream."

"A dream, Davy? No offense, old chap, but *dreams put fools in a flutter,* as the Scripture says."

"True, most dreams are like that. But God occasionally speaks through dreams."

"So, tell me, what do you think He's saying?"

"I don't know."

"C'mon, now, you look far too troubled for just a dream. There's something else, isn't there?"

"There is. But I hesitate to mention it."

"Out with it!"

"I saw that cardinal on Capri."

Billy's face went blank and he stared at Elijah.

"You're not serious."

"I saw him at the President's villa."

Billy looked slowly across the altar toward the cardinal. Then he looked back at Elijah. His face was stricken.

"I'll mention this to the boss. And I think maybe you should have another visit with the Holy Father. I'll arrange it. It would be better if he hears about this from your own lips."

* * *

In the days that followed, Elijah expected a summons from the Vatican. He was now assigned to the Carmelite International College in Rome and given the task of teaching philosophy and pre-theology to the novices. It was hardly a demanding chore, and he spent much of his free time in prayer and private study. The body of apocalyptic literature that had grown since the beginning of the previous century provided more than enough material for his purposes. Between Cardinal Newman's sermons on the Antichrist and the visions of numerous saints and mystics on the same subject, he was fully occupied.

A week went by. Then another. No call came from the Vatican. Finally, he telephoned the office of the Secretariat of State and was informed by a clerk that Monsignor Stangsby was out of the country on state business. Another week went by. He phoned again but the clerk said that Monsignor was still out of the country and could not be reached. Elijah asked if the clerk could take a message. Yes, he replied without enthusiasm.

Elijah gave him the number of the Carmelite house and asked him to urge Monsignor to call as soon as he returned. To which country had the monsignor gone, he asked. The clerk cordially declined to divulge that information.

"But Monsignor Stangsby and I are close friends", he argued. "Surely . . ."

"If the Father would care to telephone Monsignor's home, he

might be able to leave a message there", replied the clerk and hung up.

He succeeded only in reaching the answering machine at Billy's apartment.

"Lo, guvs," said the metallic voice, "I'm out of town on a spot of business. Home by Tuesday. Please leave a message after the beep and I'll get back to you as soon as possible."

Tuesday came and went.

On Wednesday morning, Elijah phoned the secretariat and was told by the clerk that, unfortunately, Monsignor Stangsby had suffered an automobile accident and was recovering at Gemelli Hospital.

Elijah received permission from the prior to visit him at once, and took the next city bus.

He was informed by the nursing desk that Monsignor Stangsby was in the intensive care unit and could not receive visitors. No, regrettably, there could be no exceptions. The monsignor was not yet out of danger. Father should wait a week and inquire again.

Frustrated, Elijah walked back to the bus stop. He observed the arrival and departure of his bus. He stared down at the pavement. Then, thanking God for his experience as a ghetto rat, he returned to the hospital, searched for a service entrance, and worked his way through the hospital until he found the back door to the ICU.

He waited for a moment of distraction at the ward desk, then went swiftly and silently into the unit. He found Billy in a curtained alcove. He was identifiable only by the nameplate in the slot at the foot of the bed. His face was heavily bandaged, his arms in casts, and one leg held high in traction. There were purple bruises on the patches of exposed flesh. He was wired and tubed.

"Billy", Elijah whispered.

Billy's eyes opened, swam sideways, then returned to center.

He focused on the face of the priest, and a groan came from his swollen lips.

"Dawwee?"

"What happened, my friend?"

"Caw! Blowuff. Fie! Blubby twoob ut."

He thrashed weakly and gestured toward his face.

"Twoob. Ut!"

"Should I really take the tube out? You probably need it."

"Juh suk."

"I'm sorry Billy, I don't understand. It might be dangerous to remove that tube. We'll talk another day, when you are better."

"Nah baddah. Nah nahddah deh. Now!"

Billy glared and began to thrash wildly. Elijah nervously removed the tube, intending to replace it at the first sign of distress.

"There! Thank God!" gasped Billy in a hoarse voice. "It's just a suck tube. Blasted thing! Keeps the bloody mouth clear. Gah!"

He spit blood and mucous.

"What happened to you?"

"I don't know."

"Were you hit on the street?"

"I was dozing off in my apartment. I'd just popped some candy that came in the mail and fell asleep. I was really tired. Just got back from Helsinki. Next thing I know there's a mob o' bleedin' medics wheeling me away from the ruins of the Jaguar. It was burning and looked like a crumpled accordion. 'This is cloud coo-coo land, boys', I told them. 'I'm not here', I said. 'I'm havin' a nap and you lot are a bad dream.' But they didn't pay any attention to poor old Billy."

"Do you remember getting into the car?"

"No! Not a flicker of a memory."

"Driving?"

"No, no, no! Nothing! Look, this is crazy, Davy. One minute I'm getting drowsy at the apartment, and the next thing I know

I'm in the ambulance, bashed up, in a hell of a lot of pain, and the car's on fire. Worse than that, these louts are breathing garlic on my face."

"What could have happened?"

"I've got my suspicions."

"Tell me."

"The candy. I think somebody wanted me to have a nasty car accident—permanent-like."

"What do the police say?"

"They say I was drunk."

"Were you?"

Billy gave him a fierce look.

"No bloody way", he said in a tone that made Elijah want to apologize.

"But what would make them conclude that the accident was related to alcohol?"

"There were empty bottles of booze in the car, and my clothing was soaked in gin. Which is sufficient evidence for me to conclude that it was a rigged job."

Elijah looked perplexed.

"You see, old boy, I hate gin. I absolutely never, and I mean *never,* drink it. I used to when I was a dedicated booze-artist, but I haven't been able to choke the vile stuff down for decades. The smell of a juniper bush makes me nauseous. I take a sip of wine now and then, as you well know, or a tankard of ale . . . "

"Or grappa?"

"All right, all right, all right! But *gin* —never!"

"So, are you saying someone has tried to kill you?"

"Right. And made it look like an accident."

"It is a miracle you survived."

"I expect so."

He spat more blood.

"I lost a few back teeth. Don't ask me why the front ones are still in my gums. And I got a big tear in my mouth, but don't ask me where that came from. The whole thing's pretty bloody mysterious."

"Has anything unusual happened that might have brought this upon you?"

"Gad! Any number of things. My whole life's unusual. Everything we deal with at the office is unusual. Ask me another question."

"Have you discussed Cardinal Vettore with the Secretary or with the Holy Father?"

"Not yet. I intended to, but a storm of crises broke out the morning after the African Mass."

Billy cleared his throat and spat into a basin.

"That's enough. Don't talk any more", said Elijah.

"Try to stop me!"

"No, no. You must rest."

"Talking's my chief pleasure in life, and it's been denied me since I got tubed."

"I'll call a nurse."

"Don't do that, Davy. Listen to me. There are things you need to know."

"What things?"

"I kept waiting for a chance to get alone with the boss, but we had Great Britain arriving that morning, and hot on the heels of that, we had Russia protesting the large number of conversions our missionaries are making. *Stato* kept saying, *Later, William, whatever it is it can wait.* I wish he wouldn't call me William all the time. By nightfall he had to rush off to meet with the Pope and then on to a meeting with other foreign ministers to discuss papers they're giving at The Club of Rome. The next morning I had to leave for Helsinki. *Stato* was scheduled to leave for an emergency meeting at the U.N. I went home late, but before going to bed, I made a voice memo of our conversation about Vettore, intending to have my secretary put it on paper. I meant to send the cassette by courier early the next morning and have it hand-delivered to *Stato* as soon as he got back from New York. But I overslept and had to rush out to the airport. When I got back from Helsinki it was late, and *Stato* had gone home to his place, leaving instructions that he wasn't to be disturbed. His secretary said he'd caught a bad flu. I almost drove over there and rousted him out of bed. I'd learned something big in Finland, so big that I should have ignored everything to get it to him. But then I decided I didn't want him to grump at me for disturbing his beauty sleep. And besides, I knew I'd see him at the office in the morning. What a crazy sequence of events. So I went home and opened my mailbox. There was the packet of chocolate mints—my favorite. I chewed a few as I dictated a memo about Helsinki into the cassette. The rest is history."

"Who sent you the candy?"

"Some nuns in London. Friends of Mum."

"Do you have the mailing package?"

"I suppose it's still there on the coffee table."

"And the cassette?"

"Sitting in the machine probably."

"If it's not there, what will we do?"

"Just get *Stato* in to see me pronto."

"It must be very urgent."

"It's big. Very big."

"What is it?"

"It's all on the tape. Look, I don't understand why the boss hasn't been in to see me. Can you ask him what's going on?"

"I will. Can you tell me about Helsinki?"

"I'm coming to that. Let me catch my breath."

"Billy, what information could be so important that someone would try to kill you? Certainly not the Vettore connection."

"I don't think this has anything to do with him. Not as far as I know. At least not directly. Which is probably why they haven't arranged a little accident for you too. After all, we both know about Capri, right?"

"Correct. But it is merely my word against the cardinal's."

"Right."

"One does not do this sort of thing to stop a rumor about a cardinal."

"Vettore is ambitious and blind as a bat. But he's not a killer. I think they're using him somehow. I don't think he even begins to understand what they're up to."

"Who are they?"

"His masters? I have a few names, but it's much bigger than that."

"What have you learned?"

"It's penetration."

"Penetration?"

"One of their side got cold feet. I won't say he's had a conversion to *our* side, but he's the sort who has ideals. He'd been doing some soul-searching and decided he couldn't stand what they're up to. He phoned me two weeks ago and begged for a secret meeting in Helsinki. I can't tell you who he is. If his name gets out, he's a dead man. He told me their whole battle plan for the destruction of the Church."

"Who are they?"

"They're . . . "

Billy choked and spat blood.

"That's enough for now", said Elijah. "I'm calling a nurse."

"No, no. Look, just go to my apartment. Get that tape and put it into *Stato*'s hands personally. And ask him to come and see me as soon as possible."

"Can I have your apartment keys?"

"I don't know where they are. Check the drawer in my bedside table."

"Nothing there."

"They're probably locked up at hospital security. No way they'll give them to you. Just tell the landlord I said it's okay to let you in."

"Will he believe me?"

"Tell him you need to feed Andy. He'll know you're from me."

"I pray you will be all right, Billy. God protect you!"

"Don't worry. They'll need an elephant gun to bump off this old peer."

"And pray we find the cassette."

"Go see *Stato* yourself. He'll believe you. I'm sure he'll take you to the Holy Father."

Elijah reinserted the suction tube, blessed Billy, and left.

*　　*　　*

The apartment was pin-neat. There was no wrapping paper. No candy box. And no cassette. There were no signs of a struggle. But on the kitchen counter there were three empty gin flasks beside the sink.

Elijah stared at the bottles for some minutes before it struck him that they were lined up like soldiers, or like witnesses standing at attention to give evidence against the sobriety of a certain Billy Stangsby, notorious lush. The neatness bothered Elijah. That alone suggested a "set-up". Moreover, he knew Billy well enough to believe that he was not lying about the gin. Billy's confessional nature owned up to anything. In addition, the monsignor was angry, bewildered, and a little frightened—a reaction entirely different from shame.

He picked up the telephone and dialed the office of the Secretariat of State.

It rang twice, and when a voice answered he hung up without saying a word. He looked at the ceiling of the apartment, then around at the walls. Then he left.

Elijah decided to walk directly over to Vatican City. It was a late September afternoon. The day was cool and the sky brilliant blue. The sort of weather that had always elated him. Even as a ghetto-child he had been happy on such days, no matter how hungry he was.

He walked along the Tiber and crossed over to the west bank on the Sant'Angelo bridge. Then, wanting to enter the Vatican unobtrusively, he walked north and turned west onto the Via Crescenzo.

If an individual or group of persons had made an attempt on Billy's life, it must be because he knew something that would endanger their purposes. Why then, in this city of rampant crime, of daily brutal murders, most of them unsolved, did they not simply assassinate him? Lethal poison or a bullet would have been fast and efficient, leaving few openings for detection. Why had the assassins found it necessary to create the appearance of an accident? The only possible explanation was that it was absolutely necessary for them to avoid difficult questions. A murdered monsignor in the Vatican Secretariat of State would have aroused curiosity in many quarters. It would have stimulated some messy inquiries. Almost certainly to be asked would be: What volatile information had recently come to the monsignor?

Was the "accident" ordered by whoever was overseeing the electronic surveillance of Vatican officials? Was this person or persons an exterior enemy? Or an interior one? It was preposterous to think that someone inside the Vatican had been responsible. There were many kinds of corruption in this world, but ecclesial corruption usually took the form of vice or ideological dissent. Neither of these provided the motivation to kill.

What, then, were the other scenarios? He had heard not a few alarmists spin elaborate theories of Masonic penetration of the Vatican. Mafia manipulation. Marxist undermining. There was a theory that the latter, before their demise, had planted thousands of agents in seminaries throughout the world and that some of these were now of age to accept appointments to bishoprics and sensitive offices in the administration of the universal Church. He had heard of fascist moles, Satanic moles, eurocommunist moles, invaders from outer space, and even American capitalist moles. Everyone seemed to have "evidence" to support his own conspiracy theory.

He had no doubt there were sinners and traitors in the college of cardinals, and among the thousands of bishops in the world—the press delighted in revealing their defections and scandals. He knew that the Church was just what the Lord had said she was, a net cast wide into the sea of humanity, bringing in catches of every kind, some good, some not so good. It had always been that way.

He wished he could discuss these questions with Don Matteo. The friar would have been able to throw supernatural light upon it.

Elijah felt exposed, endangered. The world had always presented itself to him as a disaster zone: Warsaw, Cyprus, Israel. But the Church? No. She was built upon rock, a cornerstone, a sure foundation.

But the Lord, speaking through the cross of San Damiano, had said: "Go, rebuild my Church, which is falling into ruins." Seven hundred years ago, Francis had picked up one stone and laid it atop another. Then another. And another. He had begun with the literal and moved to the universal. The little poor man of Assisi would have crumbled in dismay if he had foreseen what would happen because of his holy obedience.

Now the Church was falling again into disarray, but nowhere near as bad as the thirteenth century, or the time of the Borgias, or the Avignon papacy. The dark days of the Nazi occupation of Rome had also been very bad. And during the Soviet era, it had seemed that all Europe teetered on the edge of an invasion that more closely resembled the reign of Antichrist than any other tyranny the Church had faced in her two thousand years of history.

But that period was now over. Communism and fascism were dead. The world had entered an era of relative peace, though it did continue to boil over in regional conflicts from time to time.

True, the world powers were secularized, and believers were steadily dwindling in number, but did that mean the worst was indeed happening? Did that mean the Church was in ruins? Did her interior troubles really stem from the activity of a few secret agents, a few devils in the closet, or a few noisy rebels posturing at heroic dissent?

Elijah was tempted to laugh bitterly. He had suffered under real tyrants. How could these foolish Western prelates and pampered academic theologians begin to understand the nature of real tyranny! If they were to spend one day in the Gulag, they would instantly abandon their peevish malice toward Rome. They would grow up and quickly come to see their hostility for what it was—an adolescent rebellion. An Inquisitional Church, they called her. But this tyrant, curiously enough, had no police or army, no temporal power, only the voice of truth in the conscience.

Was that why she was so hated? The voice of truth in the conscience heard as a reproach, and if the guilty could not endure their guilt feelings, they must eventually silence the reproacher.

But to kill Billy? Billy, who more than anyone else at the Vatican wore his weaknesses on his sleeve and would reproach no one for sin or human frailty, though he had some pithy remarks about men in high places who preached errors. No, clearly the attempt upon his life was of another dimension. Was it purely political? Perhaps it was a shot across the bow, a warning to *Stato* that a similar fate might await him if he persisted, with that characteristic stubbornness of his, in carrying out certain policies. It might be that the "accident" had nothing to do with Elijah or with Cardinal Vettore whatsoever and was an eruption of complex international moves, the nature of which Elijah could not begin to guess.

Whatever Billy had learned in Helsinki was obviously the missing piece in the puzzle. It struck him suddenly that Billy was the only one in the Church who knew what it was. He felt momentarily afraid for him, and regretted that he had not insisted on hearing more. Then he reminded himself that Billy would relate the information directly, and in detail, to *Stato.*

Elijah arrived at the entrance to the suite of offices occupied by the Secretariat of State and asked to see the cardinal.

"An appointment would be necessary", the priest-clerk told him.

"It is really rather important", he replied.

"The cardinal is restricted by a heavy schedule."

"Could you please take a note to him? It is of utmost urgency."

The priest-clerk looked dubious, but pushed a writing pad and a pencil toward him. Elijah scribbled his name, his telephone number at the Carmelite House, and the message: "Regarding William. Urgent and sensitive matter."

"You will see he gets it quickly?" he pleaded.

The clerk was of that genre of bureaucrat who cultivate impeccable coldness as an art form.

"Do you see this?" he said indicating a basket on his desk. "That is today's personal mail to His Eminence. I have another pile, thicker still, secretariat mail that he must also read. In addition, I have a handful of phone messages, to which he must respond. The Holy Father's office has called to arrange an unscheduled meeting for this afternoon, and you are the fourth cleric who has come by this morning, without an appointment, demanding to see him on *urgent and sensitive matters.* What am I to do!"

"If the cardinal knew what it is I wish to tell him, I believe he would put all other matters aside."

"No doubt he would be moved to put aside even the Holy Father?"

Elijah sighed and spread his hands.

"Please. In the name of God."

"I am a busy man. So is the cardinal. Eventually, when he can find a free moment, he will contact you. It is the best I can do."

Elijah went away with a heavy heart and took a taxi back to the International College.

* * *

He had a course to teach after supper, but was surprised to find that the classroom was half full. All of the novices were present, yet none of the day-students and auditors had arrived.

"Where are the others?" he asked.

The novices exchanged looks and chuckled.

"Father, didn't you know? There's a big soccer game tonight. It's one of the finals for the World Cup."

"I see", said Elijah. "In that case, I wonder if there is much point in comparing Juan de La Cruz to Aquinas on the subject of the Cross."

The students suppressed their grins and stared at him to see what he would do next.

"We will try theology another night, when the big game is over. There is no class this evening, my brothers."

They stampeded out, and Elijah wondered where they would find a television set in all of this house of Carmel.

He went wearily to the chapel and prayed for an hour. His tension eased somewhat, but he continued to feel restless.

He telephoned to the Gemelli, but the nurse at ICU could tell him only that Monsignor Stangsby's condition had stabilized. He might be able to receive visitors within a few days.

Feeling agitated, Elijah went out for a walk in the dusk.

The night was cool, and a few stars pricked the brass dome over the city. The noise of traffic on the main thoroughfares had declined a little but was still jarring to his nerves. He turned away into side streets that he did not know, and he walked without any sense of direction other than a vague impression that he would make a wide circuit around the college and return to it within an hour. His ramble took him through a run-down residential district, where women screeched at children from balconies, and the streets were full of litter. Dogs barked at him. A rat was not the least concerned at his approach. The smell from the sewers was strong here, mixed with odors of offal and cooking pasta.

On a dark street between lampposts with burnt-out lights, a group of street boys surrounded him. He found it both sad and amusing to meet teenagers who spoke gutter Italian, dressed like Nazis but with haircuts like savage American Indians. They sneered and mocked and frisked him for cash. They found only a few *lire* and the stained rosary. They threw the rosary to the ground, stomped on it, shoved him around their circle, and went off cursing and laughing, without doing any serious damage to him. He blessed their departing backs.

The rosary was in pieces. He gathered up the broken fragments and put them into his pocket. He prayed for the youths and continued his walk.

A few blocks farther on, he passed an alley and saw a flame from the corner of his eye. Fearing fire in one of the tenements, he turned and went into the dark passage. At the end of the narrow canyon he came upon a crowd of children and youths hunched over a fire.

When they saw him, the youngest of them screamed in terror. Then all of them scattered, shrieking *"Prète, prète! Sacerdote!"* The older ones ran away from him more slowly, trotting backward toward the street, howling a stream of filth at him. He was amazed at the inventiveness and the vileness of their words. He was further perplexed that in the feeble light they had been able to tell he was a priest. He went over to the deserted fire and saw splinters of wood burning under an iron grate. Something black lay across the top of it, smoking. Then the black thing moved. Elijah jumped back in horror, then moved forward and tipped the grate over with his foot. The black thing rolled onto the cobblestones and began to writhe noiselessly.

It was a cat. Its paws had been hacked off and its limbs and mouth were trussed with black tape. Most of its fur was badly burnt. The stench was horrible. Its eyes flared at him insanely, glowing red, incandescent in the light from the flames. Elijah stared in disbelief.

He found a loose brick and hit it on the head. He hit it again and again until it ceased to move.

Then he stood up and looked around. The fire was enclosed within a white circle that had been drawn on the cobblestones. Within the circle and on the walls of the alley were chalked magical symbols. Elijah uttered a prayer of exorcism and sprinkled holy water in all directions. Then he walked away.

During the next hour, while he searched for a route back to the house, he saw more of humanity than he had seen since the War.

He stepped over several sleeping drunks. He passed two old women who were vigorously slapping a fat man who was laughing hysterically and staggering under the influence of the wine bottle he brandished in one hand. A little weeping girl was pulling on his free arm, crying, "Nonno! Come home, Nonno!"

A deranged youth dressed only in underwear, hunched beside a stairwell, ferociously smoking a cigarette, muttering to himself. Middle-aged men roared down the narrow streets in Porsches and BMWs, dressed in shining black leather, looking powerful, cynical, and swollen with knowledge. They made rude signs at Elijah.

He passed an old church and saw young women lighting cigarettes in the alcove of its doorway. They called out invitations and prices to him. He went over and began to exhort them to leave the life into which they had fallen, but they merely found his archaic terminology hilarious. They laughed not unkindly, and swore at him without conviction, and told him to leave them to their work. He pleaded with them to at least conduct their business at some other place than the door of a church. They stopped laughing and explained with great seriousness, and a certain civility, that the church was abandoned and the Blessed Sacrament not there, a grudging concession to reverence. He prayed interiorly to Mary Magdalen for them, and surprisingly, they left without another word. A small victory, but he was shaken.

Eventually, traveling through a maze of cross streets and avenues, he arrived back at the House of Studies. He went straight to the chapel and knelt without moving. There, in the calm of the room, he realized that his hands were trembling.

"My God," he cried, "my God. Where are you? Why can we not reach them?"

When his hands had ceased to shake he heard a voice speak to him from the tabernacle. Simultaneously, it spoke within him.

My son, I ask you to go down into the lost places. Go without fear.

"I have no strength, my Lord. I have no power to save them!"

No man can save another. Only I can save. Yet My strength is within you. My strength works most effectively in your weakness. When will you trust Me?

"What is happening, Lord? Your Church is reeling from many blows and bleeding from a million wounds."

Have no fear. Walk into the darkness and bring back souls from it. I am with you always.

"What would you have me do, Lord? What about Billy? How can I warn the Pope? I am hedged in on many sides and walled out of the very place where I must go. What should I do?"

You are to do only this: you are to look neither to your left nor to your right. You are to go neither ahead of Me nor behind Me. Wait for Me and I will act.

Then, gently, the Presence withdrew into its ordinary state. Even so, it remained with him. He felt it as a sweet fire that surrounded and gradually filled his agony. A fire so different from the fire in the alley that it was a marvel they could be called by the same name. The fire of Presence on this altar was the embrace of total love; it burned but did not consume. It gave joy, not pain. It did not bind its creatures nor mutilate their flesh. It freed them. It gave light. It consoled and it fed them. Why did men hate it so?

He went to bed and slept.

IX

Rome

Elijah waited patiently for the cardinal to contact him. But no message came that day or the next. He taught his classes and kept himself busy with private research. He prayed and read and walked a circuit of clean streets around the college. He went out one evening to the Gemelli but found Billy sleeping soundly. He looked much improved, which lifted Elijah's spirits considerably. Not wanting to disturb the monsignor's sleep, he left as stealthily as he had come.

Though he prayed and made continual acts of trust, the suspense caused by the Vatican's silence continued to mount. It was difficult to trust, even more difficult to remain without action, when all within him was crying out, *Avanti! Sound the alarm!*

But he did as he was told and waited. If there had been no apocalyptic literature in which to bury himself for long hours each day, the tension would have become unbearable.

He was growing in admiration for this Englishman, the famous Cardinal Newman, who had converted from Anglicanism in the last century. An unusual character, a man out of step with almost every level of his society. His loneliness, bordering on alienation, had given him a unique perspective. He was able to step outside the ethos of his century, the nineteenth, and observe it with an objective eye. He was serious to the point of melancholy, brilliant, sensitive, and, it was said by many, a genuine prophet. He had written and preached extensively about the spirit of Antichrist. He said that this perverse spirit was growing in the world and that a great apostasy was looming. He quoted from the prophet Daniel, who warned that the adversary's power over all nations would be obtained peaceably and by flatteries.

Newman further argued that the apostasy of the people of God in various times and places had always preceded the coming of antichrists, tyrants such as Antiochus, Nero, Julian the Apostate, the false prophet Muhammad, and the atheistic leaders of the French Revolution—each a type or foreshadowing of the Antichrist who would come at the end of history, when the mystery of iniquity would express its final, terrible illogic. The failure of believers to live their faith, Newman warned, as in previous ages, would usher in the reign of "the man of sin", who would deny the divinity of Christ and exalt himself in His place, even to the extent of entering the temple of God and demanding that he be worshipped.

Elijah read: *They shall pollute the sanctuary of strength, and shall take away the Daily Sacrifice, and they shall place the Abomination that makes desolate, and as such as do wickedly against the Covenant shall be corrupted by flatteries. . . .*

His concentration was broken by the porter rapping on his door.

"Father, a message from the Vatican! They're sending a car for you. It should be here in ten minutes. You're to go to a meeting."

"I will be ready, Brother. Thank you."

He splashed cold water on his face, straightened his habit, and bustled down the hallway to the chapel. There he prayed for a few minutes before the porter came in and signaled that the car had arrived.

"Hurry, hurry, he's circling the block."

Elijah went out onto the main steps and looked up and down the street, but there was not a limousine in sight. He was about to go back inside to question the porter when a badly rusted yellow

Volkswagen pulled up with squealing brakes. An arm jutted out of the driver's window and beckoned.

"Jump in, Father", said the Cardinal Secretary of State.

Elijah buckled his seatbelt as the cardinal tore away from the curb in a cloud of black exhaust. With a beep-beep and a lurch, he screeched around a corner, plunged into the frantic stream of nighttime traffic, and drove like a typical Roman in the direction of the dome of Saint Peter's.

"I am relieved! You have received my note, Eminence."

"Note? I have received nothing from you."

"But I have been trying to contact you since Monsignor Stangsby's accident."

"*Il colmo!* That's the limit", said the cardinal, exasperated. "It's been a circus of activity since the accident. I suspect that my staff has been screening the communications coming through the office. There's a flood of it, more than we can possibly handle right now. I must apologize. With William absent . . . "

The cardinal seemed to swallow what he was about to say.

"Your Eminence, there is something urgent I must tell you."

"And I you. I have some very unfortunate news, Father. I'm afraid our William is dead."

Instantly, the traffic seemed to slow, and sound faded from his ears. His heart gave one great thump, and an old agony returned to his breast. He stared out the windscreen, disbelieving, suspended in timelessness and a slow-motion tour of the eternal city.

The cardinal's voice broke the spell.

"I'm sorry. He was your friend."

"Yes, he was my friend."

"It's a terrible loss to us all. So many times I said to him, *William, you pray like an angel but you drive like a devil.*"

This from a man who was tearing down the Via Appia at eighty kilometers per hour.

"I saw him a few days ago and he seemed to be recovering well. Do they know what happened?"

"The people at Gemelli say they don't know why he died. Until there's an autopsy they can only guess. His doctor thinks there was a hemorrhage inside they didn't catch. Possibly a large blood clot stopped the heart. It happened in the middle of the night. The night-duty nurses failed to hear the alarm. Apparently, they were busy with another crisis on the ward, though it proved to be a false alarm. By the time they responded to William, he was gone."

"This is very bad", Elijah said.

"I know. We will miss him. He brought laughter into a place that's too often solemn. He was a gifted administrator."

"It is worse than our personal loss. Far worse."

The cardinal looked sideways at him.

"What do you mean?"

"It is very serious. Far more than I can explain during a short car ride."

"*Bene!* We'll go to my office and you can tell me what it is."

"I don't think that would be wise. We cannot assume that any place is safe."

"Father," said the cardinal gently, "William's death is a shock to you. Why don't I take you back to the Carmel? You can rest. We'll talk tomorrow."

"When I tell you what has occurred during the past few weeks you will know that I am not suffering from grief or nervous shock. William and I have discovered a grave threat to the papacy and to the nature of the Church herself. Her very foundations are in danger."

"Her foundations?" said the cardinal, looking dubious.

"Can we stop and walk?"

The cardinal did not immediately answer. Elijah could see he was weighing everything.

"All right", he said in a quiet voice. "We will go to some friends. There, we won't be troubled by uninvited listeners."

By which Elijah understood, with some relief, that the cardinal had his own doubts about the security of curial offices.

"We will speak no more for the time being", he said. "Electronic surveillance is sophisticated these days. A bug may even crawl inside a beetle."

Fifteen minutes later they pulled off the Via Appia onto a lane that wound through shrubbery and trees.

The cardinal parked the car on the grass flanking the lane, leaving the headlights on, pointing toward a small stone building that appeared to be a funerary chapel of the fifth or sixth century. He unlocked the bronze door, entered, and switched on an electric light within. Elijah turned off the car lights and joined him.

The cardinal went through a doorway at the end of the room, unlocked another door, went through, and disappeared down a long flight of stone steps. The stairway was obviously very ancient, cut through strata of alluvial soil, then a tufa mixture of gravel and earth, and finally at the lowest level, stone. The staircase ended abruptly about fifteen meters beneath the surface, opening onto a narrow, irregularly hewn gallery that drew away from them into indeterminate darkness.

"This is my only luxury", said the cardinal, shaking the key in his hand. "Come, I want to introduce you to my friends."

He led Elijah farther down the concourse and turned right into one of countless underground avenues that branched off the main *galleria*.

"You know where we are of course?"

"The catacombs."

"Yes. There are miles and miles of them down here. We are in San Callistus, in a little-known side passage. See, from here on no one ever goes. Only the crazy cardinal."

He stopped at a wooden door of great age, unlocked it, and entered. Elijah followed. In the pitch blackness of the chamber he heard the scratch of a wooden match; a light flared blindingly as the cardinal lit a kerosene lantern. He closed the door behind and shot the bolt.

"I like to come here sometimes. I sit among the graves of my brothers and sisters. It gives one perspective, no? When Rome seems especially full of corruption, and the Vatican is a hive of busy bees chewing up paper into honey, ah, then I come down here and pray to the Lord. I say, keep me simple, my Lord. Don't let me become a prince. Don't let me become puffed up with my self-importance. Let me become like these little ones, your true servants."

Elijah glanced around at the shelves set into the walls.

"Look here, Father. Read this; what does it say?"

"Praetextatus, *clarissimus.*"

"*Clarissimus.* It means he was a senator. We're not far from the grave of Saint Cecilia, the great early martyr of noble birth. This man was possibly a member of her family. Now, look across here. What does this one say?"

"Osimus, *servus.*"

"A slave. You see, these two men were brothers in Christ. They rest side by side, awaiting the Last Day."

"A peaceful place to wait . . ."

"Yes. It's full of saints, most of them unknown to history. Here are the real foundations of the Church. Many of these died horrible deaths. Torn to pieces in the arena, burnt alive, beheaded. A few even died by crucifixion. Look at this one. She's my favorite. A girl. One of the thousands of unknown martyrs. I think of her as my saint, the little daughter I never had. Do you ask yourself if I am slightly mad?"

"No, Eminence."

"A Christian lives both within time and beyond it. I'm closer to this one than to most of those walking and talking up there on the surface. Yes, she and I know each other well."

"What is her name?"

"Severa."

"Do you know anything about her?"

"Only that she died during a persecution of the third century. She was a martyr. Thirteen years old. She chose to be thrown to the lions rather than submit to sexual seduction. The family selected the words of her eulogy with tact—*a martyr for holy virginity, victorious over the lion,* it says. Beneath that inscription, there is another. Can you read it, Father?"

"*A dove without bitterness. Rest, Severa, and rejoice in the Holy Spirit.*"

"A little saint."

"Yes. Seventeen hundred years old. Our daughter she is—and our mother."

Elijah could find no words that would reach his tongue.

"For a moment you looked happy, Father Elijah. For the first time since I met you your face has lost its burden. What is it that crosses your mind?"

"A memory. My wife died young and took with her into eternity our child, in her womb, a little girl. I saw her in a dream recently."

"Your daughter is literal."

"Your Severa gives me hope that I may one day see her."

"Listen to us. If the Protestants have a bug in here they will conclude that we are demon-infested necromancers, haunting the house of the dead in search of visions and voices."

"Our communion is of another order. A union of spirit that needs no mediums and séances."

"Tricks of the devil, they'll say! Ah, the devil would feel very uncomfortable in this holy place."

The word *bug* recalled Elijah to the purpose of their meeting.

"Eminence, I have a grave matter to convey to you."

"*Bene!* Tell me."

Beginning with his trip from Assisi to Naples, and on to Capri, Elijah recounted the events of the last few weeks.

He stumbled over the account of the discovery of Cardinal Vettore's connection to the President.

Even in the wan light of the kerosene lantern, Elijah could see the cardinal's face grow pale. Though his expression did not falter, his eyes ceased to blink regularly.

At the conclusion of the Elijah's tale, he exhaled loudly and sat down upon a stone.

"It is difficult to accept. You're absolutely sure it was Vettore?"

"Absolutely."

"This is most distressing. He is considered a good man."

"I am sorry."

"It's not your fault. You have brought into the light a seemingly small fact, perhaps nothing more than a suspicion, but one upon which the future of the Church may hinge."

"I may have jumped to conclusions. Perhaps the cardinal was sent on a separate mission, at the request of the Holy See."

"It's unlikely the Holy Father would have done so without discussing it with me."

"Perhaps it was a personal mission of the cardinal's, a desire to assist the Church in her negotiations."

"This sort of negotiation is entirely out of his province. You are a novice at life in the Vatican if you suppose such a mission would ever be undertaken without consultation. I think, Father, that you're trying to throw as generous a light upon the situation as is reasonably possible."

"I may have misjudged it."

"I hope you have. What you have told me has implications beyond your grasp."

"I wish I could have told you sooner, but it seems that the receptionist who manages your visitors and mail was not helpful."

"He's a good man. Very efficient."

"Cardinal Vettore, too, is a good man."

"You say you left a message for me with the receptionist?"

"Yes, a written note, marked *urgent*. I also telephoned several times and left verbal messages."

"I see."

"There is more to tell you. I'm convinced Monsignor Stangsby was murdered. During my last conversation with him, he expressed strong doubts about the accident. He believed he was drugged and the car crash arranged in order to give the appearance of an accident."

"He told you this?"

"Yes. He told me other things too."

"Such as . . . ?"

"He was fairly certain that his apartment was bugged, but in haste one night before his departure for Helsinki, he dictated the story of Cardinal Vettore into a recorder, hoping to dispatch the message to you."

"William was not always discreet."

"He also told me that he had information far more damaging than the Vettore connection. He said that in Helsinki he had learned about the enemy's plans for the destruction of the Church."

"Did he tell you any details?"

"No."

"That is probably why you are still alive."

"He said it was all on the cassette. But by a tragic chain of events, he was unable to put it into your hands. It has disappeared."

"I see."

"And with it all proof that what I have told you is the truth."

"And so we are left with only your testimony", the cardinal said slowly, looking down at the floor of the chamber.

Elijah stood silently, praying.

The cardinal looked up. "I believe you", he said.

"The situation may not be as compromising as it appears. Vettore may be entirely innocent of subterfuge."

The cardinal looked straight at Elijah and said, "I wish that were so. But I have a feeling it is not so. What you have told me explains many things. Many small, ordinary anomalies, almost invisible, the kind of things one expects in a large office complex like ours. Daily life at the Vatican consists of a hundred thousand details, much of it insignificant. One of the details, for example, is that my receptionist, able fellow that he is, recently came to me from the Pontifical Council for Dialogue with Non-Christian Religions."

"Cardinal Vettore's office."

"Yes. There are other minor events that now appear in an entirely different light. Relationships, conferences, glances, a word here and there, an innuendo. A nudge of *romanità*. Still, this doesn't add up to a murder."

"I may be guilty of faulty reasoning, Eminence, but I cannot help noting that the accident occurred precisely when Billy tried to communicate an extremely sensitive piece of information. His death would have eliminated the only man alive who had knowledge of the Helsinki information. One man, that is, outside of their circle."

"I suspect that is the motive. However, we should not underestimate the Vettore connection to Capri."

"I agree. I do not think we should rule it out at this stage."

"If your reasoning is correct, however farfetched, then you are in harm's way. You are in danger."

"If I may add a further conjecture: if anyone knows of your communication with me this evening, then you also may be in danger."

"No one knows except your porter, and I doubt that he's a subversive, by the looks of him."

"Indeed he is not. He is a very simple fellow. In fact, he does not even know the name of the Vatican official who came for me this evening. But I will advise him to keep silent, if there should be any inquiries. Have you told anyone else?"

"No. As far as the world knows, no message from you has reached me, nor has it reached the Holy Father."

"Should we continue that illusion for the sake of a higher good?"

"Ah, I wonder what the moral theologians would make of this one! Yes, we will ride the wave of illusion."

"Tomorrow, why don't I telephone your receptionist and ask if he has passed on my message? I could beg for an interview. If he is involved in a deliberate deception, he will tell me one thing and do another. He will pass on the information to his friends, and refrain from passing on my message to you. If that happens, we will have at least an indication that some kind of conspiracy is underway."

"A splendid idea. My dear Father Schäfer, I had no idea that you were capable of such intrigue!"

"I have been at various times in my life a street rat, a member of an underground army, and a government prosecutor, among other things. Some rather odd skills lie dormant within this priest."

"I can see that. *Bravissimo!*"

"Will you warn the Holy Father?"

"I will arrange to see him tomorrow morning, over breakfast."

"If I may suggest, Eminence, it would be best if you were to speak to him about this matter as you walk in the most private sections of the Vatican Gardens."

"The thought had already occurred to me."

"How will we know if your receptionist has passed or failed his test?"

"Call the office at eleven o'clock tomorrow. In my own way, I am rather good at detective work. I will observe the morning's events with much interest."

On that note they rose and returned to the surface.

The cardinal drove back to the city at breakneck speed and dropped Elijah several blocks from the college.

* * *

At eleven sharp, he called the office of the Secretary of State and was answered by the now familiar voice of the receptionist.

Elijah asked to speak with the cardinal.

"Once again, I must inform you, Father, the Cardinal Secretary is an extremely busy man. We simply cannot answer every message as quickly as people would like."

"Did you deliver my message?"

"Of course I delivered your message! I have mentioned your telephone calls to him, and I gave him your written note."

"I see."

"Really, Father, you must have patience. If the matter is something the cardinal can help you with, he will do so, but all in good time. One mustn't aggravate him. One mustn't become a nuisance."

"I am sorry. It was inconsiderate of me. You will tell him?"

"I will go in to his office directly and advise him of yet another message from you", said the receptionist dryly.

"Thank you."

"And Father, I suggest that you not call again. If you do not hear from the cardinal, it means he has weighed the matter and has decided he is unable to help you."

"Yes, of course. I understand."

"And, Father, whatever it is that seems so urgent, I suggest you leave it to the actions of divine Providence. I recognize your name. You are a professor at the Carmelites, are you not?"

"Yes, I am."

"Then I suggest that you focus your attention on your duties and leave the management of the Church to those who are better equipped for it."

"Yes, I will think about that", said Elijah in a conciliatory tone. "Thank you. It is good advice."

"It is very good advice."

"You are right. I have been overtired lately. I may have imagined something. It is probably best to forget it."

"We have many real crises on our hands at this office, Father. We cannot deal with the doubts and imaginings of every cleric in Rome. Few things in life are as urgent as one thinks they are."

"That is true. I have been a nuisance. I won't bother you again. Please excuse me."

"It's nothing. *Buon giorno,* Don Schäfer."

"*Buon giorno.*"

During lunch, Elijah was called away from the refectory by the porter.

"Telephone for you. Imagine, at this time of day. It's nap time in Roma!"

"*Buon giorno.*" It was the cardinal's voice.

"*Buon giorno, Signore.*"

"We won't need to use names. I'm calling from an outside line, but we don't know the condition of your line."

"I understand."

"The matter was as we suspected. The garden is invaded by parasites, but not fatally, as far as we can see."

"You received no word?"

"Nothing. I stood by the door. I overheard his side of the conversation."

"Afterward, did he tell you about it?"

"Not a word. Instead, he called a certain office of which we have spoken. He advised the party on the other end that all difficulty is now averted."

"I see. Then we have our confirmation."

"We do. I spoke with Papà at breakfast. He was feeling poorly, but we took a stroll in his garden to look at the flowers."

"How are his red roses?"

"They are near the end of bloom. Some are worm-eaten. But a majority remain healthy."

"You told him?"

"Everything. Papà understands. He saw it coming."

"What does he advise? How should we save the plants?"

"He believes we must let matters take their course. We mustn't do anything suddenly. Some discreet pruning, some fertilization of the soil. Spring will come again, he says, and a new generation of roses will bloom."

"He is wise, our Papà."

"Yes. A saint."

"Can we meet soon?"

"Yes, we must. I have a message for you from Papà. Let's meet at Severa's place. Can you get a car?"

"Yes."

"Tonight, at nine?"

"I will be there."

After supper Elijah borrowed the house car and drove north through the city, away from the catacombs of San Callista. He circled, wandered aimlessly for an hour, then doubled back toward the Appian Way, certain that he was not being followed. The cardinal was sitting in his Volkswagen with the engine running and the lights off. They went down into the crypt and five minutes later were facing each other beside the tomb of the dove.

"The infestation," said Elijah, "is it extensive?"

"At first glance, it seems to extend only as far as the limits of Cardinal Vettore's circle of friends. It's not a large group, possibly a dozen cardinals and as many bishops. It may be much larger. It's difficult at this stage to untangle the associations that are connected to his official work, and those which are voluntary and connected to something hidden."

"What do you think is their purpose?"

"I'm not certain. I'm perplexed by it."

"Are they ambitious?"

"Some yes, some no."

"Personal enemies of the Pope?"

"None of them, as far as I know. Two or three speak well of him."

"That may be cosmetics."

"Possibly. I can discern not a single unifying factor in their association. No common thread of passion. They are of differing opinions about the nature of the Church."

"This does not indicate an ideological component."

"But what could possibly draw such a disparate group of men together?"

"Perhaps a spiritual bond."

"Spiritual?"

"For the sake of conjecture, let us say that these men from such widely differing backgrounds within the Church have each in turn succumbed to an *approach,* let us call it. Suppose that the nature of this offer was so veiled, so disguised as a good, that they did not recognize their peril. At some point, interiorly, they gave an assent, some subtle turning of the mind away from Christ, away from the historic vision of the universal Church. Gradually, their perceptions were bent away from Catholic eschatology."

"You mean the last things? The time of the End?" said the cardinal, dubious. "Why should that have anything to do with conspiracy? Ah, wait, I see where you are leading."

"This could be the thread that unites them. They may have been seduced by a beautiful vision of the future—a spiritual vision."

"You mean, a salvation of some kind."

"Something like that. I do not say this is the case, but I think it would explain many things."

"It doesn't explain murder."

"The situation may be more complex than we think. These poor churchmen could very well be naïve, manipulated by organizations or forces, or a combination of both, which are adept at reading human nature. Someone else may be responsible for Billy's death."

"It makes sense. It is no simple thing to turn a man of God into a killer."

"Your use of the term *parasites* is apt. I do not think that these poor bishops are our parasites. The parasites are men or powers behind the scenes, riding upon these prelates' backs into the very House of God."

"That would be an abomination! If so, it must be stopped."

"How do we stop a chimera?"

"As we always have—by prayer and fasting. We must awake the entire body of believers. They have been sleeping far too late into the day!"

"Eminence, prophets and saints, popes and teachers have been trying to arouse the faithful for more than a century. They refuse to rise."

"I know, I know", sighed the cardinal. "But some will respond. We must save what remains. Besides, the Holy Father is right. The garden is ever young. A new generation of souls will need cultivation. Our responsibility is also to the ones who are yet unborn, who will come after us."

"On a practical level, how can I help?"

"The Holy Father would like you to remain in Rome for the time being. He wishes you to await his instructions, for he wants you to proceed as you have begun. You are to be his presence within the camp of the enemy. He knows the President has his eyes on you and believes he can turn you to his purposes."

"Are you saying that I should respond to his invitations?"

"Only in a sense. Answer his invitations as far as is morally possible. You will discern the limits."

"I cannot pretend to be another Cardinal Vettore."

"But you are capable of a few mental reservations, in the interests of a higher charity."

"I can't lie."

"I have not asked you to lie."

"What are you asking?"

"To go into his camp as David went into Saul's camp, when Saul sought to take his life. You will be surrounded by enemies; you may even meet those who are responsible for William's death. We ask you to be a word of truth in the sea of falsehood with which the President surrounds himself. But you must be as clever as a serpent and as gentle as a dove, as the Lord cautions us to be. You must choose the moment wisely. Until then, you will learn much and you will increase your importance to the President, in preparation for the time when he must hear the words of Christ from your lips."

"Can this not be accomplished by a letter? Or by a meeting with the Pope himself?"

"A letter is print on a page. The world is awash in printed words on pages. As for the Holy Father, as I told you before, the President would merely use a face-to-face encounter for propaganda purposes. He wouldn't listen. Your task is to penetrate his defenses, to go deep into the levels of human intercommunion— those mysterious regions of the soul where one man listens to another."

"Is he capable of such receptivity?"

"We don't know. There is a possibility that he is not yet entirely captive, and thus we must try to reach him."

"It is spiritually dangerous."

"Yes. Very dangerous. But we know of none other whom we could send. You are free to refuse. Neither the Pope nor I would blame you for it."

"What would our friend Severa say to me?"

The cardinal looked wistfully at the tomb and touched the slab with his forefinger. He traced the word—P A L V M B A—*dove.*

"This child faced the lion and overcame it", said the cardinal.

"Can I do less?"

"Only you can answer that question."

Elijah looked at the cross, anchor, and dove etched into the marble.

"I will do it."

"Thank you", said the cardinal. "In the name of Christ, I thank you."

*   *   *

Despite everything, an air of unreality clung to the card sitting in the palm of his hand.

It was a printed invitation to a private banquet to be held at the Palazzo Giancarlo Galéone, on the Piazza Navona.

A celebration for the successful conclusion of the meeting of The Club of Rome.

It was signed by the President.

On the evening of the banquet, Elijah removed his Carmelite habit, stroking the cloth, wondering how many times he would wear it again, if ever. He stored it in the wardrobe of his cell. The Cardinal Secretary of State had told him he must begin to cultivate a new image if he was to move farther into mission territory.

"A new image? But they know what I am!"

"They know you are a priest, and that on one occasion you have acted as an envoy from the Vatican. They will assume you were chosen because of your interest in archeology, an avocation you share with the President. They know also that you were impressed by him. Regarding your motivation, it is probable that they consider you a monastic who has come in from the desert, hankering for the stimulations of a more cultured, urban life, even for more involvement in the world—hence the transfer to Rome. They understand that you teach a course of philosophy and another on pre-theology. They will presume that you are like so many others, an academic infected with just the right amount of subtle ambition and a mild disaffection with orthodoxy—without falling outright into heresy. A heretic, you see, is merely a stupid tool in their hands, and they know it. You are a better catch—in fact a prize."

"But they also realize that I know about the connection between Cardinal Vettore and the President."

"Whoever stole the cassette knows about it. But the Vettore connection may have nothing to do with what William learned in Helsinki. Do you read the newspapers, Father?"

"Seldom. Why?"

"A well-known Italian diplomat hanged himself in Helsinki on the day of William's accident."

"I see."

"I wish we did see", the cardinal sighed. "Daily it grows more obscure. These people may have nothing to do with the President and his circle. There are many demons in Rome. We should be careful about jumping to conclusions."

"We should consider the worst, at least as a possibility."

"Of course. But there could be a dozen scenarios, with hundreds of characters, some of them spilling over from one cesspool into another."

"Your Eminence, if someone in the President's party is responsible for Billy's death, and if they know that I know about the connection, why wouldn't they eliminate me as well?"

"I don't know. If this scenario is the true one, then we are presented with new puzzles. They could easily have arranged an accident for you, with fewer repercussions than the death of a curial monsignor."

"I am still alive, which means that as far as they know Billy was unable to tell anyone what he knew."

"Yes, they must believe that you know nothing about their long-range plans. The ICU was closely guarded, and the hospital staff would ensure that, for medical reasons, Billy communicated with no one."

"But why the invitation?"

"They are probably counting on the power of the President to woo you to his side. They have assessed you as a valuable player on the field, and they want you badly, for some reason which presently eludes us."

"It makes no sense. There are hundreds of teachers of theology, many of them more influential than I am."

"How many of them have connections to Israel and to Eastern Europe and to a number of figures in the West?"

"If that is their motive, they are mistaken. They overestimate my tactical value. Almost all of my contacts fell away when I became a Catholic, a quarter-century ago."

"True, but many contacts could be reactivated. You were greatly admired in your time. If you were now to renounce Catholicism, let us say, or alternatively, to advocate a marriage of Judeo-Christianity and New Age spirituality, you would be welcomed as the Prodigal Son who had seen the light. Ah, what a celebrity they would make of you!"

"Anyone who knows my views would realize how ridiculous that proposal is!"

"Without a doubt, but how many people in the world know the views of a certain obscure monk from the desert near Haifa?"

"By the same token, how many people would be interested in the opinions of a man who was famous for a few days during the 1960s? I am old. My time is past."

"Is it? Listen, Father Elijah, they are trying to win to their cause every possible player in the arts, politics, and religion. They are attempting an entire reconfiguration of world culture. Much of their work is already accomplished. Of course you are important to them! Not only your past is significant. Do you not also maintain correspondence with the chief rabbi of France—a personal friend of yours? Also with a former attorney general of the United States? And the new Catholic archbishop of Saint Petersburg—is he not one of your spiritual directees?"

"Yes."

"You see, a most useful man. You must play along with them."

"I would find it morally inexcusable to deceive anyone, even an enemy of this magnitude."

"As I said before, I'm not asking you to lie, nor even to create the illusion of a lie. I want you to be what you are—a man of God responding to an invitation to enter their camp. It's entirely within their province to think what they like. You must be like Paul in Athens. Do you remember the passage where he faces the sophists and turns the pagan altar to the Unknown God into a witness to the one true God?"

"I remember."

"Be like Paul, Father. Go into the territory that has been captured by the enemy, use what you can, and retrieve what you can. God turns everything to the good for those who love Him. You may even discover poor souls in chains who need to be rescued. Is that not reason enough for such a mission?"

Elijah smiled. "Your Eminence, it is now very clear to me why the Holy Father chose you to be his chief diplomatist."

The cardinal chuckled. "Enough! You overestimate my tactical value!"

The banquet began at eight. Elijah glanced at his wristwatch and dressed with discomfort in the dark blue suit, white shirt, and stylish Italian tie—a swirl of hand-painted fuschia and gold. He forced his feet into expensive burgundy oxfords. He combed his hair. He glanced at himself in the mirror and looked quickly away.

A silver-haired gentleman had appeared in the glass. A stranger who might have been a distinguished college professor, a bank manager, a wealthy entrepreneur. Only the eyes betrayed the costume. They were sad and dark, burdened with memories or with perceptions that saw too far into the past and the future.

He looked at himself and tried to appear less dismal. He screwed his eyes into an approximation of cheer. The effect was ghastly. No one would be convinced.

He tentatively applied a few drops of an expensive cologne the cardinal had passed on to him, plundered from Billy's effects.

"Poor William", said the cardinal. "His mamma sent him this bottle of scent. It smells like a grandmother's hanky!"

Poor William.

His glorious martyrdom had taken a form that he would never have chosen. To be smothered by luxuries and then to die in a hospital bed, without a sword at hand.

Shortly before seven he went out and caught a city bus to the

Piazza Navona. The bus was packed with weary laborers, university students haggling over politics, old women with shopping bags rearranging loads of bread and fruit, children sleeping on young mothers' bulging bellies, old men cackling and gossiping, and sullen teenagers plugged into headphones. Every voice fell silent when he entered, and every eye followed his passage to the last vacant seat.

"A prince visits the lower classes!" someone muttered. The passengers erupted in hard laughter, smirking and sneering.

"Hey, you, *Illustrissimo Signore,* where you going? Off to find a girlfriend in the slums?"

More laughter. Elijah gazed out the window.

An old woman sitting across from him watched the fun without blinking. She stared at him with a piercing look that was far more ferocious than his mockers. She shifted a string shopping bag off her ample lap, swung around, and snapped at them, "*Basta!* Shut up, you stupids. Can't you see this is a good man?"

No more comments were made, and the passengers resumed their ordinary babble.

She leaned over and patted his arm. "Don't pay attention to them, Signore. They're just young and crazy."

He thanked her. She shrugged. Without losing her ferocity, she reached down to the garish, costume-jewelry crucifix that hung around her neck and kissed it five times.

When the bus deposited him at his destination, he did not go directly to the *palazzo,* but lingered by the Fountain of Neptune. He studied the sheen of copper sunset reflected in it. The old pagan sea god was in flames. The windows of the upper story of the *palazzo* were burning with the last reflected light of the fleeing sun. The ancient pagan world was returning with the night, and what remained of Christendom was under siege.

He struggled to overcome a feeling of revulsion against the evening's proceedings. He desired more than anything to walk away from the web of illusions that lay before him, to return to his monastery, and to spend the remainder of his life in the more fruitful occupation of prayer. He would ask the Lord to send a better foot soldier than himself into the field. He prayed for that now, but the answer was not the one he desired.

The Palazzo Giancarlo Galéone was not the most opulent mansion on the plaza, but it was the most distinguished. During its four centuries of existence, it had been the home of counts and concubines, doges, cardinals, and corporate magnates. It was now owned by *Globaltek,* the international corporation that produced computer imaging technology, the primary shareholder of which was the current President of the Europarliament. It was decorated in the style of the late Italian Baroque period, replete with thick rose-colored carpets, mint green walls, and paintings by Caravaggio and Guido Reni.

A footman bowed to him at the entrance, asked his name, and bowed again. He conducted him into a marble-tiled grand entrance hall, and then through a set of gilded doors into a ballroom that struck Elijah as being both spacious and intimate. There were approximately twenty people there, gathered around an orchestra that was playing a medley of romantic pieces for strings, derived mostly from operas of the previous century. People left and entered the room at random, some obviously preferring conversation in quieter spots of the *palazzo.*

The footman introduced Elijah to the official welcomer of guests who turned out to be—Roberto!

"Signore Schäfer, a great delight! The President asked me to convey his greetings to you, and to tell you of his pleasure that you are able to attend tonight's festivities."

"Thank you so much. I look forward to seeing him again."

Roberto raised his eyes to the ceiling in a gesture of affectionate disgust. "My employer is presently ensconced upstairs with the delegates from the World Bank. Poor man, he is never finished with these meetings! But I have strict orders to interrupt them shortly before dinner."

"So we will see him at dinner."

"Yes. He expresses a hope that there will be time during this evening's festivities to speak with you."

"Yes, I hope for that also."

"Please, allow me to obtain for you a glass of something to warm the spirits. Yes? Red? White? No? Champagne? Oh, but I am embarrassed, I should say positively *mortified,* to admit that our wine provisioner has been remiss. He has given us a champagne that is inferior to the *beaujolais.* Please, may I press this dry red upon you? You will not be sorry."

"You are always so gracious, Roberto. Monsignor Stangsby and I were so grateful for your kindness when we were detained on the night of the storm."

"Yes", said Roberto, his face falling. "I have heard about the demise of poor Signore Stangsby. My sympathies for the loss of your friend. Such a funny man."

"He was."

"Now, you will excuse me, please, for I must greet a few latecomers, and after that I must go to ensure that *il boss* is not detained by the tortures of world economics. So boring!"

He deposited a theatrical grimace and went away. Elijah wandered into a large banqueting hall, its walls hung with Renaissance tapestries, its floor shining parquet, and its long, damask-covered dining table set for forty guests. The tableware was silver. Candles were lit, crystal sparkled, bunches of roses sent their fragrance throughout the room. Footmen bustled around making last-minute arrangements.

He wandered back to the hall and crossed over to a small library where eight people were standing, scattered about the room, some sipping from their drinks, and others warming their hands by a blazing log fire in the hearth.

The vivacious mood of the guests did not release Elijah from a tension caused, in part, by the realization that most of the faces he saw were identifiable only because they appeared regularly on the front pages of international journals. He noted three heads of state, the publisher of the largest daily newspaper in France, the American ambassador to Italy, a world-class Israeli violinist, and a much-published English economist. There was continuous traffic in and out of the room. No one made an attempt to welcome him into the circle of discussion, nor did they exclude him. Elijah did not recognize the eighth person present, a woman in her late forties. She was talking to the violinist, who was attempting to convince her of some point by using his face and hands with considerable animation.

When the violinist caught his eye, he stopped in mid-sentence, and beckoned to Elijah.

"Hello there. Why don't you join us! Shalom! You're Schäfer the archeologist, aren't you?"

"I am."

"A fellow Israeli", he explained to the woman.

"How do you do", she said in a quiet voice.

"Look, Schäfer, we need an intervention here. You've got to rescue me from this woman. She's getting the better of me on a very difficult topic. It's completely unfair of her. After all, Anna, I am an artist, dominated by the right brain. You are a creature of the left brain! Did I say creature? Ha! I should say a *monster* of logic."

The woman smiled and turned to Elijah. She put out her right hand and said, "I am Anna Benedetti. You are . . . "

"Elijah Schäfer."

"An archeologist, Uri informs us."

"Well, he's a bit more than that!" the violinist said dryly. "Aren't you, Father?" He took a long sip of his drink.

"I am a Roman Catholic priest", Elijah said evenly. The woman looked at him curiously, but there was no hint of the hostility he had come to expect when moving in the regions of the intelligentsia.

"An interesting combination", she said in a friendly tone.

"Not an uncommon one."

The violinist, a high-strung man in his early thirties, wandered off into another room, waving at guests as he passed, shaking hands here, embracing there.

"You mustn't mind Uri. He is young and very famous. A genius, but a little boy inside. He likes to make himself look wicked."

"He didn't seem wicked to me."

"He's not. He plays at being a cosmopolitan who says witty and devastating things to innocent victims of distressing social situations."

"Such as myself?"

"Yes. Do you mind so much being here?"

He looked at her thoughtfully. A kind person, with honest eyes and intelligence. She was probably the wife of one of the dignitaries. But there was no wedding ring on her hand, he noted, and he wondered if she was involved in some kind of modern arrangement.

"I did mind at first", he said. "I'm not used to this sort of milieu."

"Good, then why don't you stick by me and you won't have to simulate casual conversation with prime ministers and geniuses."

"That is kind of you."

"Not at all. It relieves me of a similar burden."

She smiled at him, and it warmed the chill that had settled on him from the moment he entered the *palazzo*.

"What would you like to talk about?" she said.

"I don't know. Nothing. Everything. I have many questions, but they are inappropriate."

"Inappropriate. Really?"

"For example, would it be too forward to inquire about your connection with the President?"

She laughed with genuine hilarity.

"Not forward in the least. You are a gentleman, I see. You

would be surprised at how the number of gentlemen in the world has decreased in recent years."

"I suppose it would depend on what you mean by a gentleman."

"I mean a *chevalier du roi*. A man of good will and good word."

"It lifts my heart to hear there are some who still value such things."

"There are some. But to answer your question: I'm a member of the Board of Directors of the President's Foundation for the Development of Archeology."

"Are you an archeologist?"

"Strictly an amateur."

"Then why . . . ?"

"Because my family has a great deal of prestige, and because my name is useful to him."

"You are very forthright."

"Life is short. I don't think we human beings have much time to waste on the creation of misleading images."

"I agree with you."

"So, you see, not only has your inappropriate question cleared away the fog, it has uncovered the fortuitous fact that we have something in common. We can discuss ruins until dinner time."

He was struck by the gentleness of her voice, the consistent clarity of her glance, revealing both modesty and honesty and a more elusive quality . . . virtue. He liked her and realized with some surprise that he had made an ally.

"Now, I am free to ask the same inappropriate question. Why are you here?"

"I have been invited, but I don't know why. I met the President only once, a few months ago. I was simply a courier."

"Simple couriers do not receive invitations to gatherings such as this."

"Then I suppose he thinks I may be useful to his cause — in some way that eludes me."

"He always has a purpose", she said without emotion.

"Do you admire him?"

"He is an extraordinary person."

But again he noted the absence of enthusiasm.

"Do you admire him, Father Schäfer?"

"As you say, he is an extraordinary person."

She did not reply, but continued to look into his eyes as if waiting for something.

At that moment the dinner bell rang, and the guests began to move toward the dining hall.

"Thank you for this conversation", he said. "You have made it easier for me. I wish you well in your enterprises."

"I also wish you well. Perhaps we will meet again one day."

She turned and went ahead of him into the hall.

That was that, Elijah said to himself. He lingered by the door, uncertain as to what he should do. He watched Anna Benedetti locate her place card halfway up the right-hand side of the table, and seat herself. He observed most of the guests proceeding to their positions at table with a certain knowing, as if they had a faculty for estimating their degree of importance.

Roberto and a few other servants guided the stragglers, Elijah among them, to their places. To his surprise, he found himself positioned beside Anna. He had come to think of her as Anna. She looked up and smiled. He smiled back.

"Archeology", he said.

"Yes, that must be it. Someone has done his homework. They always do, you know."

To his right sat a woman who rustled in black satin, appointed with diamonds. They introduced themselves, and then she turned to the man on her right, with whom she resumed a vigorous discussion in a Balkan language. Elijah guessed from the names of classical composers bobbing on the surface of unintelligible words that they were discussing music. Anna was chatting with the elderly man on her left, the American ambassador.

Elijah looked down at his own name card. It read *Professore Elijah Schäfer.* So, it had been determined what his public image would be—the academic. He shot a glance at her name card. It read *Signora Anna Benedetti.*

She was married. A married woman without a ring. A widow?

The President entered the room flanked by two men. Some of the guests burst into applause. All conversations stopped in mid-stride and the applause became a storm; the guests rose en masse to their feet. Elijah stood up with them. Anna caught his eye, but her face remained expressionless.

The President seemed embarrassed by the attention and waved them to silence.

"*Grazie, grazie!*" he said, then he made an Italian pun that elicited much laughter. It was clear that the guests not only esteemed the man but felt affection for him.

"Now, really, you must forgive me for this inexcusable delay. I had hoped to be able to greet each of you as you arrived, but I was kidnapped by these two sinister fellows and held at ransom. I have made every concession within my power, and thus I am now set at liberty. This international terrorist on my right will return to the London School of Economics with his bag of cash, and this other one on my left will return to the IMF with his loot. I am now free to enjoy—to enjoy *with you*—the pasta!"

More laughter, applause, and cheers.

He was a gracious host. He conducted the two economists to their respective places near the head of the table. The heads of state were at that end also, and two or three personages whom Elijah could not identify.

When everyone was seated, the President remained standing.

"My friends," he said in a voice that carried to the end of the room but remained warm and virile, "my friends, welcome to this festive day. We have completed weeks of deliberation, composed masses of documents, and now we must play. No speeches, no position papers, no honorifics are permitted this evening. Enjoy yourselves. *Viva Roma!*"

"*Viva Roma!*" the crowd shouted and raised their glasses.

"*Viva Roma!*" said Anna, sotto voce, looking at Elijah with a raised glass. He touched his glass to hers and said, "To the wisdom of history!"

She smiled at him and then sat down smiling to herself.

During the meal, the American ambassador continued to engage her attention. He was a charming extrovert and had a great many opinions to offer on a variety of subjects. They spoke at length about laws that would likely be passed by the Europarliament at its next session. Elijah was intrigued to overhear Anna's grasp of fundamental principles of law and to hear her argue, relentlessly and with considerable skill, against a piece of proposed legislation, the substance of which Elijah did not hear because of a guffaw from the direction of the Balkans. When he again caught the thread of their discussion, he found that it was winding up quickly. The ambassador was shaking his head, saying, "Well, you may be right about the principle, but for the good of societies one must be flexible. Law must serve man, not man the law."

"That is true", she replied. "But one must be careful of sophistries. Law must serve universal principles in man, grounded in natural law. Law cannot serve man properly if it is blown this way and that by every wind of opinion, fashion, or prejudice."

"Hmm," said the ambassador, "that's too philosophical for me."

He turned to the woman on his left, leaving Anna to eat her meal.

"You are no ordinary housewife, Signora Benedetti."

She looked at him.

"Professore Schäfer, I am of the opinion that when one gets to know a housewife, any housewife, one finds that she is never ordinary."

"That is a noble sentiment."

"It's also a fact."

"You know, tonight I learned that very thing."

"Oh?"

"I discovered a great secret of the cosmos."

"Did you? And what is this secret?"

"I learned that the universe is held together only because of a few extraordinary souls. It is kept from crumbling into ruins by the power of fierce old women who carry string shopping bags."

She put down her fork and laughed outright. "*That* is a noble sentiment, Professore."

"It is also a fact."

"I think you mean it."

"I do."

"Good."

Over dessert and wines, the President worked his way along the table, welcoming each guest personally.

He came to the musicians and told them how eagerly he was looking forward to their performance.

He moved along to Elijah and gripped his shoulder with the right amount of firmness.

"Father Schäfer, I'm so very pleased you were able to come. You honor us. If I may presume upon your patience, there are so many guests and few of them could bear to be neglected. It would be a pleasure for me if we could meet together later this evening."

"Of course, sir. I will leave it to you to let me know when it is convenient for us to meet."

"Anna! Always a joy. How are you?"

She answered that she was well. She used his first name. He inquired after the health of people unknown to Elijah. She reported accordingly. She was friendly, open-faced, but reserved.

He moved on to the American ambassador.

"Edgar, can Europe ever repay such a gift of credit and wheat from your people? Bread is life! Hope is life! When the fall session begins I will have Parliament draft a formal letter of thanks. I have already commissioned a sculpture — titled *Freedom* — which we wish to donate to the American people. I think your Congress and President should have a tangible memorial of our gratitude. Your generosity has averted a disastrous war. Russia, Ukraine, Georgia, the millions of lives you have saved . . . "

"I think, sir," said the ambassador rising, shaking the President's hand, "that if facts be known we should be thanking you."

"Now, now, none of that! I want none of your Louisiana nonsense!"

The ambassador roared appreciatively and slapped the President on the back.

And so it went up and down the table.

The guests were invited to move into the main salon, the red room, thickly carpeted and hung with Renaissance portraits. The guests arranged themselves on brocade couches and gilded chairs. The President entered and chose a seat in the front row. Some of the men remained standing, twirling their brandy glasses. Anna sat by herself in a stiff-backed chair off to the side. Elijah came and stood beside her. She did not seem to notice his presence.

The orchestra had positioned itself on a low stage at the far end, and the woman in the black satin dress now went forward and stood with them.

Candles were lit throughout the room; the ceiling lights were dimmed.

The woman, speaking in accented Italian, said, "Mr. President, and honorable guests, tonight you will hear three romantic pieces: Telemann's *Aria*, Puccini's *One Fine Day*, and Dvořák's *Hymn to the Moon*. These works express the deepest mysteries of love. I wish for all who gather here a happy stirring of the powers of the heart. Love is the medicine which will cure our sick world. I dedicate this trinity to the man who is rejuvenating our times — to you, sir."

She bowed to the President. He stood and returned her bow.

There followed a wave of gentle applause.

The woman repeated her introduction in French, English, and her native Slavic tongue.

The orchestra struck its first notes and began the passionate sweep through the *Aria*. Elijah gave himself up to the music and felt his emotions stirred. Ruth's face came to him, Ruth as she had been under the pomegranates, Ruth with the rose light of sunset on her brown cheeks, Ruth with joy. Ruth with child, slow and happy, her slender feet rubbing the black-and-white goathair rug, her fingers deftly cutting red peppers into a bowl of sliced avocado, orange, and lettuce. Ruth with her heart pounding hard under the roof of their bedroom. At the morgue with her body torn open.

The wells of agony and loss burst and flooded upward from his interior.

I am old. All love now lies in memory. All love exists beyond an impassable gulf.

Insanely, he wanted to kneel and lay his head on Anna Benedetti's knees and tell her that in his long life he only ever had one home, had only once dwelt as a man was meant to dwell with a woman. One home. For two years.

"There was a garden in Eden", he would whisper. "And a man was formed there. A deep sleep was cast upon him, and from his flesh there was formed another, she who was made to be his companion, to be cherished as his own. And he, in turn, was to be her own, and neither the powers of the heavens nor those of the earth could split them in two. They were one soul."

But she would not know the meaning of this. Her face would remain expressionless. She would see before her only a man groveling.

It is a secret of the cosmos, he would say to her, aching to convince. *It is one of the great things, but not the greatest.*

Is that a noble sentiment? she would reply. *Or is it archeology?*

Anna, if the heart is dead, love is only archeology.

I am strictly an amateur, Professore, strictly an amateur.

Applause for the aria.

Then Madame Butterfly's longing poured out of the singer's throat and became the lament for all human loneliness and loss, all aspirations for union, all hope for permanent joy. A new form of ache transfixed his heart.

He felt time sliding again. Music filled the entire created order. Existence was music itself. Music reflected back the glory of existence to itself.

Ruth, I thought I could escape the unbearable moment. I thought I could bear to live without you. I have lived without you for all these years, but as a butterfly that wriggled under the pin, tore loose, leaving behind a fragment of itself, beating upward on the wind, sustained by an image of itself as whole. But not whole.

Applause. He was jolted back into time. He looked down at Anna Benedetti and saw that she continued to remain motionless. He noticed that her chest was swelling and her eyes were wet.

Anna, have you been stirred as predicted? Did they apply the effective recipe for emotional release? An evening of catharsis as social sport?

The Hymn to the Moon began. The singer knew her art, knew the unique powers of her voice, and knew Dvořák's intention. Elijah's eyes followed her gestures, his hearing absorbed the massing, controlled passion of this love cry until it united with some long-buried movement of his own heart. He closed his eyes and listened until it was completed. When he opened them, the applause burst into sound. And Anna's seat was empty.

He wandered through the ground floor looking for her, but she was nowhere to be seen.

"You are searching for Signora Benedetti?" Roberto asked, eyeing him.

"Yes."

"She has gone."

Elijah stared at the doorway.

"Gone?" he said.

I am making a fool of myself. You are a priest forever. David, Elijah, David, Elijah, Elijah, Father Elijah. My brother, my daughter, my father, my sister, my mother, my friend, my love. You have been a priest for so many years and still you wriggle on the pin? Five pins? Five kisses. Eli, Eli. Pawel. Papa. Ruth. Anna. You are a priest forever. With my whole being I do give my life to you. Lord. Jesus. Protect. Me. By. The. Blood. Of. The. Lamb.

"Signore Schäfer is feeling unwell?"

"I am feeling dizzy. I must sit down."

"Let us go out onto the balcony. You can sit there in the cool night air. The circulation is bad in these old places. Come with me."

He followed Roberto through a set of French doors onto a marble *balconata* that overlooked a miniature garden enclosed within the walls of the *palazzo*. A single flowering tree grew there, a fountain whispered, night birds sang. He sat on a wicker chair and breathed deeply. Gradually, his head cleared, though what was left of him when the spinning stopped was meager indeed. He felt himself to be a void surrounding a lump of sick dread.

"Would you please give my regrets to the President. I am feeling quite ill. Would you call a taxi?"

"Certainly, Signore."

The taxi arrived within minutes. Later, Elijah would recall nothing of the journey to the college. He remembered only stumbling up the front steps, entering his cell, looking with disgust at his own image in the mirror, tearing off the fine clothing, laying down on the bed, pulling his habit over himself and clinging to it tightly. He lay trembling in the dark, not knowing what was happening, afraid of it—no, terrified of it. Eventually, toward dawn, his breathing slowed and he drifted into troubled dreams, tearing loose from a skewer of old pain, beating into the sky, leaving a fragment of himself behind, leaving many fragments falling, falling, as they had so often, spinning slowly back to earth as he climbed, sustained by an image of himself as whole.

*   *   *

He lay sick in bed a day. He got up to teach his classes, but he was merely a voice delivering information. The students knew there was a difference. They stopped taking notes and merely listened. At the end of the class one of them suggested that he return to bed and stay there until he was well again.

Gradually, the fragments pulled together and the memory of flight faded into a symbol in the mind. The ache declined steadily. The sacraments strengthened him. He was convinced that once again he had failed. He contacted the Cardinal Secretary at his residence, continuing to communicate in cryptic language.

The cardinal picked him up one evening, and they drove far out into the countryside.

"You penetrated the darkness without armor", said the cardinal. "You tried to go in by your own strength! Really, Father Elijah, you mustn't do that again. You should ask for prayers when you go into such places. You must plead for the necessary graces."

As a restorative, the cardinal instructed him to read Ephesians 6:10–20. He scolded Elijah humorously, with the air of an urbane Italian *nonno,* but his eyes were worried.

"This woman who troubles you, do you think it's an attachment of the heart?"

"It may be. It's not ordinary romance. It's not sexual desire. I simply liked her and felt that here was a soul with whom I could find friendship."

"Friendship? Many priests have fallen in this manner. Love is kind; love is charitable; but it must also be prudent concerning matters of the heart."

"I know. How many times have I cautioned my spiritual directees about seemingly innocent attachments? Loneliness is the human condition, I tell them. Even the most happily married

229

couples must face this condition at some point. Only God can fill this emptiness."

"And yet you find it difficult to take your own advice?"

"It happened so fast. What worries me is the totality with which my senses reeled and my prudence evaporated."

"You rely too much on yourself. You are a solitary man. But certain kinds of solitude are not truly monastic."

Elijah agreed. And then protested. "Is there no human love for me? Must everyone I love be killed?"

"How could I possibly justify your many losses? But at least understand this: God didn't kill the ones you loved. God's enemies did."

"I draw close to this woman's soul, but from afar, only within the enclosure of my heart. I will never see her again, for if I were to love her, some enemy would kill her."

"I'm sure she's a fine person. I'm sure there was no sin intended."

"Of course not! She is a very wonderful soul."

"How swiftly the knight rises up to defend this lady."

"Eminence, please don't make more of it than it is."

"Father Elijah, do not make less of it than it is. This woman, whoever she is, could demolish everything that is truly you. And yet, she has done you the good service of opening up your heart with a scalpel. Perhaps the Lord wants you to let Him reach inside and touch an old wound that didn't properly heal."

* * *

Some weeks after the foregoing discussion, when Elijah felt himself largely repaired, he went one evening to peruse the *Jerusalem Times* in the reading room of the House of Studies. He saw the face of Anna Benedetti looking at him from the cover of a news magazine on the periodicals rack.

The feature article recounted the appointment of Doctor Anna Benedetti, judge of the Supreme Court of Italy and advisor to the Commission of Human Rights in Geneva, to the position of judge of the World Court in The Hague.

* * *

A month passed during which the President made no attempt to pursue a meeting. Elijah assumed that he had failed once again, due to presumption on his own strength and lack of spiritual preparedness. He taught his classes, studied the Apocalypse, and applied the remainder of his energy to the exercise of monastic life in an urban setting.

After a warm autumn, a heavy snowfall came in December, covering the city on the Feast of the Immaculate Conception. Children everywhere ran outside, squealing with delight, soaking their feet, rolling snowmen, waging wars, and catching colds. The city's traffic was impeded by the freak weather. Late in the afternoon, Elijah went walking in it, feeling deliriously happy, remembering the happiest days of his childhood in Poland, before the war. A city in winter sun. A city of many bells, of horses, and of children.

Bound temporarily in a gown of melting snow, even a monstrous metropolis such as Rome could become a beautiful thing. Its cacophony muted, except for the cries of children and torrents of water running everywhere off the roofs, the city was so quiet, so without frenzied motion, that it no longer resembled itself. It was restored to the human dimensions of a community.

In his mail slot there was a letter postmarked Brussels.

My dear Father Schäfer,
The duties of government have kept me from writing this letter. I am so sorry that you were unwell on the evening of the Galéone party. I had hoped to speak with you that night about a forthcoming event, to be held in Warsaw in the spring of next year. I am arranging, with the assistance of other concerned organizations, a conference on the restoration of the culture of the West. There will be

a large number of workshops approaching the problem from several directions. It would be remiss of us if we were to overlook the cultural insights of the See of Rome. I would be grateful if you would come to Warsaw at our expense and conduct a workshop on biblical archeology in the light of the Dead Sea Scrolls and the New Testament codices recently discovered at the Dead Sea. Would you consider integrating this topic with your own valuable (and I think unique) insights into a new spirituality of biblical criticism? I await your reply.

The letter was signed by the President.

Elijah contacted the Cardinal Secretary of State. The cardinal was pleased by the proposal, and reminded Elijah that the conference offered a double opportunity to continue the contact with the President and to insert orthodox scholarship into what would almost certainly be a media event.

Elijah wrote a letter of acceptance.

He wrote also to his prior at Mount Carmel, and to various other contemplative communities where he was known, describing the spiritual ramifications in general terms, and asking for their prayers. In a longer letter to Don Matteo, he outlined the situation as it had developed and went on to describe in detail a dream or a "vision" that he had just experienced.

Don Matteo, I now turn to a phenomenon about which I am uncertain. I will describe it to you, and leave it for your discernment.

This morning, after a peaceful sleep, I awoke well rested. A few seconds after the return of consciousness, I saw an interior vision that was almost visual in its clarity. I was staring at the wall beside the bed, and I saw a sphere. I knew—I don't know how I knew—that the sphere represented the structure of the book of Revelation.

Revelation has always fascinated me, its lush symbolism, its drama, and majesty. But it is also frustrating because it is a mystery that refuses to be unlocked by analytical methods. All methods fail to make it understandable. Those that seem to succeed do so only by limiting the significance of the work, especially if one infers a linear historical structure to it. One can safely do that to the Gospels, which are derived from a chronology, an actual sequence of historical events. But the events in the vision of Saint John had not occurred at the time of its writing, and have not yet occurred in their fullness.

Without any rational analysis or knowledge imparted through words, I understood that the book of Revelation is the record of a series of visions that were given to Saint John *in a multidimensional form.* Yet, the evangelist was restricted to writing it down in a two-dimensional form— a string of letters on a page. Pages are read from one side to the other. Lines are read from one side to the other. Letters themselves are read in the same way. There is flow and consistency, all of which affects the sense of time and immediate reality for the reader. The work itself has a beginning and an end. And thus, through its very form, the written word impresses deeply within the subconscious of the reader a sense of chronology, a feeling of time's passage from point A to point B in a linear historical process.

But the "sphere" of my interior vision (I hesitate to call it an inspired vision; let us just call it an insight) was a presentation of the end of history as a spiritual *condition* during a state of climax. The events it depicts are real. They will occur. They will one day become historical. Yet a repeated reading of Revelation imparts the sense that there is great complexity to this period. Because of its complexity, those living within it might be easily misled. Man perceives all things with varying degrees of subjectivity. He can easily miss the essential things, details, which in the pedestrian language of narrative may strike him as peripheral, when they are indeed central. He may over-focus on the flourishes of startling detail and miss that subtle core which is his most dangerous enemy. Thus, the Holy Spirit employs powerful symbols to help the reader suspend his normal ways of perceiving and draw him into a much larger awareness of the vast, multifaceted conflict between good and evil that will occur as the culmination of history. He is interested not so much in imparting information as implanting in us the tools of awareness.

In the literary form of the book, we do not find only one chronology of events—though that is often how it is read. I saw that it is actually a *layering* of symbol-events, as if one were looking into a globe of glass, or into a sphere of water, in which numerous stories are taking place, many of them simultaneously. Many of them overlap, some in time, some in geography, still others in both time and place. The sphere contains a number of chronologies, but they are not strung out, one after the other, into a single line. Within Revelation there are, of course, a number of consecutive events following each other in rapid succession, but one must not conclude that the entire book is simply that, especially in the earlier stages where the various streams of the vision are gathering. Only gradually do they draw together toward the final events. Within the multidimensionality of the whole there is a gradual progression toward the "eschaton", the final battle and the Second Coming of Christ. In this sense, it does have a beginning and an end. Yet, the primary structure of the vision takes the form of a creative *being,* a work of art that is not flat but rather contains depths into which the reader plunges for insight.

The vision is a prophecy, but more than prophecy in the sense of mere foretelling. It does not preoccupy itself with dates and lengths of time, except in an oblique way. Those believers who will one day find themselves living within the actual events predicted will see things laid out all round them, and then the times and places will become clear, like lenses coming into focus. Whether or not the revelation of John describes a period stretched out over three and a half years or twenty-five years, a century, or a millennium is as yet uncertain and remains the subject of debate among biblical scholars. Jesus Himself reminds us that no man knows the hour or the day of the return of the Son of Man. It would not be good for us to know. Most people would probably lapse into a kind of reverse legalism, indulging in all sorts of disorders, assuming that we can rehabilitate ourselves as the time draws near for His return. For the health of each individual soul, therefore, the Holy Spirit found it necessary to avoid overt descriptions, precise details.

The vision of John is not rendered in a purely literal approach for another, and perhaps more urgent reason. One day the Antichrist will come. But we often forget that in every age the spirit of Antichrist has been active, capable of deluding souls and dragging to perdition entire nations and peoples, without resorting to the high drama of an Apocalypse. There have been many apocalypses since the time of Christ — the reigns of Nero, Hitler, and Stalin, for example. They are prefigurements of the reign of the Man of Sin. They are also warnings. Reminders that we must not perceive the struggle against Antichrist as simply a magnificent mega-drama reserved for a distant future. The actual battle against that spirit is waged from the very beginning of human history and continues uninterrupted to this day.

If the vision of John had been rendered in literal terms, similar to many in the Old Testament, there would be an even greater danger of misinterpretation for those who are alive when the actual Man of Sin rises to power. Because natural human psychology tends to interpret the surrounding landscape and one's own time as normal, however extreme it may be, it is difficult to recognize in it *the* decisive moment of history. Only the person developed in spiritual perception is able to interpret the warning and apply it to his seemingly ordinary universe. Thus the vision of John had to be delivered in forms that are universal.

Because it is materialized in symbols, the prophecy takes on its own life within the imagination of the believer of any era. It is not merely stored away as one more news item, one more piece of religious information, one more scenario—that would be especially unfruitful for modern man, who suffers massive oversaturation of theory, knowledge, and scenarios. Instead, the revelation takes a form that is a loud shout in a world growing deaf. The authority of its horrific imagery guarantees an absolute claim on the imagination. We are intrigued, puzzled, frustrated, alarmed, and ultimately encouraged. In short, we are aroused to a kind of *attention* before the mystery of human history as it unfolds, precisely because we do not know when or how the ultimate danger is to be incarnated. With prayerful reading, the book assists in the conversion of *attention* into holy *vigilance,* the spirit of the watchman.

That, my dear father in the spirit, is all the sense I can make of my "dream-vision", but I submit in peace to your discernment on the matter. Is it vain imagining, a deception, or merely an intuition? Is it a teaching from the Holy Spirit?

I do not suffer the blows that you endure in your battle with the enemy. Mine are interior, and not the least of these is an abysmal self-doubt. I have asked the Cardinal Secretary, and through him the Holy Father, to relieve me of this mission, but they have refused. And so I must proceed in a condition of total weakness. How close you must be to the Savior, if He has given you the task of bearing His wounds in the world. When you speak with Him, beg for strength for me.

Your son in Christ,
Father Elijah Schäfer

*　　*　　*

A reply came on Christmas Eve, a hand-written note delivered by a young Franciscan friar.

"Hello Father, I like it to see you again."

"Jakov!"

"I want it you get letter from Don Matteo. I carry it on train. Sorry for mess it."

Elijah clapped him on the shoulder in welcome. The giant bobbed his head repeatedly.

"It's good to see you, Jakov. Is all well with you?"

"Everything good. My head it not break; my heart it get fix."

He assisted at Elijah's Mass, during which the young man's face radiated such light that several of the novices could not keep their eyes off him. Throughout the liturgy, Elijah half-expected to turn around and find Jakov floating above the ground, but nothing of the sort occurred.

He would not stay to dinner and refused a ride to the friary where he was to spend the night before returning to Assisi.

"This Christmas night, Father. Tonight the Holy Family walk on the earth. I look it for them, maybe find a place for them can sleep. The Holy Family, they like to play. They come to us but they not look like the Holy Family. But I find them", he said grinning, wagging his index finger as if to scold the Holy Family for such tricks.

He went off into the maze of streets with a backward grin and a wave.

After vespers, Elijah remained alone in the chapel and read the note.

> My brother, Elijah,
> Your vision is from the Lord. Trust in Him and He will act. Fear nothing, yet guard your heart in all things.
> With constant prayers,
> Don Matteo

X

Warsaw

The jet banked, and he saw the city.

He had anticipated this moment many times in his life. He had been sure he would feel excitement, or terror, or joy.

He felt nothing.

Warsaw simmered in the spring sunshine, a sprawling metropolis of close to two million people. As the wheels of the aircraft hit the tarmac, many faces arose in his thoughts. His mother. His father. Brothers, sisters, cousins, uncles, and aunts, childhood friends, neighbors—all missing, perished in the fires of the *Shoah.* He saw children at hopping-games on sidewalks. He saw Mother wafting the smoke of *shabbes* candles and covering her face. He saw Father stitching, stitching, stitching as Grandfather read to him from the tractates. He smelled the rankness of fish and the narcotic aroma of baking bread. He tasted the sweet stickiness of purple wine. He heard the babbling tongue of hagglers in the market, the whinny of horses, the shouts of brave youths hurling words at tanks, the screams of the violated, the whine of bullets, and the crack as they chipped the sidewalk beside him.

He saw many other faces. The guards at the ghetto gate. The bookseller, Pawel Tarnowski, his face turning white as he hid him in the recesses of the attic. And the other one, *the bent one,* his face burning red in the act of betrayal. Faces, faces flying through memory like birds flushed from deep woods, where light exposes certain details only on the bleakest days of winter, when everything is stripped down to its essential form.

The taxi driver who took him into the center of the city kept up a running commentary, pointing out this or that tourist attraction: religious monuments, the grandiose architecture of the communist régime, the new theatres and nightclubs sprouting on every corner. The cultural center of Poland, some called it, though Krakow, the ancient capital, probably deserved that title. They passed many street exhibits, painters, musicians, acrobats, old people selling flowers, smiling, shouting, laughing, grumbling; countless young people in groups, chatting boisterously. A city of the young and the very old.

The streets careened with heavy traffic. Jerozolimiski Avenue was as crammed with the roar of automobiles as any major thoroughfare in Rome or Tel Aviv. The driver dropped him at the Marriott Hotel, and within minutes Elijah was checked into his room on the top floor. It had all been arranged. The paper work had been completed by someone—no, the management could not say who precisely—would Father care for some coffee? No? Father should please ring for whatever he wishes.

After his experiences in Israel and Rome, such politeness was a pleasurable surprise.

When room service was gone, he sat on the luxurious bed and stared out the large plate-glass window at the treetops punctured by office towers. This city which had been home to him for the first seventeen years of his life had become completely unintelligible. The Nazis had destroyed it, but a new city had risen on the gridwork of the streets. Only Old Town and New Town, the ancient medieval core, had been painstakingly reconstructed from the rubble left in the wake of the invasion.

He saw the Vistula bending around the core to the east, and then he knew that if he looked north he would see Muranow district, which had contained the ghetto. Piece by piece he located the original shape in his mind and superimposed it upon the parks and modern buildings. In the northeast he identified the most familiar area of all. The tenement block on Zamenhofa was gone. Only then did he realize that his hands were trembling and that for a very long time he had contained a secret room within his soul. It had always worried him that he had felt no longing to recall the life he had lived. He had assumed that what came afterward was of greater importance, and the past merely a shrouded memory. Of course, he had occasionally recalled the festivals and the prayers, the scoldings and the kisses, and the solemn discussions on philosophy. But these had faded into a theatrical background, vague, unexamined, a tone, an atmosphere, a world that had drifted away steadily as his life assumed an entirely different shape and name. On occasion, he had been pierced by split-seconds of longing for the beloved faces, or for the dirty gray apartment block and the three rooms on the fourth floor that had been his home. But never had it come to him as now that an entire portion of his existence had been cleaved from his consciousness. That he was a Christian, and a Christian priest, was beyond questioning. It was his life, his joy, and the fulfillment of all that was authentic within his character. Yet, there had been a keystone missing from the structure. He had been a child once. A Jew. Everything from that former existence had been demolished, and yet it had remained within him, dormant, still alive. He had sealed it away. Now the door was opening.

He said Mass on the desk facing the north window. The portable Mass kit had been given to him by a German bishop on the day of his ordination many years ago.

"This chalice, this paten, these candlesticks were made secretly in Dachau by a German priest", said the bishop. "He died for the faith you have embraced. It is my greatest treasure. I ask you to accept it."

Elijah had taken the gift numbly, understanding the symbolism of the gesture, grateful for the meaning of it, but largely unmoved. Why had he been unmoved by it? He had corresponded with the bishop for many years, and they had become friends. But the small, remote zone of numbness had remained, had eluded explanation. Forgiveness? Yes, long ago he had forgiven everything. Perhaps it was simply a matter of failing to grieve. He had hated and later forgiven. But had he simply *grieved* to the very depth of his soul?

After Communion, he sat in the light streaming through the window and felt the heat of the Presence within himself. He worshipped and embraced It. He rested against the Heart that beat within his own heart. The sense of disorientation and anguish diminished, and peace gradually filled his being. He looked out at the place where the ghetto had been and prayed for the hundreds of thousands of souls who had suffered there. Flocks of birds flew past the window in sprays of white and gold, red and black.

He prayed for the souls of his family. When he had completed the final words of the liturgy, he prayed in Hebrew the *kaddish,* the prayer for the dead.

* * *

After lunching in his room, he went down to the lobby. The desk clerk signaled to him and handed him an envelope. It contained a message from the President's appointment secretary, inviting him to the opening reception of the International Conference, to be held at the Palace of Culture and Science, at seven in the evening, four days hence. The commencement address would be delivered by the President. Would Professor Schäfer please join the President and his party for dinner beforehand at the Canaletto in the Hotel Victoria Intercontinental, five o'clock? R.S.V.P. There was a stamped reply envelope, which Elijah filled in and posted in the lobby mail box.

He strolled out onto Jerozolimiski and was hit by a wave of heat. The sun was high over the city, the air was humid and noisy, but filled with the fragrance emanating from the flower stalls along the avenue. He walked east for ten minutes, fending off gypsies who wanted to read his palm, vendors who offered him tin cups of *woda gazowa,* and young, healthy, well-dressed beggars. He crossed over at Marszalkowska and went north toward the ghetto's east side. A half-hour's stroll brought him to Nowolipki. He turned left, went one block, and turned right onto Zamenhofa. He continued north a few blocks, as far as the corner of Mila.

He stood and looked at the place where his apartment should have been. The buildings were completely different. New trees grew there. Children played on the sidewalk. If he squinted his eyes, there would be nothing different about them, except that they did not have skullcaps or earlocks or the tassels of the *tallis-kot'n* showing beneath their garments. They were dressed like modern children everywhere. Cars rushed up and down the street. A teenage boy went past strumming a guitar. Old ladies sat smoking cigarettes on the front steps of a Soviet-style tenement.

"Are you lost, Father?" called one.

"No", he replied. "Can you tell me, Pani," he said in Polish, "are all the street numbers the same as they were before the war?"

"Eh?" said one, looking at the other. "I don't know. We didn't live here then."

"I'm looking for 112. I used to live there as a boy."

They looked him up and down.

"The Jews used to live here. You are a Catholic."

"I am a Catholic. And a Jew."

The women looked perplexed and turned away, ignoring him.

He walked slowly up the sidewalk. The street seemed much narrower than he remembered it. There was more light. More trees. Approximately halfway up the first block north of Nowolipki, on the left. Yes, yes, surely this was the place. Rows of new buildings had replaced the tenements that had once lined this section. He looked down at the pavement and found a patch of cobblestone. Yes, there was the cracked stone that resembled a horse's head.

"I played here", he said. "My feet touched these stones . . . "

He did not stay long. He continued to walk aimlessly through the maze of avenues, courtyards, and alleys. Eventually, he found himself leaving Muranow and moving toward the waters of the Vistula. He did not know where he was going, nor where he wanted to go. The thought of returning to the lush sterility of the hotel did not attract him. He thought perhaps that he might see the river. He passed the corner of Nalewki where he had escaped from the ghetto by squeezing past a cart that was going through the gate with a load of brushes. They shot at him—there. He stopped and stared at the spot. Yes, there.

He ran from them. He was hungry and extremely weak, but in a final burst of desperation he galloped away from the whistles and the ugly German shouts, *Halt! Halt!* The *tallis* flew out behind him, and his feet were soaked in the slush from the cold rain. He heard the whiz and ping of bullets.

Going by intuition more than memory, Elijah now retraced the route of his terrified flight. He walked slowly toward Old Town. More than fifty years had elapsed. Yet he saw the boy fling himself down the streets with two big soldiers clomping hard on his heels; he heard with his own ears the pounding of his heart, felt the aching of his throat and the wailing of wind in and out of his lungs. Tearing in and out. In and out. This way three blocks, then right into the old quarter, left into an alley, right, left, double-back, a courtyard. A dead end. Despair. The approach of death. He hid in the alcove of an entrance. The jelly of his legs collapsed, and he fell backward into the bookshop of Pawel Tarnowski.

Father Elijah's interior compass did not fail him and within fifteen minutes he was standing in the courtyard, staring at the day's second resurrection.

The lime tree was gone. The buildings appeared much the

same although many of the finer details had changed. The frame of the shop window was painted bright yellow, not green. The door was new. The gold letters of Sophia House were gone, replaced by a gaudy sign advertising Galician folk art. In the window were brightly colored boxes, wooden dolls, tapestries, cheap icon prints laminated on wood.

He went in. A bell on the door jingled, but the shop remained unattended for some minutes. He stood staring at the interior, astonished that it was completely transformed yet mysteriously familiar. The windows and the doors were situated where they had always been. The lighting was modern. He knew that behind that curtain there was a staircase leading to the apartment on the floor above, and that it would have a ceiling of ornamental stucco, and that inside a bedroom closet there was a secret staircase to the attic, and that in the wood-paneled attic there could be stacks of boxes, a window to the roof and a burst of memory that might be unbearable.

"Can I help you?"

A young woman had come out from behind the curtain. She was heavily made up and wore her hair spiked like an American rock star.

"No, thank you, Pani. I merely wish to look, if you don't mind."

"To look is cheap. Look your fill." But she did not seem happy about it. He smelled hot sausage, frying onions, and boiling cabbage. A television was screeching hysterical cartoon plots in the back room, and two young children were squabbling about changing the channel.

The woman stood watching him with a bored expression.

"You looking for a souvenir? A gift for somebody?"

"I used to live here", he explained. "When I was a boy. During the war."

"Oh, the war. Before my time."

He pointed to the ceiling.

"I lived up there."

"All that's been locked up since I came. Nobody ever goes there. Maybe it's empty. Maybe it's got treasure", she chuckled. "The landlord has the key."

"This was once a bookshop. The man who owned it, his name was Pawel Tarnowski. Have you heard of him?"

She shook her head.

"I don't know him."

"Do you know what became of him?"

She shook her head again and looked toward the back room. She shouted at the children to turn down the volume of the television.

"Maybe the landlord knows", she shrugged.

"Can you give me his name?"

"Why not? Everyone knows him. He's owned this place since the war. He was a communist. Of course, nobody's a communist any more. Right? Old Boleslaw always lands on his feet. He's a capitalist now. An aristocrat." She laughed with a mouth full of rotten teeth.

She wrote the name and address on a scrap of paper and handed it to him.

"There you go. Watch yourself. He's a snake. But don't tell him I said so. Wait! On the other hand, please tell him I said so!" She opened her mouth wide again, but Elijah did not stay long enough to hear the laugh.

He found the address, south of New Town, in a quiet, tree-lined street of fashionable apartments overlooking the Vistula. The landlord's suite was on the fifth floor, the top. A brass plate on the door said, *Boleslaw Smokrev, Broker, Dealer in Antiquities, Assessments, Estates.*

A hard-looking man in his thirties answered. He gave Elijah's religious habit a sharp look.

"Yes?"

"I wish to speak with Pan Smokrev, please."

245

"Who are you?"

"I am Father Elijah Schäfer, a visitor to Warsaw. I wish to meet him."

"For what purpose? You want to buy or sell some items of significance?"

"No. It is a personal matter."

"The count is ill. He can't see anyone."

"My regrets. May I leave a message for him?"

The man nodded curtly.

Elijah wrote his name on the back of a piece of paper, the name of his hotel, and the message: *Regarding Pawel Tarnowski.*

"I will give it to him when he wakes. If it is a matter to which Pan Smokrev can respond, you will be contacted shortly. If it is a matter that he can't be troubled with, you won't hear from him, and you won't call again, please."

"I see. Thank you. Good-day."

The man did not return the greeting. He closed the door.

Elijah returned to his hotel on foot. He had walked several miles and arrived quite exhausted. He slept until early evening when room service knocked and brought him coffee. On the tray was an envelope.

The note said: *Come tomorrow, 9 A.M., B. Smokrev.*

The handwriting was shaky, blue ink on thick card stock, tinted mauve.

The sky had opened its dams the following morning, and the streets were awash with heavy runoff. The smash and patter of the rain was a delight to his ear. The heat gradually lifted. Shortly before nine o'clock, he managed to hail a taxi. Minutes later he was riding up an antique brass elevator to Smokrev's apartment. The same hard-faced young man opened the door and beckoned him in.

The suite was spacious, carpeted with oriental rugs, and appointed with antique furniture of the heaviest, most oppressive kind. The walls were covered with paintings from various periods. The atmosphere was one of opulent gloom.

"This way", said the man. He led him down a long hallway and into a bedroom. They were met by a uniformed nurse who conducted them into a second bedroom connected to the first by a glass double-door. There, on a four-poster covered with red silk, lay a wizened man. He fingered a remote control in his hand and a miniature Japanese television at his elbow flicked off. The old man was covered with brown spots, and his pale eyes leaked a stream of yellow fluid. His expression was sardonic, his glance guarded.

"Count Smokrev," said the manservant, "this is the one who left the message."

"Ah, yes", said a small croaked voice. "You wish to purchase my icon collection. You're the art expert the cardinal said he would send. You tell that wicked fellow he will not cajole me out of what's rightfully mine. I bought my collection legitimately, and I did not (here the old man roared with an amazing volume), did *not,* confiscate them from churches. You tell him that if he continues to spread those slanderous rumors, I am seriously going to consider a legal suit against him — *and* his entire Church. The Church in Poland will reel for decades from the shock! If he wants my icons, he must pay, just as everyone else does!"

"Count Smokrev, I have not come from the cardinal. I come as a private individual. I am from Israel."

"Israel, eh?" he said suspiciously. "Why do you want to see me?"

"I am the man who left the message about Pawel Tarnowski."

"What do I have to do with him, eh?"

"During the war he was a resident of a property now owned by you in Old Town."

The manservant whispered in Smokrev's ears, and the old man grunted.

"Yes, yes, now I remember. You left a note yesterday", he groaned. "An elderly person isn't permitted to rest."

"May we talk together? It is a matter of great importance to me."

"Leave us", he said to the manservant and the nurse. They went out and closed the glass doors, but the nurse sat on a lounge chair within sight and bent her head over some embroidery.

"I don't know anyone by the name of Tarnowski. Was he from Tarnow?" he cackled.

"No. From Warsaw. He was a bookseller."

"I knew no booksellers. My circles were entirely different. The intelligentsia."

"He also published books before the war. I suppose that's a kind of intelligentsia. He also wrote a play that was published in Germany after the war. It came out under a false name. It was later republished in German under the name of its true author. It appeared for the first time in Polish only after the fall of the communists."

"What is your interest in him?"

"I knew him."

"So?"

"He helped me."

"What is that to me?"

"He saved my life."

"How did he save your life?"

"He hid me."

"You were with the underground?"

"No."

"A Jew?"

"Yes."

Smokrev cackled again.

"A Jew! A Jew! In a priest's costume! How delicious! Always a delight to meet a traitor to his race!"

Elijah remained silent.

"A betrayer of his faith!"

Smokrev calmed himself down, and when the cackling had

ceased, and he had wiped his eyes, he snapped, "I repeat—what do you want of me?"

"I see that you know nothing of my benefactor, sir. But it would be a great kindness if you would permit me to visit the premises now owned by you in Old Town."

"The little shop where that hag sells imitation folk-art to the Americans?"

"The little shop, yes. Above it is the apartment and the attic where I lived. It would mean a great deal to me."

"Why should I do you a favor? Who has ever done *me* favors?"

"I beg you, sir."

"He begs me", snorted Smokrev.

Elijah's heart sank.

"He begs me", muttered the old man.

Elijah stood, bid him good-day, and left.

*　　*　　*

He woke at seven the following morning. He said Mass at the window overlooking the city, prayed for the victims, prayed for wily survivors like Smokrev, and for the success of the papal mission. He experienced a period of consolation after Communion, a touch from the Lord that reassured him. Still, he felt a lingering sadness that he had discovered no more about the destiny of Pawel Tarnowski. He spent the morning reading through the Apocalypse and praying for the success of his meeting with the President. The day after tomorrow he would face the lion, if indeed the President was such a beast.

After lunch, a hotel boy brought a mauve envelope to the door. Inside was a black key and a message.

> Dear Tourist from Israel.
> Go, look inside the empty box of your past. Then do me the favor of reporting to me what you see.
> Smokrev.

When he entered the shop, the woman looked up from the newspaper she had been reading, a rope of red licorice dangling from her lips.

"You're back", she said irritably.

"Count Smokrev has given me permission to see—"

"I know, I know", she grumbled. "The old snake's toady phoned this morning. Well, come this way."

She led him behind the curtain and down a hall to a staircase. Mops and brooms were lying across the steps. He cleared them out of the way and began to climb.

"If there's treasure up there," she quipped, "I get my share."

"It is unlikely there will be anything other than the treasure of memories. Thank you for your help, Pani."

"Don't mention it. Treasure of memories! Ha! Can you eat memories? Memories are garbage. You live your life and then you take out the garbage. That's all."

She went off shrieking at her youngsters who had burst into the hallway, fighting.

At the top of the stairway he unlocked the door. It squealed as he opened it and a wave of cool, musty air rushed out to meet him. He closed the door behind and shot the bolt.

He stood for a few moments looking about him. The apartment was recognizable only by its shape and by the light coming through a dust-covered window in the kitchen/sitting room. The toilet closet was in the same place, but the plumbing had been removed. The ceiling did not seem quite so high as he remembered, but then he had been a youth at the time, an underfed, undersized boy. Nor was it any longer embellished with plaster ornaments—a casualty of the bombing. There were no furnishings. The hardwood floor was strewn everywhere with bits of crumbling plaster and mouse droppings.

The small bedroom came closest to the template of his memory. The windowpane he and Pawel had replaced with a tin sheet for the smokestack of the wood burner was no longer there. It had been restored by glass. But the dimensions of the room were the same. He stood in the echoing silence and listened once more to the stories Pawel had told him. The tale of the artist who saw Christ hidden in the ruined face of an old sinner. He recalled especially the tale of a prince without a kingdom, who found his heart. Here too, the orthodox Jewish boy, David Schäfer, had told his Polish benefactor the tales of the Hassidim. How often had Pawel looked at him with puzzlement? How often, in return, had he failed to understand the older man? Yet between them there had grown a mutual respect that had set aside for a time the barrier between their cultures. They had learned much from each other. Pawel had become like a father to him, because his father and his mother had perished in the *Shoah.* He had become like a son to Pawel because Pawel had no wife or child, and because Pawel was a prince without a kingdom, who searched within himself for a father's heart.

Years later, after the war, when he was rising in Israel, a lawyer with a reputation for outrage and justice, a public figure destined for a political future, he had received a message from this man. A crumpled note wrapped around a tarnished religious medal. An angel delivered it to him while he was on a speaking tour in New York. The medal said, *Mądrość* — Wisdom! This small coinage had dislodged him from that certain future, had raised the fundamental doubt which set his life upon an entirely different course. A few words on a scrap of yellow paper.

> David, my son, my friend,
> Never have I wanted to live so much as I do now. I go down into darkness in your place. I give you my life. I carry your image within me like an icon. This is my joy. I go down at last to sleep, but my heart is awake.
> Pawel.

The messenger said it had been hurled from a train during the war. The messenger had kept it for many years until an angel had spoken to her and told her that the famous Israeli was the man to whom the note was addressed. But David Schäfer had ceased to exist. By then he had a new name given to him by the Haganah. During the War of Independence, this name had solidified and become his public identity, and the past became merely a form of garbage that must one day be taken away. Eventually, he grew famous with this name, and it bore no relationship to the name on the note. There was not a soul in the world who would remember his true name, aside from those who kept a certain file in the basement of Haganah headquarters. How could a simple Polish woman from Florida know him? How? Impossible, he thought at the time. But she knew him with a kind of knowing in the soul, and she credited the angels with that knowing.

Had Pawel Tarnowski gone down into darkness? Was the train really bound for Oświęcim? Perhaps the woman's husband, the trackman, had been mistaken. Even if he were right, and Pawel had been taken to that place of death, he may have survived. A few had survived. If Pawel lived, Elijah knew that he must find him.

The curtain that had once covered the staircase to the attic was gone, its secret exposed. The door was unlocked and swung open without difficulty. He went up.

The attic was one long, empty room, paneled with strips of dark brown wood. The household cooking aromas from the first floor were stronger here, but the smell of aging varnish dominated everything. Elijah went to the far end and looked out the small window. The roof tiles were the same. The view of the roofs of Old Town were identical, a faithful reconstruction. The horizon was completely different, dominated by Soviet and capitalist architecture.

On the day of their betrayal, he had escaped out through this window and run across the roofs to another block. He had walked to the river, trying not to attract attention, and when he came to the sand banks, he struck east along the shore for a kilometer until he found thick bushes. He hid in them until nightfall and swam to the opposite shore, then traveled cross-country until he came to woods. In these woods he found partisans. He told them that he had directions to a place of refuge at Mazowiecki, on the farm of Pawel's cousin Masha. They advised him against it. He looked too Jewish, they said. Even disguised as a farm laborer, he could never remain undetected. He had no papers. He would be dead within a month. The Poles passed him on to another group of partisans who lived in a forest to the east. They were young Jews, bitter, tattered, and poorly armed, trying to find the Soviet front. He stayed with them for a week, left them, and moved east by night. He was soon starved, sick, half-crazed. He stole food when he came upon unguarded fields. Gentiles attempted to hand him over to the Germans more than a few times, but he always managed to escape.

Once, caught sleeping in a barn, he was beaten and locked inside a tool room while the farmer went to get the SS. He tore up a floor board and squeezed out through a gap in the stone foundation and crawled across a muddy field, slithered into a creek, and waded downstream for hours until the barking of dogs grew faint behind him. Others, righteous Gentiles, recognizing a half-mad Jew boy, hid him in haylofts and fed him entire meals. Some along the way, mistaking him for a holy fool, gave him bread, an egg, a tin cup of milk, a slice of stale sausage. South of Lvov he came upon the Dnestr River. He traveled for three nights along the riverbank until he tripped over a punt half-sunken in the shallows. He dragged it up on shore, turned it upside down and slept beneath it. In the morning light, he saw that it had been punctured by bullet holes and that dried blood was spattered on the gunwales—an old event. At dusk, he filled the holes with bunched reeds, put it back into the water, got into it, and lay down. The current carried him south throughout that night. A man, fishing in the dawn, hailed him from the shore. He cooked a fish. The boy ate it ravenously. The man observed the manner in which he consumed it. He gave him cheese and a shot-glass of harsh, home-distilled vodka. He talked to him in a strange language. He made jokes. The boy did not laugh. He made sign language for guns, gestured in a mock Hitler salute, and pointed down the river, by which the boy understood that the Germans were on the river, not far below. The man made the sign of the cross on his breast and raised his eyes to the heavens, a glance that conveyed a mixture of long-suffering and irony. Then he took him to his farm, fed him for several days, and throughout one long night led him by a footpath across forests and fields to the banks of a different river.

"Prut! Prut!" said the man emphatically, pointing downstream.

David Schäfer thanked him in Polish, Yiddish, French, and pidgin Russian, to which the man replied with broad grins and nods. As the sun set, the boy walked away from him, south along the banks of the River Prut, which bent around the foot of the Carpathians and meandered toward the Black Sea.

*　*　*

The banging on the door pulled him back across a half-century of time.

"Come on. Aren't you finished? What's up there?"

"I will be down soon", he called.

"Let me see. Maybe you found treasure after all, eh? Maybe you want to keep it just for you."

He went down and unlocked the door.

"Come up and see for yourself."

The woman went through the top floors carefully, clicking her tongue in disapproval, commenting on the bad insulation, the cost of heat, the mice, the "snake", the problems of trying to raise good children now that the old order had disappeared.

"The communists were bastards," she said, "but at least they kept things in line."

"The War was worse."

"Everybody talks about the bad old days," she complained, "but I tell you, this time looks bad enough to me. How can an honest worker hope to own a home, I ask you!"

"Believe me, Pani, the War was beyond imagining. It was the reign of evil."

She grunted but did not argue.

"I would like to be alone awhile longer, if you don't mind. There is no treasure."

"All right. But I have to go out at noon. I need you gone so I can lock up. Not that I mistrust you . . . "

"I understand. Give me a little time."

She grumbled down the stairs, closed the door, and abandoned him to silence. This silence was of inestimable worth to him, for when he sank into its arms forgotten passages of memory came out of the shadows and spoke to him.

"I listen in the darkness for God", Pawel said.

"That is a beautiful thing", said the boy.

"Like Elijah on Mount Carmel, listening for the words of God in the gentle breeze."

"Is it a lonely thing?"

"Sometimes it is. I live here in this great city like a *monachus,* a solitary one. I pray. I work. I put good books into the hands of people. Perhaps good thoughts are born in their minds. That is my calling."

"I am returned to not-understanding. Why does this prevent us from sharing the bed? Five blankets are better than two. You are like a brother. You are my friend. We would sleep well at last."

"The warmth of another heart beating close would be too great a consolation for me. Don't you understand?"

"I will never understand."

"I would forget the great heart beating through everything and everywhere at all times. I would cease to move toward Him. I would love the creature more than the Creator—and in the end I would cease to love the creature too. I would not love anything."

Father Elijah sat on the floor of the bedroom and leaned against the wall. He closed his eyes. He recalled the bitterly cold nights when Pawel would not permit him to share the bed, when the host had given him his extra blanket instead. A natural reserve perhaps. Modesty. Pawel was always a distant man, wrapped within himself. He did not reveal much of his heart except in stories.

"Am I like a son to you, Pawel?"

"Yes, a little like a son."

"And a friend?"

"Yes, that too."

"But a young friend who says childish things."

"*Może,* perhaps. But also the man who is becoming. A good man who one day will walk with me beside the Vistula, when this war is over, and who will correct my poor philosophy."

David Schäfer smiled. Father Elijah smiled.

"I see now that you are not angry with me, Pawel."

"I have never been angry with you."

"Yet I am a burden to you."

"You have never been a burden to me."

"But there is another thing. I see it there, in your heart. It remains."

"Some day, on a spring morning when the invaders have gone, we will walk in the sun beside the river, and then we will speak of this thing."

"Is it a thing which makes you unhappy?"

"Yes."

"Of which you are ashamed?"

"Yes."

"Is it *sitra ahra?*"*

"It is a wound inflicted by the *sitra ahra.*"

*Sitra ahra: literally, *the other side,* the kingdom of darkness.

"It hurts you?"

"Yes. It hurts me."

"Is it like a stone in your heart? Like the prince?"

"Yes, like that."

"We will remove the stone and throw it in the river."

"You are very young, David."

"Sometimes the young see things that the old don't see."

"More often the old see things the young don't see."

"Pawel, I think it is a holy thing to be a son in the realm of the soul."

"Then it is a holy thing, also, to be a father of the soul."

"It is a thing we can make together, you and me."

The Germans and a Polish traitor had eliminated that possibility. *The bent one,* Pawel had called him.

"*Far groys tsores zolttsu zikh nit farbrenen . . .* ", David Schäfer had cried into Pawel's coat on the day the Germans battered down the door.

"*Do not burn for sorrow, do not burn for sorrow . . . ,*" he had cried, though he did not understand why he should utter the words of a ghetto song at this very last moment.

"Go!" Pawel said sternly. "Go!"

"I cannot leave without you."

"They are already here. I will hold them off for a short while, enough time for you to get away."

"I will not go!"

"Go! Go!"

Those were the last words the man had spoken to him before shoving him out the attic window onto the roof, into his future.

* * *

"The count has been expecting you," said the nurse, "but he is sleeping. Please wait in the drawing room while I wake him. He will need some attention to his needs, and then, if he is able, I will bring him to you here."

The hard-eyed manservant placed a tray of tea and biscuits on a side-table. Elijah did not take them. Despite the large windows, the front room was saturated in perpetual gloom, unrelieved by black and burgundy portraits of ancient noblemen, scowling from their chiaroscuro, badly painted, in monstrous gold frames. Two life-size sculptures stood guard at each end of the room. They were male nudes carved from marble, a dying satyr (probably Roman), and a runner (classical Greek). Both were stained and chipped. They might be genuine antiquities or clever frauds.

"So, you are admiring my collection", said a high-pitched voice behind him. The nurse was wheeling the count across the room toward a chaise longue. She and the manservant shifted the old man's body onto it and left them.

"Please, sit. Tea? No? It isn't poisoned. No doubt you think you have fallen into the boudoir of a Medici?" He cackled and then had a fit of coughing.

"Ah, *sic transit gloria mundi!*" said the count pompously. "All flesh is grass, is it not? You people are the experts on *that* subject. But I could tell you a thing or two."

He coughed again, and when he had settled himself and rearranged a purple velvet rug over his legs, the count cocked his head becomingly and draped an arm along the back of the lounge.

"Now, I don't wish to miss a single detail. You must tell me *all!*"

"I didn't come to intrude upon your time, Count Smokrev. I wished to thank you personally for permission to visit your premises in Old Town."

"A mere nothing. You have my key? Please give it here."

"Of course. Here it is."

"So. Was it as you remembered it?"

"It is essentially unchanged. It was really quite kind of you to allow a stranger a moment's nostalgia. I thank you."

He rose to leave, but Smokrev fluttered his hands, commanding him back down: "Sit, sit, sit! I haven't quite finished with you."

"Indeed? There is not much more to tell."

"Tell me how you came under the protection of this man. Tarkowyski, you called him?"

"Tarnowski."

"Yes, yes. Well, tell me. Tell me *all.*"

Father Elijah noted the hungry glint in the old man's eye and decided to humor the whim of a lonely soul.

"I was raised in Muranow, up on Zamenhofa. When the Germans came, as you remember, we were cordoned off. In the summer of 1942, my entire family was taken and put in a train at the *umschlagplatz* for resettlement."

"Aha! You know what that meant, of course."

"Yes."

"Treblinka."

"Yes. Treblinka."

"But not you? They didn't take you?"

"I hid in the sewers. I lived like a rat. In September I broke out by the northeast gate. I ran. I didn't know where I was going. I just ran. The soldiers chased me, but I lost them in the maze of Old Town. I fell through the door of the very shop which is now owned by you. The proprietor hid me. I lived in the apartment and attic above the shop throughout the winter of '42–'43. Then I made my way south."

"When was the last time you saw your protector?"

"Late winter, early spring of '43. I was forced to flee, you see. I was discovered by a Pole. He reported me to the Germans."

"The traitor!"

Smokrev lit a thick cigarette with trembling fingers and blew a cloud of noxious smoke across the room.

"I never found out the fate of my friend."

"A pity."

"I was put in a camp on Cyprus after the war and got into

Palestine on an illegal ship in '47, just before the War of Independence. Those days were frantic, very exciting for a young man. After the birth of Israel, I had more time. I wrote to the Polish government seeking information about Pawel Tarnowski, but, of course, there were no replies."

"But of course. By the way, did my nurse tell you I'm dying of lung cancer? No?! Did she mention my age? I'm in my nineties, you know, although I look in my early seventies. Don't deny it! Don't violate an old tart's vanity. I survived the collapse of the nobility, the Nazis, the Russians. It's the new crowd who will bury me", he sighed and exhaled a stream of smoke.

"I developed a taste for these foul Russian cigarettes in bed. I liked the Russians. Especially their boys. You would be simply amazed at how often a *coquette* is to be found beneath a hulking farmer in a uniform. Ah, those sweet, vicious, mongol eyes! Paradise!"

In an instant, Father Elijah saw the exact contours of Count Smokrev's life. He said nothing and looked into the not very great depths of the man's soul.

"Remove that insulting glance of pity from me, please!"

"You are not a happy man, Count," said Father Elijah gently.

"I am a *very* happy man. I have had everything I wanted from life."

"Your life is drawing to a close. Have you not given a thought to eternity?"

"I sold my soul a long time ago, dear fellow. The rest is all cosmetics and parlor games. Nothing that you say, you admirable, earnest apostle, will touch me in the slightest."

"Are you so sure? Isn't every man a mystery to himself?"

"I have plumbed every depth of depravity known to man. I have exhausted it all. You have no idea. Don't waste your time."

"It wouldn't be wasted time. You are a human soul. You were not created for this . . . "

"Ooh, dear, dear, you came very close to saying something

tasteless. You were about to say *depravity,* or *corruption,* or *damnation,* weren't you?"

"I was about to say that you were not created for this lovelessness."

"Love? What is love?"

"To give one's life away for another."

"I am a taker. Not a giver. No conversions are possible here."

"You seem adamant about that."

"Simply free from illusions. I know that there is no love in the world. We are all creatures of various kinds of desire. Even the idealist who talks of love, love, love all the day long will make a few sacrifices to convince himself of his fantasy. But I tell you, his fantasy is a *pleasure* to him; he *desires* it to be true, but he will abandon it at the very instant it becomes unmitigated suffering. I am a creature who cultivates a certain kind of desire, that's all, merely a variation on your idealist who *thinks* he loves. I love in my own fashion, just as he does. But let neither of us call it pure, unsullied, unselfish love. There is no such thing. You think me a deformed creature. I admit it. But everyone is deformed. Not a soul on this planet escapes it. The idealist is deformed by his theological romance. I have been deformed by history and by your religion, and by my darling mother and by . . . "

Here the count stopped and lit a second cigarette. He inhaled and precipitated another fit of coughing. He lay back and struggled to catch his breath.

"In all your years of living," said Elijah, "has no one told you that it is possible to be restored to what one was created to be?"

"They have told me in a thousand ways. I have heard more sermons than you've ever given. I have listened to the exhortations of the zealous, the compassionate, and the strident, the saints, geniuses, and cretins, all in the employ of your beloved Church. And I tell you that nothing touches my unbelief."

"You cling to your unbelief like a Medici clings to his bottle of poison."

"Ah, *touché! Formidable!* A delightful turn of phrase. I'm warming up to you. You have a literary streak. Marvelous. Do go on."

"Life is short, eternity is long."

"If there is a God, let Him advise me that the end is near. I will repent on my deathbed."

"Did you know, Count Smokrev, that deathbed conversions are quite rare? Any priest will tell you that."

"As a matter of policy?"

"As a simple fact. Many people think they can postpone repentance till the end. This is an illusion. Most men die as they have lived. If death is sudden, there is no time for it. If it comes gradually, there is usually little energy for the revision of an entire way of being."

"Tsk, tsk! You won't frighten me with such dire warnings."

"Nothing I say touches you, does it?"

"True. But don't be discouraged, dear fellow. You *are* mildly entertaining. Quite a relief from my nurse, who wishes to preserve her job as long as possible, and my manservant, who labors with excruciating persistence in the cause of my damnation. They are dull characters interested in various kinds of profit."

"If I were to wrestle for your soul, would you wrestle with me against the things that entrap you?"

"No. I would wrestle against you and call upon a legion of demons to assist me."

"Then what, precisely, is the purpose of this conversation?"

"Entertainment."

"I see."

Father Elijah stood.

"Ah, yes, well done. You will now leave with great dignity. Just as I choreographed it. This dialogue has been perfectly predictable, yet enjoyable."

"I leave with a great sadness in my heart. I see a gifted man who believed a lie."

"What do you mean? Ah, yes, your theology. Well, it doesn't matter. Good-bye."

"I will pray for you."

"Don't waste your effort. Good-day."

"Good-day."

His legs shook on the steps leading down to the street. His hands trembled and dismay filled his mind. He had heard the confessions of countless people. He had encountered many great sinners. He had met brutal men, corrupt men, liars and cheats and murderers and adulterers and seducers of the innocent. But he had never yet encountered one so completely without a hint of shame. This dying soul, this Count Smokrev, was one who appeared to know he was damned, who had chosen it, who delighted in it. Elijah, appalled and helpless, walked away from the apartment and went blindly up the street.

At the end of the avenue, he happened upon the entrance to a convent. An order of contemplative nuns. He rang and explained to the portress that he felt unwell and wished to have a few moments of prayer. She let him in to the chapel, and he knelt in front of the Blessed Sacrament for close to an hour. He was at first agitated, beseeching help for himself and for Smokrev, for the President, and for the Church that was now bleeding copiously from more wounds than he had imagined. After some minutes he became calm but bereaved, then gradually fell into a state of interior recollection. Eventually, all sensation of time disappeared.

A voice spoke within him:

I ask of you an extraordinary immolation of your heart.

"Yes, my Lord."

I ask you to love My enemy in My name.

"I will try to do this, my Lord, but I beg You for the necessary grace."

Where everything is given, nothing is lacking. Fear nothing, my son.

"I am afraid, Lord, I am afraid. Soon I must face the lion. I fear him greatly. This corrupt one, I fear him also. He exhausts my every resource, and he has weakened me for the meeting with the lion."

My strength is most effective in weakness.

"It is impossible. I have nothing left. I wish to return to Mount Carmel. I beg You to send another messenger to him."

I have chosen you.

"Have You given me two impossible tasks? Both are beyond my strength. I do not understand."

I have given you but one task and that is to trust Me as you go down into the darkness of men's hearts. This depraved soul is My child. I see what he once was and may be again. He fights you fiercely because he longs for you to resist him. Resist him with love. The other, the man of power, is a foe of a different order.

"Lead me, Lord, I am shaken."

I ask you to fear nothing. I have brought you forth like a brand from the burning in order to address the foe and for the good of many souls. I carry you always. You must trust in Me especially during times of desolation.

"You are the heart of the world. I place my trust in You."

Cling to Me in everything that is about to happen. You will bear many more wounds for My sake.

"You are my life."

You are My friend and disciple. Elijah.

The interior light faded and time poured back into his consciousness. He got up and went out into the foyer and rang for the portress. His legs were still weak. He asked her to call a taxi to take him back to the Marriott. Upon his arrival there, he collapsed onto his bed and fell instantly into a deep sleep.

XI

The Confession

I wish to confess, said the note. *Come quickly.*

The nurse let him into Smokrev's apartment and led him down the hallway to the bedchamber. There, he found the count sitting up in his enormous bed, a stack of newspapers beside him, books, trays of medicines, and drinks spread across the brocaded coverlet. He was reading a theatre paper from New York and smoking his Russian cigarettes. The room smelled ghastly—a mixture of tobacco and the urinary incontinence of old men.

The nurse cleared her throat, and Smokrev looked up, waved at the priest, and broke into a smile that resembled the leer of a delighted weasel.

"You came! Well done, good and faithful servant!" he muttered and glanced to the heavens. "I can always spot a true disciple. They will go to the most degraded places on the planet in search of a single repentance. They will kiss tax collectors and prostitutes at any time, night or day."

A sarcastic note lingering just below the ironic tone did not ease Elijah's tension.

"You asked me to come. Is it true that you wish to confess?"

"It is."

"I am glad. I am very glad."

"I dressed for the occasion", said Smokrev, pulling at the lapels of his crimson satin housecoat. "Red for the scarlet woman. Black lapels for true contrition. White shirt for restoration to my pristine purity."

"I am surprised by this sudden change of heart. When we parted yesterday you had convinced me that no such change would ever occur. May I ask what has brought it about?"

"Something you said about nostalgia. That did it."

The simplicity of it puzzled Father Elijah. Even so, he removed a purple stole from his pocket and unrolled it. Smokrev watched him place it over his neck; he observed with a little smile as the priest drew a chair close to the bed and bent his head to listen.

Smokrev erupted into high-pitched, hysterical giggles.

"You misunderstand me. I wish to confess to you as one man to another. I didn't mean your sacrament!"

Elijah's heart fell.

"I see."

"Always on the lookout for someone to rehabilitate, aren't you?"

"Yes, I suppose that is true, though you put it crudely. If by *rehabilitate* you mean restore a soul to a world of love, yes, it is true."

"Ach! There you go again. The preacher! Please, please, all I ask of you is that you listen. I would like to tell you some stories about my life."

"Why me, Count Smokrev? If you disagree so adamantly with the very thing that is *my* life, of what service could I possibly be to you?"

"You have one redeeming quality, one very minuscule, but altogether rare quality, and that is that you are not ambitious. My servants listen to my babbling because they are paid to do so. My customers from abroad listen to my monologues because they think they will learn something useful for their businesses. You are the first person I have met in many years who doesn't want something from me."

"I want to bring you back to life."

"Ah, I see. One more soul dragged into Paradise by the hands of holy Saint Elijah? Is that it?"

"You are trapped within a cage. You think there is nothing beyond it. But there is something so great, so much better, that we can scarcely believe. There is life. In abundance. And joy."

"The brief, bright hopes that are conjured up by the small of the earth. They have no power to create their own reality, and so they spin their dreams; they live in their fairy tales. You are the servant of a myth."

"If I am so deluded, why do you wish to tell me a story?"

"Because you are human, and because you have expressed an interest in a portion of my past. And, I suppose, because you are an honest, though deluded, man."

Elijah smiled.

"Thank you for the compliment."

"I was flattering you. It's a talent of mine."

"Do you not grow weary of playing with people?"

"Sometimes. It can make one feel so alone when everyone you meet proves vulnerable to tactics. Everyone can be bent or bought, you know."

"That is untrue."

"You would think it untrue, of course. A perfectly predictable response. You haven't yet been offered a large enough bribe."

Elijah shook his head. "I would like to hear your story."

"It's not a pretty one."

"I have loved stories since my childhood."

"Comedies, tragedies?"

"Yes, everything."

"Sleaze?"

"Comedy and tragedy contain everything."

Smokrev snorted and coughed.

"I have heard many thousands of sacramental confessions in my life. There is nothing I haven't heard."

"You are beyond shock?"

"I won't say that. It is possible that man can devise new forms of violation. But the essential sin remains more or less the same. Each of us, including the best of men, is tempted to make himself into God. The murderer makes himself master over life and death; the thief over material goods, the tyrant over man's freedom, the occultist over spiritual powers, the adulterer over love, and so on."

"And by implication, I too wish to divinize myself?"

"All of us. None excepted."

"How very shocking. Your attitude seems to be a far more perverse and pessimistic view of human nature than mine!"

"I saw many horrifying things during the War and later, during the wars in Israel. But nothing quite prepared me for the variety of human sin that I heard in the confessional."

"Tell me some."

"That is impossible."

"Ah, yes, your oath that you will never betray the secrets of the confessional. Charming. A most interesting part of the romance."

"Why do you say that?"

"Because of all the traffic in lusts and addictions that I have fostered and fed upon, none, I tell you, none has the power over the personality that information has. Scandal, slander, details, facts, and especially gossip."

"You may be right. The trade in information is a way of having knowledge of good and evil, a way to have power over others."

"A subtle deification."

"That is why we so carefully protect the sacrament of penance. It is a moment of radical exposure. We guard it with our lives."

"Ah, such chivalry!"

"Such realism."

"All right! All right! When are you going to cease your monkish prattle and let me confess?"

"You may begin at any time."

Smokrev smoothed the coverlet, adjusted his crimson sleeping cap, took a long drink of carbonated water, and lit a cigarette.

"Let us begin. I cannot tell you what a pleasure this is to have someone wrestle for my soul. You will lose, of course, but we will have a great deal of fun along the way. Ah, so serious, so serious. Smile, Father Elijah."

"Please, begin."

"I would like to tell you about my first great sin. It was my primeval choice. I'm sure you'll hasten to add that it was my Garden of Eden. No? Nothing to say, Father? Well, I said it myself, didn't I? Let us call it my original sin, my first conscious choice for evil. It set in motion a number of forces that have brought me to this bed loaded with delicious guilts. I have grown old in wickedness. But in the beginning I wasn't like that. Oh, I was guilty of all the usual boyhood faults. I stole a cookie or two; I told harmless lies; I slapped my nanny and made her promise not to tell Mama, and she didn't, for fear of losing her employment. My mother was a countess, you know, a vain, shallow woman, an extraordinary beauty, the usual pathetic little story from the gentry. A nobleman marries for beauty, ignores character. He pays the price for the rest of his life. A dreary tale that has been told a thousand times over. A *real* fairy tale. But I'm getting ahead of myself!

"My father ran away from the slow strangulation that, as it soon became obvious, would be his lot in life. He was always away 'on business'. He helped Pilsudski stop the Red Army at the Vistula in 1920. He was well known and admired. A patriot. The Nazis killed him when they destroyed the aristocracy."

"Why didn't they kill you?"

"I was in Paris during the thirties. I became a fascist, and the

Germans found me useful for cultural affairs after the occupation. But once again we are leaping all over the map. There is so much to tell you, I'm easily distracted by this crime or that one."

Smokrev peered at him with amusement and lit another cigarette. "Well done. You didn't blink an eye at the Nazi connection. Bravo!"

"Are you testing me, Count Smokrev?"

"Precisely. You have passed, *summa cum laude.* Now, where was I?"

"Your boyhood. Your first great sin."

"Ah, yes." Smokrev stubbed his cigarette and lit a fresh one. He did not speak for several minutes and appeared to be thinking over the details of what he was about to disclose. His eyes lost their chronic look of sly humor.

"It is not easy to tell. I will ask you to try to imagine an eleven-year-old boy, the son of aristocratic parents, screwed like a tiny jewel into the gold setting of his family estates. This is his world. He knows nothing else. His parents pay for every pastime, every distraction, toy, and pleasure.

"He is a lonely child. His father, whom he admires, is not often at home. He has important matters to attend to at the capital. He is making a better country for the sake of his son's future. For the sake of the blood line that will come from his heir. His one heir.

"Try to imagine, if you will, a sensitive, imaginative boy, trained in the arts: he plays Mozart at age seven, he draws landscapes and clouds, writes poetry. He is given a white Arabian for his tenth birthday and rides it well. He loves to race with his borzoi across the lawn enclosed by the hedges of the estate. He is good at archery, fencing, swimming. He achieves exceptionally high marks in his studies—he is privately tutored—and is preoccupied by an ongoing correspondence with several literary scholars in Poland and Paris. Busy men of letters, they are well disposed to exercise a certain kindness to the child of their benefactors. The boy reads the novels they recommend, German and French works, and he understands few of them, learning only that the world is much more complex than the little stories he writes, composed for his own entertainment—stories full of sword-fights, camaraderie, wild beasts, ships, trains, and abandonment in exotic places.

"He is not an attractive child. Yet he is pleasant in appearance and sturdy in bearing, and he moves with a certain grace and precision that imitates, if it doesn't actually express, nobility. Once or twice a year, he is conducted across Europe on a tour of museums, salons, fashion houses, and the homes of the aristocracy. He finds them boring. There are few children in this circle of beautiful, accomplished people.

"More than this, he is devout. He longs to throw his life into heroic causes, to have many adventures of a religious nature. He fasts, wears a hair-rope under his shirt, and sleeps on the floor of his bedroom for almost the whole of his twelfth year, until his secret is discovered by the nanny, and he is ever afterward forbidden by Mama to do such a strange and worrisome thing. He continues to talk to God in the privacy of the chapel, which is situated in the west wing, on the floor above his room, in the main house. He rises often in the night to visit this Presence which never replies. No words are exchanged. Even so, the red vigil light is a comfort to him. It pulsates in the darkened chapel. Old incense lingers on the air. There are glints of fire on the silver and gold threads of the tapestries. He sinks into the gentle warmth of this atmosphere, as if into an ancient refuge, a sanctuary, though he did not have words for such a feeling. Almost, he can feel the beat of a mysterious heart on which he rests, the warmth of arms enfolding him. He feels a profound peace that is always shattered by the dawn.

"Nevertheless, he wishes to be a saint and to participate in glory. The chapel priest notices his attention to prayer during the Mass, and it is suggested that the young count may have a religious vocation. Perhaps he should attend for a year the seminary school at such and such a city, where the fathers are devoted to the education and edification of the young. But Mama won't hear of such a thing! He is just a child! He is the only heir! Also, he is her main company in this vast house. The little count reads difficult novels to her at night by the fire, while she sips English sherry and practices her petit point. She seldom prays. She gossips heavily, aloud, to her son. She complains about his father, in subtle, exquisite terms. The little count does not raise the question of a religious vocation with Papa during his infrequent visits. He does not think to ask for a different life. He does not inquire into the meaning of his own life. He merely lives it. He is not moved to ask why he was born.

"He has one fault, at first a very small thing, but a dangerous fault. Because he is fawned upon by his mother and neglected, except in a most formal manner, by his father, he does not learn to give when it costs something. He is the recipient of all that is best in civilization. Yet he does not know what it is to lack anything. He is ungrateful. He is proud. He is a master of throwing fits when he doesn't get his way. He wants to have everything, do everything, be everything. He expects to achieve greatness in all that he tries, even sanctity, but has little opportunity to measure the meaning of greatness aside from the continuous stream of mental and physical disciplines that are set for him to learn. In time he becomes an attractive, intelligent, accomplished adolescent. He has everything. And he has nothing."

"Why does he feel such a thing?" asked Elijah.

"He feels that he has everything on the *outside* of his life, and nothing in his interior. He is lonely. In his thirteenth year, he begins to taste the sweet, rotten fruit of the imagination when passion is joined to a profound loneliness. But the passion is unexplainable and undirected. He drives his Arabian mercilessly, and she falls and breaks a leg. It is necessary to shoot her. He breaks household objects, small things at first, bumped off tables by an errant elbow. And then increasingly more valuable *objets d'art*. There are worried consultations with Mama and Papa. There are lectures. There are disciplines. As punishment, he is consigned to spend a day entirely alone in his room. A maid brings him meals he does not eat. He hurls lead soldiers across the room. Their bayonets stick into the wall. He ceases to make his nocturnal visits to the chapel. He begins to think that the sensations of peace and enfolding were a fantasy. He feels growing reluctance to attend Mass.

"He regularly steals the butler's cigarettes and vomits afterward. He drinks a half-bottle of English sherry and nearly drowns in the fountain, but is saved by a servant who agrees not to tell. On a few occasions, he wanders through the village at night and looks in the windows at the family life of the poor. He kicks the horses, and they learn to fear him. He throws stones at his borzoi, who always forgives him. He takes his faults and sins to confession, but freedom from the impulse to hurt and to waste lasts only a few days, a week at the most. He asks for daily Communion, but Mama, anxious lest he return to his religious fanaticism, refuses. Eventually she tells the old chaplain not to return to the estate, and the family and staff partake of the sacraments once a week at a convent, a short carriage ride away. Mama prefers the landau pulled by two horses to the new motorcars that are so unhealthy, considering their fumes and the terrifying speeds at which they travel."

Smokrev paused and lit another cigarette, which precipitated a fit of coughing. When he was settled, Elijah said, "You were very unhappy."

"You are an observant fellow."

"Surely there is more."

"During the summer of that unhappiness, an extraordinary thing happened. I met my first friend.

"I was walking moodily through our old orchard on a late summer day, and I came upon a boy gathering windfall apples from around the base of a tree. He looked at me, startled. We stood and stared at each other.

" 'Who are you?' I asked him.

" 'Piotr', he said.

" 'Why are you taking apples from my trees?' I demanded.

" 'My mother sent me to get them. My father is Stanislaus, your father's gardener.'

"I knew Stanislaus. I knew that the gardener didn't like me, because he had seen me do things of which he didn't approve. In addition, it was he who had been told to shoot my Arabian when it broke its leg.

" 'Is it allowed?' asked Stanislaus' son. He wasn't much older than I, a year or two at the most.

"I was so sorely tempted to shout *No!* at him, that these were *our* apples and he had no right to pick them without my mother's permission. I wanted to exercise my superiority over his father, but I was stopped by something in the boy's face. It was trust. It was as if he trusted that I would say yes, because that is what a good person would do, you see. Good people say *Yes.* Good people are generous. He had faith in me. He was projecting his heart upon the world, in much the same way I was projecting my own upon him. I expected him to be an unwanted parasite because I felt unwanted, unwanted by the whole world except by my lonely, affection-starved mother. I felt like a parasite. He expected me to be a kind master. But the truth of it is, he was the kind one.

"He moved like a young god in an arcadian paradise. He pulled a small golden ball off the tree and handed it to me with a glance of friendliness that was completely foreign to me. 'Here, take a bite. They're really sweet', he said.

"I hesitated. After all, they were my apples. But the gesture touched me so much that I accepted it gratefully. I took a bite. The fruit was sweet and highly flavored. To this day, I can taste that first rush of pleasure on my tongue. It will forever represent for me the taste of friendship.

" 'Sit down', the boy Piotr commanded me, not unkindly.

"I sat down beneath the tree, and he threw himself down on the grass beside me. He was tall and lithe, dressed in a heavy cotton tunic and baggy trousers. His hair was a sheet of gold, his eyes blue. His face was poised, clear, beautiful, and manly all at once.

" 'You see this?' he said opening a burlap sack. 'My mama's going to boil it down, and do you know what it will make?'

" 'No.'

" 'One jar of apple jelly.'

" 'That's not much.'

" 'We'll save it for Christmas dinner, to eat with the goose.'

" 'Why don't you boil more apples and get more jelly?'

" 'Because Mama said we're allowed only one sack of windfalls. The rest go to the count's—I mean your father's—cows. Oh, they'll get fat here!'

"I laughed, and he laughed too. It was a glorious feeling.

" 'Look,' he said, 'it's a hot day. Would you like to catch a fish with me?'

" 'Yes', I said, barely choking out the word.

" 'Come!'

"He jumped up and ran off toward the thicket of birches bordering the southern extremity of our estate. A river meandered through it, a cool deep run, full of sun-speckled shadows where fish lazed.

"Piotr threw in a string with a hook and slice of pork rind attached to it. In a minute, a brown carp was flopping on the bank. He put the string into my hand and showed me how to pitch the hook into the warm pools. The line sang in my fingers as it flew. The jerk and tug when a fish took it were delirious happiness. I shouted for joy when it tried to pull me into the water. Piotr bent double, roaring with laughter. Then, hand over hand, we pulled it in together. He left the final victory to me. I dragged the great golden carp out onto the shore and stood looking at it with amazement. I had had no idea that life contained such delights.

"We took the fish home to his mother, and I saw for the first time the house in which they lived. I had known that most people live in pitifully small accommodations, but it had been a theoretical knowledge. Here I was for the first time in a peasant's house. Piotr was the eldest of thirteen children, and so you can imagine the noise and activity in that place. Swarms of children came leaping and shouting round him. They hung on his arms. He was so good. You could see how his younger brothers and sisters loved him. He was like a little father to them. I envied them.

"His mother greeted me with a bow and a smile, and thanked me for the apples. When we presented the two fish to her she was very pleased, for combined they would easily make a meal for the entire family. This woman, I tell you, was one of the few genuine saints I have ever met. Her lot in life wasn't easy. Stanislaus was not an even-tempered man, but she managed him well. The house was full of icons and crucifixes, and noise and joy. There were fervent prayers before the meal. Yes, the little master was invited to stay. Never before or since have I tasted such a meal as that.

"Afterward, the parents and the thirteen children got down on their knees, lit a candle beneath a very primitive icon of the Mother of God of Częstochowa, and prayed the Rosary. I had prayed the Rosary in chapel, with the priest, and occasionally with visitors. But never like this. You felt a surge of religious energy, the marshaling of all religious powers of the soul. You heard the sounds of prayer penetrating heaven's gate and achieving a hearing at some far, far throne. It was then that I understood my wretched condition. I saw with stark clarity that these people were truly rich and I was a pauper. I made my excuses and ran home, where I received a scolding from the nanny for being absent and worrying the entire staff half to death. I slept well that night, after a brief visit to the chapel. I had intended to thank the Presence above the red light, thank Him for this extraordinary day, thank Him for giving me my friend Piotr. But the light was extinguished and the tabernacle door wide open. From boredom or fear, I never could tell which, Mama had chosen that very day to attempt a reform of our lives. She thought that a more social existence, less traditionally religious, more cosmopolitan, would restore me to what she called 'balance'.

"Throughout that fall and winter, Piotr and I frequently met in the woods and talked of many things. We hiked throughout my father's holdings as if they were Piotr's and I were the visitor. He pointed out to me the many species of tree on our land, and I learned their names from him. He taught me to make small toys from chestnuts. He strung me a longbow and cut arrows for me, and fledged them with feathers from pheasants. He listened patiently to my stories about ships and the adventures of abandoned boys. He laughed at my first feeble attempts at jokes. He clapped me on the back when I did things well; he grew quiet and turned our attention to other things when I failed. He was like a brother to me. Sometimes we prayed the Rosary together, walking along the snow path around the perimeter of our grounds. Prayer became very sweet to me, a companionable thing, a mystery shared. I came to love him as brothers love each other. I was happy.

"I recall the day when desire burst through the membrane that separates chaste love from lust. It was a spring day. The last of the snow had just disappeared. He was showing me the new bunnies produced by his rabbits. They were his own animals, a special project. Wire cages behind their cow shed contained two large, gray females, a mournful brown buck, and dozens of offspring. Flemish giants. It had been a harsh winter, and Piotr was running low on hay. I told him that we had hay to spare up at the main barn. Also, more carrots were buried in our sand-bins than we could hope to feed the horses. I asked him if he would like some for his rabbits. He agreed enthusiastically.

" 'Can Camilla and Ludmilla come with us?' he asked.

" 'Good idea! Maybe we'll see some greens on the way and they can nibble. Bring a sack for carrots.'

"It was one of those hot spring afternoons that come early in the season to melt the ice in the soul. After filling sacks with carrots and hay up at the main farm, we turned and retraced our steps. The large mother rabbits lay heavy and docile in our arms. We took a shortcut through the woods, crossed the footbridge that's over that way, and came upon a clearing on the other side. I hadn't ever been across. It was new to me and seemed a perfect sanctuary of light in the dark copse. It was sun-filled, and fresh grass was pushing up. We lay down in it and immediately the rabbits began to eat furiously. Piotr and I rested content in this pool of amber light and grew drowsy. We talked for a while, then I closed my eyes. I must have dozed for a long time, for when I awoke the light had shifted in the clearing. Afternoon was moving toward the evening. Still, it was quite warm. I saw that Piotr was stretched out alongside me, and in the heat he'd removed his boots and socks, and his shirt. One of the rabbits was grazing beside his legs, and he was holding the other in the crook of his muscled arm. He was kissing its ears, which twitched back and forth, back and forth. He was amusing himself by this game, and the rabbit seemed well content to indulge him.

"I watched them for a long time, and against my will, not understanding why it should be so, my heart began to beat like a hammer. Never had I seen such a perfect form of beauty. In this drowsy peace, in this exaltation of light, he looked like a form into which heaven had poured liquid gold. I stared at his face, so handsome and tender, so virtuous and oblivious. I must have swallowed hard, for he looked at me and whispered, 'Sshh, *bratko, dziecko.*' He called me *brother, little one.*

"It was as if light had become love itself. I could hardly

breathe. I reached up and touched his face with my fingers. He laughed and pushed my hand away. Mesmerized, I touched his lips with my fingers. He frowned.

"'Don't do that, *dziecko*', he said calmly and turned his attention back to Ludmilla.

"Heat coursed through my body, and my heart hammered even harder. My face felt as if it were in flames.

"'Can't I touch your face, Piotr? It's so nice.'

"'*Nie!*' he said firmly.

"'Please!'

"'Why do you want to touch my face?' he said, looking at me strangely.

"'I don't know.'

"He sat up and dressed himself in haste. He said nothing, but I was troubled by his frown. At the time I was too young to understand. Years later it came to me that he must have been suffering what the astoundingly beautiful often suffer. Their looks attract all eyes, but who sees them for themselves? Who cares if they have a self, isn't it so? Women put up with it all the time. But rarely is a man forced to endure this sort of humiliation. It's experienced particularly by men who are too handsome. Usually youths who don't know what to do with the emotion. That was Piotr's pain. He didn't like his own face; he considered his appearance unmanly. That it was causing problems for another *boy* was doubly distressing for him.

"As for myself, I wasn't in the least distressed. I was intoxicated, enamored, captivated, obsessed, rendered speechless with awe. It was worship."

He looked up at Father Elijah.

"Do I detect the preliminary stages of disgust upon your guarded visage?"

"I am merely trying to feel what you and your friend felt that day. Two very different emotions."

"Precisely. Which was the source of the trouble that was about to break loose like furies from hell."

"What happened next?"

"The brother I had so recently become disappeared, and the selfish little count rose up in me like a fiend. I would *not* be denied such pleasure. If I could not be held in the arms of sanctuary, then I would reach out to touch it. I would *take* it! It would be mine. It *was* mine.

" 'I want to feel your face', I said curtly.

" 'That's stupid. Don't!' Piotr said.

" 'You have to let me!' I insisted.

" 'I don't have to let you!' His voice rose, and I saw the first trace of fear in his eyes.

" 'Yes, you do. You work for us. You belong to us.'

" 'We work for you, but we don't belong to you.'

" 'You have to do what I say!' I yelled at him. Piotr looked at me as if I were mad. He had never seen me throw a fit. He just sat there and stared. As if possessed, I reached over and began to stroke his face. Suddenly, his eyes filled with tears and his mouth twisted in rage. He didn't hit me. He didn't curse me. He merely stared at me with a look of comprehension. If he had kicked me, I probably would have forgotten the whole incident soon after. Instead, he leapt to his feet. Without a word he scooped up Camilla and Ludmilla and strode off into the woods in the direction of his home. He didn't bother to take the sacks of hay and carrots.

"That night I twisted and turned on my bed, confused and terrified by what I had done. I thought of running down to his place before sunrise to take him the hay and the carrots, to ask his forgiveness. I considered it and rejected it. After all, I argued, he's our servant. Why should I beg for his favors? Why should I, who one day will be the count, be forced to grovel before a peasant who has sprung from a family of ignorant peasants? Slowly, as the hours ticked away, I gave into the urge to resent him for his beauty and his goodness. Above all, I hated him for his refusal to permit me to hold his glory in my hands, to possess him. My Piotr. Mine! Gradually, the resentment built and built in the darkness, surged and swam with a burst of sexual desire. Hatred, hurt, anger, and lust boiled together, seeking release.

"In the morning, it found release. I saw him coming across the field in the dawn, coming toward the house. I thought, *He's going to tell my mother.* I thought, *He's going to mock me and then I'll feel small and ugly. I'll feel a cursed thing. I'll be beneath him.* My hatred of him burst like an abscess, and I ran downstairs swiftly. The borzoi whined at the door. I took him outside but held tightly to his collar.

"Piotr stopped a few meters away. He was holding one of his big gray rabbits in his arms. He waved at me and grinned. 'Boleslaw, you feel better? You were crazy yesterday. But let's forget it. Today's another day, right? Let's go fishing!'

"I said nothing in reply. I stared at him with a hatred colder than death. Piotr quickly lost his smile. 'I'm sorry I didn't say good-bye yesterday', he said in a quavering voice. 'But, look, I thought maybe you'd like to hold Ludmilla. Maybe you'd like to stroke her. She likes it. If you want to, you can keep her.'

"For a moment I hesitated. His goodness washed over me like a wave, and it nearly broke my resistance, but I knew that if I gave in he would be above me again. He would be superior. *I am the count,* I said to myself. *Who is this peasant to play the prince!* Piotr stood waiting. I strode over, went up to him, and took Ludmilla by the scruff of the neck. I tore her from his arms and I hurled her onto the ground beneath the jaws of my dog. She landed with a thump and a squeal. The dog took one look and tore into her.

" 'Stop him!' cried Piotr.

"I said nothing. I folded my arms and watched as the borzoi tore the legs off Ludmilla and ripped the rest of her to pieces. She screamed, and it sounded like a baby in agony. That sound was a pleasure, a deep, delicious, black pleasure.

"I heard the sobs of Piotr. I observed his face twisted in horror and grief, and that too was a pleasure to me. He turned and ran away and never again came to the house. Did I feel remorse? Sadness? No, I felt fine. I felt a sense of mastery. I was *above*. I was lord of life and death. Granted, it was a small life, a small death. But it seemed to me that it was the first step in a long career that might one day lead to being above many things, many people, and that it might give me the power to rule over everything. I would never again feel small and ugly and unlovable."

Smokrev sat back with a smile. He reached over and lit another cigarette and began his cycle of puffing and coughing. When it was finished he said, "Time for intermission."

Elijah exhaled and could not raise his eyes from the floor.

Smokrev rang a bell. The manservant entered and placed a tray of coffee and biscuits beside the priest. He went out and returned shortly with a tray of medicine for the count.

"You are silent."

"The tale was not a comedy."

"Have I managed to shock you?"

"No."

"Why don't you look at me?"

"I am thinking."

"I can imagine your thoughts."

"I am thinking that a confused boy, gifted in so many ways, could have taken a different course in life, if he had had a little direction."

"Absolutely. You are coming close, close. Keep thinking. You will eventually arrive at the conclusion to which I am leading you."

"You cannot control everything."

"Yes, I learned that eventually. But I can rule rather a lot."

"You cannot capture men's thoughts."

"Those are the easiest things of all to capture."

"Not this man."

"We shall see."

Oh, God, he prayed interiorly, *grant me grace to stay with him, grant me strength to walk down with him into the pit of his soul. Help me, help me to resist him with love.*

"Tell me why, priest. Why didn't God stop me from becoming what I have become?"

"Shall we begin a dialogue on the nature of freedom?"

"Later, later. Just tell me why God didn't rescue me. Why didn't he rescue Ludmilla from me?"

"It is not God who is on trial here. It is Man. To be more precise, a man. You. Why didn't you stop yourself?"

"I couldn't."

"Is that true?"

"Aha!" Smokrev cried gleefully. "I have heated you up. There is anger in your voice."

"Do you want me to pretend that tearing a creature to pieces doesn't make me angry?"

Smokrev shrugged but said nothing.

"I am, in fact, angry at the forces that manipulated your life, that made your parents what they were, that tempted you, and into whose jaws you fell. That makes me angry."

"*Touché!*" whispered Smokrev, pensively. "I shall have to search hard for a riposte to that one. Well done!"

"This is not badinage, Count. This is life. This is the fate of your soul."

"Ah, yes, yes, yes. But let's get on with it. There is so much to tell you, and I have only begun."

"Tell me, first, did you ever approach your friend Piotr again? Did you ever ask forgiveness?"

"Yes, actually. Some fifty years later. But that is a boring incident."

"I am interested."

"All right then. Needless to say, I couldn't help loving Piotr even though I now hated him as well. He preoccupied my thoughts incessantly for years. I always held out the hope that he would one day come and beg for my forgiveness, would apologize for his rudeness. It wasn't to be, of course.

"When I was working for the communists, it struck me one day that I should drive out to our old holdings. They had passed into the hands of the state after the war, and I had always felt quite bitter about that. I hadn't seen the place since the nineteen-twenties, when I left for studies in Paris. It was as if I had been released from a cage. I felt such loathing for my birthplace that I hoped somehow it, and my parents along with it, could be burned or bombed without losing any of our capital. Believe me, I felt no nostalgia for the estate for the longest time. When I returned to Poland after the Germans arrived, I found it confiscated by the General Government and in the hands of Hans Frank. It was used as a watering hole for high-ranking administrators. After the War, the communists did the same thing with it. But my parents had been smart enough to liquidate some of our other land holdings before the invasion, and our savings were in gold, in Swiss banks. As a result, I have never suffered extreme want. But the invaders, one after another, inhabited the *palace.* In Paris, I developed the habit of calling my ancestral home a *palace.* It opened many doors. My mother was a Habsburg, you know, and if about thirty or forty people ahead of me in the line of succession had been wiped out, I would have become the crown prince of the Austro-Hungarian empire. However, that was demolished in 1919. By then I was at the Sorbonne studying decadent modernist literature. Nevertheless, my title was quite useful. It unlocked the doors of many palaces, studios, and bedrooms."

"You were telling me about meeting Piotr again. About forgiveness."

"Well, sometime during the Jaruzelski régime, when Solidarity was starting to make its nasty moves, and that Pope was pulling the foundations out from under everything, it struck me that the Soviet influence could very well be gone from Poland in short order. And I thought, what if the new régime decides to restore the old estates to their rightful owners? As it turned out, my chequered past had followed me; the government had peered into a rather fat dossier about me that had been put together by various governments. It decided that I was undeserving. But before it did so, I was possessed by a whim to see what remained of the old place.

"It was a half-day's drive. Going out there I felt a thrill of expectation such as I have rarely felt. But the *palace* turned out to be a disappointment. It seemed incongruously small compared to my memory of it. The grounds were well kept, but apparently the original lands had shrunk considerably. I wasn't permitted to enter the house because it was now a government retreat center, and high-level visitors were in conference there that day. Nevertheless, I went on a tour of the grounds. The orchard was gone. The barn was gone. There were several new farm buildings constructed of metal. The stone stables were still there. The woods were now a thick forest of enormous trees. But the river was unchanged. I walked the paths alongside the water for hours, but I couldn't find the bridge or the clearing. Later I drove to the village on the other side of the forest.

"It had become a large town. It had many stores and a discotheque. On the outskirts, I found the place where our former gardener had lived. The lot was empty. I asked a neighbor if he knew where I might find Piotr's family. 'You mean the baker!' said the neighbor. 'Sure, I know them. They used to live here before the War. Piotr's in town now. He runs the bakery.'

"On the main street, I discovered the Star of Mazovia Bakery. I went in feeling some trepidation. My driver kept the Daimler purring outside in case there were any scenes. The shop had a bistro attached to it. I sat and ordered coffee, prunes, poppy-seed cake, and a hot croissant.

"An enormously fat man brought it out and set it on the table. 'Here you are, sir', he said. 'Sorry for the delay. The kitchen boy's sick today. My grandson. A good lad but something of a lout. Lazy—like all the young generation.'

"Yes, that is what the apollonian youth had become. A baker. A large, jolly man, bald, wrinkled, red-cheeked, wearing a greasy apron. The eyes were almost perfectly preserved. They were—yes, after fifty years—they were still kind.

"I must have stared at him without answering, for he cocked his head at me curiously and said, 'Are you from around here, sir?'

" 'I grew up near here. I left in the twenties.'

"He could see clearly that I wasn't a peasant. When I told him my name, he scratched his head as if recalling a memory of the vaguest sort. 'Oh, yes, the count and his family. My papa used to garden for them. You weren't their boy, were you?'

"I nodded, unable to speak.

"He smiled. I couldn't believe it. He smiled.

" 'Now I remember. We used to go fishing, you and me!' He burst into a hearty laugh and thrust out his hand. We shook hands.

" 'Here we are, two old men!' he said. 'Who would believe it!'

"Then suddenly his face fell, and I thought I was in for trouble. 'I heard,' he said, 'I heard about your papa, the count. I remember when the Germans took him away. They killed him, didn't they?'

" 'Yes, they killed him.'

" 'So many things happen in a life. So many.' Piotr's eyes filled up with tears, and he wiped them with his dirty apron. 'My wife, she died last year. Cancer. God rest her soul.'

"Still I couldn't utter a word.

" 'Say, why don't you have supper here? It's almost closing time. I'll make you something nice. Do you like sausage? A sip of beer? We'll talk about what it was like before all the troubles, when we were boys. It was beautiful then, wasn't it? It was always summer. Do you remember the river, the fat carp, the bells ringing for Mass, the sound of wind in the poplars on autumn nights? Hey, you probably don't know this, but I almost was a priest. I went into the seminary in '28 and lasted a year. I wasn't cut out for it. I met my wife in '32 and apprenticed with Wajda the baker. He gave me this shop before he died.'

" 'How many children have you?' I managed to ask.

" 'Nine. Not as many as my mama and papa. But we're a fertile lot. Six married, one nun, two priests; one of them works with the bishop in Krakow. All of them happy. It's been a hard life but good.'

" 'You have much to be proud of.'

" '*Dziękuje!* Tell me, what do you do for a living?'

" 'I sell paintings and statues in Warsaw.'

" 'You like that?' "

" 'I like it.'

" 'A good life?'

" 'Yes.'

" 'I'm glad', he said.

"Then he looked into me with perfect penetration, and I realized that he remembered everything. He had all along. It was his nature to refrain from recrimination.

" 'Do you remember Camilla and Ludmilla?' I asked him.

" 'No', he said in a very quiet voice.

" 'I think you do remember.'

"He didn't answer me. Then, after a long pause he said: " 'I remember a little boy who was alone too much. I liked him. I always wondered what became of him.'

" 'You are good', I said.

" 'Who's good?!' he smiled. 'Nobody's good.'

" 'You forgave me.'

" 'Nothing to forgive, *dziecko*. Nothing to forgive.'

"His kindness was too much. I controlled myself, stood and thanked him for the tea, made polite excuses, and left.

" 'Come back some time', he said as I got into the Daimler. In a minute, I had roared out of town and I never returned.

XII

Another Confession

Smokrev shook himself and let out a long sigh. He looked up at Father Elijah.

"Had enough?"

"The tale is improving."

"Don't worry. It gets worse. If you hang on long enough, it gets really bad."

"It is late. I should leave you to rest."

"Why don't you stay for supper? Do you like sausage? A sip of beer? Why don't we talk about what it was like when we were boys, before all the troubles? It was beautiful then, remember? It was always summer."

Elijah could not ignore the faintest note of pleading beneath the irony.

"If you wish."

After supper, the nurse drew back the curtains of the bedroom window and turned down the lights. Only the bedside lamp remained aglow. Elijah went to the window and looked out at the river. The lights of the eastern shore were scattered brightly along the edge of the water. A tourist boat went past, trailing dance music and raucous laughter.

"Why are you here in Warsaw, priest from Israel? Really, why?"

"I am here to attend a conference on culture."

"I heard of it. It's big. The President of the Europarliament is speaking at it."

"His opening address is tomorrow night."

"I will watch it on television, then we can discuss it the following day."

"I am afraid that is not possible. I must leave for Rome the day after his address."

"Then this is our final meeting. I have only a few hours left in which to refute your defense of God?! It's not fair! I have amassed an enormous indictment against Him. You can't get away so easily."

"A few hours? How can I possibly justify the ways of God in so short a time?"

"It needn't take long. I have arguments to make which I believe are irrefutable. If they can be refuted, why not simply?"

"You have a point. But some answers are so simple, so true, that modern men like you and me have a difficult time grasping them."

"I will try very hard."

"Will you? Then let us attempt the impossible."

"Be seated, please."

Elijah once again took up his position on the easy chair.

"And so, the continuing epic of Boleslaw Smokrev, late of the aristocracy, late of the fascists, late of the Nazis, late of the Soviets, late of the international trade marts. Late of the intelligence community of several nations, not least of which is the Americans."

"You were an agent?"

"I was an agent. Among my many masquerades and pompous acts, this was one of the authentic ones. I was in the Allied sector of Berlin when Germany was crushed. US Army Intelligence tracked me down and convinced me to get over into the Russian sector and then back to Poland. There, for the latter half of my life, I proved quite useful to them. The CIA kept me in the style to which I was accustomed."

"Then you are a patriot, after all."

"Oh, I was useful to everyone, most of all to myself. A typical wastrel, I had squandered the bulk of the family inheritance just before the War. As a result, I was in reduced straights and forced to buy and sell people. I traded in human flesh. Political flesh, not sexual. Oh, well, there was some of that too. As a literary critic, I made and broke several writers' reputations. Careers. Relationships. I created and destroyed. It became my major art form. Between 1927 and 1989, I was always an international culture broker of one kind or another. I was at home in Paris, Berlin, London, Rome, Washington, Moscow—with a brief respite between '39 and '45. During the occupation, I was a consultant to the Reich Culture Chamber in Poland as well, and I had come to know many useful things. Later, after the War, I made myself most useful to the Polish communists and to the Russians. It became my task to assist in the negotiations for the return of the art treasures of Europe that Goering and the Einsatzstab Rosenberg had plundered. And on the side I made a fortune in black-market diamonds, state secrets, and art. Only the traffic in art remains to me now. But, of course, my energy is limited. I am old", he concluded, striking a match below the tip of a cigarette.

Elijah sat quietly, sorting order out of these references.

"Are you trying to convince me that you are a bad man?"

"Not at all!" protested Smokrev. "I am *proud* of these accomplishments! I'm merely setting the stage. It's all theatrics."

"Go on. I anticipate the comedy or the tragedy with great expectations."

"Tsk, tsk, tsk, that borders on sarcasm—so unbecoming in a minister of God."

"It was a weak attempt at irony, Count."

"I like you. I like your mind. You are honest. Deluded, but honest."

"You were going to tell me your arguments against God."

"That is precisely what I have been doing. And there is more—much, much more. I haven't even begun to test your resistance to shock."

"I will listen, but only on one condition. I do not want you to embellish your tales. I want you to tell me in clear language what you wish to say. Please do not make yourself out to be a monster. You cannot shock me. You cannot make me despise you."

"Really? How very extraordinary. You will be the first to survive that test."

"I am a priest of Christ. There is no need for me to pass your tests. Whether or not I pass or fail is beside the point. God is not on trial."

"Ah, but He is."

"No. Man is on trial."

Smokrev cackled: "I have the indictment prepared. He cannot get off that easily."

"I must go, then", said Elijah rising. "You are playing games. You cannot toy with God."

"All right, all right", said Smokrev, condescending, waving Elijah back into the chair. "You are so touchy. I was having a little fun."

"Life is short. My time is short as well. I give you what I have, but I ask you not to waste it."

"You are so *gravissimo!* All right, I agree."

"Then proceed. What do you wish to tell me?"

"I am undecided about my approach. Should I state the philosophical problem first and illustrate it with certain pungent details from my life? Or, alternatively, should we just slog through the chronology of my wasted years, recounting every single one of my unmentionable crimes? Which would best suit your temperament?"

"The first approach."

"You don't enjoy cheap opera?"

"No. It is self-indulgence."

"But in a sacramental confession I am forced to submit an itemized list? Isn't there a contradiction here?"

"No. In a sacramental confession, the penitent names his offenses because it is a way of taking responsibility for them before God and before man. He says, *I am a sinner. This is what I have done. I blame no one but myself. I ask to be pardoned and healed. I need a Savior.*"

"Hmmm. I have always suspected that it was intended more to shame the penitent into never repeating his folly."

Elijah shook his head. "That is what so many misunderstand. A priest of Christ knows that he is a man like other men. He too could commit the sins told to him through that screen. He stands there as a sign of contradiction set down in creation. A sign of mercy and truth. The truth sets us free, and mercy heals us. He stands as a living presence of Christ before men, and in the place of men before Christ."

"I have confessed countless times. It did no good in my case. A half-century ago I gave up."

"What might you have become if you had persisted!"

"Such a dreary custom! It became too humiliating."

"Why?"

"Some of those things I had to tell were unthinkable. Ludmilla was the first of many, you see, nor was she the only species. During the War, there were human victims as well."

Elijah's heart began to beat faster. He prayed silently for detachment from his emotions.

"Places like Treblinka, Oświęcim, Belzec—they were an inexhaustible treasure house."

Clearing his throat, Elijah interjected, "You have underlined my point. If you had persisted in the sacraments as a young man, would you not have been strengthened to resist such temptations?"

"That is academic now. It happened", he shrugged. "That is the way it was in those days. Hundreds of thousands of people destined for burning. Trash. Human waste, already erased by the state. No future, no hope. No rescue. No savior. No God. No nothing. They were already dead, even though they continued to walk around for a few miserable weeks or months or years. There were so many, many beautiful young people. I kept a stable-full."

Elijah looked down at his hands.

"Ah, the preliminary symptoms of distress. Some revulsion, perhaps? A certain loathing? Perhaps a note of hatred creeping into the heart of this priest of Christ?"

"I feel grief. Does that surprise you?"

"Entirely predictable. But do tell me, why shouldn't I have seized what was my passion, the very things that had been denied me and were spread out before me like a banquet?"

"Because you didn't own them. Because they were human beings. A man's body is his own."

"Dead souls. Characters from Gogol. Statistics. Geopolitical pawns."

"And there, Count, is the crux of our problem—precisely there."

"What do you mean?"

"Every sin is a choice to turn a miraculous being into an object for consumption. It flattens the human person, one's self and one's victim, into a one-dimensional universe."

"No, priest, that is not where the crux of the problem lies. The crux is this: Why, when man crushes his victim, is there only silence from heaven? Why did God not save me from myself, and my victims from me? Answer!"

"He will never negate your free will."

"Not even to stop me negating the free will of millions? But that is absurd."

"You are free. That is the fundamental structure of the universe."

"Ah, the problem of freedom."

"Are we equipped for this discussion? Do you undertake it seriously?"

"I will try", he said, waving his hand.

"Heaven is not silent."

"Heaven is not silent? Do you know that millions of victims were pleading with Heaven as they fell into the flames? What was the cry on their tongues, I ask you? It was this: *Where are you? Where are you, Savior of the world?* And we the powerful, we the killers and the despoilers and corruptors of the innocent? What cry was on our lips? I will tell you: *Where are you? Where are you, Savior of the world?* That taunt was on my lips as I did the things which are too unthinkable to tell even you, extraordinary priest that you are."

"Heaven was not silent."

"Ha!"

"What did you want God to do? Did you want Him to tear open the sky like a theatrical backdrop and step through? Did you want Him to send an army of angels into creation, with orders from headquarters: *Kill the bad ones! Save the good ones!* Did you expect a voice to come booming out of the clouds saying, *Stop that!* Did you expect Him to press a button and the entire cosmos would grind to a halt while the master mechanic stepped into the innards of His machine and tinkered with a broken part? Is that what you think the universe is?"

Smokrev suppressed a chuckle of glee.

"It's wonderful to see you so worked up."

"Do not sidestep this question. It is central. Heaven was not silent."

"I will never accept that. I heard no voices."

"Where were you when the papal encyclicals condemning National Socialism were read from every pulpit? Where were you when many mystics and visionaries were crying warnings? For a hundred years the people of Europe were warned. They were continuously called to repentance in preparation for a terrible outrage that was approaching. Did you heed the passages in the Scriptures which speak of our times? Did you read the words of the wise? What literature were you reading in the thirties? Many great Christian and Jewish writers saw it coming. But who listened?"

"If few listened, why didn't God speak louder?"

"What could be louder than the fact that His own Son died in agony beneath a silent sky?"

"That was a long time ago."

"Was it so long ago? We are old, Count. Wasn't it just yesterday that you walked with your friend Piotr in the forest? Wasn't it just yesterday that you destroyed the beloved creature that he held in his arms? How swiftly the years have passed."

"You are evading the central problem: Why, in the first place, does God permit it?"

"The answer to that question is another: Why has He created a universe in which there is freedom?"

"I don't know. It seems an inefficient way to run a universe."

"You are right, if the universe is just a mechanism running down. What if it is something else?"

"Like what?"

"A creative universe. A place where beauty was made to increase and multiply unceasingly, where unique beings love one another and create ever more life. Always different, ever revealing new vistas of joy."

"He could have had that without the dark part."

"Could he have prevented the possibility of evil without turning every living thing into a puppet, a mere part in a clockwork?"

"You are evading again."

"No. I am focusing on the core of the problem. You refuse to see it, because you cannot admit that it is the core. You want the darkness to be the core."

"And if I do, isn't that an argument in my favor? Doesn't it tell you that if one soul like me dwells in darkness, it negates this glorious fantasy of a lovely creation that you cling to so obstinately in your imagination?"

"Beware of that theological nuance. It is a powerful deception. Should a soul who has chosen to reject the light be permitted to annihilate the laws sustaining those who have chosen to follow the light? If so, that would be like handing everything over to a terrorist. Should he be permitted to hold the entire universe hostage? One act of evil, and he forces the laws of creation to crumble into dust? I ask you, is that an efficient way to run a universe?"

"*Touché.*"

"The problem is not only one act of evil, but many such acts. Let us say, six million Jews and six million Gentile Poles, and tens of millions of others. That is just the Second World War. Let us say that our cosmic terrorist pushes harder and harder against the integrity of God. Let us say he uses a Stalin—now we are considering perhaps fifty million, some say sixty million people, dead at the hands of this one tyrant. Should God destroy the moral structure of the universe in order to save the physical universe? That would be a superficial defense and an ultimate self-defeat. Should He give in because of the quantity of the victims?"

"You are overstating the situation. I don't see what you mean."

"It is something like this. Satan holds the chosen people hostage. He holds a gun to their heads and he says to God, *Well, aren't you going to do something! Aren't you going stop me! Aren't you going to break one of your own insignificant laws to save your darlings?* God replies, *I will not break the laws I have written into creation, for that would bring about a different kind of destruction for my beloved ones.* Satan answers, *All right, watch this!* He squeezes and crushes and rips with his jaws until the chosen ones begin to cry out to their Creator, *Save us! Where are You? Why do You not come?* Satan looks at God and says, *Well?* But God is silent. He is so silent that a darkness seems to spread over the world. Satan believes he has forced God to back up. He has argued Him into helplessness. He thinks that God has nothing left to say. He thinks he has won the cosmic debate and has obtained power *over* God. He thinks himself *above* God. But all the while a tremendous thing is happening within the heart of God. A Word begins to form. A Word that is so immense, so much larger than the entire created universe, which rests like a golden apple in His hand. This word is so vast, yet so simple, that none can hear it. Satan *will* not hear it. Man *can* not, for he has been deafened with the screams of his own agony. Matter itself can only feel it without knowing it.

"*I will go down into my own creation as once I did so long ago, when I walked with Adam and Eve in the garden. As I did when I came to Jerusalem as a man. I will go down into my creation and I will suffer in it. I will suffer with it. And this shall be My Word, as once it was My Word on Calvary.*"

"Theology again?"

"This is His reply, but it is so powerful that ears cannot hear it. Only the soul can hear it."

"I don't hear it", said Smokrev moodily.

"You are deafened by screams of agony."

"You are wrong. You may have noticed that I evaded every form of incarceration that Europe has offered since the turn of the century. I deserved all of them, mind you. But I am not a victim."

"You are a victimizer. And a victim."

"I hear no screams."

"You are deaf."

"I hear no word spoken within creation, no messengers from your silent God."

"You don't see them? You don't hear them?"

"No. Nothing. Come, come, we are bandying words here. Let us get back to my original question. The objective reality here is that there was no rescue."

"What do you mean by rescue? Escape from a concentration camp? A long life? In the larger scheme of things, it may be that the victim who goes to his death uncorrupted by hatred is the one truly rescued."

"So you just let the bad go on doing bad? You won't fight evil? You don't stop me?"

"We must do whatever is possible without going beyond the boundaries of the divine principles. We cannot take up the weapons of evil in order to defeat evil. To do so, even in the defense of good, would be to be doubly defeated. I believe that is Satan's ultimate objective. Why would a fallen angel want to kill six million, or sixty or a hundred million, or even the whole human race? What would that prove? That he is bad? He already knows that, and God knows it too. No, the prize he is after is no less than to seduce all mankind into his rebellion. And to do it in the name of the good. That would be his masterstroke."

"Well, well, well, you do attribute a great deal of perspicacity to this cosmic bogeyman. It saves a lot of soul-searching, doesn't it? Blame him. The devil made me do it."

"In a sense he did. He tempted. You chose. You believed his interpretation of the universe."

"Frankly, considering the state of humanity, I think his version is the more accurate one. You Catholics build castles in the air — then you try to live in them. As if you were all aristocrats."

"Count Smokrev, we are all sons and daughters of a King. Each one of us."

"You cannot have it both ways. You are mixing metaphors. You said this God has come into creation and suffers with us, and in us. Now you say he is a king. Kings rule. Kings live in castles. Kings establish order in their kingdoms. You are deluded. There is no king."

"Our King suffers with us. He suffers in us. When His Kingdom is established in its fullness, our love for Him will surpass that for any earthly king, because He has suffered everything that His poorest children have suffered. And suffered by choice, where we have suffered unwillingly."

"Let's have a break. I feel suffocated. Theology, literature, myth, metaphor! It's too much for this old brain. All I have is what I have seen and what I have done. It's not pretty. But it's my universe."

He rang for the manservant, who brought a tray of coffee and small cakes.

They drank and ate in silence.

After consumption of a cigarette and more coughing, Smokrev lay back and smiled to himself.

"I am really enjoying this. The thrill of the courtroom, the clash of swords, the sting of minor philosophical setbacks, that special gloating feeling when I push you into a corner."

"I don't think you have done that as yet."

"I shall."

"You mentioned the clash of swords. I think you will agree, then, that we are in a war zone."

"But of course!"

"Good. You admit that."

"Yes!" Smokrev replied with irritation.

"Why does man insist on trying to make his utopia in the midst of a battleground?"

Smokrev shrugged: "The battle ebbs and flows. Some die. Some survive. I want to survive."

"You would do anything to survive?"

"I have already done everything and anything to survive. I have survived."

"Do you agree that a battlefield is a poor place to make a utopia?"

"All right, for the sake of argument, I agree. It's not the greatest place."

"Would you follow Someone who has died in your place on the battlefield, has been mysteriously brought back to life, and now offers you a real Paradise?"

"It depends on the cost. A temporary utopia in the hand is better than a fairy-tale paradise in the clouds."

"That is the crux of our problem."

"So? We are agreed on that."

"Suppose this Man who has come back from the dead is the most good and beautiful person you have ever met. He has given His life for you."

"I haven't met him."

"You have met Him. As a child. In the night."

"Childhood! Ha!"

"He reaches out His hand and He says, come with me. I know the way back from the dead. And I know another thing, the greatest thing. I know the way to the land where there is no more death."

"I would say he is a fool and a dreamer, and however attractive he may be personally, I would not risk my life following him."

"You would prefer to risk your life dodging bullets and missiles."

"Listen, listen, listen," said Smokrev waving the image away, "this is theoretical. The validity of your argument is founded upon the presumption that this man exists and he is what he says he is. I tell you, in my entire life I have never met a man who is what he says he is or what he appears to be."

"I have met many."

"Then you are a fool and a dreamer."

"No. This Man has been tested. Countless souls have followed Him to Paradise."

"An illusion produced by fevered brains searching desperately for hope. Everything is illusion."

"It is clear that you trust nothing and no one."

"A perfectly accurate assessment. You are no mean psychologist."

"Let us say, for the sake of argument, that this Man who has come back from the dead reaches His hand out to you and says, *Come!*"

"I would laugh at him. What right has he to command me?"

"He offers you life. The landscape is confused and dangerous, a minefield full of contradictory signs. Obey Him and He will lead you to safety."

"Why should I trust him? Why should I serve him?"

"Because He first served you. He gave you His life."

"I serve no one."

"Yet you are a slave to many things."

"What do you mean?" he snapped.

"You are enslaved to your appetites and your fear. You are addicted to many things."

"So, you are like all the rest. You just came here to accuse me!"

"I know my own heart. I know what a fallen man is, because I am one. I know that if I had been born into your circumstances, I might have become worse than you. Given the circumstances of my life, you might have been a better man than I. That is beside the point. What I ask you to consider is this: no one escapes serving. We are all creatures. We exist in a hierarchical cosmos with a King reigning at its head."

"I live in a democracy."

"When it suited your purpose, you served a tyranny."

"I used them. I used them all."

"Did you think you were above them when you served them?"

"I was above them. I create, remember. I create my realities. I created the impression of servitude in the mind of those who thought they were my masters, when all the while it was I who mastered them."

"Does the double agent ever really own himself? Isn't he owned by two masters, and in your case, many masters? Wasn't it they who allowed you the illusion of being in charge?"

"If that were so—I don't admit it, but if it were so—we used each other. Everyone does it. We all use each other."

"You call that a democracy?"

Smokrev shrugged, "Yes."

"The monarchy in which I live has a King at its head. But what a King! A King who died for me. He reigns with His heart split open. Oceans of blood pour from His wounds, century after century. This is a King of such nobility that Love is too small a name for Him."

"You wax poetic", muttered Smokrev. "Stop it. I hate sentimentality."

"So do I."

"What's that drivel, then?"

"The words of a lover speaking of his Beloved."

"Beloved, beloved! Ha! To hell with castles and fairies!"

"He is real. I have seen Him. I have felt His embrace. I have touched His Blood to my own lips."

"I cannot abide cannibalism, though I have dabbled in it, merely from curiosity, mind you, not as a habit. There were rituals I attended in London that . . ."

"Please, Count Smokrev, listen to me. You combat every word of truth with a twist, a sneer, a lie. Why do you do it? Why?"

"Because I will not serve."

"But He is real!"

"What if he is real! That makes it worse. Why didn't he rescue me? Why didn't he let me touch him, see him? Why was I so alone all my life? If he is real, why so?"

"You were a child who demanded that everyone should serve you. When they would not serve you, you attempted to control them by throwing tantrums. When that did not work, you seized power. When power would not give you love, you destroyed. Can you not stand outside of yourself for a moment and look in? Can you not see?"

"You just want to make me despise myself as much as you despise me."

"The truth is quite the reverse. I do not despise you. You despise yourself far more than I ever could."

"Stop!" screeched Smokrev.

His eyes and lips twisted horribly. He lit another of his Russian cigarettes with a trembling hand.

"This has gone far enough, priest. You are playing games with my mind."

"That is not what I am doing."

"What *are* you doing to me? What are you?"

"I am a messenger from the Beloved. He says to you, *Come!*"

"Do not paint your fantasy murals in my mind. I have had enough of this. I need rest. It's time for you to go."

Elijah stared at him for several seconds, exhaled, and stood up slowly.

"I am sorry. I have offended you."

"Not in the least", said the count in a strained voice.

"I ask your pardon. I have been too blunt."

"It's all right. It's all right", said Smokrev, calming himself. "I appreciate bluntness in a man."

"I will go. I won't bother you again."

"Sit down."

"Really, I . . . "

"Sit down", he commanded.

"Do you think we should go on any longer? Perhaps it is futile after all. We are throwing words back and forth at each other. And neither of us accepts the objective reality of the other's belief."

"So passes a pleasant evening", he said dryly. "I would be watching sumo wrestling on television if it weren't for you. But I can watch that any time."

He rang a handbell on the bedside table. The manservant entered.

"Where's my medicine? It's after nine o'clock."

"But sir, you told me not to disturb you while the visitor is . . . "

"Yes, yes. Well, I didn't mean it should go as far as this, that I should miss my medicine."

The manservant went out and returned immediately with a tray. He sat on the edge of the bed, rolled up Smokrev's sleeve, talked to him in baby talk, and injected him with a hypodermic needle. Then, the manservant tucked the old man in like an infant and departed.

"Disgusting, isn't it?"

Elijah shook his head.

"So, the messenger has become a mute."

"What good are words if the messenger has no credibility?"

"You are gambling that at least some of your words will slip through a crack in my armor and wreak havoc with my self-delusions. You are investing your time in a hopeless cause, because it will provide you with some sentimental melancholic pleasure years and years hence, when I am buried. You will suck on your defeat like a rotten candy. You will offer it up to your God."

"You project a great deal of yourself onto the world."

"I am a realist."

"What is a realist by your definition?"

"He is neither an optimist nor a pessimist."

"I agree. A realist is neither an optimist nor a pessimist. He has the courage to look into the abyss of a very dark century and see it for what it is. He sees the victory of light."

"Don't misunderstand me. My realist knows that power shapes the world. He knows that pleasure motivates it. In my ninety some years I have seen nothing that contradicts this."

"I have seen an endless stream of events that contradict this."

"Why should I believe you?"

"Am I not myself, this objective flesh, this presence seated before you, a kind of word?"

"A dream-word that stumbled into my house by accident. It's a meaningless incident, but amusing."

"A few minutes ago you didn't seem so amused. Did I touch a nerve? If so, what does that nerve say to you about objective reality?"

"What do you mean?"

"You suffered extreme pain when I mentioned the fact that you do not love yourself."

Smokrev's face soured.

"If it means anything, it means that I am a realist. Nothing more, nothing less."

"I think it means that in every person's soul there is an icon of what he is meant to be. An image of Love is hidden there. Each soul is beloved beyond imagining. Each soul is beautiful in the eyes of God. Our sins and faults, and those committed against us, bury this original image. We can no longer see ourselves as we really are."

"Proceed. I'm listening. I can see the turrets and towers rising in the rosy clouds."

"When I touched the place within you where you suffer, when I touched the damage, you felt the agony of the lost image. It was unbearable and you told me to stop."

Smokrev stared out the window at the lights of the east shore of the river.

"You won't let yourself believe what I am trying to tell you because you are afraid the pain of the lost image would be too much for you to bear."

"Then what hope is there for a man like me?"

"Limitless hope! You needn't bear the pain alone."

"This man on the battlefield who died and came back from the dead. What does he have to say about all that?"

"He has much to say."

"Why doesn't he come and tell me, if I'm his beloved?" Smokrev smiled sardonically and flicked the embers of his cigarette into the bedside ashtray.

"He has come to you countless times. But you would not listen. Now, as your life closes, He is sending a human messenger to you. One whom you can see and hear."

"What does this messenger have to say then, eh?"

Elijah felt a surge of interior light.

"He says, O soul steeped in darkness, do not despair. All is not yet lost. Come to the heart of your God who is love and mercy."

Smokrev's face wrapped itself in its shadows.

"My son, My little one, listen to the voice of one who loves you."

"Love?" said Smokrev, snorting.

"An everlasting love. An indestructible love."

"For me there is no love, no mercy, no peace."

"Do not let yourself fall into a deeper darkness. Listen to me. Despair is a foretaste of hell. Do not cling to it. This is your rotten candy, your drug. Throw it off!"

"I will not serve."

"He is calling to you. But if you persist in blindness and hardness, what can He do? He will not violate your freedom. Love does not force itself upon you. Listen to Him. He is pouring out a final grace upon you. Open your heart to it. It is a special light by which you can see God's effort for you. But conversion depends on your own will. This is your final grace. You know it. You know it."

"I know nothing."

"He is mercy. There is nothing that cannot be forgiven."

"And you are the messenger of this point of doctrine?"

"For better or for worse I am. I have been sent to you."

"You have brought yourself to me. You are a sentimentalist."

"This is not sentiment. It is life and death."

"You are a romantic. Look over there, on the wall above my *écritoire*. What do you see?"

"An icon."

"Go over there and look at it. Tell me what you see."

"I see a Byzantine image of Saint Michael of the Apocalypse."

"Describe it to me."

"It is a famous prototype of the defeat of Satan. Michael is seated on a horse. He holds the book of the sacred Scriptures in one hand and with that hand he also holds a trumpet, which he is blowing. In his other hand, he holds a spear, which is also the cross. He is thrusting it into Satan, who, in the form of a serpent has coiled himself around the cities of the world."

"Mercy extends only so far", said Smokrev.

"He too would not serve. His revolt is eternal."

"Is there no mercy for him? I have always felt that Lucifer was unjustly maligned."

"That is absurd."

"He is a myth. He is a symbol of our dark side."

"Satan is real."

"If so, why not extend a little mercy in his direction? Why is that big bully archangel making Lucifer writhe like an eel on a spear."

"To stop him. Didn't you demand of God, earlier this evening, that He make an end to evil? You cannot have it both ways."

Smokrev huffed but said nothing.

"God's mercy for mankind is limitless," Elijah continued, "but He will not permit evil to go on devouring the good forever. That would not be mercy."

Smokrev sat himself up in bed. He seemed to have been struck by an inspiration.

"I have saved the best for last, priest. My confession is not yet complete. You won't like this part."

"You can no longer shake me."

"Nothing can shake you?"

"I do not think so."

"You, the messenger of mercy, you promise? Nothing will dislodge you from your merciful stance?"

"I am a human being. I am flawed like you. If you should succeed in dislodging me from confidence in the mercy of God, it proves only that I am a creature. Only God is perfect mercy. I am merely His messenger to you."

"We shall see."

Elijah looked at him quizzically. Smokrev seemed genuinely delighted.

"You see that icon of the Apocalypse?"

"Yes."

"I purchased it from Pawel Tarnowski during the war."

Startled, Elijah said, "You knew him!"

"Oh, yes, I *knew* him. I knew him very well."

"You lied to me."

"Illusions, smoke, mirrors. Part of the act."

"Why did you lie to me?"

"I foresaw the debate, old boy. I knew the height and depth of this great argument. I knew you would put forth a defense of God."

"Why didn't you tell me?" he insisted, a constriction in his throat.

"I am the master of this debate. Not you, messenger. Not anyone!"

After a silence, Elijah asked in a trembling voice, "Do you know what happened to him?"

"Not so fast. I will tell you later. First, let me say that I have saved this bit of information until the end because it is the masterstroke of my case. You shall prove my case for me."

"Where is Pawel Tarnowski?"

"He is dead."

"Of that I was almost certain. But I had hoped . . . "

"Why is he so important to you?"

"He risked his life for me. In the end it cost him his life."

"He was a benefactor?"

"Yes, he was my friend."

"A companion?"

"Like an older brother to me."

Smokrev cackled.

"How perfectly delicious! That sly Tarnowski always did have a knack for seducing the prettiest boys."

"What are you saying?"

"You know exactly what I'm saying."

"I do not."

"He was a *tapette,* every bit as wicked as me. I knew him in Paris in the thirties when he was a ne'er-do-well painter, living like a parasite off rich old lechers. He broke quite a few hearts there, you know. And he enjoyed every minute of it. He sucked his benefactors dry and then threw them away."

"That is not the man I knew. He was good."

"He was not good. He was a maggot, just like I am a maggot."

Before Elijah was able to stop him, Smokrev supplied several more details about the career of the notorious and corrupt Pawel Tarnowski.

"I know it is a lie. I knew the soul of this man."

"It is not a lie. You refuse to see what we really are. Man is a besotted, vicious animal who preys on the weak. You cannot face this fact. You want your rosy castle. I too am a messenger. I bear you tidings from *reality!*"

"This is not real", said Elijah, but he failed to bring his voice under control; his throat ached.

"You know it is true. Didn't he take you into his bed? What a pleasure it would have been to observe that. An orthodox Jew boy, as beautiful as you were, a young David plucked from the shepherd's field, laid out, and despoiled on an old satyr's bed."

"Stop!" cried Elijah.

Smokrev cackled hysterically, then went on, vomiting descriptions, names, places, details of the corruption. Elijah shouted, interrupting the flow of filth.

"He did nothing to me!"

"I don't believe you."

"Not once in my life have I felt a flicker of desire for what you are suggesting. Nor did I ever see anything of the sort in Pawel."

"Let us say, for the sake of conjecture, for some bizarre reason that I cannot fathom—impotence perhaps—he refrained from consuming you as he had consumed so many others. If that is indeed the case, it was not for lack of wanting you. He craved you like a pig craves rotten apples. He told me so."

The two men stared at each other. For several minutes neither of them spoke. Smokrev lit another cigarette and lay back smiling to himself. Elijah sat as if stunned. His head reeled, his stomach churned with nausea, and he felt like weeping. An invisible darkness seemed to suck all air from the room. He felt a flush of terror and disorientation. He wished to leap up and flee.

"I rest my case", whispered Smokrev, his eyes closed, smiling and smoking, smiling and smoking.

Resist him, said the voice.

I cannot, Elijah said to himself. I cannot bear it.

As if to seal Elijah's defeat absolutely, Smokrev said, "I killed Pawel Tarnowski."

"You?"

"Of course! It was I who sent him off to the gas chamber. I tried to buy you from him, but he wanted too much money, the pimp. When I refused, he hit me with a cane. So I gave him what he deserved, a meeting with the SS."

"You were *the bent one.*"

"The what?"

"He told me about you."

"Did he? He told me about you too. In fact I saw you. I can still remember that gangly, half-starved *shtetl* boy with fringes dangling beneath his coat. Your jet black hair, skin as white as alabaster, lips like the flesh of cherries! Sublime."

Elijah looked away.

"So lean and waiflike and hauntingly gorgeous. David."

"How do you know my name?"

"He told me. Your keeper."

Elijah's heart gave way to a sickening rage. He wished to stride over to the bed and slap the man. He wished to find within himself a word or words that would utterly demolish the old dragon's pride. But there were no such words within him. Only a cloying sense of decay. He felt the entire structure of the universe slide sideways, then pitch in a long, slow collapse into the abyss, which in the end would suck down everything.

He held himself in check and did not move for many minutes. He had no strength. He was trapped in utter powerlessness. Love was indeed a dream that fled at the first cold blasts of reality. As love died, he felt terror rising. Smokrev watched him closely, as a scientist might observe a specimen dying under a glass.

"You have two choices", said Smokrev. His tone was relaxed and pleasant. "You can run from this room as fast as you can and never look back. But know that we will chase you to the ends of the earth, and there we will eat you alive. The other choice—well, you can do what your emotions prompt you to do—come over here and put your fingers around my neck and choke the life out of me. That's what you want."

Elijah said nothing.

"Then you will be master", prompted Smokrev.

Elijah stood up, his face an expressionless mask over a pool of agony. He took a step toward the bed.

"Good, good", whispered Smokrev, his eyes slitted, his mouth grinning, exposing yellow, gold-filled teeth.

Elijah knelt down beside the bed and reached his hands up to Smokrev's head.

"Do it now. End my wretched existence."

He took Smokrev's face in his hands, and he kissed him on one cheek, then the other. Deep sighs rushed from the priest's mouth and tears streamed from his eyes. The tears fell on Smokrev's forehead. The old man pulled back in horror.

"Get away from me!" he hissed.

"Can I touch your face?"

"Get away. You are not my Judas", he screeched.

"No. I am not your Judas."

"You think you can just go around kissing people! This isn't real! This isn't real!"

Smokrev's eyes were terrified. He pushed the priest away.

Elijah reached out and touched his face. "Shhh, *dziecko.*"

"Why do you want to touch my face?" Smokrev screamed hoarsely.

"Because I love you."

The darkness fled outward to the farthest corners of the room. Elijah closed his eyes, and he saw an interior image of a small boy in a golden crib. The child was crying in the night. He screamed but no one came.

Smokrev began to shake violently. Elijah put his arms around him and drew him in. He was amazed at the smallness and frailty of this fierce creature convulsing in his arms.

The old man gave a dry retch. A long, pinched wail burst from him. Then a sustained screech that was just above the level of sound, a sound so ugly that Elijah winced and turned his head away from the mouth. When it was finished, he looked again at the face resting against his chest. Smokrev was sweating heavily, trembling. The eyes were closed. The face exhausted. It resembled the expression of a runner who has fallen to the ground at the finish line.

The spotted, clawlike hands gripped his arms. Then Smokrev began to sob. He cried for such a long time that Elijah ceased to think or to note the passage of the night.

Eventually, the old man's snores informed him that the worst was now passed. He lay Smokrev down against the pillows and pulled the satin blanket up over his shoulders. He removed a brass tube from his pocket, opened it, and wetted his fingers with the oils it contained. He blessed Smokrev's forehead with the sign of the cross, anointed the palms of his hands and the base of his feet. He prayed over the man, asking for deliverance. When he did so, Smokrev twitched and muttered, then appeared to subside into a deeper sleep.

The nurse, in slippers and nightgown, clutching her throat, met him at the door. She looked worried.

"I heard some awful noises", she whispered. "Is the count all right? Does he need me?"

"He is asleep."

"What happened to him? He usually needs his drugs in order to sleep."

"He is at peace. I will return in the morning."

*   *   *

He woke early, feeling exhausted. The strain of the previous night was not relieved until he had said Mass at the window overlooking the city. When he consumed the sacred species, he fell into timelessness, rested in the radiant warmth of the embrace, then prayed the concluding prayers. A look at the clock informed him, to his surprise, that his meditation after Communion had taken more than an hour.

It was midmorning before he arrived at Smokrev's apartment.

The manservant greeted him coldly at the door. "He's not here. They took him to the hospital."

Elijah dug more information out of him and half-an-hour later strode into Smokrev's hospital room.

The old man was surrounded by intravenous jars and connected to various tubes. A doctor gave Elijah permission to stay for five minutes.

"He is *in extremis,* Father. He doesn't have long to live."

"Is he conscious?"

"In and out. Do you want to give him the last rites?"

"Yes. I need to be alone with him."

"Of course."

The doctor went out and closed the door behind him.

The old man wore a green hospital gown, tied around his thin neck. His manicured hands lay alongside his body, palms down on the sheets. Elijah unrolled his violet-colored stole, kissed it, and put it over his shoulders. He repeated the ritual of anointing that he had performed the night before and added the prayers for the dying. When he was finished, he saw that Smokrev was awake, watching him.

"I am dying?"

"Yes."

"Will you hear my confession?"

"Yes."

"This time, the real one."

Slowly, painstakingly, in a weak voice, Smokrev retold the priest the events he had described so luridly the day before. He told it simply and added certain facts he had omitted. When he received absolution, two streams of water slid out of the corners of his eyes. This profound weeping bore no resemblance to the hysterical sobs of the night before. It was soundless, and Elijah could see that the old man was resting in deepest peace.

"There is something else I have to tell you."

Elijah nodded.

"In my confession, I told you about my lies. There were a million lies."

"Leave it to the past. It is drowned forever in the mercy of God."

"But the effects of my sin live on. There is one lie, above all, that I must correct."

He gasped for breath.

"Do not talk. You are very ill."

"David, David. I beg you to forgive me."

"I forgive you. Everything is forgiven."

"I must repair the damage. I can do little now, but I must try. Permit me this consolation."

"What is it?"

"I lied to you about Pawel Tarnowski. Those things I said about him. They were lies. It was true that I knew him in Paris. But he wasn't what I said he was. He was good, and that's what made us hate him. He ran from us when he saw what we wanted. That made us hate him even more."

"I knew it in my soul."

"He had many difficulties. He suffered much. He too longed for love, though it was denied him. A man like that! He could have had the whole world. But he wouldn't take it."

"You said that he tried to . . . "

"To sell you. That too was a lie. He struck me and drove me out when I tried to *buy* you. That's when I destroyed him. I almost destroyed you too."

"Do you begin to see, now, the structure of the universe? Do you still think there is no reason behind things? Why has God sent the very one you would have destroyed to tell you about His love for you?"

"That is beyond comprehension. Is He cruel?"

"You know it isn't so. He wants you to know that nothing you can do will ever destroy His love. He has sent a man back from the dead to tell you this."

"I do not understand."

"We do not understand because we are small creatures. You and I. All of us. Very small. To hide in His arms, that is the best thing we ever do."

Smokrev's lips broke into a weary smile.

"I see why he loved you."

"He loves everyone."

"I mean Pawel. He loved you."

"I loved him too."

Smokrev asked for the oxygen mask and breathed in it. His color improved slightly.

"I left something for you. When the ambulance came last night, I told the nurse you would come back. I told her to give you some things. One of them is the icon of the Apocalypse. It is yours now."

"I cannot accept it."

"You must take it. It is not rightfully mine. I bought it from Pawel Tarnowski during the War. It was worth a fortune then, but I paid a pittance for it. I cheated him and he knew it. He sold

315

it so that he could feed you. Pawel Tarnowski gives you this icon. You cannot refuse it."

Elijah tried to speak but no words came.

"There is another thing. A tin box. In it you will find the soul of a man."

With that, Smokrev began wheezing and gasping. Elijah put the oxygen mask over his face and rang for the doctor. While the medical team did what they could, he continued to sit beside him and hold his hand. He whispered *dziecko* just loud enough for the patient to hear. He prayed. Eventually, the hand became cool to the touch, and the doctor removed the mask and looked at the priest. He clicked his tongue and said, "Well, the old count is dead."

XIII

The Conference

The Canaletto was once considered the best restaurant in the city. It had fallen from popular favor in recent years, rivaled by the Bacciarelli in the modern Marriott and by the Wilanow, where tourists could feed, amidst hunting trophies, on roast pork in plums.

But at the Canaletto, situated in the Hotel Victoria Intercontinental on Kralewska Street, one could still dine in old-world splendor, served by waiters in bow ties, accompanied by the music of piano and harp. One could eat wild boar and snails in garlic sauce, smoked trout and mushrooms, and complete his meal with a flaming crêpe.

Simplicity, silence, poverty, he thought as he entered the hotel's main foyer. The environment of the hotel seemed the antithesis of monastic ideals. In spite of himself, he felt disgust.

An elderly maitre d' spotted him and hurried over.

"Professor Schäfer?" he said in Polish with a French accent. "I am Philippe. Please to accompany me to the banquet room of the *ristorante.* Your party is waiting for you."

It was not clear just how the man had recognized him, but Elijah followed obediently. At the door to the banquet room, the maitre d' pinned a small red rose to the lapel of the dark blue Italian suit that Billy had purchased for him on his arrival in Rome several months before. This was the first time he had worn it, and he hated its luxuriance, hated the expense of it, and the discomfort of a costume that was so removed from the truth of his interior life that he wished to make apologies for it to whoever might listen. He shuddered at the maitre d's touch and overcame an impulsive dislike for the man's affected waxed white moustache, the professional eyes, the overfamiliarity of certain kinds of servants who are on a first-name basis with the famous.

Then, as the man fussed with a pin, Elijah looked at him and felt compassion. Few human beings escaped the dictates of their position, he realized; rare indeed was the soul who remained unaffected by his own public image.

"Ah, I see that monsieur is a trifle nervous. Monsieur should not be. The President is a great man, to be sure, but he is a kind man, and a man of the people. Great and small are welcome at his table", he added with a flourish. "Ah, *bon, bon, bon*", he concluded, dusting a skiff of dandruff from Elijah's shoulders.

"Thank you, Philippe."

Elijah entered the large dining room and saw before him a gathering of two dozen people. The President rose from the head of the table and came up to him with his arms extended. He shook Elijah's hand warmly and once again the priest felt a wave of admiration for this man's sense of presence.

"It is a pleasure to have you join us this evening, Father Schäfer. Are you as unprepared as I am for the talks we must give? Ah, yes, I see that you are! Then I am reassured! We are two actors with butterflies in the stomach, aren't we?"

"Yes."

"Come, let me introduce you to some of our fellow sufferers. Tonight the eyes of the world will be upon us, but for the next hour we will calm our nerves and be friends together, without pretense. I believe you may know some of them."

Elijah was introduced to a heavy-set woman who was the Polish minister of culture. Next came a young Chilean poet, thin and shy; then an American academic who was described as a writer on the Jungianization of culture; followed by the coordinator of the conference, an elegant, middle-aged man in a tuxedo, whom Elijah recognized as the premier of a former Soviet republic, a man hailed as one of the chief architects of the new democracy of the East. His was the first face that failed to convey an emanation of relaxed conviviality. After that came several names he did not recognize, professors, artists, writers, the curator of a British museum—every one of them exuding a mood of quiet elation.

Then a name that he recognized: "A confrère of yours," said the President, without the slightest change of inflection, "Dr. Felix von Tilman."

Von Tilman, the theologian, in the flesh, was excruciatingly charming, but Elijah felt certain that his was the practiced charm of a very political animal.

"Archeology, aren't you?" said von Tilman. "Archeology and spirituality? Fascinating. I look forward to your presentation, very much—*very* much."

"As you know, Felix is a co-religionist of yours. He will be speaking on the spirituality of pan-mythology", said the President.

Elijah cleared his throat. "Pan-mythology?"

"Yes, my dear fellow," explained von Tilman, "the universality of all religious belief. It is becoming quite a broad field, and of course it is central to any successful transition into the new era. I expect that the substance of our talks will overlap to some extent."

Elijah was still searching for a reply when the President guided him along to the next guest. His heart skipped a beat.

"You have met Anna before, I think."

"Professor Schäfer, how very nice to see you again", she said, without rising. She extended her hand, and he shook it.

"It is nice to see you again, Dr. Benedetti", he replied. His voice was higher than he intended, but he hoped it expressed an amicable detachment.

"Why don't you sit here", said the President. "Anna, will you permit me to place him beside you, strategically, out of harm's way? He is not a social creature."

He smiled at Elijah and squeezed his arm.

Anna Benedetti replied in the affirmative, using the President's first name, just as she had done at the party in Rome. "I will make sure he is comfortable."

"Thank you, my dear. You see, he is a monk, a man without guile. This sort of gathering is totally alien to his temperament, and I want you to tame him."

"That would be a grave error", she bantered with a slight smile. "He would not survive any alteration of his essential form."

The President's laughter was in no way condescending, merely a jest between equals.

"Please relax, Father. You are among friends here", he said.

He turned away suddenly, distracted by an oriental man who had just entered the room, looking, if anything, even more uncomfortable than Elijah. He wore an ill-fitting black cotton jumpsuit with enormous lapels. Around his neck draped a purple silk scarf.

"Excuse me, please", said the President. "There is the representative of the Dalai Lama." He walked away to greet the newcomer.

Elijah sat down beside Anna Benedetti.

"Once again we are thrown together, like two gawky adolescents at their first dance", she said.

"If they do not know what to do with me, they should not have invited me."

"There, there", she soothed. "He invited you because he is drawn to you."

"Or because he thinks I will be useful to him."

She sipped from a wine glass.

"I am sorry. That must have sounded cynical."

"Only a little", she said pensively. "You should have more faith in human nature."

"Please forgive my rash words. The President is a most admirable man."

"An idealist", she prompted.

"Yes, even a visionary."

"A visionary", she echoed tonelessly.

The candor of her glance disarmed him, just as it had done at their first meeting. He could not have said why she invited his trust. She said some of the things one might expect from a person in her position, apparently a proper devotee. And yet, he sensed that she would always be separate from the general flood of the President's admirers. She was her own person and would remain so in whatever company she found herself.

"I spoke without thinking. Forgive me, I am very tired tonight, Signora."

"Please call me Anna. I hardly know you, and yet I feel I have known you a long time."

"That is because of the generosity of your temperament."

"I don't think so. I am not generous by nature. I am generally suspicious, if the truth be known."

"You should have more faith in human nature", he replied with a smile.

She gave him a wry look and said nothing.

"And yet, since our last meeting, I have learned that you are a judge. It is in the nature of juridical people to be suspicious, is it not?"

"An occupational hazard. Tell me, don't you also have a cautious streak?"

"That is because when I was young I too was a lawyer."

"Oh, yes, I heard that."

"You did? Who would have told you that?"

"I can't recall. Tell me why you are so tired."

"I have been through something of an ordeal during the past few days."

"Here in Warsaw?"

"Yes, I have been involved with a man who, through a strange chain of events, was connected to my life without my knowing it."

He recounted the story of Count Smokrev. She listened attentively. She leaned forward when he told her that the man had been responsible for the death of his friend, a friend who had saved him. At the end, when he described the count's conversion, she appeared moved but made no comment.

Then the lighting of candles and the lowering of the chandelier lights in the dining room signaled a call to supper. Dinner bells chimed. Large silver salvers were borne in by uniformed waiters, and when uncovered, revealed roast chicken and duck à l'orange. The meal was begun amidst general revelry, to the accompaniment of a stringed quartet, which played discreetly in the background.

They both were soon engaged in discussions with other guests. Anna, on his right, was preoccupied with the curator of the British Museum, who was clearly enamored of her; Elijah made strained conversation, in the German language, with the young Chilean poet, who sat at his left. When he informed Elijah that he was a New-Marxist, the priest could not suppress a smile, which the poet interpreted accurately. He looked insulted and furious, and for the remainder of the meal refused to acknowledge Elijah's presence. Still, Elijah preferred this seatmate to the gregarious von Tilman, who was entertaining most of the people at the far end of the table with wicked and witty gossip about Catholic prelates. The President was obviously enjoying the court jester, but every so often his glance would dart toward Elijah and Anna without lingering overlong upon them. Within that glance was a great seriousness.

The coordinator of the conference was two places up from Anna, on the other side of the table. He reached over and handed a sheet of paper to Elijah.

"Before I forget," he said coldly, "here is the itinerary. The time and place of your talk are listed there."

"Thank you."

"You will be discussing the recent findings at the Dead Sea, I understand."

"That is correct."

The coordinator turned to the person on his left and muttered in English, just loud enough to be heard, "The emissary from the Dead See of Rome."

There were embarrassed chuckles from those around him.

Elijah looked at Anna, but she gave no indication that she had heard.

"Tell me, Father, when is your presentation? And where?" she said.

"At ten tomorrow morning, at the Palace of Culture."

"I would like to attend."

"I would be honored."

The sting of the coordinator's comment gradually faded.

Over dessert and wine, the President rose and bid the party adieu. He must go to prepare for the opening address, scheduled to begin in an hour from now. Please, he said, the guests must take their time over dessert and make their way to the palace at their leisure. And if, alas, they should arrive too late for his talk, rest assured that they had chosen the better part, for wine and friendship were the highest truth of all.

This was greeted by hearty reproaches all round. Of course they would be there! They wouldn't miss it for the world! No one else could do what he was going to do tonight! An historic occasion! Best of luck! *Bravissimo!*

Kisses were thrown and much applause spattered around like shrapnel.

Elijah, warmed by two glasses of white wine, was feeling flushed and weary, but happy — inexplicably happy, considering

323

his predicament. He entertained a desire to rise and go after the President, to take his hands in his own and wish him well. Light-headed, he tried to rise but failed to complete this maneuver. He fell back, soaked in a glowing beneficence, a rejuvenated optimism, a conviction that perhaps a second chance was being offered to mankind in this good and noble man, the President.

Two glasses of wine? he said to himself. *What an extraordinary change in my attitude. What amazing spirits are in this bottle?*

He laughed aloud, and Anna shot a perplexed glance at him.

"Anna", he said.

"Yes?"

"Nothing—just Anna. Such a lovely name, so gracious on the tongue, so sweet."

She touched his sleeve. She gave him a severe look. "No more wine, professor. And please, eat your duck."

He found this hilarious and began to laugh uncontrollably, but the laughter was inaudible, compressed within his body. He shook with the power of this savage humor, and then when it dissolved into a pool of grief, he wished to weep. But the weeping also was kept within, emitting not the least exterior evidence. No lawyer, jury, or judge in the world would have found him guilty of inordinate emotion.

Shortly after, the dinner party broke up, and it was announced that the private guests of the President were to be taken by limousine to the Palace of Culture. Standing on the sidewalk in front of the hotel, Elijah and Anna let the others go ahead. Anna waved away the last car that stood waiting for them.

"It's not too far", she said. "Why don't we walk and get some fresh air?"

She took his arm and led him west on Kralewska, then turned south on Marszalkowska, heading toward the massive tower of the Palace of Culture. It took them twenty minutes, during which Elijah's head began to clear.

"What is that building?" he said.

"That is a monstrosity the Soviets built. There are many meeting halls, cinemas, and auditoriums in it. The conference is being held there."

"It is unspeakably ugly."

"The people of Warsaw say that from the tower of the Palace of Culture one has the most beautiful view of Warsaw, because from there one cannot see the Palace of Culture."

He laughed.

"The Polish government is planning to build a new facade over it," she continued, "to disguise the last vestiges of Stalinist architectural realism."

"Let us hope the face-lift comes quickly."

"One step at a time. At least the streets have been changed back to their prewar names."

"It is a step, as you say. But the city cannot be restored to what it once was."

"You were born here, weren't you?"

"I was. I left during the War."

"You were very young."

"I was young, but the memory is as sharp as if it had happened yesterday. There are few sensations in life stranger than returning to a place that was one's whole world and finding that it is gone."

"Surely it's not gone entirely?"

"Not entirely. I have been walking the streets of my boyhood, and I have found remnants of it. My past was real. It was here."

"Doesn't it still live within you?"

"Yes, it does. Like an icon in the mind, an image of something that was once known and beloved, but which exists no more."

"And yet it survives, submerged in memory."

"Anna, you sound as if you have experienced this yourself."

"I was born after the War. But loss and transformation are universal human experiences. We try to hold onto what once was, in the hope that it may be again. And we find that it can never be what it was. Life points us always toward the future."

"I wonder if the people who went through the years of reconstruction have an advantage over people like me."

"In what way?"

"After the War they saw the rebuilding of their world step by step, piece by piece. One reality gradually evolved into a new reality. They observed its progress daily. They even helped to lay the new stones. There was no radical break. Their minds shifted with the gradual changing of their world."

"But you . . . ?"

"Men like me must live with a split in the mind."

"Is that so hard?"

"It is very hard. Man longs for a permanent home. But he does not know it until it is torn away from him."

They climbed the steps to the palace in silence. She stopped at the entrance and turned toward him. "I would like to see the remnants with you."

"The remnants?"

"Sometime before this week is over, would you take me to the places you knew as a child?"

He nodded assent. Then they went in.

* * *

Their invitation cards guaranteed Elijah and Anna a place in the front rows of the congress hall, main auditorium. They were led by an usher to seats in the second row. The crowd of several thousand delegates behind them was charged with electrified anticipation.

The stage was bare. An enormous white banner filled the back wall—a blue and green planet earth encircled by gold letters, written in several languages: *Unitas—A New Civilization for Mankind.*

The rumble of conversation died as the congress coordinator strode from the wings and took the solitary microphone at stage center. Gone was the man who had made the sarcastic comment at the dinner party, and in his place was a figure of great poise. His bearing was so replete with the mystique of his high station that the crowd was reduced instantly to silence; his manner, his clothing, and the set of his shoulders revealed a statesman at ease in public, but no less aware of the import of his role.

"Ladies and gentlemen, delegates, honored guests", he said. "I bid you welcome to what may be known by future generations as a seminal moment in the development of human civilization on this planet."

Headphones attached to every seat in the audience offered simultaneous translation in a dozen languages.

"I share with you the excitement that we all feel this evening. In a very real sense, this moment has been approaching for centuries. It is my task to do what one could never hope to do adequately, that is to introduce the man who will inaugurate our congress. He is no stranger to current affairs, and yet I wonder if anyone here fully realizes the significance of his coming among us. A man of vast erudition and profound humanity, one who has poured out his skills, his personal fortunes, and his immense concern upon the human scene, in a heroic effort to bring together the disparate, and often contentious, communities of mankind. Those of you who know his writings, or have listened to his speeches, or who have heard within the quiet confines of your own hearts a voice that bears witness to his role in the evolution of human consciousness will know that I do not exaggerate. In fact, the problem before me is how to so sufficiently reduce his significance in your minds" subdued laughter came from the audience, "that you will not accuse me of flattery."

An outburst of appreciative laughter.

The coordinator beamed at the audience, enjoying his joke with them.

"You know him. You love him."

A storm of applause.

Returning to a serious tone, he went on: "The energies accompanying this man's emergence on the world's stage are truly phenomenal. By sheer moral force, he has made possible the transition of the former totalitarian states to economic and cultural communion with the West. He has reduced the tensions between other fractious states and has made significant progress in the struggle to end world hunger. In addition, he is emerging as the man of vision for the next millennium. In a series of bold strokes, he has captured the imagination of both the cultural elite and the common man, the masses of humanity for whom there has been so much suffering in our times, and for whom there has been little hope, until now. He is known by many names: Doctor, Professor, Visionary, Moderator, Author, Negotiator, President, and most recently, in last week's declaration by UNESCO, a *Worldhealer*. I call him simply, the Teacher. I bid you welcome the keynote speaker for our congress . . . "

The applause was deafening. The entire crowd leapt to its feet as the President walked onto the stage. Elijah stood and clapped uncomfortably. The surge of adulation that flowed all around him was disconcertingly like worship. The applause continued for several minutes, until at last the coordinator and the President were able to quiet the crowd with hand gestures.

A hush fell as he took the microphone. He appeared handsome in a perfectly ordinary fashion, yet princely in a democratic mode, heavy with thought in a manner that did not discount joy. Overriding everything was a profound dignity that was neither pompous nor affected in any way whatsoever. He seemed a self-contained individual, composed and humble, yet within that containment was a quality that not a single soul present could fail to understand as greatness.

Elijah saw instantly that here was the quality he had misread until now. Not without reason did the myth of the Great Man prevail in all eras and cultures. Nature produced such figures from time to time, as if to remind mankind of what it could be. And here was one who rode high above the other great ones, beside whom the coordinator was reduced to normal proportions. Here too was a puzzle, thought Elijah. Was this not the humorous host, the man who had touched him and joked with him so disarmingly no more than a few hours ago? Was this not the scholar in his study at Capri, and the clear-eyed director of a flourishing business conglomerate? Was he a visionary or a pragmatist? He was both, it seemed, and the juxtaposition, or rather the perfect *integration,* of these seemingly incompatible qualities was startling. At the very least, it gripped the attention with a kind of magisterial authority. Only a fool would not listen to his every word.

"In this most warlike of centuries, we are invited to a joyous rebirth", he began in a quiet voice.

He paused. The hall was filled with an immense listening.

"For millennia of existence, we have proceeded through time and space, going about our affairs on this little spinning planet as if *being* itself were not a miracle. We have lived in blindness. We have been burdened by guilt. We have huddled in fear. And as a result, we have produced a planet teeming with warring tribes and hungry children. This must cease."

He paused again and stared out over the thousands of faces.

"The millennium that is fast approaching is a transcultural event of epic proportions. It is a climax that occurs once every thousand years, a psychic convergence felt by every soul on earth who is living at the time. It is a moment of tremendous blessing for mankind. And yet, throughout history we have misused this opportunity. We have watched it approach with dread or we have seen it as a time to strike an enemy or plunder a neighbor, to cringe before a mythological divine punishment, or to watch for the collision of stars. We have crawled into caves and awaited the end, searching the black skies for judgment. And when the judgment does not come—and it never does come, for it is entirely a creation of the human mind—we crawl out again and begin to reconstruct our little encampments, surround them with stockades, rearm, and continue on as always, projecting our terrors upon the cosmos and upon the neighboring tribes."

His voice rose in intensity: "No generation until our own has discovered the great secret of the universe."

He paused.

"The universe breathes!" he cried in an impassioned voice.

A ripple of awe washed through the audience, and all around him, Elijah heard the intake of breath as the power of the President's words penetrated the consciousness of his audience. The sound of the room was just within the range of hearing; it was an indefinable radiation, a suffusion of expectancy.

"The universe lives. And we whom she has created are part of her. It is time to sink our wells deep into the earth, and to discover in the depths of her being what all wise souls eventually discover; there we shall see that at the source of everything is an underground river. There are African wells and European wells, aboriginal wells and Sufi wells, Jewish and Christian, Muslim and Buddhist, Hindu and Jain wells. There are Gaia wells and Confucian, and red and black and white and yellow wells. There are animist and wiccan and spiritist wells. And even, beneath the dry wastes of fundamentalism, there is a choked well, a yearning toward the one great truth. Each and every one is a point of access into the ultimate truth of human destiny. There we shall discover a primal awe, and an original sacredness. Every person in this room is radiating glory!"

He cried: "When will we begin to see ourselves for the first time and know ourselves? When? When will we come into the light? I tell you that we shall come out into the light on the day we lay down our weapons and our judgments and divisions and look into each other's eyes. For in our own eyes, we shall see at last the radiance of divinity. *Doxa!* Glory! And on that day we will begin to worship in spirit and in truth!"

The ardor of the President's voice hung in the stillness of the air as the crowd absorbed these words. Gradually, a soft rush of applause gathered momentum and crashed against the stage in wave after wave of euphoric intensity.

The President did not acknowledge this requited passion, did not drink it in, as some might have done. He merely looked down at the floor and waited until it was finished, and then he continued. He spoke movingly of the ecological revolution and of the various humanitarian movements that for more than a century had been groping with the problem of man. He praised them, each and every one, as prefigurements, as forerunners of the people of this generation who were converging toward a leap of consciousness into the age of universal harmony.

More applause, deeper, longer.

He spoke of the suffering of indigenous peoples, of women, and the poor. He displayed a flash of righteous anger against those unnamed forces still at work in the world that spread division and defended the destructive split in the human consciousness. Elijah shivered. Fear began to work its way up his spine. He understood now what was coming.

"Those who are committed to pessimism have condemned themselves to a tragic ending. They create their own demise. And I tell you, my friends, it is not for us to seek to bring the dead structures back to life. Systemic social philosophies, systemic religion, systemic economies, systemic forms of oppressive government are all dying, and no human being on earth can prevent this death. We who are called to usher in the new world order must leave the dead to bury the dead."

Intense applause.

"Periodically, throughout history, civilization reaches a great turning point. As one era ends and another comes into being, there is a difficult transition period, during which societies undergo a series of crises threatening their very existence. It becomes painfully clear to all that the old systems and the old solutions are no longer working. At those times, individuals gifted with authentic vision must work together to restore peace and harmony, must unite in a marshaling of all human powers to spread *worldvision* to a frightened human community. An overwhelming convergence of truth has occurred in our century, and it is no accident. Even as the forces of death have vented their last outburst of rage upon the suffering human community, a new age is beginning. The tyrants are dead. A race of creators is being born. Great thinkers, artists, spiritual teachers, and mystics have appeared all around us, each bearing a flame of that universal light. If this congress is to assist successfully in the birthing of a new world, then we must lay aside our fears of one another, lay aside our endless suspicions, our dogmatism, and our cosmic dread. It is time for man to forge a new creation story, to reinvent the ancient myths without discarding them. By drawing upon the riches of our global cultural heritage, we shall do this!"

Applause.

"We shall do this!" he cried more emphatically.

"That is why the hopes of the world are turned upon us at this very moment; that is why the communications media of the planet are here this evening, enabling us to speak to billions of people through the miracle of modern technology. The generosity of several nations and private benefactors have made possible the broadcasting of the proceedings of this congress and its individual seminars to the entire world. In the coming days, the people of the planet will be able to hear speakers from every field of human endeavor: the arts, the academy, the sciences, the various world religions, and those selfless individuals who work within the existing order, leaders and government officials who understand politics as the art of birthing a truly human, truly global community. In all this vast banquet of culture, you will hear the cry of man, and the cry of divinity: *Unitas! Unitas! Unitas!* Come home, mankind! Come home from exile and *live* within your own body and soul. Find on this earth the ultimate meaning of our common destiny!"

He bowed to the audience and without ceremony walked offstage.

The crowd leapt to its feet, roaring and clapping. Elijah remained seated, stunned, trying to collect his thoughts. Anna stood and joined the applause, but hers was calm, measured clapping, and her face was expressionless.

Floodlights poured over the image of the globe, and an orchestra in the wings began to play, competing with the roar of the crowd. People broke up into hundreds of groups, discussing the speech with enthusiasm. Surging above the mayhem, the music was sensuous, sensitive, stirring, with a note of exuberance that was kept just below the level of stridency. It perfectly matched the mood of the crowd.

Several people came over to Anna and engaged her in animated conversation, but her manner, although pleasant, remained detached.

"Yes, a fine speech", she replied to one. "I agree, he knows how to blend urgent topics with a poetic gift. A master of language. Moving. Yes, I think the world will pay close attention from now on. Fine, I'll see you in Amsterdam next week. Goodbye, Thea. Don't forget the committee meeting for the show in Florence. Good, I'll have my secretary flag the documents when they come to the office. Your Excellency, how very good to see you here. I did. I was impressed with his style. He is always impressive. You are so right—he knows how to touch a crowd. Absolutely. Yes, he struck all the right chords."

She bent her head graciously toward another inquirer. "Am I excited? Well, no, not actually. I am just a little under the weather. A touch of the flu. Please give my regards to Eleanor. You too! Indeed. *Buona notte! Adieu!*"

Lines of people poured toward the exits leading to the reception foyer. Uniformed waiters circulated amidst the crowd offering trays of wine. Long banquet tables laden with delicacies were besieged.

Elijah exhaled and stood, struggling into his trench coat. Anna stared up at the empty stage, her eyes clouded.

"Well," said Elijah, "you must go now, mustn't you? I expect there is a private reception. He is waiting for you. Or are you waiting for him?"

She turned to him with an unreadable expression.

"I am not waiting for him. He is not waiting for me."

"You seemed preoccupied a moment ago."

She shook her head and put on her evening coat.

"I am feeling unwell. I think I will go straightaway to the hotel. Thank you for your company, Father Schäfer."

"Can I hail a taxi for you?"

"If you wish."

Because of the crowds, they stood in a light rain for some time before there was an available taxi. When Anna told the driver, "The Marriott", Elijah exclaimed. "Why, I'm staying there too. May I ride with you?"

She said, "Of course."

They rode in silence. In the hotel lobby, he told her that he hoped she would soon be feeling better. She replied that a good night's rest would help. She did not wish to miss tomorrow's presentations. Which room would he be speaking in? He told her, and she bid him good night.

Elijah went to his room and lay on the bed. He stared at the ceiling for a long time. It seemed impossible to him that so much intense experience could be packed into a single day. Only that morning he had helped a dying man in his final moments—it seemed ages ago—and then the events of the evening, so heavy with significance, were like a mountain falling into the sea of consciousness. Wave after wave of memory raced through his mind, tormenting and mesmerizing.

Not the least of the day's happenings was the barely perceptible movement of his heart toward Anna Benedetti.

He looked into the mirror of the dressing table and said aloud, "Who are you, Elijah Schäfer? Why has it become so easy to penetrate your detachment? Do twenty years of priesthood simply vanish in the presence of a woman?"

He looked at his reflection and did not like what he saw. An anguish, solemn with grief, was written there.

"Who are you?" he said aloud.

A thought flashed through his mind, *I am David.*

He shook it off.

"I *was* David. I was married for a brief time to Ruth, but I am no longer married. I am a monk. I have become a new being, marked forever with the anointing of ordination. My soul is a different soul than it once was."

And what of your heart?

"My heart, like all human hearts, will bear the mark of the fall of man until the very end. The true test of a man's identity lies in his will. How perfectly he conforms to divine order is the real measure of his love."

Elijah — David, does love negate love?

"When one gives his life to another, it is with the totality of his being. If at times the heart slips back, or looks away from the Beloved toward a human love, it is a moment of testing. It does not negate the original gift. In fact, it may be a chance to prove love and strengthen it in the forge of adversity."

You committed no sin, told no lie — yet you made a gesture of intimacy.

"At table I murmured a few words that released a message of longing."

Longing for what?

"For union with another heart."

Long ago you gave away your heart.

"I did. I know I did. But tonight, when that mad impulse ran through my veins, I did not realize what I was doing. It was a moment of weakness."

Understand, My son, that your heart belongs to Me alone, and in this way it is poured out for all mankind. There is no greater love than this.

"The longing was an intolerable sweetness."

You took your gift back into your own hands. It became a possession.

"I know, my Lord. I know."

Countless souls depend on your fidelity. In Paradise the love that awaits you far surpasses your present loneliness.

"I am so tired. I cannot think."

Rest in Me and pray, and I will be your strength.

His body, he realized, was utterly exhausted and hyper-tense. He knelt, prayed his breviary, and eventually lay down again in peace.

* * *

Elijah's talk was delivered in a small meeting hall on the third floor of a wing of the palace complex. Four times a day, delegates could choose from among several presentations given simultaneously. Each talk was to be recorded for broadcast on world television, and also would be available in video format.

Of the thousands of delegates, no more than a dozen filed into the room. One of them, Elijah was glad to see, wore the white habit of Saint Dominic's order. He and the others sat waiting for the cameraman to finish preparing his technology. When he was ready, he flashed a sign at Elijah, a red light winked on, and the priest began his lecture.

He had taken care to wear his Carmelite habit. Dressing in his hotel room that morning, he had recalled the Holy Father's request that all professed religious wear their habits in public, as a sign of their consecration, a visual witness to lives given wholly to God. Few obeyed him any more. Indeed, this request had been bandied about in the Catholic and secular press alike as a symptom of the Pope's "legalism" and had been hotly debated where it was not simply dismissed with a laugh. Although Elijah had received a dispensation to wear secular clothing in deference to his new "mission territory", he felt that if he was the one representative of orthodox Catholicism speaking here today, then his witness should not be without a cohesive unity. He did not wish to give even the appearance of disdain for the requests of the Pope. The audience, such as it was, eyed his robes with curiosity, as if he were a character in a new and daring opera, set in a quaint past.

He had completed a brief historical sketch of biblical criticism when a few delegates put up their hands. With apologies for the interruption, they informed Elijah that the simultaneous translation service was not operating properly on their headsets. Elijah was speaking in German. It was soon determined that the German and Spanish channels were functioning, but the other language channels were dead.

Making a silent prayer that his listeners would be able to follow, he proceeded in German to describe the theologian Bultmann's influence on biblical criticism, and the ensuing decline into naturalistic explanations of the miraculous—the so-called "demythologizing" schools.

Three people got up, shrugging, pointing at the headsets, shaking their heads. They left the room.

Elijah, distracted, attempted to collect his thoughts, consulted his notes, and pressed on. It was going badly, he knew, but when Anna came in quietly and took a seat at the back, he felt a burst of cheer.

He described the first discoveries of the Old Testament scrolls at Qumran, which authenticated the precision of later translations of the Bible. He went on to describe with enthusiasm the extraordinary material recently discovered in other caves near Ephesus and the Dead Sea, texts that achieved three immensely important things: they were far older than the earliest known manuscripts of the Gospels; one of them was written in plain Aramaic, accompanied by a facing text in Greek, the work of a scribe-scholar who was either taking the dictation of a living apostle, or was checking his translation with the same living apostle, ensuring that the exact sense was being rendered for future generations. The manuscript effectively dated the New Testament to the lifetime of the evangelists, and thereby demolished, in a few bold strokes, the school of biblical criticism that sought to "demythologize" the New Testament.

It had come to be believed that certain first- and second-century Christians had rewritten the life of Christ to suit their particular theological outlooks, colored by the crises of their day. The recent discoveries, Elijah asserted, refuted this theory. If one considered human psychology, it was less likely that those who had witnessed the events of the Gospels, or who had written parts of the New Testament under their direct guidance, would project their personalities upon what to them were shattering events of the most recent past. Theological coloration was far more likely in the present age, so dominated by theory and myth. Could it be that modern exegetes had projected their own disbelief, styles, and temperaments back onto the people of the first century? If this was true—and the discoveries provided convincing evidence that it was—it was no small failure. The loss of objectivity, not to mention professional detachment, pointed to a tragic blind spot. Many had simply presumed that they knew better than those who had gone before them. They had assumed that the advance of time confers a near-infallible superiority. This, Elijah underlined, was really a form of myth, the myth of the evolution of intelligence.

"Perhaps," he added with a gentle smile, "perhaps it is the demythologizers who need to be demythologized."

One or two uneasy laughs came from the audience.

He went on to say that intelligence, training, knowledge, however advanced they might be in this century, were clearly no guarantee of immunity from man's abiding handicap: *subjectivity.*

"Pride blinds us to our own blindness," he said, "and there is no pride sweeter to the taste, and so enslaving, as the illusion of superior knowledge. This is especially true when one has a great deal invested emotionally in one's own theory. In the end, the need to demythologize the sacred Scriptures is rooted not in the exigencies of scholarship or science, but in profound spiritual problems. Man loses wisdom when he persists in sin . . . "

The Dominican stood up dramatically in his swirling white habit, and said irritably in French, "Are you saying that those who question your simplistic notion of God are living in sin! Fundamentalist nonsense!" He stalked out.

Elijah took a deep breath. Undaunted, he went on, speaking at length about specific passages from the new codices, comparing a sampling of verses in the Aramaic text, its Greek companion, and several reliable modern translations. The effect was stunning. But there were only eight people left in the room, including the cameraman.

When it was over, no one came forward. Everyone filed out, except the technician and Anna. She was writing in a notebook, and when she looked up she gave him a look of sympathy.

The technician was muttering and cursing in Polish, flicking switches and bobbing all over his machinery.

"Is there a problem?" said Elijah.

"I don't believe it! All the settings were correct!"

He threw up his hands and growled, "I'm sorry. It didn't record a damn thing!"

He went out snarling to himself, carrying the rebellious equipment with him.

Elijah exhaled loudly. "Well, it seems a complete disaster", he said.

"Not entirely", said Anna. "I found it fascinating. Should we go for lunch?"

On the staircase, they met a flushed young woman running up from the ground floor with a sheaf of papers under her arm. Anna introduced her as one of the President's press secretaries.

"Quickly, quickly", she gasped. "We need you downstairs."

In the crowded lobby, the President greeted Elijah with his customary warmth and asked him to stand beside him. To his surprise, von Tilman came out of the crowd and stood with them. The President put his arms about the shoulders of both men, one on either side. Cameras began to flash and several media technicians filmed the moment.

Then an interview with the President commenced, and Elijah felt that he was no longer needed, or wanted.

"Lunch", whispered Anna and took him away.

The private banquet room set aside for conference speakers and associates was also crowded. Anna and Elijah found a corner table and sat drinking their soup and munching on sandwiches.

"What was that about?" he asked.

"Publicity, I suppose. He is doing it with every speaker and national delegation. Hundreds of such sessions I would guess."

"Von Tilman and myself represent Catholicism?"

"I imagine so", she said. Her serious tone had returned, and along with it the mask of emotional neutrality. He had come to think of it as a mask. Why a mask, he wondered? Masks disguise, protect, evade. What was it she did not wish him to see?

"When is your presentation, Anna?"

"Three days from now."

"What is your subject?"

"I will be speaking on human rights from the perspective of new models of international law."

"That should draw a good crowd."

"Undoubtedly. I have two talks scheduled for one of the cinema auditoriums. My first should draw several hundred delegates. There won't be so many at the second."

"Why is that?"

"My presentation won't be what the organizers expect."

"Really?" he said intrigued. "Why?"

"There is an unspoken uniformity beneath all the eclecticism you observe here this week. It revolves around a single vision of existence. It is the ancient worldview of *monism*. Monists believe that all divisions are ultimately illusion, all conflicts can be negotiated, all dogmatism is essentially a violation of freedom, and so forth."

"And you don't think that is true?"

"No, I don't."

"Is the President a monist?"

"One might call him a neomonist, a new kind of spiritual politician."

"That is the first hint I have had from your lips that you aren't at peace with what is happening here."

"It is rather euphoric, isn't it? I distrust that. My juridical background, no doubt."

"So, it is not so much disbelief as professional caution."

"Yes, I think that would be more accurate to say. I am observing. And I am thinking about many things right now."

"But you are not happy about monism, even though it comes from the hands of such a remarkable man?"

"He wishes to bring peace to the world. He speaks everywhere of unity. These are truly great objectives. But monism is only superficially about unity. As a judge, I have developed an inner ear for the difference between impressions and facts."

"And you have detected a distinction?"

"Monism is a pleasing concept; it resolves many difficulties. But I believe that it also creates many destructive tendencies in society."

"And so, you will raise this caution during your presentation."

"Yes. In the morning seminar, I will discuss the principles we find in existence, upon which all civilized law is based. I will demonstrate that certain concepts of man may appear to be humanistic and at the same time result in the violation or destruction of human lives."

"Who could object to that?"

"I think the objections will arise not so much in the *mind* as in the emotions. My audience will instinctively recognize a threat to euphoria. And to utopia. And yet I wonder if this is an

exercise in futility. Few have the intellectual apparatus to understand what I am going to tell them."

He said nothing.

"You see, I am proud, Father Schäfer, but it is not sweet to my
tongue. It is a bitter thing."

"Why is it bitter?"

"I will tell you about that some day. Not now. Not here."

"All right. To return to your subject: it seems to me that you
are discussing the basic problem of law. In theology, we maintain
that social law must be grounded in natural law—the principles
God has written into creation."

"I don't know who or what wrote them there in creation. But
I do know that they *are* there, and I know also that disaster
follows upon disaster for any society which ignores those principles.
It is that which distresses me. I must speak about that."

"You may do more good than you think."

She sighed, "I hope so. But I suspect that most human beings
aren't really interested in the truth. They think in a chain of
impressions, and they have been fed on pleasing impressions for
more than a century. I am disappointed to say that there are
numerous signs of impressionism here this week."

"And in your second talk?"

"I will speak on law and conscience."

"Have you read the Pope's encyclical on this subject?"

"I have. He is obviously a man of outstanding intellect, and a
visionary in his own way. There is much in it that I agree with."

"But not everything?"

"Not everything. I am not a believer."

"I didn't know that, though I suspected."

"Because of the company I keep? You don't understand me in
the least."

"I am sure that is true. But I think I understand you a little
better now. I am grateful."

"If you come to the second talk, you may be among an
audience smaller than your own."

"I regret that I will have to miss your talks."

"When do you return to Rome?"

"Early tomorrow."

"So, your contribution to the congress is finished?"

"Yes."

"You seem dispassionate about that point."

"Do I? I suppose I am. There is much about the proceedings that disturbs me. I will need time to consider many of the things that have been said here."

"Including the President's remarks?"

"Yes. He appears to have made some kind of departure."

"Departure? From what?"

"The real question is, *to what.* I think he has taken this opportunity to move to a new level of public activity."

"He could hardly be more public than he already is."

"I mean another level of *revelation,* if you will. A kind of epiphany of his vision that has not yet been seen by many."

"You mean, of course, his opening speech last night."

He nodded.

"It disturbed you?"

He looked her straight in the eyes and said, "Didn't it disturb you?"

She looked down without replying.

A minute later she looked up.

"If you are leaving early tomorrow, there isn't much time to see the places you knew as a child. You said you would show me. Are you free this afternoon?"

His heart beat a hard stroke, against his will.

"I am. Would you like to come with me?"

She suddenly broke out in an unguarded smile. And Elijah felt a rush of pleasure.

*　　*　　*

After lunch they took a taxi to the northern end of the ghetto. In the passing streets, there was nothing to indicate that a city within a city had once occupied this area. Nothing cried out, no voices protested the catastrophe that had occurred here. Trees flowered all around them. Children played happily in the public gardens. He did not speak, and she did not attempt to break his silence.

Standing in front of the marble memorial at the *umschlagplatz,* he said, "The Nazis dispatched hundreds of thousands of ghetto Jews from this embarkation point. The rail line began here. It led to Treblinka."

"Your family went on the train?"

"All of them."

"Did any survive the war?"

"None."

They went down the street and turned onto Zamenhofa. She took his arm without comment. He felt numb, wondering why the gesture did not move him.

I am old, he said to himself. *The people who look at us, if any, see only a young woman taking an old man for a walk. A niece with her uncle. A daughter with her father.*

At the corner of Mila, he showed her where he had lived as a boy.

"I lived on the fourth floor, in the apartment block that once stood here", he said. "But everything was demolished. The Germans blew up the ghetto, building by building."

"Nothing remains?"

"Nothing."

Then he remembered the crack in the stones that resembled a horse. He found it and pointed it out to her. During the past few days someone had colored in the shape with white chalk. A child, almost certainly. A child.

"I was a boy here. I played on this spot. I recall how we used to pretend, my brothers and sisters and I, that the knight who killed the great dragon of Krakow came here after his victory and cut this shape into the stone with the tip of his sword, as a memorial to his brave deed."

For the remainder of the afternoon, they went through the Pawiak prison and the Jewish History Institute. At four o'clock, she asked if they could find a café. She needed to sit. She was hungry. He continued to feel the hideous numbness, although beneath it was a growing tension.

At the edge of Old Town, they found a bistro. Anna ate a small meal and drank a glass of wine. He sipped at a cup of coffee.

"Do you have a family?" he asked her.

She looked up sharply.

"I am a widow."

"I am sorry. Did you lose your husband recently?"

"Several years ago."

"Is there anyone else?"

"Two children, both at university."

"What are their names?"

"We should talk about my life another time. This day is for you. I want to know about your past."

"There isn't much to see", he apologized.

"There is a great deal to see."

"It's all in the memory, you know. When my generation is gone, it will become entirely a page in a history book."

"Do you think so? I think the world won't forget. Warsaw is a haunted city. So many dead. So many little plaques on every corner commemorating the fallen."

"The memorials are admirable. But it's not the same."

"The same as what?"

"It's not the same as growing old with the living. Millions of stories were not passed down to the next generation. The next generation perished. We few who survived grew old when we were still children."

She watched his eyes for some time. Eventually, she ventured: "No doubt it's the lawyer in me, Father, but I sense that there is more — something you are not telling me."

"If I were to begin to discuss the *more*, it would take forever."

"I have time", she replied quietly.

"There is a place that is important to me, as important as the site of my home."

"Will you take me?"

He nodded.

Minutes later, they entered the side street in Old Town and stood in front of Sophia House.

"One whole winter I lived there, in that building."

He told her the story. When he was finished, she asked him about his protector.

"His name was Pawel Tarnowski. He was one of the *hasidei umot haolam* — the ones we called *righteous Gentiles*. He risked his life to hide me. He fed me with his meager supply of food. He demanded nothing in return."

"How extraordinary. What kind of man was he?"

"A solitary soul. A devout Catholic. A book-lover. This was a bookshop then. He published some things, too, before the War."

"You are sure he didn't survive the War?"

"I am sure."

"How did he die?"

"He was gassed at Oświęcim. Auschwitz."

"Tell me, how did it happen? How was he arrested?"

"We were betrayed. It happened very suddenly; there was no time to think; no time to discuss anything. He gave his life for me."

Elijah recounted the last night he had spent in the House of Wisdom.

"He stood in the way of evil, you see. He stood as a bulwark, and he let the full force of what was intended for me land on himself. He did this for a boy who didn't value what he believed in; he did it so I would have life."

"Why did he do it?"

"I really don't know. He was a philosophical sort of man—actually a young man with everything to look forward to—but for him, I think, life was only as good as the principles he lived by. He died as much for that as for me."

"Was he a friend?"

"Yes, a friend, in a way. I was only seventeen. He was as much a friend as a man like that can be to a child."

"What do you mean?"

"He was old in a way that I have become old, but in a different way. He had suffered something very difficult, but I never knew what it was. Some grief perhaps, or a lost love. He wrote an interesting little play I stumbled upon a few years ago. It was published in East Germany after the war, by a former officer of the Wehrmacht who had stolen it from him. Pawel lost everything, you see."

"Everything except his principles."

"That is true. Interestingly, the plagiarist repented toward the end of his life and admitted publicly what he had done. It ruined his not inconsiderable reputation. The book was published recently in Polish, under the name of its real author."

"What is the title of the play?"

"*Andrei Rublev.* It is an imaginative re-creation of the life of a famous Russian icon painter. Have you heard of it?"

"No."

Elijah sighed, "No, you wouldn't have. It's not well known outside of the Polish literary community, where it has a small following. It's probably not a great work of literature. But he poured his heart into it. It's about the search for beauty and for love in a fallen world."

"A well-examined theme in literature."

"The favorite of serious writers."

"One might even say, the favorite theme of the human heart."

"I suppose that's true."

She pointed to the second floor. "You lived up there?"

"Above it, on the top floor, hidden in the attic."

"Can we go in and look at it?"

"I saw it a few days ago."

"Is it the same?"

"The Germans destroyed Old Town, but pains have been taken to reconstruct it exactly. It's the same and not the same."

"*You* are not the same."

"That's certainly part of the difference."

"I would like to see it, if I may."

"Anna, I would prefer not to go up there today. It was something I had to see alone. It would become something different if I went there with you. I hope you understand."

"I understand."

He looked up at the blue-black sky above the roof tops.

"What are you feeling?" she asked.

"I don't know how to describe it. Numbness mostly. Regret for the death of a good man. Gratitude. And guilt that I am living because of his sacrifice—the usual conflicts felt by survivors of the *Shoah.*"

"Is that all? Nothing more?"

"I feel—how can I tell you?—I feel that this man whom I barely knew gave me freedom. At the time, I was a child and didn't really understand what he was giving. And now that I have returned I understand it more."

"Isn't it a curious thing, that you should feel such freedom in the site of your captivity, while you felt such oppression in the Palace of Culture, where every second word is *freedom!*"

He looked at the roof of the House of Wisdom and whispered, "Yes. That is it."

"It's late", she said. "We should return to the hotel."

When they arrived back at the lobby of the Marriott she thanked him for the afternoon.

"I won't see you again", he said. "I wish you well in your talks. I will pray for you."

"You needn't pray for me. Just think of me from time to time."

They shook hands, and she went up in the elevator.

The desk clerk waved to him.

"There are some things for you. A lady left them."

There was a note from Smokrev's nurse, explaining that on the night before his death the count had told her to package up the enclosed items and give them to the priest from Israel.

Elijah went to his room and sat on the bed. He opened one of the packages and found a battered tin box full of papers covered in handwriting. The other package contained the icon of Saint Michael of the Apocalypse.

Pawel Tarnowski gives you this gift, the count had said. *You cannot refuse it.*

He stared at the gift until the evening sky turned black and the first spring stars appeared.

He sat at the writing desk and wrote:

Dear Mr. President,

A man's life is a small thing, but he holds it in his hands and gives it to another as the greatest thing in the world. I do not know your plans for the future. I cannot know for certain whether your vision will prove right or gravely mistaken. But I have learned that if one's gift is not founded on absolute love, it merely contributes to the heap of violated lives that has amassed in our century.

The One who is my life, and through whom I live, would speak to you, if you would hear Him. He would tell you that no man can save the world, least of all by saving a fallen humanity from itself. There is but one Christ. He, and He alone, is the Savior of the world. And He who was God did not count equality with God a thing to be grasped, but emptied Himself, taking the form of a servant. And being in human form, He humbled Himself and became obedient unto death.

With respect,
Father Elijah Schäfer

He put the letter in an envelope, addressed it to the President, care of the congress administration at the Palace of Culture. The desk clerk in the lobby promised to see that it was delivered.

He returned to his room and sat by the window, holding the tin box in one hand and the icon in the other. The darkness in the room increased, and the network of Warsaw's lights increased until it spread before him like a vast, garishly lit battleground on which dragons and white horses clashed in confused battle.

He gazed out over the landscape of disaster, unmoving and unmoved. When eventually he pressed the icon against his breast, the numbness within him cracked, and he wept over the city and the world.

XIV

Rome

He slept through most of the flight to Rome and arrived in a rainstorm. The city was suffocating under a muggy blanket of humidity and pollution, but he was relieved to be back.

There was a note waiting for him in his mail slot at the college. Unsigned, scrawled in the handwriting of the cardinal secretary of state, it read: *Can you see the gardener tonight at Severa's place? We must discuss the spring planting. Phone my apartment to confirm.*

He made the call after supper and the cardinal answered.

"*Buona sera,* Signore Giardinière."

"*Buona sera.* You have returned."

"Yes. You wish to discuss the spring planting?"

"Indeed. Tonight at Severa's? Eight o'clock?"

"I will see you then."

"Are you well?"

"I'm well, but once again, I believe our project has been frustrated. The parasites in the garden are growing stronger."

"I know. It's all over the papers."

"Is it bad?"

"Very bad. Worse than we could have expected. I will tell you when we meet."

Elijah arrived shortly before eight. He went through the funerary chapel, past unlocked doors, and made his way down through the maze until he came to the side gallery. The door was open.

Elijah stood by the entrance and observed. The cardinal did not at first notice him. He was perched on a camp stool, reading his breviary, squinting in the poor light of a kerosene lantern. One shoulder rested against the wall, the Roman letters P A L V M B A carved in the marble beside his head. He looked older, heavier, hunched, his silver hair slipping across his brow.

When he looked up, Elijah noted the absence of his usual aplomb.

"Ah, Father, welcome", he sighed, rising. They shook hands. "It's good to see you."

"I'm glad to see you too, Eminence."

"The veteran returns. You must be weary."

"A little. You said that the situation was bad."

"Yes. A nasty turn of events to say the least. Look at this!"

He pointed to a sheaf of newspapers at his feet.

"Go ahead, take a look. *The New York Times, The Manchester Guardian, La Stampa, Figaro.* There are others."

Elijah saw his own face staring back at him from every front page, von Tilman beaming into the camera, the President between them, arms around their shoulders. Screaming headlines:

VATICAN SUPPORTS WORLD UNITAS CONFERENCE

"There will be an article in *L'Osservatore Romano* clarifying the situation", said the cardinal. "We will try to correct the misleading impression, but the damage is done. I'm afraid our attempt to bring the Catholic voice into that arena has backfired."

"It doesn't make sense. I was only one of several dozen speakers. No more than one percent of the delegates attended my talk. Furthermore, the record of my presentation has been lost—the victim of a technological blunder."

"I'm not surprised", he said, disgusted. "This venture was a piece of opera from start to finish. You were invited there only for the purpose of constructing an artificial media event." He flicked his finger at the pile of newspapers.

"We have been used", said Elijah.

"Yes. This man has no interest whatsoever in our insights. He wants our image, nothing more, just as the Holy Father suspected. He had doubts about this, but I convinced him that we should let you go to Warsaw. I have made a grave error in judgment."

"The article in *L'Osservatore Romano* will clear up the misunderstanding, will it not?"

"How many people read it?"

"But can't the Holy See ask for a correction in the secular papers?"

"We have already tried. I have been on the phone all day."

"And . . . ?"

"A ringing silence. Unanswered calls. Some rudeness. A few evasive answers wherever I can get through to the publishers. The journalists of the world, with few exceptions, have no love for us and endorse practically everything the President stands for. He's the man of the hour, the man of the year, and some say, the man of the century."

"Then it is as I suspected. My mission goes from bad to worse. Eminence, perhaps it is time for us to reconsider . . . "

"No-no!" said the cardinal firmly. "A tactical setback does not mean defeat. The ultimate purpose of your mission has nothing to do with this propaganda. It is the soul of a single man that we want to reach."

"Why is it so hard to reach him?"

"This soul is surrounded by several echelons of protective barriers. When he is not in a crowd, he is in a group of intimates; even when he is alone he is never alone, for there are powers and principalities that guard him and direct his every act. For a prophet to speak to him, that prophet would of necessity have to penetrate first his own fear, and second, the shields the enemy puts up around this servant of his."

"You call him a servant?"

"*Slave* would be a more accurate word."

"Slave. It is hard to think of him as such. He is the most powerful man in the world."

"Oh, yes, without a doubt. But he is not his own master. You can be sure that he does nothing without a spiritual army protecting his every move and deflecting every step that would approach him and call him to Truth."

"Is he possessed, do you think?"

"I don't know for sure. He may not be fully possessed at this point, but he is certainly under the influence of the Adversary."

"Can a word of warning really turn such a man from his course?"

"It's our only hope. Especially if that word is spoken in the power of the Holy Spirit and if many souls are praying for victory over the enemy spirits."

"Can we hope for such an army of allies?"

"Many contemplatives throughout the world are praying for your mission. A small number of living saints known only to us have joined with them. Day and night they fast and pray for you—and for him. I believe that there will come a moment when the President's heart will be exposed, when his unseen body-guards will be forced back, disarmed for a short period of time, during which you must gather all the courage within your soul, and open your own inner being to the full authority of the Holy Spirit. Then, whether your words be eloquent or simple, they will pierce his armor and call him to see reality as it is. He will know there is a God. For one burning, luminous instant, he will understand what darkness he has fallen into, and what darkness he is bringing upon mankind, and that he is free to choose otherwise. At that instant, he will see the inexpressible beauty of God. He will long for God and see that God longs for him to return. That will be his moment of choice."

Elijah's heart pounded.

"Once again, I must protest, Eminence", he stammered. "What if I am too small for this task? What if I fail again? Think of the consequences!"

"Think of the consequences if we don't try!" The cardinal looked him full in the eyes. "You will receive grace to accomplish all that God asks of you. It won't be from human strength or wisdom. It will be entirely a gift. Be poor, my son. Accept being a little one, and He who made the universe will fill you."

Both men fell silent. Both men closed their eyes and went deeply into silent prayer.

They remained motionless for a time, until an extraordinary thing happened. In that airless place, the door to the outer gallery slammed violently shut, and the lantern was snuffed out by an unseen force. Both men jumped to their feet. A hideous stench filled the chamber.

"Father, strike a light", the cardinal gasped. "The matches are by the lantern. Quickly!"

Elijah, disoriented and frightened, staggered around in the dark searching for the lantern. The cardinal's voice cried out with a surge of strength: "*Vade retro, Satana! Ipse venena bibas!*"[1]

Terror filled the chamber. Malice beat against the two priests, hammering against their souls for admission, for possession. A shock ran through Elijah's body, nausea gripped his stomach, his mind reeled with dizziness. He swayed and fell to his knees; he fumbled for the matches. His fingers performed their task only in obedience to a superhuman effort of the will. The cardinal continued to pray loudly in an authoritative voice.

"*Vade retro, Draco! Crux sacra sit mihi lux!*"[2]

The stench left as quickly as it had come. Elijah lit the lantern, stumbled to the door, and threw it open. All was as before,

---

[1] "Begone, Satan! Drink the poisoned cup yourself!"
[2] "Begone, dragon! The holy Cross is my light!"

ominously silent, horribly normal. Not a breath of wind stirred the air of the gallery.

The two men sat down, breathing heavily.

"Well," said the cardinal, "the old dragon still has a few tricks up his sleeve."

Elijah wiped cold sweat from his brow.

"That was the devil", he said in a tremulous voice.

"Maybe the devil. Or one of his uglier lieutenants."

"What was it all about?"

"It's perfectly clear. He doesn't like us."

The cardinal's back was straighter now, and he looked like an old soldier reinvigorated by a struggle at close quarters with an ancient foe.

"That felt good", he said. "I had forgotten how it feels to hit back."

"Hit back?"

"Before I became a bishop, I was the exorcist of my diocese. Not a pleasant job, but I did it. I was happy when they promoted me to lesser tasks. How swiftly thirty years pass! It's good to know I haven't forgotten the old prayers. Did you see how he backed off?"

"Not before delivering a few blows."

"Does it disturb you? Surely you have encountered this sort of thing before?"

"On a different level. Spiritual warfare usually takes a form the senses cannot detect."

"But when the demons reveal themselves it's not pretty, no?"

"I have prayed with a few people in Israel who came to the convent for help. Peasants who fell into magic. There have been more of them in recent years, mostly young people involved in the occult."

"It's getting bad. The cities of the West play host to hundreds of cults carrying on their arts clandestinely. Some are more bold than others, and they are getting bolder. Rome is riddled with them."

Elijah sighed and his hands shook. The cardinal eyed him. "Don't look so worried. He tried to frighten us. But it's a very good sign."

"It is?"

"It tells us that we must be doing something right if he throws this kind of ammunition into the battle. He is desperate."

"I wish I could feel your confidence."

The cardinal clapped him on the arm. "You are tired, Father. You have just returned from a different field of battle. In many ways, a more trying one. I order you to go home and rest. Take a few days off. Put aside that apocalyptic literature you have been reading. It will still be there when you take it up again. Walk in the sun. Listen to some beautiful music. Fill your mind with all that is lovely, as Saint Paul tells us to do. Now, let's go upstairs and get some fresh air."

"May I ask you one more question before we go? Why is it necessary for us to continue meeting this way? Why are we still pretending to be gardeners?"

"My unreliable clerk is gone, but there is still much that is unclear. The removal of one individual from a Vatican desk doesn't solve every problem. There may be more like him."

"Doesn't this throw everything and everyone under a pall of suspicion? How can the Curia function properly if that is the case?"

"It does present certain difficulties. There is the danger of paranoia, of course, but at the same time we must be cautious. It is no longer prudent to assume that everyone is loyal."

"And what of Cardinal Vettore?"

"Ah, yes, Cardinal Vettore."

"What is to be done about him?" Elijah prompted.

"It's difficult", said the cardinal. "There is no objective proof that he has done anything wrong. The Holy Father has spoken with him privately, and Vettore denies everything."

"Then it is his word against mine."

"Precisely."

"Does the Holy Father believe him?"

"No. He believes you. And so do I."

"Then why isn't he removed from office?"

"It's not as simple as that."

"Forgive me, Eminence, but it seems quite simple."

"You don't understand. He is a powerful personality in his way. He has said or done nothing openly against the deposit of Faith, nor against the Holy Father. We have so many interior and exterior enemies right now. The summary dismissal of a man who is considered loyal would increase the confusion on all sides. More than that, it would undermine the confidence of many good people who admire Cardinal Vettore and consider him to be *papabile.*"

"Then what is to be done?"

"The Holy Father is doing the wisest thing possible, considering the circumstances. He has gently but firmly deflected Vettore's attention elsewhere. He has given him a noble project that will consume his energies, yet demand of him a proof of orthodoxy. It is a test the cardinal cannot escape without abandoning his public image. He is to begin a series of fact-finding journeys to the Far East, assessing the condition of the Church in mainland China and Vietnam. He is to put all of his effort into this research for the coming two years. And the Pope has generously excused him from the ordinary duties of his office, replacing him, temporarily of course, with a man we know to be loyal."

"It is ingenious."

"It's the best we can do. Outright dismissal would only reinforce the widespread impression that the Pope is a hardliner who wants to return the Church to her preconciliar state, an autocrat who doesn't support his own staff, who listens to anonymous accusations that aren't backed up by proof."

"Surely, I am not anonymous. If necessary, I can testify to an ecclesial court regarding what I saw on Capri."

"And in the process destroy any hope of success for your own unique mission. No, with your cover blown, as the spy novels call it, we would lose far too much in order to gain a little."

"I see."

"These are not easy times, Father Elijah. One needs the wisdom of Solomon just to get through an ordinary day around here. Much depends on keeping our wits about us."

Elijah reached out and traced the letters of Severa's name.

"I know what you're thinking", said the cardinal. "You think we should march straight to the Colosseum and tell the guards to turn the lions on us."

Elijah said nothing.

"A heroic martyrdom is fast, simple, glorious, isn't it? Blood washes away all ambiguities. Death breaks the intolerable tensions. You would like us to braid a rope and drive the moneychangers from the Temple, then go to the cross. Correct?"

"Is that so wrong? Isn't that the pattern our Savior has shown us?"

"Indeed it is. And I tell you that we *are* going to the cross. But it is not our right to hasten that day. We must work while the light lasts. We must strengthen what remains. This is the long and lonely martyrdom. It is the most difficult of all."

The two men looked at each other without speaking. Then by mutual agreement they rose and went their separate ways.

* * *

Elijah did as the cardinal directed him to do. The academic year came to an end a week after his encounter with the *draco* in the catacombs. He corrected papers and final examinations, studiously avoided apocalyptic literature, and took daily walks in the small garden behind the college. He also read a novel that he had promised himself for many years, Manzoni's *I Promessi Sposi—The Betrothed.* The struggle between light and darkness was in it, and the author had taken care to bring his characters to the brink of absolute hopelessness before rescuing them through the intervention of a saint. Like any nineteenth-century romantic Catholic novel, it presented the struggle as relentless and full of appalling twists and turns, but it was uninfected by the existential nausea of twentieth-century fiction. At the end of the tale, the disastrous events were restored to divine order, and there was the added bonus of a spectacular conversion. It seemed a little contrived until he realized with some poignancy that his own encounter with Smokrev was, in its own perverse way, no less a miracle. *Minus the saint,* he thought to himself.

As the weeks of late spring slipped into early summer, he drew strength from the patterns of prayer, at once rigorous and restorative. The anxieties that had plagued him gradually receded, and the image of Anna Benedetti, whenever she arose in his mind, ceased to overwhelm him. He accepted an abiding sense of loneliness as a gift, as a wound the Lord permitted to remain open, exposed to the healing power of light. He suffered it gladly and made an offering of it for Anna herself, and as a sacrifice in anticipation of that future moment when he would be called to speak the truth to the President. He also offered it for the soul of Count Smokrev—and for Pawel.

Some instinct had so far kept him from investigating the contents of the tin box—an extraordinary exercise in self-restraint. If he had tried to explain it to himself, he would have said that he merely wished to keep it for the right moment. He fully intended to read the material when his peace was restored and his attention clear of all intrusion. Then, and only then, would he come to know the soul of the man who had been his friend.

That spring was one of Italy's finest. The heat was not oppressive, and day after day the sky stretched out pale blue, marbled with high, thin clouds. The scent of flowers was everywhere in the city, and even the automobile traffic seemed to have lost its frenzy. The tourists were less numerous than usual, and one could stroll through the art galleries and pray in the churches without the irritation of noisy crowds.

On a Sunday afternoon, he took the tin box out of his closet and held it in his hands. He felt a lightness that had long eluded him. He had offered the Mass that morning for Pawel and, after receiving Holy Communion, had experienced the warmth within his breast, an embrace of love that was both serene and passionate. There had been a burst of ecstasy, a brief parting of the veil that separated the human from the divine, that line of division and union running inexorably through the center of the heart. He understood that the time had come.

He went to a park near the Vatican gardens and sat on the grass beneath a cypress tree. Its perfume was delicious. The sun cast a golden light on the ornamental bushes. Riotous small birds competed mightily for attention, but their polyphony faded from his consciousness as he opened the battered, rusty lid.

Cold rain smashed against the glass of the bookshop. The doorbell chimed. Distant gun shots punctured the leaden sky with dread.

13 September 1942
Dearest Kahlia,
Things are happening quickly. I have a guest who will not be here for very long. I hope he goes soon. Not only is my position now made precarious, he places me in danger of another kind. The face is yours. I fear him. . . .

Elijah knew immediately the identity of the guest. He carefully unfolded the scrap of paper lying below the first:

Breeze-kissed, the vessel's pennant barely stirs,
The water gently heaves its radiant breast;
So plighted girls, in reveries of bliss,
Wake, sigh, then promptly sink to sleep again.
(From *The Crimean Sonnets,* Adam Mickiewicz)

*

361

5 October 1942
My dearest Elzbieta,

Why is it so difficult to write to you this night? Is it because the guest is gradually taking your place, or assuming your form? He is asleep in the attic.

The sounds of gunfire have waned into silence. The clock ticks on the wall by the bust of Paderewski. My desk has become an entire landscape. Above my head there lies an extraordinary presence, a live coal resting on a bed of old newspapers. Why has he been dropped into my hands? What madness to thrust a child upon me! I of all people . . . a man incapable of love, afflicted with introversion, and an overly sensitive temperament?

I do not dare to use the word, love. It is a word that disguises our selfish pursuit of relief from loneliness. I do not trust my own heart. But why do I feel the very feelings I once felt—and which I still feel—for you? I am afire with a passion I did not know existed, but it is not an impulse of the carnal kind.

I feel you fading upon the night wind. I would run after you into the streets if I could. Would I be running toward or from—I know not which. I long to run through the night until this ache has spent itself utterly. I would run like the wind if it were not certain that a German bullet would put an end to my silly poetic romance in short order. Oh, God, do not let me degenerate into that disordered youth I once was. I shall pull myself together. If you are there, hold me. If you are what you appear to be, then tell me that my senses are not playing false. If beauty is sacred, then how could it ever betray us? But what is beauty?

I have run out of words. For the first time since we met, there is less to say to you than there is space and time in which to say it. Love? The Greeks called it *exousia*, a breathing forth of being. My being calls to you now, come quickly, come quickly to Pawel. I am sinking.

*

Triumphant shrieks the blast; then, towering high
Out of the gurge, astride the humid crags,
Like a stormtrooper at the broken walls,
Extinction's genius stalks toward the ship.
(From *The Crimean Sonnets*, Adam Mickiewicz)

*

Warsaw, 11 February 1943
My dearest Elzbieta,

It is night. There is not enough food. Upstairs, your
little brother sleeps beneath the eaves, hidden from our
enemies. He must not fall into their hands. I could not bear
another loss.

It is almost certain that you have been taken forever by
them. You did not know me, but I knew you. You looked
at me. A look which must have cost you nothing—instantly
forgotten—yet it is my greatest treasure. Then you were
arrested and you may have been put to death. I wish there
had been sufficient courage to meet you that night after
your performance. Your handling of the Rachmaninoff
score told me more about you than a year of courtship
would have. No doubt you will think me a fool to write
this way, but perhaps you can read this from heaven. I will
ask my guardian angel to make a copy and show it to you.

When my heart was struck by the sight of you, I learned
for the first time in my life that love yearns toward completion in the being of another. I do not mean only the
meeting of the body, male and female, but more urgently,
the union of soul and soul. Where this yearning is absent,
love soon dies. Even the priests and nuns know this yearning,
although they have chosen a Beloved who returns their
embraces a hundredfold. But in all cases, love exists only as
a gift freely given. You did not know me, and so it was
impossible for this particular question to be raised between
us. The opportunity to give your love to me was but one of
countless doorways opened to a person such as you. In the
end, the enemy decided for us.

Tell me what name to give this field of mysterious communication which until now I did not know existed. I wonder what I should call it: "A Spirituality of Unrequited Love"? No—too theological. Perhaps, "The Path of Hidden Love"? Something is not quite exact in this title. Or maybe, "The Gift"? Yes, that is more my style.

I will post this now in the usual place. Perhaps there will come a time when an angel will deliver the tin box in the bottom of my desk drawer. It is bulging with our correspondence. Will you come through the front door of the shop one day when the War is over and make my heart simply cease to beat? If so, send a message ahead of you, Elzbieta, my sister, my love.

*

Dear my Host,
The alien and the sojourner have found a dwelling place within your tent. The widow and the orphan rejoice. The angels cry out for gladness.
With respect,
D. Schäfer, Warsaw, February 1943

*

1 March 1943
The Gift:
He sleeps upon a plank floor, breathing forth sighs as deep and as old as mankind. He searches for the truth. How could it not come to pass that many will desire to elevate him to the status of the divine. He is a fine boy, but he is no closer to being a god than is the Count Smokrev. He is a human being searching for the original unity, the image and likeness of the One who created us.

One must maintain a vigilance of the heart that is part of the total gift of the self. No such gift is possible without prayer, for man by himself is not able to master the drive for union and completion. Indeed, I suspect that we are not designed to be our own master. If in marriage it is three who make a union—the bride, the groom, and the Creator—then it must be so for friendship also. Friend or lover, by the gates of your heart there must stand a watchman, and that watchman is Truth. If you ignore his warnings, you must surely know that you are choosing. You alone are responsible for what must come to pass: the death of Love.

*

Elder John, startled and frightened, stared at the face of the silent Emperor. Suddenly he sprang back and, turning to his followers, shouted in a stifled voice, "Little children, it is the Antichrist!"

(From Vladimir Soloviev's *War, Progress, and the End of History*)

*

Warsaw, 7 March 1943
Elzbieta, my sister, my love,
David Schäfer is teaching me many things. I have learned that my mind is capable of deceiving me. I have long recognized this about myself, but never has it been so starkly revealed. I have projected upon him an image of what I perceive the ideal to be. He is a very good soul, but he is not the icon I created in my interior. How easily misled are our perceptions! This is a great surprise to me.

He has shown me that there is the seed of a father within me. Oh, yes, a very small father, a poor little man who does not know how to be a father. Yet, within me is a genuine love which desires the ultimate good of the beloved—yes, even to the point of sacrificing everything. This too is a surprise.

*

To reach satisfaction in all,
Desire its possession in nothing.
To come to the knowledge of all,

Desire the knowledge of nothing.
To arrive at being all,
Desire to be nothing.
To come to be what you are not,
You must go by the way in which you are not.
(From *The Ascent of Mount Carmel,* by Saint John of the Cross)

*

Paris, 1931
Chèr Paul,

You must not despair of the art scene. No one wants your paintings, you say? Ah, such pain in your letter. Alas poor solitary! Poor exile! You have tried to paint Heaven and Hell, and you think you have failed? You say your Heaven looks like Versailles and your Hell looks like the Gare St.-Lazare? I know your anguish. For sixty years I have lived in it too, and I know now I shall never leave it. I would not want to leave it.

Have you read Péguy? He is formidable! Listen to this from *Lettres et Entretiens.* He is writing about Dante's *Divine Comedy:* "Nowhere in the course of this great long pilgrimage does the author appear as an historian or geographer of Heaven and earth, as a visitor, an inspector, or a tourist—as a grandiose kind of tourist perhaps, but still a tourist. At no point here is the poet someone on a journey, a grandiose journey, maybe, but still a journey. At no point does he take up a position on the sidelines in order to observe what is going on in front of him, because what is going on in front of him is *himself*—that is to say, it concerns his damnation or salvation.

"At no point does he take up his position on the pavement to observe sinners go by, because the sinners are himself. This immense multitude is what he is himself within, not something alongside it. The whole task consists in the right orientation of mankind, turned full-face toward the Last Judgment."

Paul, we are *inside* of it, though we feel outside. Hold the ground that has been given to you. Do not try to fight on other fronts. If you abandon the very one that has been given to you, no matter how small, the war may be lost. Do not be a success too young. Go without baggage across the desert. Poverty and silence are the natural abode of truth.

Amitiés,

G. Rouault

*

Warsaw, 2 November 1942, All Souls

Words came to me last night. Broken pieces falling like large crystals from the ice-clouds that cover heaven, each flake a galaxy spinning down. They fuse in space and form a thought.

The thought is this: It is the artist's danger, being master of the form, to forget that he is poor, to think he is the master of the invisible reality which this pale scribble represents.

I am going to write a play about it. I will put the thought into the mouth of Andrei Rublev.

*

Zakopane, 15 August 1919

Pawel,

My little grandson. How brave you were today! When we climbed down into the cave of Wrog the dragon, I trembled. Yes, even grown men are sometimes afraid, but we learn to overcome fear with courage. Did you tremble too? We were brave together, weren't we?

You said to me, "Why did we not see the dragon?"

I answered, "Because he fled at our coming."

"Why did he flee?" you asked.

"Because he is afraid of *us!*"

Never forget what we learned today. Always remember it.

Do not be afraid, Pawel. It is the biggest insult you can give to a dragon. I give you this medal of the Mother of God of Częstochowa as a memorial of our victory.

I kiss you,
Your Ja-Ja.

*

There were more letters and fragments. Elijah read until the sun sank below the dome of Saint Peter's. He got up stiffly and returned to his cell. He placed the box on a shelf in his closet. He bowed toward the icon of Saint Michael of the Apocalypse, went forward, and kissed it. From between the pages of his Bible he extracted a badly worn piece of yellow paper, a paper that contained a message he had read countless times. In his bureau drawer he found a silver medallion on which were inscribed an icon of the Mother of God and the Polish word *Mądrość—Wisdom*.

Then he took the medallion and the scrap of yellow paper and went down to the chapel. There, in front of the burning light he read for the thousandth time the last words of Pawel Tarnowski, hurled from a train, written as he was borne away to Oświęcim.

David, my son, my friend,
Never have I wanted to live so much as I do now. I go down into darkness in your place. I give you my life. I carry your image within me like an icon. This is my joy. I go down at last to sleep, but my heart is awake.
Pawel.

XV

Rome

That summer was one of surpassing beauty. The dazzling light, the gentleness of the heat, the breezes that blew inland toward the city from the Tyrrhenian Sea, the fruit- and flowersellers pushing their bounty, combined to make a conspiracy of such sweetness that even the most brooding temperaments would have recanted their pessimism.

Elijah was no exception. He felt himself resting inwardly, and his physical health improved. He took long daily walks through the more congenial sections of the city and went often to Saint Peter's to pray at the shrine of the fisherman from Galilee.

For the Fisherman of this generation, however, it was not going well.

The secular press was full of speculations about "the present pope", as they called him. Their professionalism was only just maintained, a veneer of carefully worded editorials and news items beneath which was growing disdain for the "remote" aging pontiff. Rumor had it, they announced, that he was about to retire. Reliable sources in the Vatican, they said, had confirmed that he was losing some of his mental faculties. Should a man in this condition, *any* man, no matter how great he had once been, be permitted to cling to such a powerful office? He was well past retirement age, and in the "new church" (lower case *c*) was it not reasonable to suggest that a bishop of Rome be subject to the same laws that he enforced on his brother bishops? Many good administrators had been pushed from active ministry upon reaching the age of seventy-five; it was obvious that they were being summarily dismissed on a technicality of canon law, simply because they did not agree with this Pope's every opinion. Was he not the last of a dying line, an autocrat ruling in the old style, no longer capable of "facilitating" the progress the Council Fathers had mandated?

The liberal Catholic press was no better. In fact, it led the pack of critics. Strangely, the heretical Catholic journals seemed increasingly moderate in their tone. They said the same devastating things they had always said, but expressed themselves in terms that were more subtly nuanced than was habitual with them. They became models of restraint. Their subscription numbers increased steadily. People began to think of them as the new moderates; by the same token, the truly moderate were now considered ultraconservative, and the conservatives to be sociopaths.

During the previous decade, several of the more balanced Catholic journals had been turned over to new editors. The bishops, frightened by the aggressiveness of dissidents in their dioceses, and even more afraid of being condemned as preconciliar, had made concessions. One after another, they turned over the organs of Catholic information and opinion to likable, articulate editors who squirmed at the very concept of the Roman Catholic Church, but took pains to disguise it.

Since leaving Mount Carmel, Elijah had paid close attention to one American weekly in particular, *The Catholic Times*. Its editor, a certain Father Smith, a native of Idaho, had been dismissed without just cause. No reasons had been given, other than the excuse that Smith had been unable to adapt to the postconciliar age. Smith wrote to Elijah about the situation. He was a man of unusual perspicacity. He was neither conservative nor liberal—despised those political terms. He had steered his paper through the minefield of North American ecclesial politics with considerable agility and, one might even say, sanctity. He had navigated by the light of the early Church Fathers, by the Second Vatican Council, and by the writings of the Pope. He had avoided rancor on one hand and indifference on the other. He was considered to be one of the sanest voices in the modern Church. He was also a true priest, and after love of Christ, he valued obedience above all else. He believed that obedience and genuine love were inseparable.

When the superior of his order demanded that he hire certain columnists, writers whom Smith knew were infected with modernism, he declined, citing the fact that he had been given complete editorial freedom by the archbishop of his city, the man who under civil law actually owned and published the newspaper. His superior insisted, reminding Smith that he was under obedience, pointing out that refusal to comply would be unworthy of a faithful priest.

The priest now found himself caught in a confusion of obediences. He begged Elijah for advice. He also appealed to the archbishop, and the archbishop agreed with him. The archbishop, however, asked Father Smith to make a minor concession for the sake of preserving unity among the flock. Would he please admit to the company of his writers the least offensive of the dissidents? This would be a favorable sign to critics within his diocese that orthodoxy was not authoritarian, was loving, and never closed to discussion. He added that he personally had suffered as a young curate under autocratic pastors, and before that in the seminary—well, one could not begin to describe the abuses he had suffered under the old system! The new Church must always remain open to dialogue, he insisted, and it must be seen that he, the archbishop, was a sympathetic shepherd who had the interests of all his flock at heart, no matter their disagreements.

Smith, torn, exhausted, and pushed into making a snap decision by the archbishop's office of communications, had agreed. Elijah's reply, urging him to stand firm and to appeal to a higher ecclesiastical court if necessary, arrived too late. The priest, deciding to make the best of a bad situation, reasoned that one questionable columnist was a lesser evil than a paper full of them. Over the following year, he gradually ceded more and more of his authority. He was a gentle man and a perfectionist; his nervous system was not what it had once been. He lacked the talent for detecting the more subtle forms of manipulation. Piece by piece, he lost ground to a newly formed editorial committee, composed mostly of reliable people. It seemed harmless at first. When the archbishop appointed a representative of the diocesan communications office to the committee, a nun who had recently obtained a masters' degree in theology, he could think of no objection; he did not wish to be thought of as that kind of territorial male who fights rapaciously for power. But the sister had a strong personality and an agenda. Smith became discouraged, then depressed. The archbishop suggested a three-month sabbatical. He took it.

His temporary replacement was a competent man of impeccable credentials. He was a protégé of the cardinal archbishop of a larger diocese, a close friend of Smith's own archbishop. The two prelates had been at seminary together, and while they did not always agree on matters ecclesiastical, they were of one mind concerning the maintenance of unity as the highest value. The interim replacement was a gifted writer and editor. He was also adept at diplomacy and never lost his temper. He had risen in the echelons of the secretariat of the national bishops' conference and was currently the head of their communications office. He knew how to reason with unprogressive bishops and to set their fears at rest. He said many moderate things. He neither spoke nor wrote a single divisive word. He had proved himself an able troubleshooter for the bishops and was considered by all to be a conciliator.

Within a month, he had eased out one of the less popular orthodox columnists and brought in a second dissident, not an inflammatory one, of course, but one who could broaden the paper's approach to the many complex problems facing the modern Church. A second orthodox columnist disappeared from the paper the following month.

By this time, Smith was beginning to realize what had happened. He was taking his sabbatical at a Benedictine monastery in the desert of the southwestern United States. From there, he wrote in protest to his archbishop. The archbishop replied that while he was not perfectly at peace about the directions taken by the new editorial board, it would be "inappropriate" for him to use his episcopal office to interfere. The interim editor was just trying out his wings, he explained, and the paper would gradually find its balance. Father Smith must give the man a chance. The interim editor was considered a very good administrator and an outstanding theologian. Sister X was also doing an able job of keeping the more extreme rebels from getting into print. Between the two of them, they were steering the paper back toward the center. Delegation of authority was not a simple thing, and, after all, it was the age of the laity.

At that point, Smith experienced a failure of charity. He did something imprudent. He penned an angry response, quite out of character for such a gentle man. He pointed out that the archbishop had neglected to take his own advice. He had not supported him in *his* struggle with his superior. He *had* interfered. Moreover, the paper had *always* been steered on center—the true center—until the new management had taken over. Did the archbishop not see the spiritual damage being done by the present editorial approach? Did the archbishop not know that he was playing by two sets of rules? Perhaps the archbishop secretly agreed with the dissidents. Perhaps his Excellency was using the laity as a tool of revolt, one step removed from his own hands. He felt betrayed, he said, and the archbishop had played no small part in the betrayal. He signed the letter and fired it off.

A week later the priest received instructions from his superior, accompanied by a clipped letter of confirmation from the archbishop's office, informing him that he must proceed immediately to a place in California called "The Aquarius Spiritual Paradigm Center" for a prolonged period of "rest and renewal". He read the order over and over. *Aquinas?* No, *Aquarius!* The priest knew that this center had been established for the purpose of rehabilitating troubled priests who had not adapted to "the spirit of Vatican II". A friend of his had been processed there a few years back and during his internment had been invited to describe his most degrading sex fantasies in group therapy. A nun dressed only in a black body-suit, wearing a medallion of a silver moon goddess around her neck, had "facilitated" the session. When he told her that he didn't have any degrading sex fantasies, and in fact never gave into the slightest urge to entertain *any* kind of sex fantasies, such fantasies being expressly forbidden by Christ and the teachings of the Church, she gave him a pitying look. She did not believe him.

"I do like whiskey", he had offered timidly. "Perhaps even a little too much."

Smith's friend had gone along with some of it, but only in order to get a passing grade, so to speak. He had hoped to be released back to his diocese as soon as possible. No longer "dysfunctional", he would live out the remainder of his years quietly—very quietly—ministering to a poor, inner-city parish. When he was introduced to a therapy called *christo-kundalini yoga* that supposedly would help him get in touch with the serpent spirit coiled at the base of his spine, he ignored his instinctive fears. He obeyed like a lamb, but he began to feel a darkness growing in his inner life, and he lost the taste for prayer. When eventually he felt a revulsion for the Mass—a reaction he had never before experienced—he grew more confused and wondered if there really was something seriously wrong with his mind, something that demanded more intensive therapy. After that he threw himself into all the programs. One night he and his fellow priests were ordered to prance around a bonfire while dressed only in minuscule bathing suits, deer antlers strapped to their heads. They were encouraged to let fly with atavistic cries from the base of their spines. Smith's friend held back. When he observed his brother clerics trumpeting and bellowing beneath the stars, something snapped in him. He tore off the antlers, went to his room, packed his bag, and walked three hours through the desert night to the nearest bus station. He went home to his parents, slept around the clock, drank several quarts of whiskey one after another, and when his head cleared, he went out to look for a job. He had not yet returned to active ministry.

Smith telephoned the archbishop and had a heated exchange with him over the phone—again quite uncharacteristic behavior for this mild-mannered cleric. He begged him to reconsider the command.

The archbishop refused.

Smith described the ridiculous antics the priests were being forced to endure.

The archbishop replied that the ASP was highly regarded by many bishops. If such a preposterous event had occurred it was surely an isolated incident and probably was being blown out of proportion by Smith's friend, who after all was obviously a troubled priest, considering his subsequent activities, or lack thereof.

Even so, Smith refused to comply.

The archbishop demurred but offered an alternative. There was another retreat center in the northeastern United States where the approach was not quite so "creative"—the archbishop's word—which offered a more classical approach to psychological counseling. It was staffed by competent professionals, "very solid people". Would Smith comply to that?

Smith asked for time to consider.

"You have twenty-four hours", said the archbishop.

"Twenty-four hours!" Smith erupted. "Can't you give me more time than that? Why, even the Vatican gives heretics and schismatics years to reconsider their errors."

"Twenty-four hours", said the archbishop and hung up.

Smith hastily contacted a writer he knew in a city near the "classical" retreat center, a woman who had been jettisoned from the paper some months before. She was the mother of eight children and gifted with uncommon sense.

"What can you tell me about the place?" he asked.

"It's a holding tank for pedophiles, drug addicts, and various ecclesial psychopaths", she informed him. "Go there, Father, and you're marked for life."

"The archbishop says it's totally confidential, utterly discreet."

"Uh-huh. I'm sure it is. Tell me why I know so many people who have made a little visit there?"

"I don't know. The company you keep?"

"This is no laughing matter. You can do what you think best, Father, but I'm telling you, it's one flew over the cuckoo's nest, nunnish version. Depth analysis, Jungian style, pseudo-liturgies, self-revelation, and self-obsession, 'new-church' thinking woven with genuine insights. In the process, you get to strip your psyche down like an old motorcycle and put it back together again, under the guidance of the sisters. They've got university degrees coming out their ears. They know all about fellahs like you. They've got sweet voices and penetrating eyes. They speak in hushes. They're even religious after a fashion. No one will make you jump through hoops or regress you to the anal stage. But I'm warning you, you won't come out the same guy you went in."

"That's not very reassuring."

"It's not intended to be."

"What am I going to do?"

"I think you should come and spend a few months with Bob and me and the kids. If the diapers and macaroni don't drive you crazy, we'll declare you a genuinely sane human being and send you back to your archbishop fit as a fiddle."

"I'm already fit as a fiddle", he said humorlessly.

"I know, I know. I was just joking."

"It's not a laughing matter."

Thus, Smith knew what he was in for. He called Elijah.

"They've got me over a barrel, Father", he said without a trace of British accent. "If I go to either of the rehab centers there's no telling what will happen to me. I might end up like my friend, or worse. Maybe I won't even feel like throwing away the antlers. Maybe I'll like them. And if I go classical, as they call it, I could spend the rest of my life analyzing my every mood. At the very least, I'll become a permanent neurotic. On the other hand, if I refuse to go to either place they can use me as propaganda. They'll say, 'You see what these so-called orthodox priests are really like. They can't even obey.' They'll use it to justify how they've handled this whole mess."

"Don't move. Don't do a thing just yet", said Elijah. "The superior general of your order lives here in Rome. I will try to get an appointment with him. In the meantime, I want you to pray as you have never prayed before."

"All right", said Smith dispirited. "But I doubt it will do any good. He's a straight arrow, but he's also a super-nice guy. And super-nice guys don't want confrontation. He wouldn't want to go against the archbishop, and he especially wouldn't want to undercut his own regional underlings. Delegation of authority, you know."

"Then we must pray."

Elijah met with the general the following day, explained the situation, and obtained from him an assurance that he would investigate the matter.

In mid-July, Elijah received a call from Smith.

"You did it!" he cried. "You're a miracle worker! The general told my superior that he wants to find me a rehab center in Italy. I'm arriving next week."

"Where will they send you?"

377

"Here's the best part: I'm going to be rehabilitated right in the head office in Rome. The general wants me to work on the order's international magazine. It's all hush-hush, of course. I'm too political for a visible role, he thinks, but he wants me to be his assistant editor, without the title. I'm supposed to see a psychiatrist, too, but the general told me, confidentially, that he thinks we can dispense with that. It's his way of getting me off the hook without throwing the order into an uproar. He's a smart guy."

"You see, prayer can accomplish anything."

"Prayer and a certain Father Elijah! Bless you, my friend. Bless you."

But Elijah thought it might be a pyrrhic victory. Smith had been rescued, but he was also safely dispatched from the North American scene. The interim editor had been appointed editor-in-chief and co-publisher. In the ensuing months, *The Catholic Times* had shifted the attention of its readership to a new, and seemingly "more open", worldview. Step after relentless step, it led them toward a new concept of the Church. At first, it was careful to pack each issue with a plethora of the usual homely pieces about local events, which reassured everyone except the most discerning that nothing whatsoever had changed in the day-to-day life of the parishes. Gradually, it introduced reports of meetings, media events, press conferences, that gave a public platform for dissent. Each issue turned up the heat a notch. Reading *The Catholic Times,* one would likely conclude that Catholics every-where were boiling with the urgency to recreate the Church from root to branch. The paper grew heavy with the utterances of theological societies. In mild, objective tones, its reporters described their criticisms of the Pope and Vatican departments, as if these were news items of major proportions. The column that reported the words of the Holy Father, and had once occupied an entire page of each issue, shrank steadily until it was an eighth of a page, buried deep in the middle, wedged between advertisements for glow-in-the-dark statues and package tours to the Holy Land. Much space was devoted to proclamations by various bishops' conferences and their staffs and to a luxuriant growth of organizations that all seemed to press for "reform of the church".

Within eight months of taking control, the new editor had turned one of the largest Catholic weeklies in the Western hemisphere into a powerful instrument of indoctrination, with hardly anyone aware that he had done so. Hundreds of thousands of loyal Catholics were now being imbued with his concept of the Church. It was impressionism on a grand scale and it was a resounding success.

From the onset of Smith's crisis, Elijah had followed the changes closely. In early August, he noted the headlines in the latest issue:

> Rome Rejects Bible Used in English-Speaking Countries; World Conference on Religious Life Demands Greater Involvement by Women in Church Legislation; Despite Rome's Condemnation of New Lectionary, It Remains in Use Pending Clarification, Says Bishops' Conference; Catholic Education Must Become Sensitized to Inclusive Issues; Stop Discriminating against Women, Archbishop Tells Synod; German Bishops Protest Vatican's Refusal to Grant Communion to Divorced Couples; New Spiritualities Needed in Western Church, Says Visiting Animator; Dealing with Sex Abuse by Priests; Democracy Needed in Church, Says Conference of Lay Leaders. . . .

And so forth. In that single issue, there were thirteen articles that put the universal Church in a bad light and demonstrated the supposed vitality of the regional churches. There were five articles that might be interpreted remotely as orthodox. They were short and bland. Plainly, they were being used as space-fillers, or worse, as tokens. There were also two snippets from the "pope's" (lower case *p*) public talks. Elijah had read these particular speeches; he knew that they were prophetic and infused with clarity of language, moral dynamism, and passion. The newspaper had ignored the substance and extracted the driest possible scrap, practically meaningless when reprinted out of context. Technically speaking, the newspaper could not be faulted for disloyalty; yet in reality, it was at the forefront of revolt.

Elijah wondered what would come next. The answer came in the form of a highly agitated Father Smith standing on the doorstep of the college, waving the most recent issue. His eyes were snapping.

"Where can we go to talk?" he growled. "Privately", he added.

"Not here", said Elijah.

Seated across from each other at an outdoor café near the Tiber, with black coffee, the two priests read the banner headlines: "Doctors Declare Pope Incompetent".

"That is ridiculous", whispered Elijah.

"I know. Read on."

The article was written by a panel of physicians, two in the United States, one in Holland, and another in Great Britain, who had studied the recent speeches of the Holy Father, his executive decisions during the past year, and video presentations of his public appearances. There was consensus among the doctors that the Pope exhibited symptoms of a decline into mild paranoia. Citing his mistrust of loyal bishops and his thinly veiled apocalyptic musings as evidence, they suggested that a prolonged period of rest for the pontiff was in order. His physical health had also seriously deteriorated, they said. There was the chronic shaking of his hands and a recurrent trembling of his head, which could very well indicate Parkinson's disease. In addition, he displayed what were almost certainly the early symptoms of Alzheimer's disease. Then there was his reputed short temper with Vatican staffers, his inability to tolerate dissent, his growing distance from the voice of the people. *Vox populi, Vox Dei,* the doctors concluded, and the voice of the people was overwhelmingly in favor of an entire rethinking of the papal charism. Was it not reasonable in the postconciliar age to expect from the bishop of Rome the same accountability that was demanded of the world's bishops?

"I don't believe this", said Elijah.

"And well you shouldn't", said Smith. "It's a put-up job from start to finish. The Pope is an elderly man, but I hope to have one-half of his faculties when I reach his age."

"Do his personal physicians have anything to say about this?"

"They deny it. The Vatican press secretary denies it too. They say it's groundless speculation and untrue."

"The article referred to their statements. That seems fair enough."

"Oh, yes, that's journalistic cosmetics, to prop up the illusion of objectivity. Now they can say they have given all sides to the story, but what they have really accomplished is the planting of colossal doubt in the minds of the faithful. It's a classic case of gradualism."

"Culminating in a lie."

"Exactly. It's diabolical."

"Perhaps. It is also quite human."

"Elijah, I tell you I have just about had it. I want to go away somewhere and find a nice quiet monastery, but sure as shootin', the abbot would turn out to be a closet modernist. God, I'm so sick of this!"

"How are things at the general's office?"

"He's keeping pretty close-mouthed. You can tell he's disturbed by it all, but he doesn't want to make waves. He keeps smiling and smiling to everyone who comes along, and he mutters little nostrums about keeping the peace and not getting anxious. Hell, I'm anxious!"

"You mustn't be."

"What?" Smith growled. "Don't tell me you've been bit by the bug!"

"Not in the least, but I do know that if the enemy cannot trap us into error he can achieve another kind of victory by making us lose our peace. If he can provoke us to rage, he has drawn us into his schemes."

"What do you suggest?"

"Recover your equilibrium. Pray for the Holy Father. Forgive our enemies, speak the truth sincerely and calmly whenever an opportunity arises. But guard the gates of your heart, Father. Guard them carefully."

The priest looked down. "You're right", he said.

Elijah reached out and tapped the other man's chest: "Your pain becomes a powerful prayer when it is united to the Cross of Christ. He is suffering in His Church."

Smith said nothing. His eyes grew damp.

"Well, it probably won't be long anyway. The general thinks he's made a mistake bringing me here. I'm sure of it. My name appears on no official documents. They hide me like an embarrassment. I'm tucked away in a basement office all day long, editing the most innocuous little submissions. I've been directed to cut out any bit of text that even hints at controversy. The result is a custard pudding that's so utterly bland and stripped of nutrients that it doesn't deserve the name Catholic journalism. I sit there day after day pruning away every note of masculinity in those articles. We've been neutered, Elijah, and I don't like it. Not one little bit."

"You are angry."

"Of course I'm angry! Shouldn't I be?"

"I think it is a healthy thing to be angry about what is happening. The real question is what we do with our anger."

"Very wise", said Smith sarcastically, his gentle face contorted with bitterness.

"Can you take that anger and turn it into prayer? Can you take the enemy's blows and turn them against him?"

"Put it that way, I suppose there's some merit in staying in the basement."

"Think of it as a catacomb."

Smith's face relaxed for the first time, and he offered a grudging smile.

"You monks. You're incredible."

"Do you think I don't wrestle with anger?"

"You? My spiritual director and mentor? Don't tell me that beneath your unflappable exterior there beats an unruly heart."

"There does."

Smith's humor improved visibly.

"That's good news. Now tell me, what do *you* do with your unruly impulses?"

"Just what I suggested. I try to convert them. The fuel of prayer."

"Hmmm. Not a bad idea. Does it work?"

"It got you out of a bathing suit and into a basement."

"All right, you win this argument", Smith laughed. "Without you and the Lord, I'd probably be prancing around in deer antlers at this very moment."

The two priests finished their coffee, left some coins on the table, and strolled along the Tiber until they reached a bus stop.

"I'd better get back. They keep a close watch on me over there at general headquarters. I'm still officially dysfunctional, and I don't want to get the general worried. He's already taken some flack for having me here."

"It sounds as if he is not a bad man."

"There's the trouble, isn't it? He's a good man, but he's got no courage. Hardly anybody has courage anymore. That's what's so disheartening. No one wants to stop these guys who're going for power. No one can bear to be criticized. They're all paralyzed."

"The Pope is doing his best. There are many loyal cardinals. They try to maintain the peace and keep calling people back to the realities."

"The realities? I've almost forgotten what those are. Refresh my memory."

"Spread the Gospel, teach, feed, protect—and conform ourselves to the image of the One who carried a Cross and died on it."
Smith bowed his head, musing privately, until the bus arrived
and he was taken away.

*   *   *

For the remainder of the summer, Elijah resumed his studies of
apocalyptic literature. During a rummage through the stacks of
the Carmelite library, he came upon a facsimile edition of a
commentary on the Book of the Apocalypse by an eighth-century
Spanish monk named Beatus of Liébana. Saint Beatus had written the text of his commentary during the upheavals of the Arab
occupation. A tenth-century artist named Maius, a monk of the
Monastery of Saint Michael, had illuminated it with the flamboy-
ant colors and absolutely unique iconography of medieval Spain.

The imagery was dazzling. Purple dragons coiled around the
acid-yellow cities of man. Emerald seraphs spun the azure disc of
the cosmos. Indigo scorpions stung their victims. Archangels
plunged stiff from the heavens, swords outstretched, lit by neon.
Gardens exploded with ripe fruit, axes fell, heads rolled off the
martyrs' bodies like harvests in an orchard. Blood spurted, entrails
spilled. Rivers of ink spewed from snake mouths. Trumpets blew.
The messenger to the church at Sardis scowled in warning: *You
have the reputation for being alive; yet you are dead. Awake! Awake and
strengthen the things that remain.* More trumpets blew. Blood! Fire!
Flood! Two monks bore witness against the Antichrist. Hot gold
light burst from their lips. The Antichrist killed them as his
servants dismantled Jerusalem, stone by stone. Hovering over all,
the fierce face of Christ on His throne, waiting for the Last
Day—the Great Judge—far more terrifying than the beast who
gorged on the ruby flesh of saints.

The text was insightful and of historical interest. But Elijah
was especially moved by the colophon inscribed at the end of the
manuscript:

Let the voice of the faithful resound and re-echo! Let Maius, small indeed, but eager, rejoice, sing, re-echo, and cry out!

Remember me, servants of Christ, you who dwell in the monastery of the supreme messenger, the Archangel Michael.

I write this in awe of the exalted patron, and at the command of Abbot Victor, out of love for the book of the vision of John the disciple.

As part of its adornment I have painted a series of pictures for the wonderful words of its stories, so that the wise may fear the coming of the future judgment of the world's end.

Glory to the Father and to His only Son, to the Holy Spirit, and the Trinity from age to age until the end of time.

Elijah at first passed over the pun in the colophon, then returned to it: The reference to "small indeed" was no flourish of scribal humility, especially when measured against the artist's name, *Maius,* literally "major". It was a joke, and another monk, living a thousand years later, laughed.

He further noted that the Beatus apocalypse had emerged from the chaos of Moorish Spain at the same time as the Averroëst copy of Aristotle. He reminded himself that God was always far ahead of human and diabolical strategems. He also wondered why hindsight seemed to be the only faculty for discerning the ways of divine Providence.

As summer ended, Elijah put away the Beatus *Apokalypsis* and made the necessary preparations for teaching his courses. He moved from day to day in a state of peace, which he suspected was the result of the invisible prayers being offered for him across the world. With just a twinge of remorse, he was more convinced than ever that his mission had failed, although he did not say anything to the Cardinal Secretary about this. He was resigned to remaining in Rome indefinitely, perhaps even to spending the remainder of his life teaching at the International College, but he secretly hoped to return to the desert. At some point, the Pope, *Stato,* and *Dottrina* would realize that other avenues of approach to the President would have to be explored. Clearly, the letter of admonition had elicited no response. Though it had been worded with tact and imparted the primary insight with no direct confrontation, the President would surely understand his meaning: the spirit of Christ was at variance with the striving for exalted station in this life. Almost certainly the President had wiped him off the list of prospective devotees. In all likelihood, Elijah would not be invited again to enter the presence of the Great Man. This inner conviction—more accurately a hope—gave him an immense sense of relief.

During the week before commencement of classes, his relative calm was disturbed by a letter from Anna Benedetti.

> Foligno, 2 September
> Dear Father Schäfer,
> Our meeting in Warsaw impressed me greatly. In retrospect, there is much that I would have liked to discuss with you. I have a house near Foligno where it is possible to receive guests without the usual distress of public ceremony. You would honor me if you would consider a visit. My son Marco and my daughter Gianna will be returning to Milan next week. Before they leave, I would like them to meet you. You would, I think, remind them of their father, whose absence has left a gap in their lives. Would this coming weekend be convenient for you? If you will consent, I shall send a car.
> Sincerely,
> Anna B.

He wrestled with conflicting emotions for some hours before writing his reply:

Rome, 6 September
Dear Dr. Benedetti,

He crossed out her formal title and began again.

Dear Anna,
You honor me with your invitation. I would like to come to see you and your children. However, my responsibilities as the academic year draws near prevent me from accepting. Our meeting in Warsaw was significant for me also. I shall always admire you and pray for you.
Sincerely,
Fr. Elijah Schäfer

He hoped that the tone was cordial, sufficiently warm yet detached. He hoped that she would read this signal properly and approach him no more. He had placed the memory of her alongside Ruth and Pawel, alongside the many whom he loved, and who would remain outside the parameters of his sacrifice until they met again in Paradise, where all love found completion and perfection. He bore too many wounds, suffered the impulses of too much need, for him to trust his heart in her presence.

Was he being false, he wondered. But what was the truth, especially when the heart was involved? Was there anything more unstable than the heart? Would it be any more honest to say to her, *I am drawn to you, Anna, but my life belongs to another, One whom you do not believe in?* How could she possibly understand that?

He loved her. Yes, he admitted that. Without realizing it, he had allowed her face, her voice, and her soul to become intimate. He also loved Christ. And he knew that if he were to love himself in the most profound and godly sense, he must not abandon the indelible character of his life—his celibate priesthood, eschatological sign of the end of history—carrying in his own flesh a word about the final objective of love, the ultimate consummation toward which all human love strived, and which all human love fell short of on this earth.

In Paradise, he would tell her, *in Paradise we . . .*

There he was again, he said angrily to himself, having a conversation with her. He realized that his imagination was now stirred. If he did not stop it instantly, it would soon be inflamed by riotous feelings.

He had told the truth in his reply. He did admire her. He would pray for her — yes, there was no doubt about that — until the end of his life. But he needed distance. He needed to retreat to the desert as soon as possible.

He had only just put the matter from his mind when another letter arrived.

> Foligno, 9 September
> Dear Father Schäfer,
> I understand your position perfectly. Please be assured that my respect for you is total, and that it includes your life's commitment. There are few people I can trust in my present situation. Fewer still who are wise. My need is great and the matter is urgent. Would you reconsider? I guarantee your freedom.
> Sincerely,
> Anna Benedetti

She guaranteed his freedom? What was she saying? Had she correctly read whatever fragments of himself had slipped out between the lines of his terse reply and deduced the rest? If so, the situation was more impossible than ever. He could not go.

On the other hand, she was a soul, perhaps a soul in distress. Until now, she had appeared to be the kind of person who did not permit herself to experience distress. Wealth, education, status — these were an impenetrable armor. Who or what could distress her? Harm her? And what did she mean by *need* and *urgent?*

He was still debating with himself when the porter came and told him he had a telephone call.

"Hello", she said. "Have you received my letter?"

"I have."

"Can you come?"

"It's difficult."

"I beg you."

"Your letter didn't explain anything. Are you in some trouble?"

"Yes."

"What kind of trouble?"

"It's not possible to discuss it now."

"Danger?"

"Partly. Please."

Her voice was calm but insistent.

"Really, Anna, there must be others to whom you can turn. Is there anyone . . . ?"

"This concerns you as well."

The silence hung between them. Several times he opened his mouth and closed it again. He felt anguish and elation.

"It also concerns your Church."

"The Church?"

"I can't discuss it now. Please, you must come."

"All right. I will come. When?"

"Tomorrow my son goes to Rome on family business. He will pick you up at your residence in the evening, after supper, and bring you to the farm."

"All right."

Her sigh of relief was audible, and puzzling.

"If you are in some kind of danger, shouldn't I come now?"

"It would be better if you travel with Marco. I ask you not to discuss this with him. He knows nothing."

"Nothing about what?"

"I have kept my children safe from . . . from the difficulties of my life. Please don't disturb their happiness."

"Anna, you must tell me . . ."

"I can't. Later, you will understand." She hung up.

He located Foligno on the large relief map of Italy that hung in the corridor by the porter's office. It was just south of Assisi. This was providential, for he had been longing to see Don Matteo. He had written to the friar several times throughout the summer, but had not received a reply. He had telephoned the convent twice only to be told each time that Don Matteo was ill and could not write or receive visitors. Regardless, Elijah determined that he would try to see him during the coming weekend.

XVI

Foligno

After supper on Friday evening, Elijah dressed himself in slacks, a white shirt, and windbreaker, at the request of the prior, who was worried about an upsurge of anticlerical incidents in the *campagna*. He prayed his breviary, walking back and forth on the sidewalk in front of the college. A red sports car pulled up to the curb and the driver, an agile young man, jumped out.

"You're Mamma's friend", he said, pulling off his sunglasses, shaking Elijah's hand vigorously. "I'm Marco. Ready for a space ride?"

"Ready for anything", Elijah smiled back.

Marco drove with total disregard for the reality of death. They were soon out of the city and speeding along the superhighway that shot north toward Florence.

They chatted about inconsequential things for a time until the boy said, "You're a priest."

"Yes. Can you tell?"

"Not from the cool rags. But it shows."

"What are the symptoms?"

"Nothing you could put your finger on. I guess it rubs off on you guys."

"And you, Marco? What do you want to do in life?"

"I'm a law student. It's in the genes." He flashed Elijah a look.

"Is your sister also studying to be a lawyer?"

"No. Gianna's in med school."

"Is that in the genes also?"

"She's a mutant. The black sheep of the family."

"I look forward to meeting her."

"You'll like her. She's sensible, like Mamma."

"And you are not?"

"No, I guess I'm not", he said cheerily.

The sun was setting when they turned onto an eastbound highway that wound up into the Umbrian hills.

"Will there be many guests?"

"I don't think so. As far as I know you're the only one."

"Your house at Foligno must mean a lot to you."

"We spend our summers there, and Christmas."

"Each of you travels far."

"Milan's not that far."

"It's a long journey for your mother."

"She flew from The Hague. She flies all over the place. We have houses in France and Belgium, and a *palazzo* in Roma. But Foligno is the best of all."

"Is it the most beautiful?"

"Yes. You'll be surprised at how beautiful it is. It's *grandiose!*"

"Grandiose? Better than the *palazzo?*"

"Far better. It's splendid. It's opulent."

"More so than France and Belgium?"

"You forgot San Marino."

"Better than San Marino?"

"Even better. It's a mansion."

Elijah began to wonder if he would enjoy the coming weekend. He did not feel comfortable in opulent residences.

"How is your mother?"

There was a barely perceptible pause before Marco replied.

"She's really tired. I'm glad we've got company this weekend. She needs a change."

"Really? In what sense?"

"Mamma does too much. Of course she's famous. Splendid accomplishments and all that. But . . . "

"But?"

The boy shrugged.

"Look", he said, distracting Elijah. "There's Terni coming up fast! After that we go north again and then it's not so far."

Forty-five hair-raising minutes later, the car pulled off onto a dirt road that wound up the side of a mountain covered in vineyards. Slowing a little, the boy used an electronic device to open a gate that loomed out of the dark ahead of them and closed it behind. Five minutes later, he braked in front of a small sagging farmhouse, draped with vines.

"Our mansion", grinned Marco.

Elijah got out and looked. "This is opulence!" he said.

The boy laughed appreciatively.

The front door opened, and Anna came out onto the crumbling stone steps.

"Father Schäfer", she said graciously. "You have survived. Thank you, Marco."

"It's nothing, Mamma. He's a tough one."

"Marco is very hard on our guests. He has shortened the life of many."

She led them into the house. They entered a parlor outfitted in old Italian country furniture, which looked authentic, and went through to a large kitchen illuminated by gas lamp and candles. A lovely young woman standing by a wood stove put a ladle into a simmering pot and wiped a hand on her apron. She came over with a charming smile and shook his hand.

"This is Gianna. Father Schäfer."

"I'm very pleased to meet you, Father. I hope you like it here. It's rather simple."

"That is what I like best."

"This was my mother's family home", said Anna. "She was

393

born on a bed upstairs. My great-grandfather built this house for his bride in the eighteen-hundreds."

"*I Promessi Sposi*", said Elijah.

The three Italians looked at him and burst out laughing.

"I like him", said Marco. "He can stay."

"How good of you", Gianna said jabbing him in the ribs. The brother and sister wrestled for a few seconds until the boy threw her off and made for the staircase.

"I'm beat", he said going up. "I've got to be out of here at the crack of dawn. *Buona notte* everyone!"

"*Buona notte*", they called.

"He's going sailing on the Adriatic tomorrow", explained Anna. "Mamma, why don't you two go to the parlor and have a sip of wine. The cannellone will be ready in a while. I'll call you."

They went into the sitting room with their drinks. Anna sat across the room from him.

"What wonderful children you have", he said.

"Thank you."

"Gianna is so much like you."

"She is more like a sister to me than a daughter. She has always been mature, even when she was a child."

"Marco, too, is charming—a fine young man."

"He's the delight of my heart. But he is a little spoiled."

"It must have been difficult to raise them by yourself."

She looked down at the floor while sipping from her glass.

"Is he like his father?"

"Yes. Very much like him."

"Anna, you sounded so worried on the phone."

"We'll talk about it later. I don't want Gianna to overhear."

They made conversation until the girl came and called them to supper. She and her mother ate a full meal. Elijah, who had eaten in Rome, picked at his plate. Gianna asked him travelogue questions about Israel. He gave the answers. She said she would like to work on a kibbutz when she graduated. He told some amusing stories, and they lingered over their wine. Eventually the girl yawned, kissed her mother, said good night, and went upstairs.

Anna looked across the table.

"You're tired", she said.

"I am. But I will never sleep if I don't learn what is troubling you."

"You won't sleep if I tell you."

"If I have a choice, I would like to know tonight."

"It's complicated. The telling of it will be long."

"Then we should begin."

Her eyes darkened and her lips grew firm. "Because of my work I have developed a frame of mind that is analytical. I try to keep strictly to logic and law. That, at least, must be obvious."

"Indeed it is."

"I'm not a sentimental woman. I have always been—how shall I call it—*cautious* about nonobjective reality. This helped me as a young lawyer to prevail in a field dominated by men. In those years, one had to be twice as levelheaded as a male lawyer in order to be considered half as good. That is no longer so much the case, but when I began my practice it was true. I value that period of my life. It taught me a lot. Suffice it to say that I became adept at protecting my emotions. I rose in the legal profession, and as a result I am now where I am. I worked for this. I think I have earned it. But there was a cost. I rejected everything from my life that fell outside the precise boundaries of the rational. I lost my faith in God, in the Church, and in humanity as a species. I came to consider law as a teaching tool and a safeguard against the irrational forces in society.

"Then I met another young lawyer, Stefano Benedetti. He was just beginning to have some influence in the Christian Democrat party. He was being groomed for the leadership. Italian politics were a mess, full of corruption and confusion. Stefano was honest and very, very bright. He was also a man of honor, and it was said by many that within the decade he could be the next prime minister. It was an exciting time for us. We were so happy. Gianna came along in our second year of marriage, and Marco arrived a year after that. Stefano's family is wealthy. There was never any question of need. There were nannies. There were expensive vacations. Life was full and rewarding. After each birth, I resumed my practice within a few months. We climbed and climbed, without any of the usual clawing and manipulating that goes on in that kind of life. It seemed effortless. We were the golden couple.

"Then one night in 1982 Stefano left his office and never arrived home. He just disappeared, without warning, without ransom notes, without any indication of where he had gone."

"You must have been mad with worry."

"I can't describe to you the torments I endured."

"I knew nothing of this. I was buried in Carmel during those years. We had no real access to current events. Was he ever found?"

"They found his body two months after his disappearance. He died by strangulation. He had been tortured."

"I'm so sorry."

"You needn't say anything. I know how difficult it must be to listen to a tale like this."

"Did the police find the killers?"

"No. There has never been a single piece of evidence pointing in any direction, not even a misleading one. Total silence."

"Do you think it was politically motivated?"

"I thought so until recently."

"You no longer think so?"

"I have no evidence, but I believe the reason for his death is entangled with something so vast and sinister that it's appalling to think of it."

"Then wouldn't it be better to forget . . . "

"Forget? I can never forget. I had to identify the body. What they did to him is beyond belief. The children have never been told. They know only that their father was assassinated, and they think, as I did for so many years, that it was a senseless act of terrorism, the Red Brigade or the covert fascist revival."

"Has something happened to throw new light on the crime?"

"Nothing. It's not a question of juridical evidence."

Elijah shook his head: "I don't understand."

"It's intuition . . . a womanly faculty that long lay dormant within me. I must now go back several years to describe another situation, one that seems to have no bearing on Stefano's death. You are no doubt aware that I know the President personally."

Elijah nodded, unsure of where she was leading.

"Our generation was dazzled by him. He was younger then. He wasn't well known in the world, though even then he was beginning to be influential. You felt a sense of destiny clinging to him. He was very wealthy. He had connections to important banks in Italy, France, and Switzerland. He was a polymath. All those languages and degrees. He was writing books. Stefano said he was an outstanding economist, and more to his credit, a highly principled one. The list of his accomplishments is endless, as you know. He was the sincerest man I had ever met, after Stefano. He was always the humanitarian, always apolitical—in fact, some of his closest associates belonged to rival parties. He drew an amazingly eclectic group of people into his circle, and he possessed a remarkable skill for making each of us feel as if his interest were purely personal. One never felt used, even when it came to pass that this or that service would be appreciated by him. Such requests—I hesitate to call them that—were always expressed without pressure. He was, and is, a master of subtlety.

"But Stefano didn't like him. This was always a puzzle to me. When I pressed him for a reason he couldn't put his finger on anything wrong with the man; he mistrusted him, but on some level that was inaccessible to me. My husband was a devout Catholic, you realize, and maybe that gave him some antennae that I had lost along the way. He gradually began to withdraw from that circle. I went along with him, of course, but unwillingly. We begged off the wonderful parties, the cultural events, the stream of invitations. Eventually, we were no longer asked."

"When was this?"

"About three years before Stefano's death."

"Permit me, Anna, but I couldn't help noticing your familiarity with the President when we dined with him in Rome and Warsaw. At some point you must have resumed contact."

"Yes."

"Did he come to the funeral?"

"Oh, yes. He was there, but he was lost in the crowd. There were hundreds of dignitaries there, not to mention our families. I didn't notice his presence, and if I had I would have attributed it to his social graces. An official condolence, swiftly forgotten. And yet, in the years following the death, he hired several private agencies to pursue the investigation long after the police had abandoned it. It must have cost him a fortune. He quietly turned Italy upside down in search of clues, and he did so without telling me. I eventually heard about it through mutual friends, and of course I was touched. I was so grateful. I sent him a card of thanks. He wrote back. The invitations started up again. I was heartbroken and terribly lonely. I attended some events, thinking that I might meet someone who could heal the gash in the bottom of my existence. My life was hemorrhaging out of that hole. But there was no one. No one could ever replace Stefano."

Her voice trembled, but she quickly regained her composure. "If Gianna and Marco hadn't needed me so much, I would have killed myself. They saved my life."

"And the President? Did he offer companionship, consolation?"

"He tried. But even *he* couldn't get through. Despite his many kindnesses, something inside of me couldn't bear to draw close to a person Stefano had disliked so much. I put up the usual barriers a woman knows how to put up. We established a cordial relationship, which has continued uninterrupted to this day."

"Why do you remain a part of his company?"

"There are memories of Stefano attached to that circle, old friends, many connections useful to my work. I am a private person, and it is isolating to be the kind of person I am. I work far too much. The children are always complaining to me about it. So, being loosely attached to the President's circle opens some doors for me. It provides many welcome diversions."

"I thought you were an intimate."

"Everyone and no one is his intimate. There are circles within circles, and I occupy a position within an intermediate ring, far from the radioactive core, which is the President himself, but farther in than many people who consider him a close friend. It's a very odd position."

"A unique one, I would guess."

"That may be so. There has never been any romantic involvement, if that's what you're wondering. No involvement of any kind."

Elijah sipped judiciously from his glass. It was empty. Anna got up and returned with the bottle.

"I'm wearing you out. It's late and you must be utterly fatigued. Driving with Marco is a sure recipe for exhaustion of the nervous system."

"I'm fine. I would be happy to talk all night if you like."

"Where was I? Oh, yes, the post-death relationship."

"Yes, that surprises me. What was his purpose?"

"In keeping me? I'm mostly ornamental. I'm a public figure. He borrows an air of civic stability from association with me and people like me. Money is tainted. Men like him cherish a sterling reputation far more than their fortunes."

Here she paused and looked at the dark window, curtained with yellow lace.

"I've been rambling. I shouldn't do that. It's unbecoming in a judge. Where was I?"

"You referred earlier to some new light that has been thrown on the mystery surrounding your husband's death. You spoke of an intuition."

"Oh, yes. How can I describe it? Let's say that for many years I have filed away a large number of unexplained details gleaned from the social life in Europe. Most of it is insignificant, but some of it rises to the surface and has no explanation. None of it would be admissible as evidence in a courtroom. But as a judge you learn to detect things beneath the level of words, while striving to retain the fundamental objectivity."

"For example?"

"A year ago your name came up at a party."

"A year ago I was digging in the garden at Carmel."

"Be that as it may, your name came up. You were mentioned as a man who had once risen in Israel and who might have been a forerunner of the kind of thing the President is now doing. Someone—I forget who—made a sneering reference to the fact that you had 'got religion' and thrown it all away. I found that intriguing. I had never met anyone who would consider doing such a thing. I thought I would like to meet you, but of course I dismissed it as unlikely.

"Something happened during those few minutes when you were discussed. At the time it seemed insignificant, but for some reason I didn't forget it. I put it away in my mysteries file. When you were discussed something passed behind the President's eyes. How can I describe it without sounding like a writer of ghost stories trying to spook her audience with silly melodrama? I can only say that I saw a shadow pass through his eyes—behind his eyes. It took a split second. The look frightened me. Yet it was so quickly come and gone that I almost disbelieved I had seen anything. But that look triggered a memory which had been dormant for several years. I recalled a party that Stefano and I had attended at the Galéone Palace in Rome, almost twenty years before. On that occasion, we were having a wonderful time. The world glowed. Stefano was so admired. People loved him. You would have loved him too."

She choked at this point, caught herself, and continued:

"I had gone outside to breathe the night air. I was pregnant with Marco then and was feeling nauseous. I stood on the little balcony that overlooks a garden in the inner courtyard. A beautiful tree grows there, and I was fond of it. That evening, despite my upset stomach, I was deliriously happy. I wondered if there were anyone as happy as I on this earth. I went back into the small salon, the same room in which years later you and I first met. No one noticed me when I came in. There were all kinds of people there. Powerful people. Generals, financiers, politicians. Stefano was talking about the need to regenerate a moral vision for European politics. He called it Christian humanism. In those years, I found his unabashed Catholicism somewhat embarrassing. Like most of the people in the room I had rejected the Christian brand of humanism, but I loved him for his courage, and I couldn't help admiring him. I was grateful for such a husband. He spoke passionately and eloquently. It was spellbinding. Everyone listened. I glanced at our host, expecting to see in his face what I felt in my heart. I thought that he too must love Stefano. Instead I saw something that startled me. He appeared to be appreciating Stefano, but a shadow passed across and through and behind his eyes. It shocked me. I shook it off as a figment of my imagination. It sank into my subconscious where it remained until last year when I saw that same look come into him at the mention of your name. Then I understood that the man who has become the most powerful figure in the world had hated my husband."

"And by implication hates me as well."

"That may be true, if I'm right."

"It could be groundless."

"I could be", she said doubtfully.

"But you don't think so?"

"I think my intuitions are correct."

"And so, what does it mean? Are you saying he may have been involved in Stefano's death?"

"I don't know. I'm not sure. I have gone on as before, attending his banquets and committees, but with eyes wide open, watching, waiting. And my antennae are quivering at every turn. Infinitesimally small things. Signals, glances, shadows."

"As you said, nothing that could stand up in a courtroom."

"Precisely. It's not on that level of manifestation."

"I still don't understand my involvement. Why his interest in me?"

"When your name was mentioned so disdainfully, the President said something that seemed insignificant at the time, but which I now suspect had another meaning. He said that regardless of your religion you were a person of outstanding qualities and could contribute something valuable to the new order. That's exactly how he expressed it—*contribute something valuable to the new order.* No more was said, but I detected that strange mixture of malice and desire. I realized that he hated you and yet he wanted to use you for something. It totally baffled me. Why should he hate you, a man he had never met?"

"People hate each other for all kinds of reasons."

"But why you?"

Elijah thought. "It might be a hatred that has no roots in human motives. It might be purely spiritual."

"What are you saying?"

"The soul is not as simple as we think it is. Intellect, imagination, emotions, physical processes. The distinctive parts of the human makeup can overlap, blur, shift. Thoughts influence feelings and vice versa. Health influences mood and vice versa. Can anyone really know what happens in the privacy of this man's soul? And yet I suspect he instinctively recognized that I represent the antithesis of his vision."

"He didn't appear to believe that would be a problem."

"He is accustomed to influencing men's minds. If a man can change as radically as I changed, isn't it possible that I could be changed back again, back to his vision?"

"Is that possible?"

"The question is, does *he* think it's possible? Obviously, he does, or he would not have tried to draw me into your circle."

"But the malice . . . it was so instantaneous."

"His reaction could very well have been sparked by spiritual forces originating outside of the soul."

Anna looked dubious and waved away the thought with a hand.

"Devils? I'm sorry, Father, but I'm too much the rationalist to entertain that idea."

He paused and considered. Would there be any point at this late hour in trying to convince her of the reality of unseen warfare? He would leave that for another day.

She changed the subject for him:

"When I met you that first time I saw that you possessed a character as honorable as Stefano's but lacked his social graces. A man without guile, you are. Even so, as I listened to you and observed you, I asked myself if you would become another von Tilman. I wondered how they would try to reshape you. I thought they would probably succeed, because they almost always do."

"And what have you concluded?"

"You are not a von Tilman. You never could be. Warsaw demolished that fear. But you are still a mystery to me."

"It's quite simple, Anna. There is no mystery."

"Then clear it up for me."

"A man is what he loves. A man is what he will live for and die for."

"What do you love? What is real for you?"

"I love God. He is real."

"Theology isn't logical."

"Logic doesn't contain theology; theology contains logic."

"That's debatable. Oh, damn, there we go; now we're sliding into the world of abstractions, where this sort of conversation always ends."

"The love God pours out on the world is effective in our lives to the degree that we open ourselves to it. Until we do, we presume it is just an abstraction."

"Is that so? I suppose it could be. Death was an abstraction until Stefano died."

"It's the same with love."

"But tell me, you who have no human beloved, how can you speak of human love until you have loved another living, breathing human being?"

"The indwelling of divine love contains all human love."

"But I mean flesh and blood. Heat. Passion."

"That too is contained within it, though in a different form."

"Have you never loved a woman?"

He told her about Ruth, and she listened until he was finished. "I'm sorry", she said. "I didn't know."

They drank the last of their wine. Anna stood up.

"There is more to tell you, but it can wait until tomorrow", she said.

She showed him to a bedroom off the parlor.

"We're putting you in here. This was my grandparents' room and my great-grandparents' before them. They were a wonderful old couple. Very devout", she said pensively, touching a small crucifix on the wall above an antique washstand. A framed engraving of the Sacred Heart hung above the narrow bed.

"Tell me about them?"

"Nonno was a farmer. Nonna was a housewife. They didn't have much education. They were like a little banty rooster and hen, always together, never apart a day in their lives. The Rosary every night. This house was full of love. Seven children; my mother was the youngest. They saved every penny and sent her to college. She met my father there. He was from Firenze, the son of a city counsellor. Upper-middle-class people."

"Where are your mother and father now?"

"Both gone. The land was divided up among the family, but the house passed to me when Mamma died. I treasure this place more than anything else in the world. I've changed nothing. When the world gets too much for me I come here. Gianna and Marco don't feel quite the same about it. They have their futures ahead of them, and young people don't think about tradition. Gianna will understand some day. This will be hers when I'm gone."

"It's a room full of peace. I will sleep well here."

"*Bene!* It's time for you to do that. *Buona notte,* Father Elijah."

"*Buona notte,* Anna."

*   *   *

He slept well, as predicted. He got up with the sun, prayed his office, and celebrated a private Mass in the bedroom before the rest of the household was awake. Not long after, he heard Marco gunning the motor of his car, then someone clanking the lid on the kitchen stove. Coffee and bacon smells soon spilled through the cracks in the doorway.

He found Gianna sitting by the stove tending a frying pan and a pot of coffee.

"Good morning, Father."

"Good morning, Gianna. It looks like a beautiful day out there."

"Not a cloud to be seen. The forecast is for cooler weather. It won't be too hot."

She served him bacon and toast with gooseberry preserves, a bowl of oatmeal and a cup of coffee.

"Where is your mother?"

"She's sleeping. You must have visited late into the night."

"We did."

"I'm glad you're here. She needs someone to talk to. Life hasn't been easy for her."

"She has many responsibilities."

"Too many."

"She is an amazing woman, your mother."

"Yes, amazing. She gives so much. She takes nothing for herself, except this place now and then."

"She told me about your father. I am sorry about your loss."

The girl nodded and a sadness washed across her face.

"Do you remember him?"

"A little. He was very kind. I remember that he was tall, like a giant. He was handsome. Everyone loved him."

She glanced down at a book lying open on her lap.

"What is that you are reading?"

"Philosophy."

"Do you like philosophy?"

"With a passion", she said wryly. "Don't tell anyone. It ruins a girl's chances."

"You are in no danger of that. There must be a long line-up of gentlemen callers."

"Hundreds of them. I have to bar the door."

"Good. Don't accept the first offer."

"I won't. I promise."

Her bantering mood turned suddenly serious. She flipped the pages and said, "This is a passage I think about a lot. Would you like to hear it?"

"Very much."

"It's by Kierkegaard. Do you know who Kierkegaard is?"

"I do."

She looked amused and impressed.

"Listen to this: *The majority of men are subjective toward themselves and objective toward all others. Terribly objective sometimes. But the real task is in fact to be objective toward oneself and subjective toward all others.*"

She looked up with a delighted expression. "Isn't that wonderful? Doesn't he say everything in just those few lines?"

"He says an important thing."

"Mamma doesn't like that passage. She thinks we should be objective about *everything.*"

"She probably means in regard to her work."

"Oh, it's more than that. She wants everything to stay cool and detached. She wants to be separate from life. She was badly hurt, you know. I tell her, *Mamma, you don't need to be a judge every waking moment.* She agrees but can't seem to change. Her only soft spots are Marco and me and this mountain."

"She is blessed to have you."

"I think she's blessed to have found you, Father. She needs a friend."

"I'm sure she has many friends."

"Hundreds of them. She has to bar the door too."

She refilled his cup and stacked three more pieces of thick toast on his plate.

"Eat!"

"I willingly obey, Gianna."

She went back to the stove and laid slices of ham in the pan.

"You know what she said to me when she was trying to arrange this weekend?"

"No."

"She said that in all the years since Papà's death you're the first person she felt she could trust completely."

"That is quite an honor coming from your mother. I hope I deserve it."

She looked at him gravely, wondering what he meant. Then she grinned. "Such humility! I'd forgotten what religious people could be like."

"Aren't there any in Milan?"

"There are some."

"Are you close to any?"

"One. He's humble like you. But he's proud too."

She looked away, musing.

"That's all? Just one Christian at the University of Milan?"

"They move in other circles. I'm a loner."

"Aren't there any circles for young philosophers?"

"Yes. But most of them are like me. It's hard to organize a loner's club."

"What do your philosopher friends believe in?"

"When I started medical school, the people I knew in philosophy were mostly Marxists. Idiots! Well, half-idiots: they were Gramsci Marxists, not the Gulag-and-torture-chamber kind. A lot of them are sick of it now. Some have become capitalists. Quite a few became environmentalists. Some are going back to the Church."

"What happened to make them change?"

"I guess our generation just grew up. It's interesting the way the most simple minds, and the finest, eventually go back to the Church. We agnostics find that strange."

"Ah, so you are an agnostic!"

"Don't laugh at me, Father Schäfer, or I'll burn your ham."

"I apologize."

"I guess faith gives some people strength to face life. Life can be ugly."

"And very beautiful."

"That too. But no one's ever explained the ugly part. I'll never forget the first time I assisted at an autopsy. Do you want to hear about it?"

He looked at the slices of red meat she was putting on his plate. She burst out laughing.

"No, I guess you don't."

"Oh, yes, I would like to hear. Please tell me."

She stood gazing into midair, the spatula dangling from her hand.

"It was the oddest feeling. There were about a dozen corpses laid out on tables in the lab. They all had black plastic bags over their heads, to make it easier for us I guess. To hide the identity. They wouldn't want us to think they were people, would they?"

"I suppose not. That would make it difficult."

"You steel yourself, you calm your nerves, and you watch the professor cut. It's so marvelously technical. Everything in the body has a Latin name. I found it fascinating, but I kept coming back to that plastic bag. I kept wondering who she was, the old lady we were dissecting. The professor called it a cadaver. An *it!* A few of the corpses were people who had donated their bodies to science, but most of them were derelicts given to the university by the city morgue. Ours was a derelict. You could tell she hadn't been a healthy person. Her fingernails were badly stained. No one had looked after her for a long time—you could see that. If I tell you something, will you think I'm strange?"

"It depends on what you tell me."

"You're honest. I'll risk it. At lunchtime everybody went out of the lab. It was the first time for most of us and nobody felt like eating. I went back alone and took off the old lady's plastic bag."

"Why did you do it?"

"I don't know why."

"What did you see?"

"Please don't think I'm crazy, but I saw my grandmother. Not really my grandmother, of course, because she was no one I'd ever known. But I thought, *This could be Nonna.* This could be Mamma in a few years from now. Some day this could be me."

"That is not so strange."

"I'm glad you think that. Then something else happened. I started to weep for her. I cried and cried. The tears fell all over her face. I stroked her forehead. Her hair was wild, caked with dirt. She was a poor old beggar woman, I guess. She probably died alone, unwanted and unloved. I braided her hair around her head. It took a while. Then I covered her up again."

Elijah looked out the window. Gianna shook herself and went back to the stove where she made herself busy.

Anna came down the stairs at that moment and greeted them.

"You look rather serious this morning", she said to her daughter, hugging her.

"I've been telling Father Schäfer how to dissect a body."

"Oh, Gianna, spare us!"

Elijah broke in, "It was really quite interesting. You should be proud of her, Anna."

"I am, I am", she sighed theatrically. "But please, no anatomy discussions before breakfast."

She sat down to eat and said to him, "What would you like to do today?"

"Anything you wish. Do you have any suggestions?"

"We should walk in the hills. I'd like to show you a grotto my great-grandfather made on the mountain."

"Would there be time to go to Assisi?"

"I think so. It's a short drive. Why Assisi?"

"I have a friend there whom I would like to see. We wouldn't stay long."

"All right. We can go after breakfast. We'll walk this afternoon."

She backed a nondescript sedan out of an old stable, and they left for Assisi in a cloud of dust.

"I see you were getting to know my daughter."

"She is delightful. In the space of ten minutes, we covered a lot of territory. We started at philosophy, galloped through religion, and arrived at autopsies."

"That's Gianna all right. I sometimes think she's more of a poet than a doctor."

"I wondered if she would be better suited for philosophy. That is halfway between poetics and science."

"You may be right."

"You seem worried about her."

"No more than usual. I worry about my children out of habit.

410

I ask myself if it was wise to bring them into the world in its present condition."

"They will do well. You have given them that. Gianna is a good soul. She is sensitive and seems very happy."

"She's in love. There's a young man in Milan."

"What is he like? Do you think he is suitable?"

She pulled her eyes away from the road and looked at him. "Suitable? There's an old-fashioned word. How refreshing to hear it. Yes, he's eminently suitable. We're all quite fond of him."

"You don't seem enthusiastic."

"He's young, he's idealistic, and he's studying to be a lawyer. A friend of Marco's. He's not too rich and not too poor; his father is a professor of ethics; he's handsome and manly, warm-hearted, and most extraordinary of all, he's a virgin, if you can imagine. Virgin! There's another old-fashioned word for you. He told her so. He's proud of it. They've decided to wait until the wedding. Stefano was like that too. He's so much like Stefano it frightens me."

"Frightens you? He sounds like an answer to a mother's prayer."

"It's a recipe for disaster. What do you think is going to happen to a young man like that?"

"He may be one of those who bring light back into public life?"

"At what cost? I don't want to see Gianna's heart broken."

"Like yours was?"

"Like mine was."

"Is that fair to Gianna? Doesn't she have the right to risk a broken heart?"

Anna shrugged unhappily. "He's also a devout Catholic."

"He sounds better and better. Is he real?"

"Oh, yes. He's an exotic creature, but quite real."

"At one time he would have been considered normal."

"Those times are gone."

"Are they? I think they are coming back. In their heart of

hearts, most people want fidelity. They want noble spouses who are capable of sacrifice."

"It's impossible to discuss this. We're coming from two different foundations."

"Anna, if we are friends, may I venture a blunt thought?"

"Go ahead."

"I think you are being slightly irrational."

"Irrational! I'm being perfectly rational. *They* are irrational!"

"I also think you are being scandalously subjective."

She shot him a fierce look. She whipped her eyes back to the road. Then her face thawed and she smiled grudgingly.

"You're teasing me."

"A little. Do you mind?"

"I could get used to it."

* * *

"They don't allow women in the convent", he explained. "Do you want to do some sightseeing while I talk to the guestmaster?"

She went off by herself, following a group of tourists into the main church.

The little friar was as gregarious as ever, but he had some unpleasant news:

"I'm sorry, Father. We have strict orders. Don Matteo has been sick all summer. My guess is he's been bleeding too much lately, and they want to build up his health."

"Can I not speak with him for one minute?"

"Sorry."

"He has not answered my letters. He must be seriously ill."

"I hear he is. The prior says nobody gets in to see him except the doctors. News leaked out last year that we have a stigmatist here, and wouldn't you know it, the tourists started swarming in from everywhere. It's been good for us in some ways. Lots of prayers going up to heaven. But the prior had to put his foot down. Next, they'll be tearing poor old Don Matteo to pieces to make relics, he said. It's time to put a stop to the circus, he said. So, quick as a fox they take him . . . "

The little friar covered his mouth.

"Take him where?"

"Forget what I said."

"No, I will not forget. Tell me."

"I can't."

"I have a right to know. He is my spiritual director."

"He is? Oh, that's different then."

He looked confused. He hemmed and hawed.

"Brother, where is Don Matteo?"

"He's not here."

"Where has he been taken?"

"I can't tell you. I already said too much. We're not allowed to tell anyone. The tourists . . . "

"I am not a tourist. Let me speak to the prior."

The prior was located with laborious effort and came to the front wicket.

Elijah repeated his request. The prior refused.

Together they played the cycle of insistence and evasion until Elijah realized he was getting nowhere. He went into the church and saw a familiar form kneeling in the back pew.

"Brother Jakov", he whispered, sliding in beside him.

The giant threw his arms around him and pummelled him exuberantly.

"Father, it is too good you see me! I like it you come back. How you are?"

"Very well, my friend. But I have a problem. I can't seem to locate Don Matteo. Do you know where he is?"

Jakov's face screwed up. His eyes filled with anguish. "I not can tell it to you."

"Why not?"

"Prior says nobody can know it."

"I am Don Matteo's friend. He is my director. The Pope wants me to see him."

Jakov looked unconvinced. "I know it. I remember last time, Father, but now it not can be."

"You must tell me more. At least tell me if Don Matteo is well."

"I think it he sick some more. He bleed lots. He old man and they want him go to rest place."

It was Jakov's turn to cover his mouth.

"It's all right. You haven't told me anything that I didn't already know."

Jakov looked back and forth between Elijah and the tabernacle. His immense body reflected the paroxysm of agony in his heart.

Finally, he said, "You should go to Rieti. It's a nice place there."

"Rieti? Why Rieti?"

"Listen, Father," he said, grabbing the priest's shirt sleeve and tugging, "you go to Rieti. You will like it there. Saint Francis he go there too. Holy place. Holy peoples go there."

"Holy peoples go there?"

"Holy peoples go there. You go. Nice place. See it."

"Rieti?"

"Rieti. Hermitage. Pray there. I want you go see Rieti for nice pretty place. Hermitage."

He gave Elijah a knowing look.

"Thank you Jakov. Yes, I understand. You have told me nothing. You didn't disobey. I will go to the hermitage at Rieti."

The big brother thumped him on the back and winked.

He found Anna sitting behind a pillar near the front of the nave.

"I'm sorry this has taken so long. There has been a mix-up. My friend has been transferred, and it has taken me all this time to find out. Do you think we could extend our drive and go search for him?"

"I don't see why not. Where is he?"

"At Rieti."

They had driven halfway there when it struck him that the worry lines had disappeared from her face.

"I apologize for all that lost time."

"It wasn't lost time. I enjoyed it. I just sat. It was so quiet in there after the tourists left. I looked at the art and it lifted my spirits."

"I'm glad."

"I had a lovely chat with one of the friars. A funny old fellow."

"What did you talk about?"

"About life. He was quite a character. He seemed to know who I was."

"Really?"

"Yes, and he knew you also."

"What did he say?"

"Something about a lion. He wasn't all that coherent, but he really was very sweet. I felt so reassured by his presence. They must have a few senile friars still living there. They live to quite an old age I hear."

"Yes, they do."

"He said he was praying for you. How did he know you were there?"

"Anna, did he have bandages on his hands?"

"I don't know. He kept his hands inside his sleeves. Wait, he did pat me on the shoulder at one point and . . . why yes, you're right, the hand had a bandage on it. It crossed my mind that he had cut himself. It was stained."

"Did he limp badly?"

"Yes? Why?"

"That was my friend."

"Let's go back, then, if he's at Assisi."

"He may not be at Assisi."

"You're not making much sense. He's *at* Assisi but he's *not* at Assisi? You're sounding ever so slightly irrational, Father Elijah."

"I know. Let's go to Rieti."

She raised her eyebrows and drove on in silence.

Fifteen minutes later they found the road leading to the Franciscan houses in the area. They followed it until they reached a lane marked by a wooden sign that said *Hermitage.*

They parked the car at the end of the lane and walked up to a stone building surrounded by a wooden fence. Two friars were bent over weeding a flower garden in the yard. When Elijah and Anna went through the front gate they stood up and stared.

"*Pax et bonum,* brothers, we are looking for Don Matteo."

The friars looked at each other.

"Signore, Signora. This is a private convent. I regret we don't receive visitors here."

"We know Don Matteo is inside."

The friars looked strained, at a loss for what to say.

"Guests must have an appointment", one stammered.

"He is a close friend. I believe he is expecting us."

"It's not permitted."

"Would you kindly tell him that I'm here. You can let him decide."

"That won't be necessary", said a voice from the front door.

Don Matteo stood there, smiling sheepishly, holding onto the frame with a bandaged hand.

The friars rushed over to him and held him up, one on either side. They began to chide in rapid Italian.

"Don Matteo, you know what the doctor said!"

"Now, now, now", he admonished them tenderly. "Don't fret. I was expecting them. You can leave us."

"You are not supposed to get out of bed. You must go back and lie down."

"A few minutes won't hurt. Let me just sit here on the bench. We will talk for a bit. Go on, now."

The friars went away, leaving Don Matteo resting in a pool of sunshine. Elijah and Anna sat down on the porch steps.

"Hello again, young lady."

"Hello. How did you get back here so quickly?"

"I travel fast", he said, his eyes twinkling.

Elijah reached up and took one of Don Matteo's hands in both of his. He held it without pressure. He did not let it go.

"Father Elijah, you look good. How are you?"

"There is so much to tell you I don't know where to begin."

"So! Tell me, how are the gates?"

"The gates?"

"The gates of your heart."

"Battered but holding firm."

"As I thought. Very good. How is the fear?"

"Some victories, some losses."

"Yes, yes, that's normal. Now listen, I have a message for you."

"A message? From whom?"

"From our King. He wants me to tell you this: *By day and by night my gaze is fixed upon you. I see how much you suffer for me.*

"He wants you to know that he permits these adversities to increase your merit. All merit lies in the will. No other sacrifice compares with the immolation of your heart. He doesn't reward for success, but for patience and hardship undergone for His sake. No success matters as much as perfect obedience, for it is this which prepares the way for the action of divine grace in your soul. It is through your weakness that He will work most powerfully to bring mercy to mankind. He knows your fear, and He wants you to come to Him and lay your head against His heart. He asks you to talk with Him as friend to friend. He says that there is much opposition and deception coming. You must expect this and not be dismayed by it. He will console you at certain times, but the greater work is to do His will in the darkness of faith. Faith is of utmost importance.

"*Know this,* He says, *know this: I am always in your heart, and My love is released to others when you trust in Me completely. You are My son.*"

Elijah closed his eyes. All thoughts, all emotions, all impressions faded. He plunged deep into his interior and rested there, motionless, suspended in being, in perfect peace.

Anna had listened to the foregoing with amazement. She stared at the two priests, trying to comprehend what she had observed. It made no sense.

Don Matteo looked at her.

"I have a message for you too, little sister. The Lord asks me to tell you that your martyr is with Him."

"My martyr?" she murmured.

"He who shares the name of the first martyr. He who was the companion of your soul."

"Stefano?"

Don Matteo nodded.

Elijah slowly raised his head. He saw first the tender expression of the old friar and then the bewilderment in Anna's eyes.

At that moment the two friars returned with a highly agitated third, who brusquely announced that the meeting was over.

Don Matteo got up painfully and hobbled back inside, escorted by the friars. Anna did not move. Elijah took her arm and drew her to her feet. They walked slowly back to the car and returned to Foligno without further conversation.

*　　*　　*

That afternoon she took him up the mountain behind the farmhouse. A thin veil of cloud covered the sky and a cool breeze swayed the pines. She led the way on a path that wound between old vineyards fallen into disuse, invaded by tangled brambles and scrub brush. The land became steadily drier as they climbed, and the path thinned. At the crest of a hill topped by an outcropping of rock, they came to a patch of grass from which one could see the entire valley. Cut into the rock was a grotto. A plaster statue of the Mother of Christ stood there, its white paint discolored and peeling, its head crowned with a circlet of crumbling plastic flowers. Birds had built nests in the crevasses between the stones.

Anna sat on the grass at the base of the image and looked up into its serene face.

"Seven swords pierce her heart", she said. "I used to come here with my grandmother when I was a girl. We prayed beneath the image. She taught me the Rosary. My parents didn't like that. They were educated. They thought of themselves as liberated from the old superstitions of country people."

"Our Lady of Sorrows."

"Yes, that's what Nonna called her. It used to frighten me when I was little, but my grandmother loved her so much. She told me that the Madonna watched over the valley, interceding for everyone who lived below. The Lady was weeping over our sins, she said."

"She is still here."

"Decade after decade she has stood here, unmoving, unchanging. My great-grandfather built this in the eighteen-nineties. I never met him; he was gone long before I was born, but the memory of him was kept alive in the family. They told us that on his deathbed he asked the family to pass on a message to each generation that would follow. He told them he had seen a vision of the Holy Father kneeling, all alone, weeping over the Church because it was in ruins, and soldiers coming into the Vatican and hitting him with rifles. But it was a different Holy Father, he said. Rome was in flames. A vision for the future. He foresaw a time when everyone would be tempted to lose faith. They say my great-grandfather cried, a tough old man like that. He was inconsolable. He cried because he didn't want his family to go to Hell, and he thought that many of them, the ones who would be born in another century, would go there."

"What does the family think of this now?"

"I don't suppose any of them know, or if they know they've forgotten. I heard it only because my grandmother told me about it once when we were praying here. Even then I doubted it. When I told my parents, they laughed and said it was the ravings of a dying peasant, a poor old man full of fear. But Nonna said there never was a man as fearless as her father. He died in peace, looking at the picture of the Sacred Heart—the one above the bed where you slept last night. There are so many mysteries, aren't there?"

"Many. And yet, sometimes a mystery is really quite simple."

"Yes, you said that last night. A man is what he loves."

"Also, such a man may see things that others do not see. Faith opens certain doors."

She looked out across the valley.

"Anna," he said eventually, breaking her reverie, "we have not talked about Rieti. What happened in your heart while we were there?"

"I don't know. I can't talk about it now. I need time to think. Maybe it was an illusion."

"Did Don Matteo strike you as an illusion?"

"I'm not sure what I think", she said angrily.

She stared at a mountain across the valley. "You mustn't push me", she said fiercely. "I don't want this. I don't . . . "

She stopped herself and stood up abruptly.

"This mountain is a place of refuge for me. It's a memory, a heritage, that's all, a piece of my past. I can't let it turn into something else. As long as it stays what it was I can always come here and find peace. But don't make me say it's more than it is!"

"I am not trying to make you believe anything you don't want to. I am merely asking questions."

"There is still a lawyer in you, Father Elijah. You have been asking some very leading questions. Please, do not lead the witness."

He smiled at her, and her face relaxed.

"I'm sorry", he said.

"I'm sorry too. I'm a bit jumpy. Hearing Stefano's name from the lips of a stranger . . . "

"I assure you, I have no idea how he knew you, nor how he knew Stefano's name."

"Another of your mysteries?"

"It must be."

She shivered.

"Let's go", she said and led the way back to the head of the path. She turned once and looked back at the statue, then went down.

After supper that night, Gianna and Marco drove off to an end-of-summer party at the house of a cousin who lived in Spoleto. Elijah and Anna went out onto the kitchen porch and watched the sky above the mountain turn from rose to violet to deep blue-black. Stars appeared one by one.

"She's up there", she said wistfully and pointed. "There on the peak. You can't see the grotto from here, but I know she's always watching, standing guard."

"You speak of her as if she were real to you."

"She is real, but not in the way you think."

"In what way is she real to you?"

"She represents a world that's gone. It was a simpler time in history, but it had a certain beauty that no longer exists."

"Are you so sure it no longer exists?"

"Look at the world, Lawyer Elijah. Look at it, my friend."

"I see it continually."

"I too see it continually."

She got up and went in, returning a few moments later with two small glasses of wine.

"You find me a difficult convert, don't you?"

"That is not how I think of you."

"How do you think of me?"

"As a friend."

"As a young friend."

"Yes."

"A young friend poisoned by the toxic wastes of the twentieth century?"

"What kind of a friend do you want, Anna? One who lies to you?"

"Of course not. I think you have answered my question."

"The entire world is infected. This century has bludgeoned the perceptions of man with so much horror that the mind recoils. Evil of this magnitude shakes existence to its very core. One either believes or he doesn't. We choose. My wife told me something surprising once. She knew many survivors of the Holocaust. She said that for some, their experience destroyed their faith in a good God. Others believed more deeply than ever."

"The psychology of that is unfathomable."

"It's quite simple."

"For you, everything is simple."

"Not so. Remember that for many years I was far more poisoned, as you call it, than you are."

"And so you ran away into the world of religion in order to keep from going insane."

"Now, who is being simple?"

"I apologize", she said, rubbing her forehead. "That was insensitive. Forgive me."

"The ones who didn't lose faith found a meaning beneath the horror."

"What was the meaning?"

"They understood that the powers of evil must have felt threatened to unleash such malice against people of faith."

She pondered that. "You call it evil. I call it the irrational."

"But the designers of the *Shoah* were quite rational. Some of them had degrees in philosophy; some were masters of logic."

"Your presupposition is that the powers of evil actually exist."

"They exist. I assure you they exist."

"That is a statement of faith, not empirical knowledge, the kind of evidence that I as a judge must base my decision upon."

"I am not an attorney in this case; I am a witness."

"You must let me catch my breath. Too much is being condensed into too short a time."

"There is not much time left."

"Then let me settle the matter once and for all. If you want my definitive judgment, I will tell you: the human mind is largely subjective. Religious systems are the result of man's need to have hope. He projects belief onto the cosmos. It's as simple as that."

"Tell me, Anna, if man is capable of projecting his belief onto the cosmos, isn't it possible, by the same token, that he can project his *unbelief* onto the cosmos?"

She thought about that. "All right. You have a point. But it's entirely theoretical."

"Is it? I think we are continuously bombarded by a multitude of real evidence that bears witness to the invisible realities. Most people don't want to see it, and thus they gradually shut down their faculties of perception, one after another."

"You must consider us a cynical generation!"

"Not at all. I don't think it is a conscious refusal to accept truth. Disbelief is rooted in an inability to trust. It takes an effort of the will to have confidence in the ultimate goodness of life, and the experiences that mankind has been enduring for more than a century do anything but encourage trust. Above all, this is the age of fear."

"There we go again. Round and round", she sighed. "Abstractions within abstractions. As you said, our time is short. Let's go inside, shall we? There are still some solid facts you must know."

She directed him to a rocking chair by the stove. She started a fire crackling and made espresso. When they had steaming cups in their hands, she sat down on a bench across from him. She crossed her legs, made her mouth firm, and looked him full in the eyes.

"I haven't been completely honest with you."

"Oh?"

"Not that I would lie, you understand. That would be abhorrent to me. But there is something else afoot in which I'm involved. It's not pretty."

"Can you tell me?"

"We have become close this weekend. We are friends. I admire you and I believe in your integrity. You are what you are. That can be said of few people these days."

"What are you getting at, Anna?"

"I want us to remain friends. I need you as a daughter needs a wise father. She may not always agree with him, but she knows he has her best interests at heart."

"But of course."

"I'm afraid to tell you about it. Perhaps you won't like me anymore."

"Anna! You know me very little if you are afraid of that."

She looked down at the floor. "Do you remember what I said last night about my relation to the President's circle, about my position being unique? After Stefano's death I stayed there because I needed that social life as a defense against madness. I coasted along on the surface of his society for years, unthinking, unaware of the circles within circles that are the true composition of his world. Then last year, when I saw that look on his face and it unlocked the memory of his feeling against Stefano, I began to watch in earnest. I began to catch glimpses of the large number of concentric rings that surround him, the vast network of his contacts. It frightened me. I saw that I might be one of those deluded people who revolve around him like satellites, who think they are free, but who are really in effect owned by him."

"But he has no claim on you. And if you are right about him being involved—in some way that we don't understand—with Stefano's death, wouldn't you be a threat to him?"

"You don't know him. I thought for years that he was in love with me, and that I controlled the situation with my barriers.

How fatuous of me! I think he read me like a book all along. I thought I was using him, but all the while he was really using me."

"How was he using you?"

"If my suspicions are correct, I think it gave him a sort of perverse pleasure to have the widow of the man he had murdered as a devoted member of his following."

"Could he be that depraved?"

"If you had seen Stefano's body . . . what they did to him. Whoever was responsible for that was depraved."

"But why would he desire your company? What purpose would it serve?"

"I'm a constant reminder to him that he is utterly clever and utterly safe."

"Does he know that you and I have been communicating?"

"He knows about it. But he doesn't know the substance of our conversations. Nor does he suspect anything about my new awareness. He thinks I'm a loyal camp-follower, of course a high-class one. You must understand that eventually every loyal subject of his is rewarded. He threw me a great prize. It was he who arranged that I move from the Italian Supreme Court to the World Court."

"Has he asked anything in return?"

"Yes."

"What was it?"

"It concerns you."

"Me?"

"On the night before I first met you, he told me about a priest who would be attending the party, a man who had recently arrived from Israel, whom the Vatican was using as an envoy. He said that the priest was a person who many years ago had been— how did he put it—groomed as a key player in the reshaping of the West."

"That is untrue."

"He said you had backed out and disappeared from public life. He didn't explain why. He said that he wished to make certain overtures to you, to invite you back into our sphere of activity. He thought, however, that because of your simplistic religious tendencies, it wouldn't be easy to win you to our side. *Our side,* he called it. He suggested that if I were to get close to you, I would be able to make you understand the greatness of his vision. I asked him how he thought I should do that. He suggested in the most tactful language imaginable, that you were a man with an unresolved doubt, a weakness that lingered in your personality due to the horrible experiences you had suffered during the War. He told me that some human contact would reassure you of the benevolence of our vision of human destiny. You would gradually come to see that we are not a threat to the Church, that we are people of good will, and that we have the ultimate welfare of mankind at heart. It was all very high-minded."

"He directed you to win my heart."

"Yes, to win your heart for the cause."

"And to do it by winning my heart to you personally?"

"I'm afraid that's so."

"I see. That's why the uncanny seating arrangements at the dinners."

"Correct."

"Didn't you feel insulted by such a suggestion?"

"It was a mission undertaken with the highest motives."

"Yet his message was clear."

"Absolutely. He knows I'm not stupid. Beneath the subtle language, he was asking me to make you fall in love with me."

"And what did you think of that?"

"I thought it was despicable and absurd, but I didn't let on to him what I felt. I led him to believe that I would do as he wished because I believed in the cause."

"Do you believe in the cause?"

"You know very well that I have reservations about their agenda."

"Does he know that?"

"He knows it now, because of my second talk at Warsaw. But many of his supporters have doubts about this or that detail of the Plan—that's what they call it among themselves. It's not uncommon for them to have disagreements about strategies and minor points in their philosophy. He likes to create the impression of open dialogue. But he always wins. He can convince anyone of anything. My little rebellion didn't worry him in the least. I expect it reassured him that I think I'm a free agent. That's what he wants me to believe, you see."

"It sounds very convoluted."

"It's not as convoluted as it seems. If I were a perfect robot, he would be suspicious. So you see, my minor ideological disloyalty isn't a major problem."

"I hope you are right."

"He doesn't realize that I now hold a map to the structure of the maze. It no longer deludes me; I no longer wander aimlessly in it."

"But tell me, why did you go along with what he wanted?"

"I thought it would be a way of moving farther in toward the core of his activities, and thereby entering many doors that were closed to me. Behind one of those many doors I might eventually find out who had killed Stefano."

"That is a dangerous game, Anna."

"What do I have to lose?"

Elijah did not tell her what she had to lose. Her life? Gianna? Marco?

"So, now that I've told you, do you despise me?"

"No."

"I have tried to be candid. If you're offended, please forgive me."

"There is nothing to forgive."

"I went through the motions. I was at the right place at the right time. But you know I did nothing to encourage . . ."

"You did nothing to encourage a romance."

"Even so . . . "

"Even so. You have read my heart."

"That's the one thing I didn't expect. I'm sorry. I didn't want it to happen."

"Neither did I."

"And when all is said and done, nothing *has* happened."

He nodded and looked down into his hands.

She got up and went over to the cupboard and got out two glasses.

"Do you want wine?"

"No."

"Is the conversation over? I would understand if you never want to see me again. I will ask Marco to drive you back to Rome tonight if you wish."

He looked up and smiled at her. "No. It's all right."

"I'm sorry you're lonely. I'm sorry you lost your Ruth."

"I'm sorry you lost Stefano."

They sat in silence for a time, listening to the wood crackle in the stove.

"What was she like?"

"You would have liked her. You would have been friends."

He told her some of the best things about Ruth.

"She sounds a very fine person. I know I would have liked her."

"Yes, I think so."

"There isn't much more to say, is there?"

"Nothing, and everything."

"I'm glad you have your faith."

"I wish you understood it better. It's not a crutch. It's the greatest adventure of all."

"It's a hard time for Catholics."

"A time for courage."

"You're going to need a lot of that. There's more trouble coming. I hope you'll let me remain your friend. I can keep my eyes and ears open. I could let you know about things."

"I don't think you should. If what you have told me is correct, you are in dangerous company."

"That doesn't matter to me. I'm not afraid."

"I'm afraid for you. I think you should get out. Leave them, Anna. Now."

"I can't. I can't for Stefano's sake, and for my own sake. I'm going in as far as I can. I'm going to find out."

"Leave it be. God may have other designs on this man. We hope to call him out of darkness. In the end, he may open the doors of his own volition."

She looked at him with pity.

"Elijah, you don't understand them."

"It's my hope to speak to his heart and call him out, as once I was led out."

"You are naïve. They know all about your plans."

"Our plans are simple and direct. What is there to know?"

"They know, for example, that you and someone in the Vatican have been communicating all year about people they have planted in the Curia."

"They do? What people?"

"I don't know names. I don't know what it means, but I think I learned something that could be useful. I was present at a party a few weeks ago during which the President and a few of his close advisers were chatting nearby. I was busy talking with the organizers of an art show in Venice. When I heard someone whisper the name Schäfer, I listened with one ear. Then someone mentioned the Dead Sea. They were laughing over it. They didn't suspect I had overheard that pun in Warsaw about the Dead See of Rome. They thought they could discuss the Church in code words, and anyone overhearing them would be none the wiser. The room was full of people. There were all kinds of conversations going on at once, and they made the mistake of thinking no one would have the slightest idea what they were discussing.

"Because of your talk at Warsaw, they now realize you are an orthodox priest and that it would be virtually impossible to change you. They have dismissed our hypothetical romance as a tactic that came to nothing. They were discussing other strategies. They talked as if you and certain people at the Vatican were little boys playing at spies. They talked about how you and someone else—someone they called the gardener—were plotting a big counter-intelligence operation and how it would fail. The President thought you should be left to run on with your scheme for a time, because he found it amusing to watch it. There were allusions to so many things, I can't remember it all now. Something about an Englishman. China. Vietnam. Roses. Most of it made no sense to me."

"They used the word gardener?"

"Yes. Who is he?"

He stared at her, and his heart beat faster.

"Anna, will you take a walk with me? I need some fresh air."

"All right."

They went down the lane under the stars.

His night vision was not good and he stumbled. She took his arm, and they went on like that until they reached the paved road. They turned and proceeded along it toward the north.

"Are you feeling better?"

"We must keep walking."

"What is it? What's the matter?"

"You have just given me a devastating piece of information. They know our plans. They know everything. Our efforts to evade their surveillance have failed."

"Surveillance? Maybe someone told them about your plans."

"As far as I know, only a handful of people have any knowledge about my mission."

"Who are they?"

"The Pope, the Secretary of State, the prefect for Doctrine, Don Matteo, and myself."

"Then how would they . . . ?"

"Anna, how safe is the farmhouse?"

"Safe?"

"Is it possible they could have planted electronic devices here, in order to listen to your conversations?"

"Very unlikely."

"Are you sure, because if you are not sure, you are in extreme danger. They may have heard everything we discussed this weekend."

"You needn't fear that."

"Why not?"

"Because someone has already bugged my offices. It's been going on for the past two years. I know all about it."

"Who is doing it?"

"At first I thought it was Italian politics. Marxists perhaps, or fascists. Organized crime. Or some other radical on the playing field. I left the bugs in place."

"Why did you do that?"

"When it struck me that the source could be closer than I had previously suspected, I realized that it would be better for them to think they know my every move."

"But what about the farm?"

"It's the one place I keep sacrosanct. I'm seldom here, and they know it's a place I would never use for business or for matters that would be of interest to them. I'm sure they could only listen to so much of Gianna's musings and Marco's accounts of his athletic prowess. Besides, I've taken precautions."

"What sort of precautions?"

"One of Stefano's brothers owns a security company in Milan. He has no love for the President. He won't say why, he says only that Stefano didn't trust him so why should he. He has often urged me to leave that circle, so I think there is no danger he would ever be compromised. Every year, just before I arrive for my holidays, he goes through the house, inch by inch, literally. The floors, the attic, the rafters, the underside of cupboards, pin holes in the walls, the flower beds, the cracks in the stucco outside. He has special equipment. It takes about two days to cover it all. He times it so that I arrive just as he's finishing up. He's very good at his job. He's never found anything here."

"Has he checked your automobile?"

"Yes. He found a bug last year. We didn't touch it. We just parked the car in Milan, and his son loaned me his old wreck for the week. Usually I fly into Rome, and I have made a habit of renting a car at the airport. I select one at random from the lot."

"I hope for your sake he hasn't missed anything."

"I'm sure we're safe for the time being."

They turned around and went back to the house.

She stoked the kitchen fire again. They made futile attempts at light conversation. They could not shake their uneasiness.

"Paranoia is a deadly virus", Elijah said looking around at the walls.

Anna caught his eye.

"Sometimes even paranoiacs get persecuted", she said, smiling drolly.

They laughed.

He told her that he was very tired from the previous night and from his hike up the mountain.

"I am an old man. I need rest."

She made him lie down on the parlor sofa and draped a crocheted cover over him. There was an ancient victrola in the corner of the room. She cranked its handle several revolutions, set the volume at low, and put the needle on a disc. Opera music filled the room. Although it was scratched and thin, it was a voice from a vanished era, quaint, antique, and reassuring. He fell asleep. Later, when he awoke, he saw her reading in an easy chair by lamplight. It seemed to him that if life had gone differently this scene of tranquillity might have come about by other means. They might have been here together as man and wife. He shook off the thought. He silently prayed for her. Not long after, a car roared up, and Gianna and Marco crashed into the house bubbling happily. They all went to their respective rooms and slept.

In the morning they took him to the railway station. The two children were driving to Milan, and Anna would accompany them. She would go on from there to Geneva. She had offered to hire a car to take him back to Rome, but he insisted that the train trip would be a pleasure for him.

Anna took his hands in hers when they said good-bye. She told him that his visit had meant more to her than he could imagine. He said that he would not cease to pray for her. She nodded.

"*Buona fortuna*", she said.

Gianna kissed both his cheeks, and Marco wrung his hand. They showered him with repeated adieus. He climbed aboard and was gone.

XVII

Rome

"I have been trying to reach you for days", said the cardinal.

Elijah held the phone away from his ear.

"Didn't you receive my message, Your Eminence?"

"Messages! Messages! They just keep going astray and nobody can say where they went! Where have you been?"

"A short trip. I have learned something of importance. Can we meet to discuss it?"

"Tonight at the usual place. Eight?"

"I will be there."

When *Stato* arrived at the chapel of the catacombs, Elijah requested that they not go down to the tombs.

"I fear that no place is safe any longer", he explained. "Let's go farther out into the countryside."

The cardinal drove in silence, clearly possessed by an irritable mood. A half-hour later he pulled off the road onto a lane that disappeared into an olive grove. A hundred yards in, he braked his car and sat staring at the windscreen.

"So! Tell me the news. No doubt it will be bad."

"We must walk."

"*Bene!* We walk!"

He groaned as he maneuvered his ample frame out of the Volkswagen. He carried a flashlight. Elijah asked for the flashlight, dismantled it by the parking lights, examined it minutely, then reassembled it.

"What are you doing?"

"Eminence, it's a long story."

"So, begin!"

"First, may I ask if you are carrying anything on your person that might conceal an electronic device?"

"A bug? Impossible!"

"Please, can we check?"

Sighing, the cardinal turned out his pockets. They disgorged a small prayer book, a rosary, some coins, a set of keys, a bottle of medicinal tablets—"For my heart", he explained—a wallet containing cards and a few *lire*. In his breastpocket, he carried a cheap ballpoint pen and a solid gold pyx.

Elijah dismantled the pen and reassembled it.

"What is in this?" he asked pointing to the pyx.

"It's a relic of Saint Charles Borromeo. He's my patron, a cardinal-saint, a wise man. If only he were with us now!"

"He is here," said Elijah, "but there may be more than him here. May I open it?"

"Of course, but there's nothing to see. Just a lock of hair. I carry it next to my heart all the time."

The pyx contained a circular glass reliquary resting on a bed of purple velvet.

Elijah handed the reliquary back to the cardinal and pried the cloth off the bottom of the pyx. Embedded on the underside he found a miniature electronic component wired to a battery of the sort that powers wrist watches.

"What is that?"

"That is a wound through which the blood of the Church is pouring."

They stared at it.

"My God!" breathed the cardinal.

He looked down at his coat and pants. He put one foot forward and looked at his shoe suspiciously. He grabbed the lapels of his jacket and shook them as if they contained fleas.

"But this is outrageous!"

"Eminence, would you please get back into the car."

Item by item the cardinal went through his clothing. They found no other bugs.

"I think we should walk now."

"First give me that thing. I'm going to rip it out!"

"As you wish."

"No! Wait, don't touch it", said the cardinal. "Leave it on the car seat. When I get back to my apartment, I'll put the pyx beside my cassette recorder. I think we should give our listeners a real treat. I have hours and hours of my recorded talks on mystical theology. Yes, perfect. And also the retreat I gave to the papal household last year. And then the cassettes the sisters made of my Scripture courses. Weeks and weeks worth. That should keep them busy for awhile." He laughed humorlessly. "We might even win a soul!"

They walked deeper into the olive grove, the path illuminated by flashlight.

"How did they do it?"

"I expect you must sleep sometime. You take baths."

"Through such little cracks we have fallen! *Basta!* I have had enough!"

The cardinal's irritable mood had given away to one of dismay and confusion.

"What does all this mean? Who are these people?" he said.

"That is the subject of our meeting. I believe I know who they are."

He described his visit to Foligno in its entirety.

"So, you see, they have known our plans all along. The President has been playing with us as a cat plays with a mouse."

"Before he devours it", said the cardinal morosely.

"We are not devoured. And this is the Bride of Christ he is playing with. I think our Lord has a few things to say to this man. It's not over yet."

"Considering what you tell me, and what has been happening

in the Church during the past few weeks, we may be closer to the end than it seems."

"Is it bad?"

"Some cardinals have been granting interviews to the press. In guarded terms, they let it be known that the Holy Father is slipping. It's nonsense of course. He is as strong as ever in spirit, and his mind is clear. His physical health is failing, but not so much as they want everyone to believe."

"At least this reveals who is against him."

"Yes, it helps. But still it's a blow."

"Why are they doing it?"

"They want a fresh start. They say the Pope was not the right man for this time. They want someone young who can make peace among us. Bishops against bishops, cardinals against cardinals. The Catholic press is squabbling bitterly. All our family quarrels are spread out in public. Liberals are growing bolder. Many writers—even some we thought to be reliable—are clamoring for a new paradigm of Church, a democratic Church, a grass-roots Church, and claiming that their demands are the prompting of the Holy Spirit. On the other end of the spectrum, the ultra-orthodox are shouting that the Pope is playing into the hands of the Antichrist, whoever that may be. Old friends are painted in drab colors, new heroes are exalted. Cardinal Vettore, for example . . . "

"I have not heard about him lately. What is he doing in the East?"

"Great things for the Church, so says the press. And it's true. He has obtained from the Vietnamese permission for the Catholic bishops to attend the next synod in Rome. He is in China, presently, supposedly negotiating with the administration for increased rights for Catholics. The underground Church is suffering a terrible persecution, but only a trickle of news about it reaches the West. In the meantime, there is a flood of interviews with Vettore about the Patriotic Church. He praises it for its ability to survive above ground in a difficult situation. All of this appears most reasonable to our commentators. Vettore's reputation is rising. He is being called 'the Vatican's peacemaker'. The Holy Father has sent a message admonishing him to make no more statements that would encourage the People's Church, and urging him to speak of the suffering Church in China whenever he grants an interview. So far there hasn't been much response from the cardinal. It may be that censors have been cutting out any reference to the persecution. Or it may be that Vettore himself is the problem."

"What is your estimation?"

"A combination of the two."

"Will you call him back to Rome?"

"We are having trouble reaching him. He is traveling in the Chinese hinterland. I must say he seems to have no problem getting his articles and interviews out to the West."

"Isn't this clearly a case of disobedience?"

"He is very slippery. Besides, we have other things to worry about in the international situation. It grows more complex by the day. China is making mysterious moves on several levels. Russia is fragile and in a dangerous mood. Western Europe is drugged by its infatuation with the new vision offered by the *Unitas* conference. The Islamic nations are preaching holy war against the infidels in their midst and tearing each other apart at the same time. The President goes among them all, negotiating here, exercising pressure there, calming everyone. All the while, the Holy Father pours out a torrent of wisdom, never ceasing to proclaim Jesus Christ as the Lord of history, as the source of all true unity, peace, and hope. A great river of light streams from his mouth, and it runs away into the ground. No one is listening."

"Some are."

The cardinal wiped his face with his hands and sighed. "Not many. It's discouraging."

"On a human level."

The cardinal looked up at the stars that showed through a break in the clouds. He steadied himself. He turned to Elijah. "Thank you for being so patient. An irritable old man venting his frustrations. Not very edifying is it?"

"We are human. We stumble, just like the apostles. But we pick ourselves up again and go on, just as they did."

"Just so."

"Even if the devil achieves much, even if he succeeds in deluding most of the world, even then we mustn't lose hope. Was it not ordained that the Church must one day go through this second Passover?"

"I hoped it wouldn't come in our time."

"Do you believe it has come?"

"I'm still not convinced of it", sighed the cardinal. "But, it seems more and more clear. There has never been a situation like it."

"The Fall of Rome? The Barbarian invasions?"

"In those days the world had its evil masters, Nero, Tiberius, and Domitian. But even amidst the collapse of civilization, the world was crawling out of darkness. We are sliding back into it, and that is the difference. Our autocrats are not vicious tyrants. They are the architects of *worldpower;* and they manipulate all the resources of modern psychology to control the soul of man and make him an instrument of their purpose."

"In a sense they are rigid puritans."

"Oh, yes, but these puritans do evil coldly, motivated by the highest principles."

"Are you afraid?" Elijah said gently.

"Should a cardinal admit that he's afraid? Yes, I'm afraid. Afraid most of all for the many innocents who are falling into the mouth of that beast."

"What is the Holy Father going to do?"

"Right to the end, he will keep on doing what he has been doing. We must do the same. Our task is to proclaim Jesus. We must strengthen the things that remain. It's not for us to count the numbers who listen."

Elijah struggled to shake off a spirit of dread.

The cardinal turned and looked at him. "You know, if someone had suggested to me three years ago that it would happen so swiftly, I would not have believed it. I would have dismissed it as alarmism. Now, I'm not so sure. In the space of a few short years we have seen events pass from relative stability to increasing chaos. It's accelerating rapidly. I could not have foreseen the speed at which it has happened."

"There is still time. We can still hope."

"Hope? Above all, we must hope. Human securities are disappearing one by one. Each soul is being weighed in the balance. Many are failing their moment of testing. I am especially disheartened by our shepherds."

"Many of them remain loyal."

"I wonder if there will be as many when the heat becomes intolerable. At some point, it's going to become a question of martyrdom."

It was Elijah's turn for frustration. "Eminence, this more than anything else incites me to the sin of anger. I resist it over and over again. I urge my spiritual directees to resist it, to pray, to fast, to forgive. And yet in my heart, I am at war with my emotions. When Anna told me about the torture and death of her husband, the reality of martyrdom finally hit me."

"We must all make the mental leap from the pious histories we have read in the martyrologies to the reality of living flesh and blood. Our early martyrs were real men and women, with their own personalities, their flaws and their greatness. We are no different."

"If only we could face the powers of darkness as a unified body!"

"If only, if only . . . the old refrain. But it was ever thus. In all the major crises of our history, we've had to endure the treason of the very ones who should have guarded the flock! It's human stupidity and weakness."

"Can't our dissident bishops see what they are doing?"

"Blindness of that magnitude is rooted in sin, the sin most difficult to see in oneself, and even more difficult to root out—pride. The ancient device of the enemy."

"Someone must warn them!"

"They have been warned countless times. They don't hear."

The old doubts began to resurface. "Why does our Lord allow this to happen?"

The cardinal smiled sadly and put his hand on Elijah's shoulder. "Such alarm in your voice my friend. I hear from you the same cry that was torn from the lips of the apostles during the storm on the lake, when the ship was going down, when the Lord lay sleeping."

"You shame me. Of course you are right. At the final moment, He will awake and rebuke the storm. Then He will turn to us and ask us why we had so little faith."

"Precisely. In the meantime, we carry the cross. We watch the betrayal. We suffer."

"Can we do nothing!"

"You must understand, Father, that the devil's purpose in sowing revolution in the Church is to throw her into confusion. Thus, her attention is distracted and her energies scattered. In this way, we are weakened at precisely the moment of history when we need to be most strong."

"Why does the Holy Father not act? Can't he order these prelates into obedience?"

"He has repeatedly done so, and in the most Christlike fashion. But he commands no police, no armies. He has been more firm with dissidents lately. The Prefect for Doctrine has been unwavering in his efforts to reign in the revolt. A proper exercise of authority. The solution isn't authoritarianism, for that would only throw fuel on the fire of revolt. The Holy Father works while the light lasts. He calls us all back to the One who carried the Cross and died on it. In his hands, he carries only that, a cross; he speaks always of the triumph of the Cross. Those who won't listen will answer to God."

*   *   *

Smith came by that week and invited him out for coffee. They went to the café by the Tiber and sat at their customary table. They drank espresso. Leaves blew down the avenue. Smith lit a pipe and puffed it furiously. He pointed across the river with the pipe stem. The dome of Saint Peter's glowed golden in the sunset.

"Everything looks normal, doesn't it, Elijah?"

"What are you getting at?"

"Nothing. Nothing at all", he said through a cloud of smoke.

"Something is on your mind."

"Hardly anything. Well, to tell you the truth, I've been wanting to ask for a long time what you think about all these apparitions?"

"Which ones?"

"There are hundreds. Visions, miracles, weeping statues, lights in the sky. Pick one. Any one."

"I have been watching, listening, praying."

"And . . . ?"

"Of course, some are of doubtful origin."

"That's an understatement. What about that lady who's going all over the world saying Jesus told her that the Pope has to clean up his act, or He'll abandon him."

"I think she is the victim of imagination or spiritual deception."

"Right. I think so too. She's got an airtight case going there: hey, you good Christians, if you reject my messages you're rejecting Jesus who gave them to me. Now if you'll just buy my next book . . . "

"Rather hard to resist, isn't it?"

"I'll say! Now on the other hand, we've got a whole bunch of visionaries stating that if we want to stay with Jesus through this mess we need to cling tight to the Pope."

"I believe these are genuine. However, we have a spreading confusion among the most dedicated of the Lord's followers. It is to be expected."

"I know, I know. I just wish it were a little clearer. Some friends of mine back in the States have joined the schismatics. They're convinced that the more conservative you are the more orthodox you are. They're more Catholic than the Pope."

"I believe that some of the warnings are a grace sent to us from the Lord."

"Which ones?"

"The ones that speak of fidelity and mercy. There is a consistency to those messages. Practically with one voice they are saying that unless mankind repents and returns to God, a chastisement is coming upon the earth, the like of which has never before been seen."

"Not since the time of the Flood, they say."

"The Scriptures warn us that the second deluge will be worse than Noah's. Only this deluge will not be by water, it will be by fire."

"Yeah, I've read it. It gives me the willies."

"It no longer seems impossible."

"Not since Hiroshima. Look, Elijah, what bothers me is the speed. The prophecies are coming so fast and furious that you barely have time to make sense of it all. Natural disasters, wars, attacks upon the Church, martyrs, politics, intrigue, masons, devils, traitors, stigmatists, weeping statues, bleeding icons, three days of darkness, signs in the heavens, supernatural warnings . . . it goes on and on."

"It begins to make sense if we understand that this is the final confrontation between the Church and the anti-Church, the Gospel and the anti-Gospel. Thus, Heaven is pouring out many extraordinary graces."

"It seems a mixed bag of graces, if you ask me."

"If the adversary is mounting a last battle, isn't it reasonable to assume that he would marshal all his powers and seek to undermine those graces, draw people away from the real ones, get them chasing after imitations?"

"I guess so. It's happened before."

"Indeed. Add to this his effort to dominate and manipulate every facet of human life."

"That's a little dire, wouldn't you say?"

"We know from Scripture that the time of the end will be dire."

"Oh no! Don't tell me *you're* an end-timer!"

"It depends upon what you mean by the term."

Smith looked around helplessly, searching for a reply. "You know what I mean. A raving apocalyptic."

"I try not to rave."

Smith pointed his pipe at Elijah. "You went through some hard times during the War, didn't you?"

"Yes, I did."

"Maybe it gave you a pessimistic outlook."

"Perhaps it gave me eyes to see what men are capable of."

"Okay, but for the sake of argument, what if this is just one more crisis we're going through? We've weathered bad storms before, and this one looks kind of tame by comparison with some. Besides, the people of the tenth century got all worked up over the first millennium. They thought the Lord was returning too. They saw the Antichrist everywhere."

"I understand the point you are making, Father. You think a mass hysteria afflicts the world every time a millennium approaches."

"It's a thought."

"It is worth considering. But beside it one must place another thought. It is this: suppose that a man is sick and comes close to

444

death. Everyone is convinced that he will die. It is the end. But he recovers through a miraculous intervention by God. He lives a while longer in a condition of health. Then, as he approaches old age, he becomes sick once more. He appears to be dying. Should the doctor conclude that because he was once sick and recovered he will surely do so again?"

Smith pursed his lips and relit his pipe with some difficulty.

"Okay. You have a point, you talmudic scholar, you."

"Let us add another thought to the first two. Let us say that at the time of the end there's a special danger for our doctor and the family of the dying man. They won't be hysterical, oh, no, but they will lack a certain sense of urgency. They will lack vigilance."

"And the patient dies."

"We all die eventually."

"What are you saying? You can't have it both ways. Should we let the patient die *or* try to save his life?"

"We try to save his life *and* if he must die he must die."

"You've confused me totally."

"We labor to preserve the life of the body, but ultimately life and death are out of our hands. If the patient lives awhile longer, a certain kind of good will result. If God ordains that this is the time to die, another kind of good will result."

"All right, put it that way and I see it."

"The problem is not the survival of the Church."

"It isn't! What's the problem then?"

"Souls. How many will be saved?"

Smith glanced across the river. "But it's intolerable just letting it run on like this. We've got to stop it!"

"That is just what the apostles said. They could not understand why the Lord had to die."

"You mean we're supposed to say nothing while the Church is maligned and unjustly condemned?"

"No. We must say a great deal. But ultimately, it is the *doing* that is the real test."

"The doing?"

"Do we love our enemies? Do we accept walking with the Lord on His way to Calvary and stand beneath His Cross? Do we perhaps even allow ourselves to be nailed with Him? Or do we not?"

Smith shook his head. "You're saying we have to be two people. One fights the death, and the other lets death win. I don't get it."

"We don't have to get it. We must simply do it."

"It may be simple for you, Elijah, but it ain't so simple for me."

The two priests lapsed into silence.

"There's so much irrationality in all this. Some friends sent me a book on the Antichrist the other day. There are all kinds of prophesies in it. Lots of saints and popes were sure their day was the end time."

"Our sick man recovered. The spirit of Antichrist has been present from the beginning. Saint John says to the believers of his time that they are living in *the final hour.* In a sense, all of the Christian era is the last days. Is it so irrational to conclude that the period of the end will reach a definitive climax?"

"I suppose not. But is ours that time? Look, one of those visionaries, hundreds of years back, said that the Antichrist won't have an earthly father. The devil will be his father. He'll be born of a virgin. He'll have teeth and spout blasphemies from birth. He'll be educated by necromancers and magicians. He'll perform miracles. It goes on and on. He's a nasty character all round, I'd say."

"If that was a vision, it was allegorical. There are other prophecies that describe his bearing and personality differently. He will be an enormously attractive figure. The Greek and Latin Fathers say that he won't appear to be a monster. Saint Jerome and Saint Thomas, who were models of sobriety, describe many of his noble attributes. Cardinal Newman's essays warn that he will reap the harvest of a strong delusion that will fall over the minds of men. Antichrist will bite us, but it won't be with fangs. He will blaspheme, but it will be in the most elegant language. He will deny that Jesus is the only Christ and deny that He is God. In the place of the Savior, he will erect himself as an anti-icon, an embodiment of human greatness. He will lead mankind to adore its own ego, and eventually, to adore Satan."

Elijah spoke in tones of utmost sadness. Smith observed him closely, saying nothing.

"Are you getting enough protein in your diet?" he quipped.

For once Elijah did not warm to the American priest's wry humor.

"Father, it is close. The deception will be strong. We must be very little. We must cling to the Cross."

Smith sighed. "That's too dark for me. I've got real problems staring me in the face. Much more insistent than the Beast of the Apocalypse."

"What are the problems?"

"The heat's been turned up a notch, or down, depending on how you look at it. I'm getting articles sent to me at the magazine that make me uneasy. We occasionally received things like it in the past, but no more than a trickle. It's swelling into a steady stream. The general says we should be open. He's been asking himself if this new stuff is maybe the Holy Spirit trying to tell us something."

"What is the content of this material?"

"Mostly it's about not being judgmental about world religions, about making amends for our 'theological imperialism', they call it. You understand I'm talking about priests and bishops here. They want the Church to make public apologies to the Muslims for the Crusades, the Protestants for the Inquisition, the natives for converting Mexico, et cetera. There's a whole lot of breast-beating going on; just visible underneath it there's contempt for the evangelical calling of the Church."

447

"All religions are the same?"

"They don't come right out and say it, but that's the message. It makes my stomach churn every time I read the stuff. So far I've argued the general out of printing it, but he's getting more and more flack from the field. Those guys want to know why he's not publishing their articles. I told you, he's super-nice. He's not tough."

"Can he not see the damage such articles would inflict?"

"He thinks it's just academic back-and-forthing. He's not the greatest intellect in the world, you realize."

"What do you think motivates the writers?"

Smith raised his eyebrows as far as they would go and threw up his hands: "I tell you, Elijah, I don't know. Whenever they get close to making any kind of sense, you can watch their minds just swerve away real fast. It boggles me! Offer them a genuine idea, and they just blink off, fade out, or sink into a bucket of mental sludge. I've been ranting about it to the general, which doesn't help matters any."

"Really, Father, you mustn't. It pushes him in their direction."

"I know, I know, but I can't seem to stop myself. It usually takes me by surprise. It's uncanny the way that happens. For instance, the mail will arrive while the general's standing by my desk discussing the weather with me. A piece of garbage pops out of an envelope and I scan it while we're gabbing about soccer scores. A line leaps off the page about the *Inquisitional Church of this Pontificate* or some such idiotic thing, and I just erupt. I fume, my face turns red, and I make some comment in a loud voice. He stops talking, just looks at me with that poker face, wondering if I'm everything they say about me. He drifts out of the office without another word, a gentle, worried look on his face. About an hour later, he wanders back in and says something out of the blue like, we have to pay more attention to the spirit of *aggiornamento*. And shouldn't we be open to all sides, provide a forum for dialogue, keep everyone listening to each other? Listening! Hell, nobody listens to anyone anymore. He's still living in the seventies. The only thing this garbage will do is bend the heads of the simple priests and a huge portion of the faithful."

"How many?"

"We're one of the biggest missionary magazines in the world. Hundreds of priests and thousands of catechists read us. Hundreds of thousands of lay people too. Do I want to explain that to the Lord on Judgment Day? Not much."

"Then you have a duty to stand firm. Reject this material."

"I have orders to let some of it through. A token, a gesture of openness, says the general. I've resisted so far. He won't know I've failed to comply till the next issue's out in the fall. Then it's going to get real tense."

Smith's hands tried to relight his pipe.

"It's like *Catholic Times* happening all over again", he said.

"Stand firm, Father. Let our Lord act."

"Okay. Will you pick up the pieces if He doesn't act?"

"I will do better than that. I will pray for you as we prayed last year, and we will beg for a miracle."

"What happens if we don't get one this time?"

"Then I will speak with someone I know in the Vatican."

"You've got friends over there?"

"I am acquainted with some officials. They may be able to find you a place in another religious house."

"Good. Will you put in a plug for a monastery? I've always wanted to have a cell of my own."

"We will see. Pray, Father. Trust and pray."

* * *

One day in early November, a letter came to Elijah's mail slot at the House of Studies. It was typewritten and unsigned.

It read: *Remember Our Lady of Sorrows. I need to talk with you. Your mail and telephone may not be reliable. Call me on a public telephone. Ask for Maria.*

Penned at the bottom was a Rome number.

He drove to a nearby hotel and used the payphone in the lobby. A woman's voice answered.

"May I speak to Maria?"

"One moment."

He listened to muffled conversation on the line.

"This is Maria." It was Anna's voice.

"Where are you?"

"I'm at a restaurant in the east end."

"Can you talk freely?"

"More or less. Can you come here?"

"I'll be there as soon as possible."

She gave him directions, and half an hour later they were facing each other across a table in the back room of a cheap café. The orange imitation-velvet wallpaper was festooned with plaster busts of emperors and draped with strings of red peppers.

"It's not fancy, but it's anonymous."

"You said that my mail and phone may be unreliable."

"I meant secure. If I'm not mistaken, your ingoing and outgoing letters are being opened. And your line is probably being tapped."

"What makes you think so?"

"They know about Foligno."

"Oh, no", he breathed.

"They don't know much, only that you were there. It's sparked their hope that you and I . . . "

"Ah, you mean our mythological romance."

"Yes, that. The President called me in The Hague last week and hinted at it. 'Well done, Anna', he said. 'You may have succeeded after all.' It made my flesh crawl. I let him think something is growing between us. Of course there *is* something, but I didn't tell him it's an old-fashioned friendship."

Elijah sighed. "But to what purpose? Our cover is blown, as they say in the mystery novels. The spy game is over."

"Your game may be over but mine isn't. My cover is still intact. The illusion of a romance enhances his confidence in me, and with your permission I'd like to feed it a little."

"Before we go any farther, Anna, there is something I have to tell you."

He described the discovery of the bug that had been planted on *Stato.*

She looked blank, got up, and went to the washroom. She returned ten minutes later.

"It's all right. I'm clean. You had me worried."

"So, how do you suggest we feed the illusion of romance?"

"Let's start sending discreet little notes to each other. We'll use coded language that any fool could decipher."

"I see. A sort of counter-counter-intelligence operation. I still don't feel easy about it. They could use it against us some day."

"Do you think anyone cares any more about the sins of priests? They have more than enough scandal material to use against the Church. They wouldn't bother with ordinary indiscretions. It's something bigger they want."

"Which is?"

"They want you, and their appetite has been whetted again."

"There is something wrong here. They are too clever. They will know."

"They're not omnipotent. They can't know everything."

"I suppose you are right. Still . . . "

"And if you're worried about . . . " She did not complete the sentence.

"I'm not so much worried about your heart as my own."

"I know."

"Do you think it's easy for me to tell you that? Do you know how painful it is to admit that a person I care for is also a source of temptation?"

"Is that what I am?"

"I'm sorry. I said that badly. *You* are not the temptation, Anna. The temptation is all within me: the image in the mind, the dream, the memory of fairest love—it draws me toward a consolation that is not meant to be mine in this world. But you—you will always be my friend in the truest, deepest meaning of the word."

Emotion filled her eyes. She did not break his gaze.

"We have to fight them, Elijah", she said at last, vehemently. "Don't let them take everything."

"In the end, they will lose."

"But how much will they destroy in the process! Too much!" Tears spilled out of her eyes.

"Anna," he said helplessly, "I just don't see what we can do."

"You needn't do anything, really. A few notes, a few calls. Enough to keep them thinking their plans are succeeding. In the meantime, this will let me farther in. There are already signs that I'm moving from one circle into another."

"What signs?"

"Yesterday, at the President's invitation, I attended a private gathering at an estate near Rome. That's why I'm here in the city."

"What was the purpose of the gathering?"

"I wasn't privy to all of it, but it was obvious that during the weekend they were deliberately revealing themselves to me—more than they ever have up until now. It was a test of some sort. I think I've passed."

"What sort of people were present?"

"It wasn't a large group. Twelve men and seven women, including myself. The odd thing is, they weren't the usual ones who surround him at public functions. No politicians or financiers that I could recognize, no famous people. But each and every one of them exuded . . . power. These are people who somewhere on this planet exert some kind of enormous influence. But I can't begin to guess the nature of it."

"Why were you invited? Surely not to discuss a romance?"

"Ostensibly that was one of the reasons. In his subtlest manner he repeated the congratulations he had given only a few days before on the phone. He also hinted at the test case the World Court is considering next month. Though why he should bother escapes me, because they know it will go their way. The UN and the Europarliament are determined to make the antipopulation laws binding throughout the world."

"How will you vote?"

She hesitated.

"I'm sorry, that was presumptuous of me. You are a judge. I had no right to ask."

"I have spent many sleepless nights over the problem. I have come to the conclusion that the new legislation is fundamentally destructive. It will make it possible for governments to inflict many violations of human rights on their peoples. I know I can't support it. On the other hand, if I come out against it, my cover is blown. You see, it's a keystone in their move toward global power. They must have it. They know I'm smart enough to recognize that. That's why they put me there. They don't suspect my innermost thoughts on the matter."

"Then what will you do?"

"I'm torn. The legislation is abhorrent to me. Yet, if I am ever to strike back at the men who killed Stefano, then I'm going to have to play their game. I can't be ejected from their circle."

"Anna, I beg you. It's a mistake. If you vote their way, you will be using an evil means to achieve a good end. In the long run, it can never work."

"You don't understand. There will be a dissenting vote or two. But the court is going to pass it into world law. My vote will make no difference either way."

"Are you so sure?"

"I know it. He controls a majority. The rest are sympathetic to the legislation. The one or two dissenting votes are people due to retire soon. He has already won."

"Even so, it is a matter of conscience. For the sake of your soul!"

"My soul? I sometimes wonder if my soul died a long time ago. It's buried in a coffin in Milan."

"Do you remember our visit to Don Matteo? Do you recall what he said to you?"

"I remember."

"Some day you will join Stefano. All of this will be over. You will be happy together forever. Do not risk eternity for a dirty game of espionage."

"That's too theological. I can't think along those lines. I want Stefano's killer. If the world won't give me justice, then I'm going to get it some other way!"

"I beg you."

She shook her head, brushing his arguments away.

"Let's leave that for now. There is more I want to tell you. I know now that my intuition about Stefano's death is correct."

"How do you know that?"

"During this past weekend, I met his killer."

"You did?! Who is he?"

"I don't know his name. He was one of the group."

"But that's shocking! What happened?"

"You have to understand that the nature of this meeting was different from any others I have attended. The faces were unknown to me. From the moment of my arrival, it was first names only. No last names. Only the President was known to everyone there. Nothing was said. Nothing was overt. All conversations were generalities. But they were generalities about earth-shaking matters. Movements on the world scene, personalities, strategies. None of it understandable to anyone who wasn't deep inside their view of things. It was wheels within wheels, gyroscopes within gyroscopes. That part of it I didn't understand. No, not at all. But do you remember I once told you how I had learned to read personalities. How the flicker of an eyebrow speaks volumes to me, the interplay of glances, who communicates what to whom, et cetera?"

"I remember."

"I was a criminal lawyer during the early years of my practice. I can spot a murderer, Elijah, and I tell you there was more than one present this weekend. But these men are a different kind of animal—a species I've never met before. There is something utterly sane and utterly psychopathic about them. Can you understand what I'm saying?"

He nodded, remembering Eichmann's face.

"Perfect gentlemen?"

"Exactly. Perfect gentlemen with something hideous behind their eyes. It chilled me. From the moment I entered the front door of that place, I wanted to run. But I knew if I did I would never stop running."

"I think the time to leave them is now. Just walk away. Plead illness. A nervous breakdown, anything. But you must get out!"

"I'm not getting out. When I tell you the rest, you'll see why."

"Go ahead."

"Last night, after dinner, we were standing around having drinks, chatting in little groups. One of the men came up to the group in which I was standing. The President was with us. I could see that he's on some equal footing with the President, because everyone else took a little step back when he approached. It was one of those subconscious things people do that inform you a man is very important, in a class by himself. But he's completely unknown. I have no idea who he is. The deference shown to him was phenomenal. There was nothing remarkable about his appearance—he was about sixty years old, balding, of moderate height. He spoke in a quiet voice, said nothing of significance, only a few mild jokes that everyone took appreciatively. He was not introduced to me. Eventually he strolled away and the President followed him. It was casual, nonchalant, but I saw that he'd been beckoned."

"The President beckoned him?"

"No, the other way around. They stood apart from the group for a few minutes and talked in a low voice. They didn't know about my gift for listening to more than one conversation at a time. I was talking with a man from Scotland. He was telling me what a success he thought the Warsaw conference had been. I was murmuring agreement, but listening all the while to that whispered conversation not ten paces away. I heard almost nothing of it, but I'm sure I heard the President address the other man as *Mago.*"

"Mago?"

"Magus. Sorcerer."

"Perhaps you heard wrong. At that distance . . . "

"I don't think so. Then the other man said something else and addressed the President as *Architetto.*"

"Architect?"

"Yes. They ended their tête-à-tête by nodding sagely together, then the President returned to us and continued on as before."

"Were there many people there with such names?"

"A few. Most of them were introduced only as Carlo or Katerina or Edmund. Sprinkled among them were names like Archer and Abaddon."

"Abaddon?" said Elijah startled.

"Why? Do you know that name?"

"It's a name used in the Book of Revelation. It refers to an angel."

"He didn't look like an angel."

"These people may be using names that have symbolic meaning for them. According to Scripture, Abaddon is the angel-king of the bottomless pit. He holds the key to the abyss. He is called a star that fell from heaven."

"Why a star?"

"The rebel angels were once creatures of light. They became darkness and were cast down to the earth. In the Gospels, Jesus refers to Satan as one who fell like lightning from heaven. The common interpretation of the passage in Revelation is that when the fifth trumpet of the apocalypse is blown, this fallen angel will open the gates of the demonic world, which will then pour out over the earth."

"What a horrible mythology."

"It may be more literal than you think."

"Let's not get into that, Elijah. What does the name mean?"

"It means *Destroyer.* This is in sharp contrast to the name of Jesus, which means *Yahweh saves.*"

"Well, this man was quite human."

"Tell me about him."

"He was just one of many. Fiftyish, heavy-set, a closed face, a mouth that looked accustomed to smirking, but seemed mirthless throughout the entire evening. He kept to himself."

"Was he the killer?"

"He was a killer but not *the* killer."

"Who was the killer? How could you distinguish him from the others of his kind?"

"I just knew. Don't ask me how I knew. You may doubt me more than ever when I tell you what happened next. It's not much evidence to go on, but it's all I have. And my every instinct is telling me that I'm absolutely right."

"Was it anything he said?"

"Yes and no. It happened this way: like any party, it was a scene of constantly changing arrangements, individuals shifting back and forth from one cluster to the next. People drifting out of the salon into the ballroom and back again. There was music, flowers, a striving for vivaciousness that struck me as strained. People were dancing in the next room. Older men were smoking and laughing in a corner. Three women and I were discussing art. They had helped to put together the President's collection, which is presently touring America. They were knowledgeable people, very sophisticated, though they really didn't say what they do for a living or who they are. First names only. At one point, the man they called Abaddon walked by, and they drew him into our circle. They asked him if he agreed that Picasso was a forerunner of the modernist revolution in art. He agreed diffidently. He hung on. He sipped his drink and listened to us. I felt his eyes on me. Not the usual male thing. It was cold observation, and curiosity. One of the women said something about the way Picasso fragmented the image of woman, almost as if he hated them. Abaddon looked at her and said something to the effect that Picasso really wanted to get inside women because they were so alien to him. He took them apart, he said, and put them back together again.

"At that point the man they called Mago spoke up. He was just suddenly there beside me; I hadn't seen him approach. He said that if Picasso had ever had the chance he would have dismembered them alive, piece by piece, because he was really looking for the fountain of life. At that point most of us, I think, began to feel a strong desire to change this grisly subject. But Mago wouldn't let it go. He made a gesture to a little man standing nearby whom I hadn't noticed until then. 'Come here, *Chirurgo*', he said. He called him *Surgeon*. The little man came over and stood there like an obedient dog. I saw instantly that he too was a killer. Chirurgo, Mago, and Abaddon—all three of them killers. I looked into the Surgeon's eyes and I knew. He was the one."

"Stefano?"

"Yes."

"What did you do?"

"I did nothing. I looked away as if I had seen nothing. I was bereft of emotions. Something totally detached came over me. I didn't have to pretend. Something switched off inside of me because it was essential that I reveal nothing. Something else came into play that I didn't know I had in me. I suppose you could call it cunning."

"What happened next? What did Mago say to Chirurgo?"

"He said, 'Tell us, doctor, what is it like to take apart a living

458

human being?' Chirurgo didn't blink an eye. He tilted his head a little and said, 'It's a science.' I looked at the hands that had tortured Stefano and saw that they were delicate, clean hands. I smiled at him. Only an angel could have known that the smile was a fraud. Then I said something that I don't believe, but I said it because I know *they* believe it: I said, 'There are times when science must go ahead of the rest of humanity. The scientist must do unpopular things, even things others call evil, for the sake of the common good.' While everyone around me was murmuring agreement, Chirurgo stared at me as if I were mad. If he were an ordinary doctor, even an ordinary *evil* doctor, he would have been pleased by the remark. Instead, he seemed lost for words. I suppose the horrible irony of the scene must have hit him: here was the grieving wife of a man he had tormented to death reassuring him that it was all for the best."

"What happened then?"

"Mago and Abaddon stepped into the breach. Simultaneously, betraying no emotion, no concern, both of them flicked their eyes at Chirurgo and at each other. Between the three of them there passed an unspoken conversation, which took a split second to transpire. Then all three of them flashed a look at me. They could read nothing in my eyes. I turned to the woman on my left and asked her if she thought the other cubists disliked women as much as Picasso had. She launched into a dissertation, and the moment was over. The killers wandered off in different directions as if nothing had happened."

Elijah, who had listened to this story as if hypnotized, suddenly exhaled loudly. He caught his breath. "This is awful!"

"Awful? Of course it's awful—and a great victory."

"Are you sure?" said Elijah shaking his head. "Could you have imagined it?"

"No. I saw it", she said evenly. "It's my best evidence that the President's circle is completely without conscience and bodes no good for mankind."

"What will you do? Should you go to the police?"

"To tell them I saw three men looking at each other?"

"What then?"

"I can assure you I have no intention of buying a gun and shooting that pitiful little man."

"Anna, if they sense even the remotest threat from you, if they suspect that you know . . . "

"They are creatures who live in a world of shadows. They think themselves safe. There is no power on earth that can touch them."

"You spoke earlier of justice. How do you hope to bring them to justice?"

"By seeking an all-embracing justice. I'm going to go in as far as they will let me, and I'm going to learn anything I can. They are going to slip. They are going to give away something damning. And when I have it, I'm going to bring their house tumbling down on their own heads. The ruin of that house will be awful indeed."

Elijah could not shake off a feeling of dread.

Anna straightened her shoulders and looked around at the walls of the restaurant.

"I think I've had about all the orange velvet I can stand for one night. And wasn't that the fourth time they ran through their canned music? One can listen to *Goodbye Sorrento* only so many times."

He reached across the table and took her hand. "You are a very brave woman."

She shrugged. "What time is it?"

"Nine-thirty", he said.

"I don't want to end the evening on this note. Why don't we find a place to walk?"

They drove in his car back to the center of the city, parked near the college, and strolled toward the Tiber.

"I have just thought of one good thing about our reputed romance", she said.

460

"What could that be?" he replied glumly.

"We can play at spies and hope we're being found out. It feeds the plot."

"And what about real communication?"

"We must learn to read between the lines that are between the lines. There will be times like tonight when we can speak openly. In one way or another, I will let you know what's happening. We've got a fine cover."

"You must take extra pains to avoid giving yourself away in any manner", he admonished.

"I will."

"When we speak truthfully, we must be absolutely sure there are no bugs."

"Of course. And when we play our charade we must try to appear as if we're avoiding surveillance."

"And fail at it."

"Right. We'll fail at it. Can you keep all this straight in your mind?"

"I think so."

"If I discover anything definite, I'll let you know via our fake love notes. I'll say that I've found a priceless work of art and want your advice about purchasing it. Then we'll have to find a way of meeting."

She took his arm. "Don't worry. It helps the charade."

"I know. I was just appreciating it too much."

He saw her smiling up at him under the light of a street lamp. She held his arm lightly, without possession or release.

"Listen, Anna, if you insist on throwing yourself into peril I want you to do a favor for me."

"What is it?"

He fumbled in his coat pocket and removed a small brass reliquary. He opened it and showed her the contents.

"I want you to carry this with you wherever you go. It contains my greatest treasure."

"A sliver of wood and a few beads?"

"I won't tell you where the sliver comes from because you would not believe me. The beads are stained with the blood of a holy woman. A martyr. Whatever happens, always remember that you are not alone."

She took the reliquary and slipped it into her pocket.

"Do you promise?"

"I promise", she said and turned away to face the night.

XVIII

Advent

The world news grew worse. Small wars broke out here and there. The media was full of the President's valiant efforts to delay further violence. China was demanding the return of Taiwan. A cache of undeclared atomic weapons was discovered in Belarus by UN supervisors, fanning widespread fears that the former Soviet states were not abiding by the disarmament agreement and were an armed camp waiting to explode. El Salvador erupted in a bloody revolution. Mexico was in political chaos. The Japanese and American economic axis was once again destabilized by trade war. The papers regularly reported the decline of the Pope's health and the endless rumors that he would soon resign or be declared incompetent by the college of cardinals. There was much conjecture about who would be the next Pope. Among the top contenders the media listed a new name: Cardinal Vettore.

Elijah watched and waited, taught his classes, and prayed.

On the Monday after the first Sunday of Advent he received a letter in a pink envelope. It had no return address but was postmarked from Paris. The thick vellum paper inside was tinted violet. The words were in Anna's handwriting.

Dearest David,
I think of you at every waking moment. I had forgotten such happiness existed. When we were together I realized that you are restoring me to life.

Our love must remain a secret. Our reputations depend on it.
Maria

*

Dear Maria,
Life in Rome is bleak without you. I too had forgotten that such love still exists on this barren earth. I carry you like an icon in my heart.
With love eternal,
David

Elijah wrote the reply with feelings of uneasiness, but he reasoned that the words were not untrue. The invisible watch-dogs could interpret it however they liked. He mailed it to her address in France.

A letter of another sort arrived a few days later. It was from Smith. He was in Regina Caeli prison, and he was in serious trouble. Would Elijah come to see him as soon as possible?

Because Elijah was a priest, the prison officials waived the usual restrictions. Ordinarily, he would have had to converse with Smith across a desk in the visitor's room, where prisoners usually discussed their cases with family and lawyers, separated by a glass screen.

A guard conducted him to the interior of the complex and let him into Smith's cell. Smith was seated on a bunk, staring at the window.

He got up slowly and went over to Elijah and embraced him.
"Father Smith, what has happened?"
Smith's eyes were red, and his hair was dishevelled.
"The continuing saga of one stupid cleric from Idaho. Stay tuned, it's going to get worse."
"Why are you here?"
"Why? Because the Lord has ordained that at last I'm to have a

cell of my own. Like the desert Fathers", he said waving his arms about, his mouth twisting bitterly. "Do you like the *ambiance?* Charming, isn't it?"

Smith broke down and sobbed.

"I should have stayed in Boise and become a soybean broker like my brothers. Why did I ever become a priest!"

"What are they accusing you of?"

"Nothing much. A good old-fashioned crime, American as apple pie. Embezzlement or whatever the legal term is, I'm not really sure. The long and short of it is I'm being extradited back to the States for trial."

"But how did this happen?"

"You mean, is it true? Of course it's not true!"

Elijah put a hand on the shoulder of the priest. "I know that."

"Well, that's a relief! You're the first person I've met in the longest time who doesn't think a person's guilty until proven innocent."

"Who is accusing you?"

"The publisher of *Catholic Times* and the State of Illinois. They say that when I was editor of the paper I siphoned off funds for myself. Hundreds of thousands of bucks."

"But as editor you would have had no control over money or accounts."

"Right. But that doesn't phase them a bit. They've concocted some lurid sex scandal between Mrs. Evans—the accountant—and myself. We were in cahoots, they say, planning to take off to a tropical paradise with the cash. They say we built ourselves a love nest there and were interrupted only because I was transferred to Rome."

"Surely this will be cleared up in short order. There is no evidence."

"Of course there's no evidence! The whole thing's a lie. But all that money is missing."

"What does Mrs. Evans say?"

"She's in shock. My lawyer talked to her yesterday, and he thinks she's having some kind of nervous collapse because of what's happening. She's at home. They released her on bail."

"Is there a possibility that she may have done something illegal?"

Smith fixed him with an incredulous look. "If you knew Gertrude Evans you'd know how crazy that is. She's seventy-two years old and has about thirty grandchildren. As long as I've known her, she's kept three perpetual novenas on the go. A purse full of scapulars and rosaries, daily communicant, never says a mean word about anyone, arthritis of the hip, saves stamps for the missions, and thinks Grace Kelly should be canonized."

"Could she have had a moment of weakness?"

"Sure", said Smith with a scowl. "Maybe that's it. I did catch her knitting booties on company time once. There's a criminal streak in her all right!"

"When do you leave?"

"Tomorrow."

"What is the general's reaction?"

"The general?" said Smith with a laugh. "My captain, my captain? Oh, we had a cozy little chat just before the police came. He asked me if I'd done it and of course I denied it. He replied that the people who are concerned about the case—that means the archbishop's office, my provincial, and my silver-tongued replacement—have found some rather damning evidence. He suggested that my root problem is psychological and that if I'd just make a clean breast of everything, they might be able to keep me out of prison."

"What would they do with you?"

"Psychotherapy. The order has offered to replace the missing money, which is nice of them, don't you think?"

"Wouldn't that indicate to the government that they believe you are guilty?"

"Uh-huh. But I don't relish going to jail. A nice rehab center would be much better."

"Would it?"

"I might like the antlers."

"I don't think you would."

"No, I guess I wouldn't", said Smith rubbing his face. "You know, I don't think I'd mind it so much if they hadn't dragged Gertie into it. She's given her life to that paper. She had such a simple faith in all of us. She could have gone to live with her daughter in California a long time ago, but she really believed in our work, suffered through those cold northern winters for the sake of it. If they've broken her heart, I'm going to thump the bastards."

Smith jumped to his feet and began pacing. His eyes were red, snapping back and forth, his fists clenched. He uttered several imprecations in a loud voice. Then he threw himself back onto the bunk and hid his face in his hands.

"Father Smith," said Elijah calmly, "don't you think the truth will win in the end?"

"Will it? I don't know about that anymore."

"It will. You must trust."

"Trust? Look, haven't you learned anything from this? It's been three years of sinking in quicksand. Nothing stops it. We just keep sinking and sinking!"

"There is a Lord, and there is justice. He will vindicate you, even if all human agencies do not."

"And what about Gertie? Think of the humiliation for her. Think of what they're saying about us. It's ridiculous!"

"Think of what they said about our Lord."

"Yes, yes. Thanks for the pep-talk. But the reality here is we've got a really good person getting nailed to the cross. She's never done anyone a lick of harm in her life. And you can be sure that a whole lot of people, good Catholics among them, with their putrid minds plugged into this scummy society, are going to believe it. Where there's smoke there's fire, they'll say. And even if a court declares us innocent, there'll always be a cloud hanging over us."

"That is the price we sometimes have to pay for being on the front lines."

"Easy for you to say."

"Smith . . ."

"I'm sorry. I don't mean to knock you. You're a really good guy, Elijah, and you've been a big help to me over the years. But this is different. Take a look at my life. Take a look at yours. Something happened about two years ago that sent us to two different planets. You're a monk. You pray all day and you teach your classes, and that's your life. I don't fault you for it. I'm glad for you. But please, please understand that my life is over. I slaved for God all those years, and this is what I get in the end."

"Father, some time I would like to tell you a little more about my life . . ."

"I know. You've suffered. The War and all that. But this is now!"

"You are very upset, and with reason. But I want you to ask yourself if our Lord is calling you to walk the hardest way of all, right beside Him, carrying a bitter cross."

"It's bitter all right. You know what the general said? When I told him that this filthy accusation about the sex and love nest was sheer nonsense, he just looked at me and didn't say a thing. Not a damn thing! That blew my cork. I told him just what I thought about his gutlessness. I told him that I'm a priest and that I made vows I've never broken and never will break. I told him that I'm fifty-eight years old, and Gertie is an old lady who's a hell of a lot holier than Grace Kelly ever was. You know what he said to that?"

"What?"

"He just gave me one of his cowlike looks and asked me if I'd ever felt sexual attraction for my mother! My mother! That did it. I told him that he was sick, and the order is sick too, right to the core. I said a jail cell would be a refreshing change. Then I went to my office and waited. The police came and got me an hour later."

The two priests sat together in silence.

Eventually Smith stood up, went to the sink in the corner, and splashed cold water on his face.

"I keep telling myself all the right things, the kind of things you just said. But it doesn't take away the pain. I feel so betrayed. Why is this happening?"

"That is the question: Why is this happening?"

"I'm not hearing anything from heaven. Total silence. What's going on?"

"Are you praying?"

"I say my Mass. I pray my office. But the heart's gone out of it. I don't feel very religious right now."

"Your heart is full of riotous feelings. Calm yourself. Make an act of trust. The consolations will follow."

Smith sighed, "Will they? They seemed to have dried up months ago."

"But have you persisted? How much time do you give to prayer?"

"Well, if the truth be known, less and less. It's pretty dry."

"That is partly the cause of your distress. You need the peace of Christ right now."

"Don't I know it."

They talked for another half-hour until a guard came to the door and said, "Five more minutes."

Elijah stood up.

"I will do what I can", he said. "Pray, Father, pray. Nothing is impossible for God."

"All right. Holy obedience, Elijah. Maybe God sent you to me."

"Trust Him. He is always with you."

"Can you hear my confession?" asked Smith timidly.

Elijah sat back down and spoke the opening prayers of the sacrament. When Smith came to his sins, he said, "There's no greed and no impurity. What they say about me is a lie. But I *am* guilty of something: I hate them. I hate them a lot. I can hardly forgive them for what they've done to the order, and to the Church, and to people like Gertie. I ask God's forgiveness, and I ask His grace to overcome this thing in my heart."

"Anger is an emotion, Father", said Elijah. "It can rise up in us for legitimate reasons. The sin is only in the will. What do we choose to do with our anger? We must convert these feelings. Pray for our enemies. Suffer in silence. When the time comes, you will speak the truth before your accusers, but you must do it without rancor. Offer your sufferings to the Lord. He will use them as a powerful weapon to confound the devices of the enemy. Believe in the ultimate victory, and then your pain will become joy."

Smith seemed comforted by these words. After the absolution, he embraced Elijah. The guard came, and that was the last time he saw Smith.

*　*　*

Dear David,

The days stretch out endlessly. When can we meet again? I hope to go to Foligno for Christmas. Can you join me there?

Love,
Maria

*

Dearest Maria,

It will be impossible to leave the college before the 26th. It would arouse suspicion. I have permission to go after the

Christmas liturgy, and a tentative promise of a car. If that
falls through, I will arrive by train. I count the days.
I am always with you,
David

*

My David,
I whisper your name from morning until night. You are
an island of joy for me, my beloved. If I do not write every
day, it is because I savor the sweet pain of waiting, knowing that it is only a prologue.
Life is extremely busy here. The world is changing
quickly. Our President is achieving wonderful things for
unity and peace in the world. I know that you are unsure
of his motives. *Caro,* you must not be. He is a great leader
and history will remember him as the figure who stands
head and shoulders above the men of our times.
I am always one with you,
in the heart,
Maria

*

Maria,
I long for the time when we shall not hide our names.
Love does not hide. Love is the great fire which consumes
without destroying. This is our kind of love. Nothing can
take it away from us. Nothing can ever separate us.
I regret that I have been so critical about the President. The
news is full of his achievements. Perhaps I have been mistaken.
We can speak more of this at Foligno. Will we be alone?
Your David

*

Dear One,
I soon hope to have a gift for you. I am on the verge of
making the purchase. It is a priceless work of art. I will

bring it to Foligno. When you see it you will tell me I have
been impulsive, but it is worth the price.

M.

*

Maria,

I worry about your impulsive heart. You must not pay
too much. I implore you! Do not pay too much. Our love
is the gift, and that alone outweighs all treasure.

I am hoping for snow. Snow at Christmas, the world clothed in white. We will walk side by side in the hills. You will hold
tightly to my old arm, and I will appreciate it too much. We
will speak of mountains and vineyards and the coming spring.

We will speak of each other, you and me,

David

*   *   *

Elijah received no reply to this note. He assumed that Anna's
schedule was full and that she was saving her news until their
meeting. The third Sunday of Advent passed uneventfully. He
kept himself busy correcting examinations and writing last-
minute cards to friends throughout the world. On the afternoon
of Christmas Eve, he took them down to the porter's office for
mailing.

The porter teased him about the excessive postage costs.

"More? *Scandaloso!* I thought you were all finished! Look at
this: Israel, the United States, France, Russia, The Netherlands!"
he chided. "Father, when are you going to be simple?"

"I'm sorry, brother. Charity demands that I do not ignore
these people."

"You get twice as many letters as any of the other Fathers.
And you send as many too!"

They jested back and forth until the brother slipped in a question:
"Who is the lady who sends you all those letters every few days?"

"Lady?"

"*Sì,* the lady from Holland."

"A friend. How do you know it is a lady?"

"No man would use a pretty envelope like that."

Elijah smiled but said nothing.

"Now it's none of my business, but I noticed the letters have stopped." He paused and looked at Elijah expectantly. It was a weakness of this brother that he liked to assemble tiny bits and pieces of information about the private lives of the clerics in the house. When Elijah was not forthcoming with more details, the porter turned away to other business. Elijah was climbing the stairs to his room, when he came running after him.

"Father, Father, I forgot. This package came for you this morning. A man dropped it off."

Printed on the front of the padded envelope: *David Schäfer*.

David?

"Did the man say who he was?"

"No. He just strolled in off the street and pushed it through the wicket. He said, 'Give this to Schäfer.' Not very polite, if you ask me."

Elijah took the package to his room and opened it. It contained the brass reliquary he had given to Anna. He pried open its lid. Inside there was a mass of material that appeared to be semi-liquid. It was dark purple, almost black, and bits of solid matter were embedded in it. It smelled of putrefaction. He stared at it uncomprehending. The odor filled the room. He took the reliquary to the sink, inserted the plug and tapped the contents into the bowl. A gelatinous sludge oozed down the white ceramic, leaving a trail of splinters and what appeared to be gravel. Upon closer inspection, he saw that they were rosary beads. One bead floated in the center, beside a sliver of wood.

He bent over the sink and resisted the urge to vomit. His heart pounded and a wild cry threatened to escape his throat.

He scooped the mess back into the reliquary and washed its outer surface, the bowl, and his hands. He put the reliquary into his pocket, turned to the icon of the archangel of the Apocalypse, and stammered a desperate prayer.

"Holy Michael, defend us in this day of battle, be our protection against the malice and the snares of the devil. May God rebuke him, we humbly pray, and may thou, O prince of the heavenly hosts, cast into hell Satan and all the evil spirits who prowl through the world seeking the ruin of souls!"

He sat down on the bed and trembled violently. He turned to the Cross and cried out, "Save her!"

*   *   *

He drove like a madman. The traffic into the city was heavy, but the outgoing lanes were almost empty. It was raining now, and the pavement was slick. He went into a slow skid, pulled out of it, accelerated, and spun out of control. The car righted itself, and he went on. He prayed incessantly as the speedometer climbed, hoping that no highway police would stop him, hoping against hope that the contents of the reliquary were merely a warning or an evil joke.

He turned east and raced up into the hills. A slash of crimson in the rearview mirror indicated that the sun was setting behind the edge of the overcast. At Terni, where he turned north toward Foligno, the rain became sleet and the road a sheet of ice. He crawled along for an hour. It grew dark and snow began to fall in thick white flakes that blinded him with the reflected glare of the headlights.

"Oh, Anna", he cried. "Spare her, Lord!"

At Foligno, he found the road that wound up the side of the mountain. He skidded along it until he came to her lane. Twenty yards up the tires began to spin and refused to move the car forward. He got out and walked.

The gate hung half-open, and he saw by flashlight that its lock was broken and the bar bent askew. He ran and stumbled uphill until the ground leveled off in front of the looming black shape of the farmhouse.

There were no lights in the building. The door was closed,

but the window had been smashed out of it. He opened it and entered, dreading to see what lay within. The interior was cold and damp. Nothing stirred. His boots crunched on the debris scattered across the floor. He went through the ground floor, taking in the tumbled furniture, the drawers tossed in all directions, the broken crockery, pictures, books, phonograph records and papers that covered everything like the wake of a hurricane. A lap-computer lay on the parlor rug, its hard-drive missing, the hole gaping like a skull from which the brain had been removed. He searched for signs of blood, but found nothing. He climbed the stairs warily. It was the same on the upper floor. Mattresses had been ripped to shreds, chairs split open, cabinets stripped, clothing heaped in drifts. Here too there was no sign of blood.

In the kitchen, he found a lamp and matches. The golden light lit up the scene of chaos starkly. He turned around and around wondering at the totality of the wreckage.

He realized then that he was chilled to the bone. He reached behind the stove intending to grab sticks of kindling in order to start a fire. Then he saw it.

A slip of paper, palest violet in color, protruding from a heap of sticks dumped beside the upturned wood-box. A slip of paper among the hundreds lying about the room. It seemed to cry out to him.

He extracted it and read:
Beneath Nonno's heart.
Anna's handwriting.
"Beneath Nonno's heart?" he whispered. What did it mean? What could she be saying?

Nonno's heart?

He shuffled through the house from one room to another.
What is it, Anna? What do you want me to find?
He went into the room where he had slept—her grandparents' room.

Nonno's room?

Heart, heart, heart, heart . . .

The bed was demolished, the pictures torn from the wall, the crucifix broken into pieces, the picture of the Sacred Heart . . .

It was lying face up on the floor beside the bed. The glass was shattered, tearing into the oleograph heart. Christ was weeping, weeping over the world. He was calling, calling, but none would listen, none attend.

Elijah lifted the lantern higher, and the light revealed the outline of a boot print on the pieces of glass.

He picked it up by the frame and carefully removed the broken shards. He turned it over in his hands. The back of the image was covered entirely by two wide strips of wood, held in place by old-fashioned pin-nails. The top two nails were missing. He removed the others; they slipped out of their holes effortlessly, and the strips of wood dropped to the floor. A sheet of paper fell out.

The paper was not yellowed with age, and it was filled with computer script. He took it back to the kitchen, turned a chair upright, and sat down on it by the stove. He read:

Foligno, 21 December

Dear Elijah,

Marco will carry this to you. I can write openly.

I am a little worried. I have received no reply from you concerning my note of the twelfth in which I relate the news about "the priceless work of art".

We could not have hoped for better: my every suspicion has been confirmed. The surgeon, the magician, and the destroyer were definitely involved, a fact related to me by a person they believe to be secure. I have worked hard to earn her trust. As I penetrated deeper into their rings, like Dante descending through the circles of hell, I found more than one individual who was unhappy to be there. Many telltale signs can be deciphered in such wretched souls. She is one of their playthings, a poor, broken human being who could no longer withstand the psychological pressures of their activities. My presence among them, which is merely a source of amusement for the most powerful ones, is a source of agony for her. Don't ask me to explain it; I can only say that she is one in whom the last pathetic scrap of conscience has not been entirely eradicated.

I befriended her only in order to dig for evidence. In the beginning I felt nothing but revulsion for her, but gradually as I learned more about her horrible existence, I was moved to pity. I let it be known that I understood her pain. She responded. We grew close. Then, last week, the prize you and I anticipated fell into my lap. The woman could no longer bear the tension of pretending she knew nothing. She hinted that she knew something very big. Point blank, I asked her about Stefano. She admitted everything. Stefano was killed by the circle. She confessed that she had been present during some of the sessions in which he was tortured. She said *Architetto* was there and approved of everything. She regretted what they did to him because he was a brave man. He was a nice man, she said emphatically. *A nice man!* I suppose those are the only words a person like her could dredge up to describe a person like Stefano.

I recorded our conversation on a concealed microtape and made a transcript of it. I will not ask her to testify in court because she would not live a single day past the filing of an indictment. However, the material she has supplied, along with other evidence that has come to light, will be enough to convince the Italian government to mount an inquiry. It is doubtful that they will be able to send him and his associates to prison, because his tentacles reach far into the vital organs of the nation, and beyond. Nevertheless, the public scandal will slow his rise to absolute power and may even bring it to a stop. A radical doubt will be planted in the mind of the world. If any harm comes to me as a result of my legal suit, it will only serve to confirm that doubt. It is a risk I am willing to take.

Despite these victories, I am suffering an apprehension. The pattern of shadows that have surrounded me for many years has suddenly changed. In my work, and in the life of the gyroscope, there is a vague disequilibrium—nuances, odd silences—so subtle as to be nearly microscopic. Remember my intuition? You may add to it a vibration on the antennae I thought I had lost.

Why have you not responded? Did you receive my note? It was coded in our usual manner and conveyed the news that a major breakthrough has occurred. Without much effort, they could interpret my meaning. They might even make that poor woman crack. She might crack on her own and tell them everything.

No matter what happens to me, he cannot escape justice. I have made several copies of the material that relates to the case. The dossiers are stacked here in front of me, and I will have Marco deliver them personally when I see him in Milan on the second of January. One to my lawyer, several to the legal powers of Italy. I will send others by courier to the UN and to the secretary of the Europarliament. Copies will go to the leading newspapers of the West. They can hardly ignore an indictment of this caliber, considering that I am one of the highest jurists in the world. (Yes, it is true, I am still proud—but no longer bitter.) In the unlikely event that these many copies are intercepted, I have placed one in the hands of her whose heart is pierced by a sword, where the sparrow builds her nest and the swallow finds her home. She guards it well.

Please come to Foligno. I am here until New Year's Day. After that, Milan, and then on to The Hague. Marco is in love at last and has begged my permission to spend the holiday with his beloved. My Gianna is with the family of her prince. It is the first time I shall be alone here. And yet I am not alone. I feel Stefano very close. On Christmas Day, I will go down to the chapel of Blessed Angela, a local saint, a wife, mother, and widow, and hear Mass for the first time in twenty years. Oh, do not hope for too much from me, Lawyer Elijah. I am not prompted to such rash devotion by the faith you want from me. Though, perhaps it is a kind of faith, a return to the beginnings to see if what was lost may again be found. In solitude, in exile, we come to know what cannot otherwise be known; we remember what we saw and see it for the first time.

Dare I tell you that there were moments when the charade of our romantic notes blurred, and I began to feel in earnest the words I wrote to you, as if they were my own, as if we were what we pretended to be? I know you will tell me not to say such things to you. You will say that your heart cannot bear it. Good, I will say no more on that. But just this once I will tell you that your heart *can* bear it. And needs to bear it! Love bursts forth from the springs of the heart as raw material. It takes many shapes. It asks us to go forth and die, over and over again. It always asks this terrible price. It wants our life—all of it. Then gives it back again.

You need never fear me. Nor should you fear your own heart. You are a father without a child. I am a child without a father. Let us be this kind of love for each other. It is no less a love than what has come to Gianna and Marco. The form of it changes, and the season, and the harvest. But it is love.

Well, my father-friend, the hour is indeed late. I am so weary. I am so happy. We have beat him, Elijah. We have won. I have swum in dark waters and survived. And yet I sense it is not yet over. Large shadows are moving beneath me in the abyss, though on the surface there is hardly a ripple.

I will ask Marco to drive down to Rome and deliver this to you personally.

(Signed) Anna

Here the computer script ended. Below it, handwritten in a hurried scrawl:

O God. They are here.

* * *

Elijah read and reread the letter. He felt like weeping, then crying out in rage. He leapt to his feet then sat down again helplessly. Should he go to the police? But what could they do? Was this single letter sufficient to connect the President to her disappearance? The name *Architetto* would mean nothing to them. It was obvious that all the evidence had been confiscated by whoever had savaged the house and taken Anna.

He trudged downhill to the car and tried to reverse it out of the lane, but the tires spun and dug into the half-frozen mud. No amount of pushing or praying would dislodge it.

"Why, my Lord?" he cried. "Why?"

The snow fell down heavier. The cold was increasing, and he wore only his light raincoat. If he tried walking to the town, he might lose his way and freeze to death. In the surrounding hills there were no other lights as far as the eye could see. He went back to the house.

He dragged a mattress into the kitchen and spread it in front of the stove. He stoked the fire and lay down.

He saw how it must have been. She had just completed printing out her letter to him when she felt rather than saw the arrival of the captors. Perhaps there were lights below on the lane, and she heard the faint clang of the crow-bar on the electronic lock, bending back the metal catch. There might have been men coming up on foot, silently, while the others opened the gate in order for the vehicle to drive through. She must have known somehow that this was the moment she had dreaded and hoped to avoid. She wrote, "*O God. They are here,*" at the bottom of the letter, then calmly folded it—she never did anything in haste. Then she walked to her grandparents' bedroom and slipped the paper into the pocket behind the image of the Sacred Heart. They must have been at the doors by then, hammering for entrance at front and back, smashing the glass. She had a few seconds to scribble the final message, *Beneath Nonno's heart,* on a scrap of violet paper and throw it behind the stove, as the doors splintered and they poured in.

He tossed and turned and prayed throughout the darkest hours of his life, an eternal stretch of desolation rivaled only by the final days of the ghetto and his cross-country flight from Warsaw as a boy.

In the middle of the night he heard voices. He sat bolt upright, straining to hear what they were saying, but it was only the wind whispering, *She guards it well; she guards it well.*

The first light arrived, a baleful gray smear on the eastern summit above the farm. He boiled a cup of hot water, and it drove the chill from his bones. He read the letter again. *In the hands of her whose heart is pierced by a sword, where the sparrow builds her nest and the swallow finds her home.*

The words leapt off the page.

She guards it well; she guards it well.

He found the footpath that led up the mountain through the devastated vineyard. He slipped repeatedly on the snow-covered trail. His feet were soon soaked, and he bled from shins and elbows, where he had struck the stones. The beating of his heart became irregular and his chest ached. He pushed himself onward, gasping for oxygen, and the sharp whistle of his breath became a cry, mingled deliriously with prayers and Anna's name and inarticulate protests. He clawed his way up inch by inch, tugging on thorn bushes and roots, branches and stones. His hands were chapped and bleeding. He was scrambling on hands and knees when he finally came to the top.

The statue stood there at the crest, reposed beneath her blanket of white, infinitely peaceful in her grotto. Cups of snow filled the nests the sparrows had built around her.

He fell to his knees at her feet and grabbed onto her waist. The statue rocked and nearly fell, but he righted it.

He sat in the snow, panting and groaning. He ached from head to foot and for a time could not make his body obey. He lay his head against the chipped paint of the pedestal and prayed. The prayer was little more than a cry of anguish, but he recognized that it was a current of genuine communication, reaching out across the abyss of the long dark age in which he had been born, across space and dimensions, through barrier after impossible barrier, to the throne of grace.

"Help us, O help of Christians, help us, Mother", he cried.

And then a word came in return. It had no origin in human psychology or biology, had no other source than the springs flowing from the throne he had believed to be so distant.

I am here.

Warmth filled his body. Light filled his mind. A stillness, which was part of that original stillness before the first word of creation, was reborn in him. He looked up at the statue and saw in its crudely painted face a reflection of man's hunger for his eternal home. He saw heaven reach down and touch this poor piece of plaster and reshape it in the forms that exist beyond the blind groping of man. Love was upon the face, and love was within it.

Do not be afraid, little one, she said. *I am with you. Love is with you until the final consummation.*

The current of heat now flowed through him like clear, warm water, containing hidden delights, cleansing his wounds, bathing his soul. His body, one massive sack of pain, was also soothed and reinvigorated, though its aches did not cease.

She guards it well, she guards it well, said the wind.

Then he knew.

He stood up and embraced the statue, and tilted it at an angle toward the rear of the grotto, where it came to rest against the stone. In an exposed cavity beneath her feet, he found a plastic bag. He removed it and tilted the statue back upon its base, recovering the hole.

The bag was sealed against moisture. He tore open the top and withdrew its contents: documents, transcripts, cassette tapes, a detailed history of the case in Anna's handwriting, descriptions of plots and subplots, names, dates. There was more. Much, much more.

He made as if to go back down the mountain, but stopped and looked back at the statue. A pathetic, lifeless madonna, devoid of artistic sense, and yet a symbol through which the Mother had come. It was her way, of course, for she had been a small poor maiden of Nazareth. Images of her were crowned in cathedrals throughout the world, icons painted by saints and statues carved by geniuses. She was loved and glorified through these mighty works, and through them she drew souls to glorify her Son, the One to whom she always and everywhere pointed. And yet she did not spurn the lowliest images, for they too were signs lifted up in the darkness of history, without false glory or human pride of accomplishment, words made from the clay of the earth and painted with pigments wrung from the earth by gnarled hands that toiled in the earth and hoped for Paradise.

Little one, my son. Fear nothing. The beast that impersonates a lamb approaches the sanctuary in order to destroy it and to take the throne of Jesus, the true Lamb of God. He will succeed for a time in obscuring the light of heaven in many places.

"Holy Mother. What am I to do? Is everything lost?"

When the enemy thinks he has won everything, that is the moment he will be defeated. Before the end there will be much suffering. You are to be a witness for Christ. You are to be a sign. Fear nothing. Speak only what He shall give you to say, and it shall be for the salvation of many souls.

"How shall I save Anna?"

You cannot save her. Pray for her soul. I am with her.

"Where shall I go?"

Pray to the Holy Spirit, and He will guide you.

The anointing within his spirit faded steadily, and he was left alone, a man standing on a mountain. It was Christmas Day.

* * *

The mud ruts were still frozen when he reached the car. He started the engine, put the gears in reverse, and backed it out easily. The pavement on the road was bare. He drove down to the valley and south to the highway. Every so often he turned and looked at the package of material on the seat beside him. His heart contracted repeatedly, and he prayed for Anna over and over until the words became a torrent of confused pleading.

He passed several petrol stations, all of them closed, but at Terni he found one open. He went into the bathroom and washed up while the attendant, an adolescent wearing headphones, cavorting to soundless music, filled the tank. In the deserted grocery attached to the station he saw his own face and Anna's staring at him from the front page of a newspaper. In an instant his eyes took in the words, *missing* and *lovers*. He did not waste time reading the rest. He took the paper to the counter and paid for it.

The attendant punched numbers into the cash register. Elijah turned his face away from him, but he need not have bothered, for the boy paid him no attention. He took Elijah's money and threw some coins back onto the counter.

"*Buon Natale!*" he drawled mechanically as Elijah went out the door.

"*Buon Natale!*"

From Terni he went southwest until he neared the turn onto the Rome–Florence highway. He pulled over to the shoulder and read the front page of the newspaper. It reported that a justice of the World Court had disappeared, and the police were investigating. Criminal involvement had not been ruled out, but there was strong suspicion of a domestic homicide. Certain letters had come to the attention of the state prosecutor, indicating the involvement of a Roman Catholic cleric, also missing, with whom the jurist had been involved. There was much to support the police theory that she had been trying to extricate herself from the compromising relationship, and that the cleric, a one-time envoy of the Vatican, had liquidated her in a failed attempt to avoid scandal. A wide-ranging sweep of Italy's major cities was underway. The article gave the names of both parties involved.

Elijah sat frozen at the wheel. He considered turning north to Milan, where he might be able to track down Gianna and Marco and learn from them any news of Anna. Would they believe him? They might, especially if he showed them the documentation. But what if their residences were under surveillance? No, it was impossible.

Obviously, he could not return to the college in Rome, for that would be closely watched. Where to then?

He closed his eyes and invoked the Holy Spirit. Interiorly he heard the word, *Roma*. He gunned the engine, turned onto the southbound lane, and drove for the eternal city.

* * *

He reached a northern suburb by midday. At a public phone booth he called *Stato*'s apartment.

A woman answered.

Elijah asked for the cardinal.

The woman's voice hesitated. "I regret, Signore, he's had a heart attack. He's been taken to the Gemelli."

"Who is speaking, please?"

"This is his sister Margaretta. Would you like to leave a message?"

"No. No, thank you. I will go to him at the hospital."

"I don't think they'll let you see him. He's in intensive care."

"Was it very bad?"

"He's had a scare. The doctor says it's a warning." Her voice trailed off and she hung up.

He got back into the car and fumbled in the glove compartment. He found sunglasses—the porter wore them, rain or shine—and put them on. He drove across the city and parked several blocks from the hospital. He walked the rest of the way, avoiding people's glances, hoping that no one would notice the suspicious rips in his clothing and the spatters of mud. He arrived at the main entrance without incident, but stopped himself from entering just in time. Two policemen stood by the reception desk, talking to a nurse. He stepped back and walked quickly down the block and around to the back of the building. There he found the service entrance through which he had entered the hospital months before in his attempt to see Billy Stangsby.

Five minutes later he was on the floor of the ICU, in a janitor's room. He cleaned his clothing with a rag, combed his hair and straightened his coat. Assuming a confident expression, he strolled along the corridor and went through the double doors of the unit, not knowing what would greet him on the other side. An alarm bell was ringing. Nurses were scurrying away down the hall toward a flashing light, pushing a machine. A list of patients' names at the deserted desk informed him of the cardinal's room number. He was inside the private room in seconds, breathing hard. He closed the door.

Stato was sleeping. His color was bad. Wires trailed from his body in all directions. Elijah stared, afraid to wake him.

"Who's there?" the cardinal said in a hoarse voice.

"Father Schäfer", Elijah whispered.

"Schäfer!" the cardinal said. "Come closer. I can hardly see you."

Elijah approached the bed. "Are you in pain, Eminence?"

"It hurts."

"I'm in serious trouble."

"I know. I saw this morning's paper."

"I need your help."

"How can I do anything? I have been flattened!" he groaned. "I needed so much to be strong."

"Please, try to help me. I could be arrested at any moment."

"Why? Why? Why is this happening to us?" The cardinal twisted his head back and forth. He looked years older, and his face was slack, beaten. His eyes blurred then refocused on Elijah.

"I have evidence that will destroy the President's career. He is a liar and a murderer." He held up the package of documents. "It's all here."

The cardinal's face brightened. The old fire welled up in his eyes for an instant, and he screwed his brows together and set his mouth in a straight line.

"Is it true?"

"It is true. We are close to defeating him, but it is not yet accomplished. I must put this information into the hands where it will be most effective. Whom should I bring it to?"

"I don't know. I'm so tired. . . . Maybe my friend the judge from Brescia. Wait, go to *Dottrina*. The Cardinal Prefect is the one. Oh no, I forgot! He's in New York, trying to settle a dispute between the American bishops. If I could have just a few minutes of strength, just a few more. I could make a phone call. You must take it to the Holy Father. He'll know what to do."

"But how do I get inside the Vatican? I'm sure they are watching for me at the gates."

"You could get in the back way. Then find the master of the Swiss Guards. I know him. He's a good fellow. I'll write a note for you to give him. Give me that note pad."

Elijah propped the pad on the cardinal's belly, and *Stato* filled it with unstable handwriting. He took off his bishop's ring and gave it to Elijah.

"If you need to use this, go ahead. It could open doors."

"Thank you, Eminence."

"Come closer."

The cardinal reached up and with his thumb and forefinger traced the sign of the cross on Elijah's forehead.

"There. Now, you bless me."

Elijah prayed the prayers of the sacrament of the sick and anointed the cardinal.

"I will return as soon as possible."

"You took a great risk coming to me. Better you don't come back here; who knows what's going to happen."

The cardinal looked him up and down.

"You're a mess. Take my coat and pants from the closet. We're about the same size."

Elijah changed into the cardinal's clothes. They fitted him approximately, but were loose about the waist.

"Now, my coat."

The heavy felt parka weighed on his shoulders. A green plaid scarf and leather gloves completed the disguise.

"The biretta too. Don't be shy."

Elijah put the red cap on his head, feeling distinctly uncomfortable.

"It suits you", Stato smiled wanly. "Now, how are you getting around the city?"

Elijah told him.

"That's foolish. Your community car will have been reported missing, and they'll be looking for it. Go to my apartment. I'll ask a nurse to phone Margaretta. She'll give you the keys to my Volkswagen. That should give you more time."

"I don't know if we will see each other again, Eminence. Whatever happens, please know that I shall always pray for you."

He took *Stato's* hand.

"May God go with you. May the holy angels guide you."

"May His peace remain with you. Please rest, Eminence. The Church needs you."

"The Church needs you, Father Elijah."

He retraced his steps out of the hospital and walked several blocks to a thoroughfare, where he hailed a taxi. Fifteen minutes later, he rang the bell of the cardinal's apartment.

A heavyset woman came to the door. Her face was a female version of *Stato's*, a plain countrywoman, gray hair gathered in a net. The apartment behind her smelled of frying onions.

"Margaretta?"

"Sì. Are you the man from my brother?"

"I am."

She handed him a set of keys.

"The hospital just phoned. I'm supposed to give you these, Eminence."

"Where is the car?"

"Downstairs in the garage. Be careful, Eminence, don't scratch it when you're going up the ramp. He's fussy about that car."

She began to cry.

"Don't worry, Signora. He is strong. You will have your brother back again."

She dried her eyes on an apron. "Maybe. Maybe not. He works like a dog. He never rests. I told him so often, you've got to give God a little room to do something. But, no, he has to do it all."

Elijah reassured her again, then went down to the garage. The cardinal's ancient rusting Volkswagen hardly deserved the concern that was lavished upon it. But it started at the first turn of the key and chugged up the ramp, leaving a trail of blue exhaust.

He drove across the Tiber bridge onto the Via Crescenzo, circled the Vatican and parked two blocks south of the railroad entrance to the walled city. He tucked the package of evidence under his arm, locked the car, and walked toward the gates.

Workmen were replacing a track beside the gates, which stood open.

"*È permesso?* Can I go through?" he waved to them with a smile. "It saves me time."

They tipped their hats at him with respectful disinterest and nodded permission.

The angels are busy, thought Elijah.

He worked his way through the gardens until he encountered his first gendarme. He asked to be taken to the commander of the Swiss Guards. Five minutes later he was led into an office at the foot of the Palace of Sixtus V.

489

"Colonel, this cardinal wishes to speak with you."

A vigorous sixty-year old man, dressed in the uniform of the Swiss, stood up behind his desk.

"How can I help you, Your Eminence?"

"May we speak alone?"

The colonel shut the door and offered Elijah a chair. He seated himself, folded his hands on the desk before him, and fixed his penetrating gaze on Elijah.

"You are not a cardinal."

"That is true", said Elijah removing the biretta.

"That young man is new here. Otherwise, he would have known you are not what you say you are."

"I have told no one that I am a prelate. He merely assumed it. I am a priest."

"Why are you here?"

He handed the colonel the note from *Stato*.

"This is most odd. The Cardinal Secretary is in serious condition in a hospital."

"I have just been to see him at the Gemelli. He asked me to show you this."

Elijah placed the ring on the desk.

The colonel's face did not reveal his thoughts. "That is an episcopal ring. There are several thousands of them in the world. How do I know you have come from the cardinal?"

"You do not know, but I ask you, in the name of God, to believe me."

"This is very shaky handwriting", he said, tapping the paper.

"Surely you recognize the cardinal's handwriting?"

"It could be a forgery."

"It is not a forgery."

"Do you know how many people, some of them in scarlet, some in black, come to this office trying to obtain a private audience with His Holiness?"

"I don't know."

"Several every week."

They stared at each other across the desk.

"Do you have a message from God for His Holiness?"

"No. I am not a visionary."

"Perhaps a private revelation?"

"Of course not. Please, colonel, I am not a madman or a neurotic with a cause. I am bearing a message from the cardinal. I have been engaged in a special work for the Secretariat of State and the material in this package contains matters of highest importance for the Church."

The colonel looked unconvinced. "Most of the people who want to see the Pope tell me the same thing. They all want to speak to him about matters of highest importance."

Elijah closed his eyes and prayed.

"They all pray too", said the colonel.

He reached for his desk phone. "What is your name?"

"I suppose it doesn't matter now. If I tell you my name, will you guarantee that this package reaches the Holy Father?"

"I will examine the contents and consider the request. Your name?"

"Father Elijah Schäfer."

The colonel removed his hand from the phone. He stared at Elijah and his eyes blinked.

"Schäfer."

He leaned back and exhaled loudly through his nostrils.

His hand moved to a button beside the phone, hesitated, and retracted.

"Why would a man wanted by the Italian police on suspicion of murder wish to speak with the Pope? Do you think he can help your case?"

"I have killed no one. The situation is a crisis of much larger proportions. There is a subterfuge—too complex to explain to you now—which threatens to undermine the Church."

"How am I to know you are not part of that subterfuge?"

His hand flashed out and hit the button. Instantly two Swiss guards entered the office.

"Stand by the door", he said to them.

"May I see the material?"

Elijah gave him the package. He went through its contents slowly, examining the documents, scanning the titles. He put each item carefully to the side, then returned to Anna's largest manuscript, the one in which she described the details of the case.

"This is written by the woman who has disappeared."

"Yes."

The colonel nodded to the guards. They went out and closed the door behind them.

He read silently for five minutes. "Obviously, this involves state matters."

"Matters of extreme sensitivity. The Holy Father would be reading this material right now if it hadn't been for the cardinal's unfortunate heart attack."

"I see that you are in a predicament."

"We are all in a predicament, sir. The situation Dr. Benedetti describes is utterly grave. You must believe me."

"Perhaps you composed this yourself."

"I did not."

The colonel stood and buckled a large double-handed sword onto his waist. His face was hard.

Elijah lowered his head and rubbed his brow.

"Please. Believe me", he whispered, knowing that it was no use.

"Stand up, Father. You will come with me."

Elijah groaned, stunned, heartbroken. A black wave washed through his mind.

"Where are you taking me?" he said disconsolately.

"To see the Pope."

XIX

In Pectore

"Put the biretta back on", he said. "You will need this too."

He handed Elijah the ring.

"Wear it."

Elijah did as he was told.

The colonel put *Stato*'s letter inside the breast of his uniform, gathered up Anna's files, and put them into a leather envelope, which he placed in a valise. He shut it, spun the numerical code lock, and gripped it in his left hand. Right hand on sword-hilt, he led Elijah out of the office.

In the outer reception annex, the colonel signaled to the two young guards to accompany them.

"This way, Father", he said. Elijah followed.

"There may be difficulties", he advised over his shoulder. "You must do exactly as I say."

"I will."

As they proceeded through the labyrinth of the Vatican, Elijah was struck by the contrast of the modern valise and the colonel's medieval uniform. If he had not felt so disoriented, he might have smiled at the startling juxtaposition, although the gravity with which the Swiss conducted their duties would have precluded any outright amusement.

As they approached the entrance to the papal throne room, the colonel pointed to a small parlor off the main hall.

"Go in there, Padre, and stay until I call you."

The colonel went forward into the throne room and seeing a group of churchmen gathered by the far door, he went up to them. The Prefect of the Apostolic Palaces and the *Maestro di Camera* were in consultation with a burly layman wearing a dark trench coat. He instantly recognized the studied expression in this man's eyes, the way he rocked back and forth on his feet, and his air of professional superiority. This was a personality that knew human nature from top to bottom. This was a personality that the colonel understood quite well.

Police, he said to himself.

The privy chamberlain introduced the man as the chief inspector of Rome's homicide bureau. The colonel was introduced as the commander of the Swiss Guard, chief of security for the Vatican, and protector of the person of the Pope.

"May I ask the nature of your business here?" he said in a formal tone.

"It's an official inquiry regarding a former employee of the Vatican, a certain Father Schäfer, who is under suspicion of abduction and murder. We have reason to believe he may seek refuge here. I want to secure the administration's assurance that you will not harbor the fugitive, and that if he is found, he will be turned over to my office in the interests of justice. I must have your assurance."

When he had completed this declaration, the inspector fixed his most adamantine, serene, and intimidating gaze upon the colonel. He had never met the colonel before. The colonel appeared to him as a member of that genre of silly old men who liked to caper about in plumes, brandishing steel blades. He was dressed in yellow hose, buckled shoes, bulging striped pantaloons, and a black cap tied with red strings. In addition he wore a theatrically oversized sword.

"I repeat: I must have this assurance before I can leave."

The colonel returned the inspector's gaze. If anything, his was even more serene, underpinned by an equally adamantine foundation. He peered unblinking into the inspector's eyes until the latter began to squirm, without showing it, and looked away.

"I remind you that you are a guest on the soil of a sovereign state. It would be appropriate for such a guest to express his desires in the form of a request, not a demand."

The inspector shrugged. "Have it your way. I *request* that you turn over to my office anyone who answers to the name of Schäfer or who fits his description. Read this!"

The colonel accepted the sheet of paper that the inspector thrust at him. "I assure you there are no criminals here."

"If I could have your *assurance* that you will report to us if he arrives."

"I will consider it."

"You will consider it?" the inspector repeated with the subtlest tone of mimicry.

"You are making it more difficult for yourself at every moment. Your manner has forced me to feel less inclined to consider it than when you first raised the subject."

The inspector's face went red and he glared.

"I want to talk to somebody who's in charge here!" he barked.

"You are talking to him."

"I mean one of the big boys. The Pope or some other higher-ups."

"You will not be seeing the Pope. In fact, you will not be seeing anyone else in the Vatican today. You will now leave these premises. These two young men will escort you to the gates."

"You ridiculous buffoon!" growled the inspector. "This case involves a capital crime, and one of your people is connected to it. Don't play any stupid court games with me. Do you know who I am?"

"I know that you are about to violate international law, unless you leave at once."

The inspector blustered. The colonel put his hand on the hilt of his sword.

"If you do not comply immediately, we shall be forced to register a complaint with your government. You can explain the situation to them."

The inspector clapped a hat furiously on his head, turned on his heels, and strode toward the door, followed at a trot by the two young Swiss.

The chamberlains looked at the colonel and at each other.

"You were quite rude", said one. "Really, colonel, you have alienated him. We should try to be on good terms with the Italian authorities."

"With respect, Eminence, however tiny we may be, we are a nation. This is the center of a spiritual community that encompasses almost a billion people."

"You were not humble."

The colonel looked pensive. He looked at the floor and pursed his lips.

"You are right. I was not humble. It is a fault of mine. I apologize."

He returned to the outer hall and called Elijah.

"Come, we will go in now."

The maestro and the prefect of the Apostolic Palaces intercepted their march to the door of the papal offices.

"Just a moment, colonel. We don't recognize this cardinal", said the maestro. "Who is he? Is he really a cardinal?"

The colonel explained that Elijah was *in pectore*. The chamberlains raised their eyebrows. They knew what he meant by that term: there were a few unknown men scattered throughout the world who had been secretly ordained as bishops for various sensitive political reasons, primarily to avoid capture in totalitarian states. The chamberlains stood aside and let them pass into the *Anticamera Segreta*, the outer chamber of the Pope's private office.

The Pope's secretary rose from his desk and greeted them.

"*Buon Natale*, colonel!"

"*Buon Natale,* Monsignore! I have with me an emissary from the Cardinal Secretary of State. He brings an urgent message to His Holiness."

"Can it wait? The Holy Father is resting after this morning's Mass. Then he must prepare his homily for the Christmas Mass at Saint John Lateran."

The colonel handed the secretary *Stato's* note and the police report. He reemphasized the absolute necessity of a meeting with the Pope.

"One moment."

The secretary disappeared through a side door. While they waited, the colonel unlocked the valise and gave Elijah the leather envelope.

The secretary returned a few minutes later and signaled that Elijah could enter. He went through the oak doors, and the secretary closed them behind, leaving him alone with the Pope.

The pontiff sat at a window. A cane rested against the wall beside his chair.

Elijah knelt before him and kissed his ring. The Pope accepted the gesture and did not make him rise as he had done on former occasions. His hands shook, his head trembled rhythmically. His face was thin, older than Elijah remembered.

"Be seated."

Elijah sat facing him. The Pope's eyes contained an ocean of sadness—and strength.

"Your face has changed more than mine, Father, and in such a short period of time."

"Much has happened, Your Holiness."

"Time accelerates as we grow older, doesn't it? Time and events are telescoping."

"Events of great import to the Church are taking place right now."

"Yes, I know. The Prefect for Doctrine telephoned me from New York this morning. Your situation is precarious."

"The danger encompasses the universal Church. I have evidence for you to examine relating to that. We now know for certain that the President is responsible for the death of Stefano Benedetti, and that he is involved in Anna Benedetti's disappearance."

"The police say you are a suspect."

"I am innocent."

The Pope reached out and touched Elijah's arm. "I know you are innocent. You need not reassure me of that."

"The accusation is but a small part of a conspiracy that seeks to scatter the organizational structure of the Church."

"The Church will survive everything. Our most immediate aim is to resist the President's rise to global power. You say you have evidence?"

"Conclusive evidence."

He opened the envelope.

"Documents, letters, tape recordings."

"I will ensure that copies are made and that it reaches the proper authorities. Put it on my desk."

When Elijah had done so, he slumped back in his chair, and an audible groan escaped his lips. He realized suddenly that he was exhausted and that his body ached.

"You are very tired, my son."

"So much has happened since yesterday afternoon that I can scarcely begin to speak of it."

He related all that he had experienced since Christmas Eve.

"I am afraid for my friend Anna. Almost certainly her life is in danger. She may be . . . "

"She is dead."

"Oh, God. How?"

The Pope handed the police report to Elijah.

"It states that she was murdered, and the crime disguised as an automobile accident in the Apennines. The autopsy indicates that she died on the 21st."

Elijah suppressed the sob in his throat.

The Pope remained silent until Elijah composed himself.

"I was afraid this would happen", he whispered. "Somehow I knew it would happen."

"When did you last see her?"

"Several weeks ago."

He removed from the leather envelope the letter she had written at Foligno on the night of her abduction.

"It is dated the 21st."

"She did not suffer long. I will offer the Mass at Saint John Lateran for her soul. She was a brave woman."

"A brave woman", he echoed in a broken voice.

"She gave her life."

"Holy Father, her life must not be wasted! We must do all we can to bring her killers to justice."

"Justice will be done, in God's time."

They sat in silence, each lost in his own thoughts.

Eventually Elijah said: "There is something I do not understand. Why would they disguise it as an accident if they wanted to lay the blame at my feet?"

"I suspect that they thinly disguised the accident and left sufficient signs of murder, in order to create the impression of a crime hastily covered up. This would point the accusing finger elsewhere, say to an amateur seeking to cover his sin. People of this sort do not leave a trail leading to themselves. They are professionals, masters of deceit. Clearly, they wished to kill two birds with one stone, Dr. Benedetti and yourself."

"Why haven't they tried to dispose of me?"

"They are hoping to achieve something more than the elimination of a troublesome individual. They want to create a scandal, thereby contributing to the public image of a Church in the last stages of degeneration."

"In any event, it is over."

The Pope looked at him sadly.

"Oh, my son, it is far from over. We have not seen the worst yet. We must not suppose that these are master criminals and nothing more. Their assault upon the Church is waged on many levels."

They were interrupted suddenly by a knock.

The Pope's private secretary hurried into the room and closed the door behind him.

"Your Holiness, Cardinal Vettore wishes to speak with you."

"Vettore? But he is in China!"

"He is here, Holiness, and he is very agitated. He demands an audience. Shall I tell him to go away? There is an opening in your schedule on Tuesday."

"No. I will see him. Give me five minutes."

The secretary went out, and the Pope, his face resolved, turned to Elijah.

"I want you to hear what is about to transpire. Please go into that room and leave the door open a crack. Under no circumstances reveal yourself or interfere in any way."

Elijah went through to a small chamber beyond the Pope's desk. The room was little more than an alcove, bare except for a small cot and a prie-dieu. A red vigil lamp burned beneath a tabernacle set into the wall. He genuflected before the Presence, then stood by the door, listening.

"Cardinal Vettore, Holy Father", said the secretary's voice. The door to the outer office clicked shut.

"*Buon Natale,* Your Holiness."

"*Buon Natale,* Cardinal Vettore. Welcome back to Rome. Your return is unexpected."

"Important events have come to light that make my presence necessary. There are developments that have consequences for the Church. We must discuss them immediately."

"I am glad you have come to me. And on such a day as this! Please be seated."

"Thank you, I prefer to stand."

"You bring news from China?"

"There is much to tell you about China, but there are more pressing matters we need to discuss."

"Tell me, my son."

"It has come to my attention that there exists within the walls of our own house a conspiracy."

"A conspiracy. What is its nature?"

"I know it will be difficult for you to believe, but I must inform you that there are members of the college of cardinals who are not loyal."

"Not loyal to the Church?"

"Say rather that they are not loyal to your person."

"To the papacy?"

"Well, not exactly. It is your pontificate which seems to have disturbed them. There is a group of bishops, several hundreds I understand, and many cardinals, who have indicated a need for consideration of retirement."

"Retirement?"

"Your own retirement."

"I see. What are their reasons? Do you know?"

"From what I can gather, there is a consensus among them that your reign was not what the consistory had hoped for. When you were elected, they had anticipated that the objectives of the Council would be implemented full-force. They feel that your recent encyclicals and the manner in which your disciplinary decisions have been carried out are a return to the preconciliar Church."

"And thus a dangerous confusion has resulted among the faithful?"

"Exactly. They believe that a younger man, one more imbued with the thought of the Council Fathers would be able to redirect our course and take us as a unified body into the third millennium."

"What do you think of this idea?"

"I am surprised, of course. Obviously, we are disunified. However, I do not think the present state is necessarily unhealthy. Change is never easy. It may take two or three generations for the Church to stabilize."

"You perhaps recall that I was a newly ordained bishop at the Council?"

"Yes, I recall that."

"You were a young man at the time."

"I was a seminarian. But our professors were quite involved in the Council; some of them were *periti,* and they communicated their expectations to us. It was an exciting time."

"Do you think the fruit of the Council is what we had hoped for?"

"There have been some mistakes. But I think on the whole the changes have brought about a more creative approach."

"There have been misinterpretations of the Council texts."

"In some regions, there have been imprudent innovations. There have been excesses. However, this group seems to think that the problem lies in another direction. They believe that conservatives have been exerting undue influence and that they have gained your ear."

"Does the group believe that I have slowed down the process of renewal?"

"Unfortunately, they do."

"And you, Cardinal Vettore, what do you think of this question?"

"My commitment to you is firm."

"Do you agree that the widespread conflicts in the fields of doctrine, education, and liturgy are the result of a misinterpretation of the Council?"

"Undoubtedly."

"By modernist prelates?"

The cardinal did not answer.

"Perhaps by conservative prelates?"

"This group seems to think the latter."

"But you, what do you think?"

"You know that I am loyal."

"Yes, you said that before."

"The dissidents are clearly out of order, and yet they have raised some important questions, which may be a valid contribution."

"Which questions?"

"Well, to be frank, the problem of collegiality."

"What, precisely, is the problem?"

"Do we or do we not trust the Holy Spirit enough to open the way to a more democratic process?"

"The papacy is therefore a stumbling block in the path of the Holy Spirit?"

"Not exactly. We are presently in a period of transition, and thus, we can expect the normal difficulties of adjusting to a new paradigm of church."

"How do you envisage this paradigm?"

"I should clarify, Holy Father, that I am not so much referring to my own views as to the opinions of this group. They feel that the national churches would function more efficiently and proceed with a more realistic process of inculturation if we did not pour our dwindling resources into preserving a monarchical model of church."

"I think the Council was clear on that point, was it not? The Pope is *Petrus*. He is chief of apostles. His brother bishops validly shepherd the flock of Christ only in union with the chair of Peter."

"I agree entirely. But the bishops merely wish to ask if they can maintain the line of authority while exercising greater autonomy."

"Have they considered the lessons of history?"

"I beg your pardon?"

"Have they considered the fourth century, when almost all the bishops of the world bowed to the will of an Arian emperor? Only the Pope and a handful of bishops united to him preserved the Christianity of the Gospels. What does this tell us about the Holy Spirit?"

Vettore did not reply.

"Have they given some thought to the behavior of the English bishops during the reign of Henry VIII? Only one bishop remained loyal, if you recall. And have they forgotten how in our own era, the communist party commandeered an autocephalous church, the Orthodox Church in Russia, and used her to subdue her sister churches and to pervert the World Council of Churches?"

"That is the past. We are a new breed of Christian, and we face new dangers."

"Christ is the same yesterday, today, and tomorrow. We face no new dangers. They are merely variations on ancient themes."

"I wish it were as simple as you suggest, Holy Father."

"What do you suggest?"

"I believe that we are facing an uncertain future. We have been weakened by dreadful fragmentation into theological camps. The dissident group will soon begin agitating for a destructuralization, a movement to a more horizontal model of church. The conservatives, as we know, are becoming increasingly hysterical. They condemn not only the Council, but also your pontificate as a betrayal."

"Ah, so you are suggesting that we strike a course straight down the middle."

"Exactly."

"But what if the middle has shifted?"

"Has it shifted?"

"Oh, yes, it has shifted. The true center can never be the exact midpoint between two extremes, for poles are always unstable, ever changing. The true center is *above.*"

"Regardless, we are dealing with a conservative revolt on one hand and a liberal revolt brewing on the other. That is the painful reality."

"Those terms—conservative and liberal—they are political terms. They are misleading when applied to the Kingdom of Christ."

"They are flawed but useful."

"These conservatives and liberals whom you speak of—do they love the Pope?"

"All but the most radical recognize that the petrine office is a charism. We will always reverence that office, regardless of the model of church. The problem is: What are the precise limits of the office?"

"The Council and two thousand years of tradition are clear on that point."

"It is not as clear to modern Catholics as it once was."

"And why is that? How has it become so unclear?"

"Perhaps the natural confusion that arises during a period of change."

"And so we return to our starting point. Who, or what, is Peter?"

"Could the Holy Spirit be asking us to grow? Perhaps it is time to rethink some of the old structures, including your office. Change is not evil."

"I repeat my question: All these people, left, right, and center—do they love Peter?"

"Love? I am not sure. Everyone admires you."

"Admiration is an easy thing to generate. Do they *love* me?"

Here the first note of impatience crept into the cardinal's voice: "I do not know."

"They love me—but they will not obey me."

Vettore's reply was inaudible.

"Do you know what love is, my son?"

"Of course. The theological . . . "

"Love is obedience unto death. And rebirth."

"Obedience sometimes necessitates a courageous dissent. In a free relationship . . . "

"Any attempt to deemphasize the true community of the universal Church in favor of the supposedly more democratic model of regional churches is a grave mistake. One of the consistent tactics of tyranny is to divide and neutralize its opponents, to isolate those movements or voices that stand in opposition to the dissolving of identity."

"But Holy Father," Vettore replied in a reasoning tone, "the tyrants are all dead. The age of confrontation is over. The hideous wars and revolutions of our century were the result of various kinds of dogmatism. The time has come to dialogue on every side, to build bridges. Too long have we walked backward into the future, obsessed with our past, trapped within it. The human race is now approaching a quantum leap forward. We must turn and face the future. This and this alone will ensure the saving of the planet!"

"And what is our part in this?"

"We will show that we believe in Man. We have too long alienated the larger human community with our judgments and condemnations, fostering divisions on every side."

"Cardinal Vettore, beware of that sophistry! If a man says that the sky is blue, is he causing division? Is he being unreasonable? Is he unsympathetic to the man who believes that the sky is red?"

"Sometimes the sky *is* red."

"Yes, as the light of day ends, it is sometimes red."

"You see my point."

"But take your point farther. Suppose during that brief moment when the light dies, your man proclaims to the world that the sky is *always* red. He argues that people need only look up to see the evidence before their eyes. The people who live in the confines of our cities have fallen into the habit of not looking up. They live their whole lives in these concrete mazes, illuminated only by artificial light, and they say to themselves, 'At last we see the sky, and moreover, we see it as it really is. It is red.'"

"You are stretching the point too far."

"Am I? The Roman Catholic Church defends diversity within her universal community—genuine diversity—and she is able to do so precisely because she is a community founded on truth. That is why she will always be strong in a way that earthly kingdoms can never be strong. Every effort of man to replace the City of God is doomed to failure."

"Why? Why is it doomed to failure? Because we say it is? Have we tried to make a decent civilization on this planet? Have we cooperated with the City of Man? Have we honestly expended every effort to make peace between nations?"

"We have", said the Pope simply.

"We have not done enough."

"What would you have us do? Say to unbelievers that we were wrong to offer them the Light? Wrong to speak about the world's darkness? Wrong to defend the full range of human and divine absolutes?"

"I wasn't saying . . . "

"What are you saying? Your position is riddled with contra-dictions."

"I didn't come here to be snapped at. I came here to help you."

"Did you? Yes, I suppose that is how you must see it. On Christmas Day, you come to bring the world a gift. This group that you represent, do they also see their vision as a gift?"

"I do not represent them. I am merely . . . "

"If you wish to help the Church, you must tell these dissatis-fied cardinals and bishops that the sky is blue. The Church is not a human structure. That is why so many varying cultures and peoples find their identity within her. The growth of regionalism in some corners of Western Catholicism only appears to foster a heightened sense of identity; in reality it contributes to the corruption of identity. Can you explain why the revolt tends toward a numbing uniformity beneath the superficial 'creativity' of its individualism?"

"Holy Father, our conversation is becoming sidetracked. The theology of church is complex. Let us return to the problem at hand."

"That is precisely what we have been discussing."

"Be that as it may. I have to tell you that your approach will no longer work."

"And you have a remedy."

"Yes. I do. With all due respect, I must tell you that there is a growing consensus that you should abide by the rules you have enforced upon your brother bishops. You should consider retirement. A consistory will elect a new Pope, one who is neither liberal nor conservative, who will build upon your very real accomplishments and bring the Church back on course."

"You are implying, with not very great subtlety, that I have led the Church off course. This indicates to me that you, like these dissidents, also have lost faith in the petrine promise, the unique charism of Peter, the keys of the Kingdom."

"That is not so. I did not say that. We are not questioning your defense of faith and morals. This is a pastoral crisis. Popes are human. Our history is a long tale with many twists and turns. Many great and not-so-great personalities have occupied your chair. For the moment you are still respected as a man who has achieved much. You will be remembered as a great pontiff. But no one is above criticism. It is for the ultimate good of the Church that you turn the keys over to others who can take up where you have left off. Better that you resign at the height of your greatness than to preside over the steady disintegration of the Church, a tragedy for which you would be blamed by future generations."

"I see."

"I hope that you do, Holiness. I mean no offense."

"Of course not", said the Pope gently.

Elijah listened without moving. A loud silence filled the Pope's office.

"My son," said the Pope at last, "leave him."

"Leave him? Leave whom?" said Vettore startled.

"Go no more to him. Return to your faith."

"What are you saying? I haven't left the Faith."

"He is using you."

"Who?"

"You do not know what you are doing. I pray to God that you do not know what you are doing."

"It's true what they say about you. Your mind is slipping. I don't know what you're talking about!"

"Disentangle yourself."

"This is absurd! I've tried to help you. It's no use. I'm going."

"Sit down", said the Pope.

Vettore sat down.

"Break his hold on you. For the sake of your own soul, if nothing else."

"No one owns me."

"Not even Christ."

"What!"

"You think that no one has authority over you, and thus you make yourself vulnerable to the darkest powers of all."

"You're raving. This is all in your mind."

"I know the truth. I adjure you, leave that man."

"To whom are you referring?"

"Leave the President."

Vettore did not answer at first. Even at that distance Elijah could hear him breathing loudly.

"I told you last year that those accusations are false. Whoever planted them in your mind is an enemy of Christ."

"He is a friend of Christ."

"You believed him."

"He is not a liar."

"And I am?"

"At the very least you have been tricked."

"*You* have been tricked! Schäfer is a murderer. He is a liar. Why do you take his word against mine?"

"How do you know the name Schäfer? I did not mention it."

"You told me last year. I'm sure you did."

"I know that I did not."

"Of course you did."

"You are a shepherd of the Church, Cardinal Vettore. The destiny of many people hangs upon your fidelity. Turn away from him. Return! Now, before it is too late."

"What do you mean by too late?" the cardinal said slowly.

"You see that dossier on my desk. It contains evidence that will shortly be presented to the authorities. The President is responsible for the death of innocent people. He is not the good man you think he is. You must cease to align yourself with him. I do not know how or why you have been seduced into serving his cause, but I believe you can walk away from him without fear."

"I am not afraid", said the cardinal coolly.

"God is merciful. Come back to Him."

"This conversation is becoming tedious. You are an obsessive-compulsive personality, and I will not stand this insult!"

"My son," said the Pope in a pleading voice, "I am sorry if my words offend you. I do not mean to. But you are in spiritual danger. You are a soul. You are one of my flock. Do not let the wolf drag you from us without resistance."

Vettore stood up and towered over the pontiff.

"He is not a wolf. He is the one who seeks to bring to the world a peace it has desperately needed."

"You are saying peace where there is no peace."

"Peace — *real* peace — now lies within the grasp of all mankind."

"The peace of Christ is coming. Do not turn aside chasing after false peace."

"The peace of Christ is coming? When, I ask you? When? The days drag on, the centuries drag on, and no vision ever comes to anything."

"The days are at hand and also the fulfillment of every true vision."

"Who is the wolf? You are the wolf, for you will not permit the flock to graze in the pastures of peace. If men such as you insist on standing in the way of reconciliation, then be forewarned, you will be swept aside."

"And how will this man of peace sweep me aside?"

"It doesn't matter how. The survival of the earth depends on his victory. You would dominate the world with your pessimism, your ritualism, your legalism, your refusal to bend before the dynamics of progress."

"Oh, my son, my son, you are blinded by a beautiful ideal. You are naïve about human nature. Man cannot extricate himself from his own fallen nature. Do you think a President can do it?"

"He will do it."

"And what will he destroy in the attempt?"

"He is a creator, not a destroyer."

"And what will he ask of us—that we say the sky is red? A little compromise here, a little there."

"Only what reasonable people should give to each other: listening to one another's side, accommodation, negotiation, compromise—it's not a dirty word, you know."

"I would a thousand times rather have a persecuted Church than a compromised Church."

"If you do not step aside, you will get your wish."

"So you want to spare us that."

"Of course I do! Do you think I want to see the world running with the blood of Christians? We must survive. We need time to regroup, time to present our case to the world. We can indulge ourselves no longer in pessimistic spiritualities. We can wait no longer for a *deus ex machina* to be lowered out of the skies. Man must build the City of God."

"Man cannot build the City of God. The Scripture says that the New Jerusalem will come down from Heaven as a gift from God, after the devastation of the earth by man's sin and error."

"Prophecies!" snorted Vettore in disgust. "The world is crawling with rampant imaginings. In the President, destiny has given us an eminently sane human being, one who will build the City of God for us if we won't build it ourselves. He will lead us to worship in spirit and in truth, freed from our ancient mythologies."

"Now I understand. Now I see the crack through which he has penetrated your mind."

"It is you who stagger through a smoke-filled dungeon. You have abandoned the heart of religion for a shell, just like the Pharisees before you. You bind up men's souls with your endless laws."

"The law is a teacher and a test. If men cannot be faithful in little things, how will they ever be faithful in great things?"

"That is the shell of religion. Where is the heart?"

"What is your definition of the heart?"

"Definitions, definitions! More rationalism! Haven't we had enough of that? When men are free they will naturally embrace the ways of peace."

"Is not the heart of religion to love the living Jesus as Savior, as God, and to love one's neighbor as oneself?"

"I believe in a religion that finds salvation in the world, not above it in a faraway castle in the sky."

"He is in the world *and* above it. You continually posit an either/or situation. You say that souls must embrace either an immanent God *or* a transcendent one, either the heart of religion *or* the structure of religion. You would have us believe that structures inevitably kill the heart."

"I rest my case."

"Your case is superficial, and I am astounded that a man as intelligent as you fails to see it."

"I am not astounded by you. You are pitifully transparent. You are Dostoevsky's Grand Inquisitor. You want to rule over a feudal system where everyone bends the neck before your will. That is Phariseeism."

"Who is the real Pharisee? Do not your rebellious prelates bind up men's souls by helping them to make their peace with sin, thus rendering them incapable of entering the Kingdom?"

"Sin, sin! Can't you ever talk about anything else? What about love?"

"Love does not lie. The truth sets us free to love."

"Don't you see what a depression you make in the human psyche?"

"You would relieve man of his anxieties by saying there is no danger? You would relieve him of his feelings of guilt by saying he is not guilty?"

"What is he guilty of? All men are conditioned by their pasts. There aren't many people on this earth who have committed real sin."

"You think not?"

"I know it. At the worst, we are all victims of invincible ignorance. We are not culpable. No one really goes to Hell."

"Who knows the numbers of ignorant who will go to Heaven? Perhaps many. But I tell you one thing for certain: there are many bishops and priests who are going to Hell for creating that invincible ignorance."

Vettore's voice rose: "I have called you *Holy Father,* but I see now that there is nothing holy about you. You are a little man who came to a big throne by accident, and by the naïveté of a consistory that could not read the signs of the times."

"The times are full of signs. Have you read them aright?"

"You fool!" bellowed Vettore.

A sharp smack cracked like a shot.

"Your time is up, *Holy Father*", said the cardinal, bending the last two words with sarcasm.

Another sharp crack sounded. Elijah was locked in immobility. *Under no circumstances reveal yourself or interfere in any way.*

Elijah struggled with himself. Then he leapt to the door and looked through the gap, only to see the back of Vettore disappearing into the outer office.

The Pope was on his knees, holding his face in his hands. His reading glasses were askew across his forehead. Droplets of blood fell onto his chest. Elijah fell to his knees, held the old man, and steadied him. The Pope's body was shaking. His eyes were full of tears, and his upper lip was bleeding.

"He struck you!" said Elijah astonished.

"Yes. It's all right. It's all right. Help me up, please."

Elijah lifted the Pope into his chair and wiped the blood from his face. Two angry welts were rising across his cheeks.

"This is unbelievable. Has he lost his senses?"

"Pray for him, Father. His mind is captive; his soul is very ill. Don't be angry."

"Don't be angry!" Elijah breathed. "He has struck the vicar of Christ!"

"He and many others have been striking me for a long time. Now the darkness becomes visible. Now is the hour for the servant of the servants of God to go with Christ to be glorified."

"I don't understand."

"It had to be this way. He has revealed himself. Now we go to Calvary."

Elijah stood back and looked down at the Pope, uncomprehending. He rushed to the outer office and met the secretary and the colonel.

"What has happened?" said the colonel. "Cardinal Vettore went out like a storm."

"He has hit the Pope. Stop him."

Both men stared at him unbelieving. They rushed into the inner office and surrounded the Pope. After reassuring themselves that he was not badly hurt, they ran out again in pursuit of the cardinal.

Elijah went back to the Pope and went down on his knees.

"I will call a doctor, Holy Father."

"There is no need for a doctor. But I would like to lie down for a while. I need to pray. The Eucharist is such a consolation to me. The Lord is so beautiful, so beautiful. He deserves so much more from us. We are so poor! Our little hearts are so poor! Love is not loved, Father Elijah, Love is not loved."

He helped the pontiff to his feet and led him into the bedchamber, lay him down, and pulled a blanket over him.

"Thank you. Thank you. Now let me rest for a while. I'm fine, I'm fine."

Elijah went to the outer office and stood there not knowing what to do. He waited, pondering the things he had just witnessed, until the secretary returned.

"Well, he has disappeared. This is shocking! What possessed the man?"

"Where is the colonel?"

"He went running off to organize security, and I expect to try to track down Vettore. I doubt he'll catch him."

"What will you do?" said Elijah.

"What can we do? I suppose the Pope will face the cardinal and demand an apology."

"Do you really think so?"

"No, you're right, he won't. He's too gentle. He forgives everything." He sat down shaking his head. "This isn't happening. This is unreal."

At which point the colonel stomped back in, looking both furious and bewildered.

"I must see him."

He went into the Pope's private chamber and remained there for some minutes. When he came out again, he said to Elijah, "The Holy Father wants you."

Elijah went in and stood by the bed. The Pope reached up and took his hand.

"I am giving you an obedience. You must do as I tell you and not ask why. It is within the plans of divine Providence, and you must trust in this, even if all should appear to be lost."

"Whatever it is, Your Holiness. I will serve, however you wish me to serve."

"*Serviam!*" the Pope said, smiling at him. He got up slowly from the bed and led Elijah over to the tabernacle.

"Kneel."

Elijah knelt.

The Pope placed both hands on Elijah's head and prayed. He removed a silver tube from the pocket of his soutane, opened the lid, and anointed Elijah's forehead with oil. Then he resumed praying aloud in Latin. Elijah understood what was happening only as the Pope made the final sign of the cross over him.

"Please rise, Bishop Schäfer."

The Pope embraced him.

"I appoint you titular bishop of *Panaya Kapulu.*"

Elijah held the Pope's arms, looking at the floor. Then he raised his eyes and met those of the old man.

"It is too much. I do not know what it is to be a bishop."

The Pope glanced toward the tabernacle.

"You may discuss your doubts with Him. But I know you will be an obedient servant and accept."

"I accept, Holiness."

"You are to be a bishop *in pectore,* unknown to any save the Lord and a few chosen servants."

"Where is *Panaya Kapulu?*"

"It is an ancient See in Asia Minor. It is in the region of Ephesus, where the Church was once great and for centuries has dwindled to almost nothing. A few souls at the most. There may be no one left. It is a few square kilometers of ruins and barren hills—a deserted place."

"Do you wish me to go there?"

"Yes. You cannot remain in Italy. You must go out into the desert to a safe place and remain there until the appointed time."

"What will my duties be?"

"You must feed the flock of God amidst many tribulations, my son."

"With permission, Holiness, I don't understand. I am to be a shepherd who feeds a flock where there is no flock?"

"The Holy Spirit will reveal your flock to you. From this time forward, my people will be ravaged by wolves. Confusion will cover everything. Doors will be locked and others will open. The foundations will be shaken. Things now standing will fall. The great shall be cast down, and the lowly shall be raised up."

The Pope sat on his cot and picked up a handbell from his bedside table. He rang it and the secretary promptly entered.

"Please ask the colonel of the Swiss Guard to come in."

The colonel entered a moment later.

"Colonel, I want you to see that this man leaves Vatican City without being apprehended. Once you are outside Rome give him a staff car and sufficient money for his journey. He must reach Bari and board the ship the Cardinal Secretary has arranged."

"But Your Holiness! I must ask you to reconsider. That ship stands in readiness for you."

The Pope turned to Elijah and smiled. "My protectors have arranged several escape routes in the event that Rome becomes unsafe for the pontiff. The Prefect for Doctrine wishes me to go with him to Switzerland. The Secretary of State has argued that I should fly to America if necessary. Others have urged me to take refuge with the Patriarch of Constantinople. The ship at Bari was made ready for the latter purpose."

He turned back to the colonel. "Would you save me from this hour?"

The colonel looked nonplussed. "It is my duty, Holiness."

"My friend, you and Saint Peter have much in common. He too wished to save the Lord from His final hour."

The colonel stammered, at a loss for words.

"Many things must yet come to pass", said the Pope. "The

517

time is close, but not so close that the Pope must run away at the first sign of danger."

"In any event," said the colonel, "the documents Father Schäfer has brought will confound our enemies. I believe we have enough evidence to ensure the security of the Church."

"With this material we may be able to delay a decisive confrontation. Yet even if the President is brought down, the enemy will raise another like him."

"Your Holiness, Cardinal Vettore has probably gone to contact the Italian police. If we are to remove Father Schäfer from the Vatican we must make haste."

"You are right. Go with God, my son", said the Pope, giving Elijah a final blessing.

They left the bedroom and reentered the papal office. The colonel asked for permission to make duplicates of the dossier on the President, and the Pope urged him to have this done without delay. He named the institutions and officials to whom the copies should be sent, adding that the material should be transported secretly by Vatican couriers.

The colonel picked up the leather envelope and opened it.

"There is nothing here", he said.

The three men stared at it.

"Cardinal Vettore", said the Pope.

*   *   *

On the outskirts of Rome two cars slowed and parked on the shoulder of the highway. The colonel, who was driving the first, turned to his passenger, and handed him a packet.

"Here is a road map and directions to the port of Bari. The ship is called the *Stella Maris*. She's a trawler of the Pescatti fishing company and is waiting at anchor. Go to their office at the docks and ask for the captain of the *Stella*. While you were changing clothes, I called him. He is expecting you."

"How will he know me?"

"You will introduce yourself as Signore Pastore. He knows only that you are working for the Pope and that he is to take you to the coast of Turkey near Ephesus. He is a very good man. He's my sister's husband, one of the Pescatti brothers. Here, this bag contains toilet articles and a change of clothes. Also, you will need a visa for the Turkish authorities if the ship is inspected and a passport. It's made out in the name of Pastore."

Elijah opened the documents and remarked at their perfection. The man in the photograph was himself, dressed in a suit and tie, the epitome of an academic. His hair was combed the wrong way, and he wore glasses. The photograph was embossed with an official Vatican stamp. He could not recall posing for such a photograph.

"How did you make this?"

"Never underestimate the power of the computer."

"But in such a short time!"

"Our friend the Cardinal Secretary of State is a man of some prescience. He ordered it made weeks ago."

"He anticipated this?"

"He confided in me that there was trouble on the way and that you would probably be maligned."

"Then may I ask, colonel, why you put me through such an interrogation when I came to your office this morning?"

"I had to be sure. *Stato* trusted you, of course, but it's my job to trust no one—outside of the Holy Father, that is. A thousand pardons."

"All is forgiven."

The colonel handed him a pair of reading glasses and a comb.

"Try to make yourself look like the *professore* in the photo. Put on these glasses. Don't worry, they are not lenses, just plain glass. It's not much of a disguise but it's the best we can do."

Elijah fumbled in his pocket for *Stato's* ring. "Would you please see that this is returned to the Cardinal Secretary?"

The colonel furrowed his brow, took the ring, and turned it

over and over in his hand. "Why don't you keep it for now? You might need it."

He gave it back, and Elijah pocketed it without argument.

"*Bene.* Here are the keys."

"I hope we meet again, colonel."

"Oh, I'll be seeing you again, after my many years in Purgatory."

"I shall beg a full pardon for you."

The colonel laughed. "*Grazie!* The Lord be with you."

"And with you."

The two men shook hands. The colonel got out and went to the other car. It tore onto the pavement, made a U-turn, and roared back toward Rome.

Elijah inspected the map to get his bearings. It would take approximately an hour and a half to reach Naples, then two hours east on the highway that crossed the Apennines toward the coast of the Adriatic. A total of four, possibly five hours to reach Bari. It would be close to midnight by the time he knocked on the office door of the Pescatti Fishing Company.

The petrol gauge registered full. The little blue Toyota was capable of going all the way without stopping, but he determined to break his journey near Naples in order to refill the tank. The sky had cleared off in the dusk, and the road was bare. The southbound traffic was light. He pressed the accelerator and eased into the fast lane.

He drove without thinking, aware only that his flesh was aching and that his senses were clamoring for attention—hunger, fear, exhilaration, exhaustion, the dull pain of cuts and bruises—it all merged into an amorphous mass of discomfort.

Gradually, his thoughts began to sort themselves out, and he replayed the events of the day in his mind, as if viewing them on a screen. He was amazed that he had begun by shivering on a mattress in a deserted farmhouse in Umbria. He retraced his steps up and down the mountain of Our Lady of Sorrows, through the Gemelli hospital, through the colonel's interrogation, through the corridors of the Vatican, through the dialogue between Vettore and the Pope, arriving at his hasty ordination to the episcopate.

"I am a bishop?" he said. He was hit simultaneously by the reality—and the unreality—of it.

Then he remembered Anna, and his heart plunged. It fell and fell, and his head began to spin. His eyes blurred. He pulled over to the curb and shut off the engine. He rolled down the window and took several deep breaths. He held his face in his hands. He sat without moving. He closed his eyes.

When he awoke he no longer felt dizzy, and the general malaise had eased a little. He drove on, wondering how long he had been asleep. By the look of the sky, it could not have been more than twenty minutes. He realized then that he had not properly slept during the past thirty-six hours. He hoped that he would be able to complete the trip to Bari without dozing off at the wheel.

A service station appeared on the right, just as the glow of Naples began to fill the sky ahead. While the attendant filled the tank, he went into the washroom and bathed his face repeatedly in hot water. Then he splashed a handful of ice-cold water across his eyes. It revived him sufficiently to realize that his stomach was crying for food. When he had combed his hair according to the passport photo and donned the glasses, he went into the *drogheria* to pay for the petrol. He purchased a loaf of bread, cheese, and a liter of orange juice. Back in the car he forced the food down his throat, chewing mechanically by an act of the will, for though his flesh was insistent, his spirit felt nothing but revulsion.

Soon after he saw the illuminated sign with its arrow pointing east:

Nola, Avellino, Bari, Ferry to Athens

He saw it and understood it. He knew that he was supposed to go there. He realized that the next necessary movement was to turn the car onto the exit lane and go into the mountains. Instead, he kept driving.

At first he did not understand why he had done so. It was merely the thing he would do, although he had not yet articulated the decision to himself. There was no emotion attached to this knowledge, still less any consciousness of a plan. There was no *should* or *must* about it. He felt an infusion of peace, his first since the events of the past two days had begun to gather momentum. Then, in the lingering certainty of this condition, a certainty that had neither object nor contours, goal nor image, he understood what he would do.

He was not sure of the way, for the night he had passed here with Billy had been storm-tossed, darker than this star-filled sky. The dome of light over Naples receded behind him as those of Sorrento loomed ahead. He saw the restaurant by the ocean where they had eaten lasagna and drunk ale. From there on it was easy to retrace their route. He saw the paved driveway leading uphill from the highway toward the "boathouse", and a minute farther on he came to the gravel lane that struck off toward the right, down to the sea. The way was barred by a padlocked iron gate. He stopped, reversed back along the highway and found a side road. He went down it until he spotted a clearing in a grove. He maneuvered the car among the palmettos until it was hidden, got out, and walked back to the gate. He climbed over it and went downhill on the crunching gravel. At the bottom he saw the boat rising and falling beside the dock. The marina was deserted. There were no lights visible in any direction. The hood of the cruiser and its chromium gunwales flashed rhythmically in the motion of the waves, reflecting the moon's crescent.

He jumped from the dock onto the deck and fumbled about in search of the cabin door. It was locked. There was a deck-wheel and a storage cabinet beside it, also locked. His experiences with the Haganah now stood him in good stead. Using a plastic credit card, he sprung the cabinet door and found a metal box inside. It contained a small flashlight lying on top of wrenches and screwdrivers, and a black plastic case, which contained a key. He slipped it into the ignition and turned it, praying. The motor sputtered and caught. Guiding the boat by the deck wheel, he took her out onto the Gulf of Salerno. He let the motor rumble softly until he was well away from shore, then pushed the throttle forward. The cruiser roared, increased speed steadily, and began to bounce on the light chop. When the coast was a good deal behind, he turned on the running lights and pointed the bow toward Capri.

XX

Capri

The lights of the palace compound appeared on the crown of Monte Tiberio. Elijah put the helm over to port, away from the north side of the island. In order to avoid recognition at the President's dock and helicopter pad, he steered for the large public marina, easing into a fleet of cruisers and private yachts. He found an empty berth at a wharf, moored the boat, and walked up through the village toward the mountain.

The dial on his wristwatch showed that the evening was far gone, after ten o'clock. The houses and cafés were brightly lit, and judging by the revelry coming from them, Christmas festivities were still in progress.

The road to the peak was dark, and he climbed steadily, fighting a babble of voices that came out of nowhere and seemed bent on invading his mind. He pushed them away. They came again and again, and he forced himself to ignore them, to resist the urge to debate with them.

You cannot win. You will die.

The night air was cold, and a north wind tore at his coat. He wore no hat or gloves, and his ears began to sting.

You will be torn limb from limb.

He became aware of the extreme exhaustion of his body, and the fragility of his will.

Go back, go back, go back.

At the halfway point, he stopped on the side of the road and sat on a tussock of grass, breathing heavily, his hand pressing the hammer of his heart.

He is not here, he is not here.

Automobile lights shot around a bend in the road, coming down from above. He rolled over into the bushes and held his breath. The car rolled slowly by. He got up to continue the ascent, but another set of lights rounded the bend, and he was forced to throw himself down again. His knees hit rock, a sharp branch scraped his face, and he cried out as the second car crawled past.

What happened to her will happen to you.

Making his way through the bracken and stunted trees growing along the righthand side of the road, he continued to climb and rounded the bend. Ahead lay a gate flanked by chain-link fencing that disappeared into the woods to left and right, encircling the heights. Two men stood on the far side of the gates. They leaned against the metal bars, talking to each other, smoking cigarettes beneath the arc lights flooding the gate area.

Elijah darted into the woods to the right of the road and scrambled on hands and knees at an angle that would take him close to the fence, beyond the circle of the lights. He went blindly now, adding to his cuts and scrapes, praying all the while, hoping that the wind was covering the sounds of cracking twigs and rustling branches.

When he passed a heave in the side of the mountain, beyond their field of vision, he flicked on the miniature flashlight and found the fence. It was eight feet high, topped by barbed wire. He went along it searching for a break in the links, but found nothing that would admit him into the compound. The fence line began to plunge back toward the south, and the moonlit sea appeared through the pines clinging to the rocks. He saw that he would have to return to the road, cross over without being seen, and try to enter on the north side.

He was about to go back when, from the corner of his eye, he saw a flicker of light between the trees farther down. He felt an instant of panic, wondering if a search party were scouting the perimeters of the compound.

We know you are here, we know you are here.

He crouched in a cleft of the rocks and tried to make himself small.

You cannot escape, you cannot escape.

He waited. The light came no nearer. He peered from his hiding place and saw that it came from no artificial source and was in fact a fire. It was burning at some distance, perhaps twenty meters away. Wood smoke drifted toward him. He listened but there were no voices. He wondered who could be out so late at night on a rocky precipice. Possibly a lonely soul looking to the sea, seeking consolation on this most social of evenings with the company of fire, water, and stars.

Even so, whoever it was might be associated with the men in the compound, and it could be suicidal to risk exposure.

Go back, go back, go back.

He closed his eyes and prayed, "It is impossible, my Lord. I must go back."

The fire leapt higher for an instant, and Elijah saw a human form silhouetted against the flames. The figure was alone, standing with its arms spread wide, facing toward the place where Elijah lay in hiding. It waved in his direction.

Impossible! For at that distance, he was beyond the glow, and the rocks concealed him. Nevertheless, it waved again. Elijah saw that it was pointless now to continue. Better to approach and risk the consequences. If he fled abruptly, the figure might sound an alarm, might have a radio that would alert security and send guards swarming over the mountaintop. His only chance lay in going forward, pretending that he was a wanderer who had lost his way in the dark.

When he came up to the fire, he was surprised to see that the figure was a boy of about eight years of age. The boy smiled at him.

"Who are you?" said Elijah.

"My name is Rafael."

He was barefoot, dressed in white shorts, and a light cotton jacket. The wind tossed his golden hair.

"What are you doing here? It's late. It's cold."

"I'm not cold", said the boy. His voice was pleasant, even sweet. His eyes contained a composure that rightly belonged to men of great age.

He continued to gaze at Elijah without speaking, offering no explanations, demanding none. Eventually he turned toward the sea and pointed at it.

"The morning star will rise when the night is almost over", he said with an expression of joy.

"You shouldn't be here. Where is your mother, child?"

"My mother is waiting for me."

"You should go. They will be worried at home."

"They are not worried."

"Little one, you must go now."

The child looked at him gravely. "But if I go, who will guide you to the top of the mountain?"

Elijah thought that he might not have heard correctly.

"It's Christmas!" he protested.

"Yes, it's Christmas", said the boy, his face blazing with the leaping firelight.

"You shouldn't be alone."

"I am not alone."

"It's dangerous here."

In answer the child walked to the fence and said to Elijah, "Come."

He obeyed. Just inside the radius of the light, the boy parted the bushes and showed him a dip in the rock.

"We can go through here."

527

He squeezed under the fence on his belly, tearing the back of his coat. It took a minute to disentangle it from the wire, and when he climbed out on the other side, he saw that the boy had already gone through.

He led Elijah up into the woods. The moon and stars lit their way. They proceeded for several minutes until a pale track appeared in the ground at their feet.

"The little sheep used to walk here", the boy said. "We will go on this."

The narrow path cut through the rocks and the straggling bushes, winding higher and higher. Elijah did not feel any strangeness in this wholly unexpected situation. He did not understand it, but explained to himself that divine Providence had arranged for a village child to be on the mountain, and that he would know, perhaps through intuition, that Elijah sought to go up to the top. The boy had assumed, no doubt, that the lost stranger must be a visitor to the house of the famous man who lived on the peak.

They came to an inner circle of fencing. The boy opened a gate looming out of the darkness, and they went into an ornamental garden. There were many statues inside and walkways of white flagstone. The palace complex and the President's house came into view beyond a maze of hedges. Then Elijah saw the helicopter pad and the visitor's pavilion.

"You must go back now, Rafael", he whispered. "From here I go on alone."

"No. I must take you."

Without waiting for reply, he strode across the lawn to the plate-glass wall of the security foyer and stood by the door. He looked back at Elijah. Elijah walked over warily and peered inside. The guard seated at the desk was leaning back with his hands crossed on his stomach, his head nodding forward on his chest, asleep.

Elijah pulled the handle. It was locked.

"It's no use", he said.

The boy reached up and pulled on the handle. The door opened.

"You can go in now."

Elijah stared at him. Dazed, he walked through the entrance and past the guard. He turned back to look at the boy but he was gone.

He went along the corridor into the window-lined semicircular room overlooking the Gulf of Naples to the north and the Gulf of Salerno to the east. The back wall was as he remembered it, paneled in rosewood. Far below, the lights of boats moved like stars on the sea.

The building was not deserted. There were voices conversing behind a closed door. From another direction, he heard the ordinary kitchen sounds of dishes being stacked and the purr of machinery. He crossed the pale amethyst carpet, noted the blue-bronze sculpture of the horse and the stripped thornbushes whipping at the window. A scent of jasmine hung in the air.

He walked stealthily along a glass-encased causeway over a tumble of rocks and potted bonsai trees into the larger building, the residence. At every moment he expected to be apprehended, but more than once a door would close just as he was about to pass, or footsteps would disappear down a corridor. He passed through two security checkpoints, at one of which a cigarette smoldered in an ashtray on the desk; at the other a guard appeared to have momentarily abandoned his station for a washroom. Elijah slid past the sound of a flushing toilet and entered a hall that opened onto the majestic living room. The room was as he remembered it, almost a full circle, fully 300 degrees of which was floor-to-ceiling glass. He passed through to another annex and entered the library.

The President sat in a highbacked wing chair, beside a blazing fireplace. He was reading from a sheaf of papers beneath a single lamp and did not appear to notice Elijah's entrance. A few moments later he pushed his glasses onto his forehead and lay the papers on his lap.

"I won't be needing anything else tonight", he said. "You may retire."

When Elijah did not respond, the President looked up and saw him standing in the shadow by the doorway.

He stared at him for a full minute. Then he smiled.

"I wondered if you would come."

"You killed her", said Elijah solemnly.

"They said someone was coming."

"Why did you kill her?"

"Of course, I didn't know who it would be. There was only a hint of disturbance among the guardian spirits. They must have been diverted by the rebel angels."

"You killed her husband too. How many others have you murdered?"

"How did you get through?"

"That doesn't matter."

"What are you going to do? Shoot me?" The President uttered a short laugh.

"Our side doesn't kill people."

"You don't know your own history very well."

"Men on all sides have done evil in the name of good."

"How nice to hear—a stroke of self-revelation."

"I have not come to harm you."

"Have you not? What do you propose to do? Convert me?"

"I have come to speak to you."

"Speak to me? What do you wish to say?"

"I bring you a message."

"Ah, tidings of great joy to men of good will?"

"Yes."

"Not very original."

The President put the papers on a side-table and laid his glasses on top of them. His expression, which up to this point had been merely amused, revealing only a hint of concern, now grew serious.

"You are tired, and you seem to have a few cuts", he gestured casually.

"I was once where you are."

"You were never where I am."

"I was on the path to the seat in which you are sitting."

"You were one of many who were cultivated for this position. There are hundreds like you."

"I was graced to see how empty it is."

"Empty? I sit atop the world. I cross it back and forth without any man stopping me."

"There is One who will stop you."

"No. He cannot stop me."

"He has already broken the power of darkness."

"Ah, theology", the President sighed. "It is late. I am not in the mood for a long argument which, in the end, will lead nowhere."

"I was a boy during the War. I saw darkness visible. I saw its true face."

"Why, then, after all you had seen, did you go so far and rise so high, if you believe we are the powers of darkness?"

"Because I thought that darkness had only one or two faces. It took me a long time to learn that it has many, and that its worst face masquerades as light."

"You are a gifted man. But you are trapped within your tragic past. Those experiences wounded you. You are not judging the present situation correctly."

"The sacrifice of Anna Benedetti disproves you."

"I did not kill Anna."

"I have seen the documentation. I know that you did."

The President shook his head. "You have been misled. Documents are the easiest things in the world to manufacture. Signatures can be forged. You are a victim of an elaborate deception."

"I know it."

"You don't understand my meaning. I am not the one who has deceived you. I have tried to save you and to save your Church, for there is much good in it. There are atavistic forces at work in the world that men of reason must resist. You and I are not enemies, no matter what you may think."

"I know that you are master of deception. I have come here to warn you that your deceptions will plunge the world into a darkness greater than any before seen on earth."

"You are simply mistaken, my friend", he replied with gentle severity.

Elijah's certainty faltered. It came to him that during the past year he had indeed been involved in a mirage of shifting horizons, illusory signs, and wheels within wheels—gyroscopes within gyroscopes, Anna had called it. Could he have misread everything, translating the cryptic events according to the dictates of his beliefs?

You are blind; you are blind; you are blind; whispered the voices.

The background chorus that had disappeared at the coming of the boy now resurged into his consciousness. He felt suddenly unsteady on his feet. He swayed and leaned against the wall.

"Your ethical system is an image in the mind, an abstraction", said the President quietly. "The people of our times are trapped within many such structures. Their mazes, their myths, their mental constructs, lead them to misinterpret the very shape of reality."

Myths, myths, myths.

"And let me ask also, what are the fruits of your belief? Do Christians love one another?"

Elijah felt a dart of shame for his flawed Church. "Two thousand years," he stammered, "so many mistakes can happen in such a length of time."

"You are pinned beneath a limited culture. But you are one of the few capable of becoming free by your own efforts."

Now Elijah began to doubt his own mind. He had long ago learned to mistrust his senses, had counted on the power of reason to sort order out of the world of impulse, had found a template to measure against a disordered universe. Had he made a god of reason and given unquestioning allegiance to that most reasonable of religions, Catholicism, blinding himself to what was irrational in its makeup? Perhaps the President was right, and he had been fundamentally damaged by the experiences of his youth. Had he fled into the Faith in order to save his sanity? The human mind could not long endure the dismembering of reality. The child beaten to death by rifles in the ghetto—*this rat was smuggling potatoes,* said the soldiers—Ruth's body mangled by a splinter bomb—*as you can see she was carrying an embryo,* said the morgue doctor. The many faces he had loved swimming frantically and hopelessly as they were sucked into the vortex of Treblinka and Oświęcim? The face of darkness materializing in monster forms? Had he coped with the horror by throwing himself into a dream of a world restored to Eden?

This is a good and noble man, said the voices. *He will restore the world to sanity.*

Confusion swirled through his mind.

You have misjudged him; you have misjudged him; you have misjudged him.

"Sit down", said the President. "Here, by me."

Elijah took the armchair facing him and covered his brow with a hand.

"I am so exhausted", he said. "I have not slept in two days."

"You can stay here. You can sleep. Tomorrow we will go to the Italian police. I will vouch for your innocence. I know that you did not kill Anna."

"You do?"

"Of course. You could not kill anyone. I know who killed her."

"Who?"

"The same people who liquidated Stefano Benedetti."

"Who are they?"

"Mafia, working in conjunction with certain rogue elements in the Masonic Order."

"And you had nothing to do with it?"

"I swear by all that I hold dear that I had nothing to do with it."

"You weren't involved in any way?"

"I won't lie to you. I was unwittingly involved with some of these people on more constructive projects, but I had no idea they would do such things. I have remained in contact with them only for the purpose of determining the full extent of their crimes. I am not a criminal, Father Schäfer. My entire life has been devoted to the principles of civilization. You know this is true."

Elijah recalled that there was no blemish on the President's public record.

"Aside from the fact that violence is abhorrent to me, do you think I would compromise my work by associating myself with such activity?"

"No, I suppose you wouldn't."

"When you have rested, I will advise the homicide bureau in Rome that you are making yourself available to them for questioning. This will be a gesture of good will on your part and will be interpreted by them as a fair indication of innocence. At the same time, I will turn over to them the facts which have reached me regarding Anna's death."

"Can these people really be brought to justice?"

"I think we can do it."

Elijah stared at the floor, his thoughts scattered.

The President looked at him compassionately.

"Have you eaten?"

"Thank you, I am not hungry."

"Father Schäfer, you have been through trying experiences."

Elijah sighed heavily. "The worst of it is Anna's death. How could it have happened! Why did it happen?"

"We don't know all the details. Almost surely it's connected to her refusal to accept bribes from organized crime. Last year, when she was a justice of the Supreme Court, they wanted a certain decision in their favor. She refused. She sent some of them to prison. They delivered a punishment."

"I knew nothing about this."

"Her life was complex. She had many enemies."

They sat together in silence for some time.

"You loved her", the President said at last.

"Yes, I loved her." The words came from his throat strangulated, broken.

"Who could not love such a woman?"

"Did you love her?"

"Yes, I loved her too."

Elijah heard the cessation of the voices as one might hear the hushed silence in a symphonic hall after the consummation of a long and difficult performance, in that moment which hangs between the final stroke of genius and the storm of applause.

His hand slipped into his coat pocket. He felt a small round brass container and gripped it—an object he had once known and had forgotten.

His mind was empty for those few seconds only, yet into it there came the face of the child who had led him on the impossible paths. Into it also came the fairy tale that Pawel Tarnowski had told to him on a night of darkness and numbing cold, more than fifty years before. He saw dragons spewing black pigment across the canvas of creation. He saw hearts laden with stones and larks instructing orphans about a missing king. He saw wind and trees and rivers of tears. Then other scattered fragments of his past blew into the skies, wheeling like flocks of birds: light splashing through the holes in Don Matteo's hands; Gianna braiding the hair of an old discarded woman; yellow plastic flowers dropping from heaven, and purest snow on the earth like a blanket pulled over a bed sprinkled with the blood of birth. He saw storms at sea and doves planted like seeds in tombs, waiting to sprout, peaks and caves, leaves blowing down ancient streets and prayers going up like incense across the ravaged world. He saw an angel, armored and Byzantine, plunging through the clouds toward the cities of the night, and a dark archon rising to meet him in a clashing of swords. He saw the pantaloons of a buffoon and a shrivelled potato rolling ridiculous off the end of a soldier's boot. He saw a heart pierced by a sword and a tiny womanchild floating in the glass sea of the womb; he saw his mother kneading bread, and his father stitching, stitching, stitching with the patience of ages, while his grandfather read from the tractates. He saw a chalice raised on a million altars, and a white horse scratched in stone, and blue horses rampant, slicing with their steel hooves into living flesh.

Night fell and morning came. Night and day and night and day, centuries upon centuries, the moon speeding along its course, and a woman clothed with the sun, crowned with stars, standing upon it. Mercy and truth were in her eyes. She looked down, and there at her feet was Pawel's gift, and the clean, wise love of Anna, the fat baker dispensing forgiveness as love, a one-eyed fool carving a cross from the olive wood of Bethlehem, and a man coughing smoke from his lungs, pleading, pleading that someone, anyone, would accept his disguised love, his single unselfish act. And all the burnt people drifting up into the sky as smoke. And with them went their songs and stories and supplications like ribbons of many colors encircling the fallen planet, and rising with them, the memory of the God of little men, kept alive from generation unto generation by the power of their sacrifice. He saw fire — and fire.

Elijah looked up, feeling that he had been away from the room for many hours, though it had been only seconds.

"Stefano Benedetti?" he said. "What did you feel for him?"

"Stefano Benedetti was my friend."

Then a shadow passed across and through and behind his eyes. Elijah saw the thing Anna had described. He saw hatred. He understood then the magnitude of the lie that was encircling his mind.

He removed the brass reliquary from his pocket and opened it on his lap.

The President stared at it, betraying no emotion. There was no curiosity, neither antipathy nor attraction. It was this masklike, neutral expression that convinced Elijah that the President recognized it.

"Put that away", he said.

"You know what this is."

"No. I don't."

"You know very well that it contains a splinter of wood soaked in Christ's Blood. Here also are beads from Africa, where holy blood was spilled. And here too is Anna's blood."

The President reached across the space that separated them and picked the reliquary off Elijah's lap. He held it in his fingertips with an expression of distaste.

"If you are ever going to progress beyond your pathetic fallacies, you must cease to clutch these amulets."

He tossed it into the fireplace where it came to rest on a bed of live coals.

Elijah watched as it turned brown, seared with darts of green and blue flame. The heraldic cross embossed on its surface smouldered.

He knelt and picked up the reliquary in his right hand. He barely noticed the scream of protest from his palm, the stench of burning flesh.

The President barked at him: "What are you doing!"

Elijah stood.

"This is the sign that has defeated you and will continue to defeat you until the end of time."

The President rose up and faced him, his mouth twisting with disgust.

"You are insane."

He plucked a black device from the inside pocket of his sweater. A miniature red light flashed on its surface. His finger hovered over the button.

"Listen to me, Schäfer. You are a doomed man. I can turn you over to the police instantly. My servants can be here in a minute, and they will throw you over the cliff if I order them to do it."

"Like your forefather before you. Like Tiberius."

"Shut up, you fool. You think you can come against an army with that trinket. The former age is over, I tell you. There is no power in that thing you cling to. Your only hope is to throw it back into the fire and listen to me."

"I will not listen to you. From your mouth comes only deceit."

"You will listen."

"I bear you a message from the King. Will you not listen?"

"There is nothing he can tell me that I do not already know. He is of the former age, and I am of the one which is beginning."

"Christ is One. There is no other Christ. In Him everything in heaven and on earth was created, things visible and invisible, whether thrones, dominations, principalities or powers; all was created through Him and for Him."

"Silence!" the President roared.

From his mouth there poured a stream of blasphemies. Elijah averted his head and prayed the name of Jesus until the flow was stemmed, and he could cut through it with the authority rising up within him.

"The Lamb is the firstborn and the height of everything. It is through Him and by Him that all creation is reconciled to the Father, by the merits of His sacred Blood!"

In reply, a voice roared from the President's mouth. It shouted denial of the primary and singular sonship of the Lamb, denial that this Jesus was the Christ, denial of the victory of the Cross, denial of the One who had come into the world.

"There is no light left in the world save one," he concluded, "he who is the light-bringer, the angel of light who was cast down by the jealousy of God!"

"The jealousy of God? Think of what you are saying. Are your words not insanity itself?"

"I and no other shall bring mankind into the fullness of its destiny", he shouted. "No other!"

The President's eyes were focused with a distillate of malice that shot across the room toward Elijah like a jet of black fire.

He felt the force of it in his spirit, and shock waves passed through his body.

The President took a step toward him.

"Do you wish to degenerate to a hurling match of magic tricks", he sneered. "Shall we play a little knight facing Dracula! Will you play the hero-martyr and end as a notation in a dusty Vatican codex? Shall I be your monster, your bogeyman? Is that what you think this is all about? Do you really think that a display of conjuring could stop the work for which I have been destined from birth, from before the beginning of the world? Your tricks are nothing compared to what I can do. By the power of him who is darkness and hath the form of black flame, I command thee to fall!"

Elijah trembled, and he felt many presences swarming around him, screeching in chorus, spitting blasphemies, cavorting, throwing horrors into his imagination and unearthly sounds into his ears.

He felt himself fading, and the strength of soul by which he had spoken began now to fall back toward powerlessness. Then he spoke the name of Jesus. The word echoed throughout the room, and there was a silence in heaven and on earth for the space of a heartbeat.

"Jesus", said Elijah, "Jesus."

"Speak that name no more! I tell you to leave the Nazarene. Why do you stand looking back to what is past and shall never come again? Come to me and stand with me. We shall look together toward the future. You who would play the prophet, I shall make you into a prophet the like of which has never been seen before, nor will ever be again."

"If I am a prophet, I am a little one. I do not want to be a great one. My only task is to bear witness to the Lamb of God, He who was, who is, and who is to come. He is the First and the Last. He is Alpha and Omega. He comes swiftly, riding upon a white horse, and His name is Faithful and True. He has conquered you."

"Oh, you poor little man. Has he conquered me? He has no army left on this earth. Billions follow me."

"Your army is like the retreating German army at the end of the War. They were already defeated, though they could lash out as their empire crashed about them."

"My army grows daily, and we spread across this planet. Leave him, you fool. He was a little Christ. He is dead. The Christ of *this* age stands before you, and you do not recognize him."

"You are not Christ. You never will be. There is only one Christ."

"Leave him! Leave that man."

"He is the Root and Offspring of David, the Morning Star. Behold, He is coming. He is coming soon!"

"He died two thousand years ago. Is the precursor greater than the one to whom he points? Is the shadow greater than the living flesh?"

"There is no debate. Your powers are limited, and you can no longer ensnare my mind."

"Oh, what a prize you would have been if you hadn't turned from the way. But it's not too late. You can still turn toward the light."

"Christ is the Light of the world."

"Lucifer is the light-bringer!"

"He is darkness. He is *Satan* — the enemy."

"He is the Morning Star."

"Christ alone is the Morning Star."

"My lord will lead mankind to its highest truth."

"Your lord is *the devil* — the slanderer. May the Lord rebuke him!"

Elijah put the reliquary into his pocket and slipped the bishop's ring onto his finger. He raised both hands to heaven in the *orans* position of prayer, palms open toward the President. The scorched flesh in the shape of the cross was lifted high over the most powerful man in the world. As the President looked at the sign, hating it, and yearning toward it, he staggered back.

He tried to form a screech in his throat, but could produce nothing. He tried to bolt for the door, but his legs would not submit. He tried to tap the button on the device in his hand but his finger would not do it.

"Get out! get out! I'll let you go if you just get out now!"

"Not until you have heard the word the Lord Himself sends to you. He tells you this: Though you have sold yourself a thousand times to the angel of darkness, you are granted a final choice. You can still leave him. Though the devil's time has come and his fury has no limits, yet he shall soon come to an end. And unless you turn from him now, you shall go with him to the punishment that awaits those who lay siege to the Kingdom of God."

"Be silent!" roared the President.

"No! You be silent!" cried Elijah.

The President made as if to walk toward the door, but he hesitated. Confusion wrestled in his eyes.

"Be still!" Elijah said. "The hand of the Restrainer is upon you. You cannot strike until God Himself permits the hand to be removed. Now you must listen! This is the moment of choice. He offers it to you because, regardless of your crimes, you are a child of Adam. You were created in His image, like all others born of woman. You are a man, no more, no less. You have been led into captivity, but this bondage is not yet absolute. Turn from Satan! Turn away from him and come home to your Father!"

The President's mouth fell open and closed again.

"I adjure you, Satan, leave him!"

The President's eyes rolled up and the whites of them showed. His mouth opened and closed like a fish cast up on a shore, gasping for breath.

"*Vade retro, Satana! Vade retro, Draco! Crux sacra sit mihi lux!*"

The President's body fell to the floor and writhed. Bestial noises came from his mouth. Then he shuddered and lay without moving, his eyes unblinking, staring across the carpet. Elijah, fearing that he might have died without repentance, knelt beside him and administered the sacrament of the dying. But he saw that the man was still breathing. Then the suppressed writhing began again. At one point, he opened his eyes wide and stared at Elijah. The personality that looked out through those eyes was not the President's. Elijah resumed prayers of exorcism, and eventually the man closed his eyes and collapsed into unconsciousness.

Elijah started, for he saw a pair of bare legs standing beside the body.

"Rafael," he gasped, "what are you doing in here? You shouldn't be here!"

The child looked down at the figure on the floor with an expression of profound pity.

"He will awake in a few minutes", the boy said. "Then he must choose."

Elijah stared at him.

"Your work here is completed. Now you must go."

Speechless, Elijah allowed himself to be led from the room. They passed many closing doors, footsteps disappearing down corridors, and sleeping guards. As if in a dream, they walked out of the building and back through the garden to the cliff. The moon was riding high, and the sheep path was well illuminated. They went down without speaking, and Elijah followed like a small child being led by his elder.

Later—he could not tell how much later—they stood on the wharf, and Elijah went aboard. He turned to say good-bye. The boy raised his right hand. His expression was infinitely tender and strong. His eyes—his ten-thousand-year-old eyes—were set in a face so pure that Elijah felt conflicting impulses to stare and to look away. He glanced at the instrument panel for a second, turned the ignition switch, and looked back at the wharf. The boy was gone.

The boat rumbled out of the harbor, and he steered it to the east. The sea was calm now, and the boat skimmed across the surface. The cold wind hit his face and refreshed him. He felt relief. It was finished.

He looked back once and saw Monte Tiberio crawling with lights. He heard bells and sirens and understood then that the President had chosen.

He veered far to the north and proceeded without running lights. A helicopter passed to the south, playing a spotlight over the sea. He kept close to the edge of the peninsula of the mainland until he was near Salerno. As he approached the shore, about two miles from the President's private marina, he saw that it was ablaze with arc lights and that many figures were moving about the dock. He killed the engine and drifted along the coast. Beneath the stern seat, he found an oar and a rubber dinghy. He inflated it, dropped it over the side, and climbed down into it. Making no sound, he paddled toward a wooded area that spilled down from the heights. He beached the dinghy and searched through the trees until he found the blue Toyota in the palmettos.

He drove east through the mountains, passing no one, meeting few vehicles. Dawn was breaking as he drove into the port of Bari. Rising above the sea was the morning star.

XXI

Panaya Kapulu

The ruins of Ephesus stand in the marshy and unhealthy plain below the village of Aya Solouk, a few miles inland from the Aegean coast. A river, now silted up, once carried ships to the city, which at the time of Saint Paul's three-year sojourn there was the capital of the Roman province of Asia Minor and a center of its commerce. It was also the seat of the cult of Diana, which attracted multitudes of visitors. Here, Paul's miracles and preaching were responsible for the conversion of large numbers of citizens. So great was his impact on the populace that the city's magicians, astrologers, and soothsayers voluntarily burned their books of incantation and arcane knowledge. The decline in the trade of idols sparked riots from which Paul was forced to flee for his life.

On a typical day, hundreds of tourists prowl about one of the world's largest ruined cities, strolling along the Roman streets from temple, stadium, and theatre, through the early Christian basilica, and the mansions of the wealthy. One morning in spring, a man moved inconspicuously among them. He did not attract the eye in any way, for he was dressed unobtrusively. He might have been a visiting archeologist, or a retired professor from Istanbul, or perhaps merely an old man with nothing to do. From a vendor he bought brown bread, white cheese, and a cup of sweet black coffee and stood consuming them in front of the ruins of the Church of Saint John. He checked his wristwatch from time to time but appeared to be in no hurry.

Just before noon, two men approached the church from the direction of the ancient forum. One was old, the other young. They came up to him and shook hands. Little conversation passed between them; any passersby would have heard comments about the weather, journeys, the historical merits of the tomb of Saint Luke. The three men turned and walked together to the city gate that led to the hills. Children threw pebbles into stagnant water of roadside pools out of which broken marble columns rose like drowned forests. They went through the gate into the countryside, and soon were passing farmers tilling the soil around the outskirts of the city's remains and women trotting by on donkeys, carrying loads of firewood.

For half an hour they climbed into the hills. On the side of a mountain overlooking the Aegean sea and the ruins of the city, the road ended at a small structure built of rough stones.

"What is this place?"

"This is *Panaya Kapulu,* the House of the Holy Virgin."

"Is it true? Can it be the one?"

The three men glanced at the doorkeeper who sat outside on a stool reading a Turkish movie magazine. They went in and stood gazing around the dim interior.

"Here the Apostle John brought Mary the Mother of Christ to escape the persecutions of Christians that broke out at Jerusalem. Here she lived."

"In this very house?"

"More than nineteen hundred years ago! Is it possible?"

"Can't you feel it?"

The building was about twenty-five feet long and as wide. They passed through the main room into a small chamber at the back, and from there into a little side room.

"This is where she slept, and where she died."

After glancing hastily over their shoulders to make sure that the building was empty, they knelt and prayed in silence.

545

The stillness in the room was a palpable presence. Ancient yet timeless, older than the reconstructed mansions in the city below, and yet younger. It was the dwelling of a poor woman who had only just departed, as if on an errand from which she would return momentarily. They felt that she would come in the door and recognize them, and though they had not met her face to face, they would know her. They had always known her, she whom they had called *Mother* from their birth.

"We have a long climb ahead of us", said Elijah. "We must go."

From the house of the Holy Virgin, they set off by a footpath at the road's end and went farther into the hills. An hour later they entered a narrow gorge flanked by steep inclines, overgrown with wild shrubbery. A stone hut nestled at the bottom. A terebinth tree twisted nearby, and a young almond bloomed beside a well. A hen pecked in the gravel of the dooryard. A tethered white goat browsed at the base of the slope and greeted them with loud naahing.

"Elijah," said one of the newcomers, "your flock is welcoming you."

"*Shtiler, shtiler*", Elijah cajoled the animal, stroking the back of its head. "Quiet, quiet. You will get your grain at sunset. Give us extra milk tonight, little sister; we have company."

The three men went into the hut, escaping the heat of the afternoon sun. Elijah served them bread and cheese, onions, herbs, raisins, figs, a mash of spiced lentils, and draughts of cold water.

After the meal, the young man lay down on a cotton mattress in a corner and closed his one eye. He was asleep in minutes.

Elijah turned to the other and said, "Father Prior, I thought I would never see you again."

Replying in German, the prior said, "I too did not think we would meet again. It is a grace we did not foresee."

"God is good."

"He is greatly to be praised."

"In all times and in all places."

"Tell me what has happened to you since we last met."

"You have read the papers?"

The prior nodded. "Of course we didn't believe it. Our Elijah a murderer! I knew it was nothing other than a sign of how greatly you have impeded the enemy's plans."

"It is so."

"Still, he goes about his business as if no one can stop him. He comes to Jerusalem in September. The preparations in the country are nothing short of a royal welcome. I have never seen anything like it. The pagan cults and some Jewish sects are already acclaiming him as a new messiah. The Christian journals are also full of praise for him."

"A strong delusion. It falls on wise and foolish alike."

"What are we to do, Elijah? Did the Holy Father give you any directions for the near future?"

"He instructed me to wait and to pray—until the appointed time, he called it."

"Until the appointed time. I wonder what he meant?"

"We will know when it is necessary to know, and not until then."

The prior sighed, "As always, the Lord demands faith from us. First faith, and then help comes after."

"You too have been through many trials since we last met."

The prior bent his head. "Your letter reached me at Nazareth just as I was close to utter discouragement. When the riots started at Haifa in January, some of the fathers wanted me to take the community to the Christian settlements across the Jordan, but I refused. I said we must show confidence. If we begin to run, I argued, our enemies will only chase us harder and farther. But when the New World people sacked the monastery, I had no choice. We went to Nazareth, those of us who were left."

"How many died?"

"Eleven fathers and seven brothers."

"Who survived?"

"Myself, Father John, this brother here, and old Photosphorous who was in the hospital down in Haifa. I don't yet know his fate."

"The small one is exhausted."

"Brother Ass? Yes, he has done more good during the past few months than you can imagine. He saved my life."

"He has changed. His face is older and he is no longer noisy."

"We thought of him as the least of the brothers, didn't we? Simple, uneducated. We, with our advanced degrees and our finely nuanced theological homilies, we smiled upon him benignly. Brother Ass we called him. We, who were oh-so-humbly superior, are lesser men than he."

"How did he save you?"

"The rioters beat us and left us for dead. I don't know where he disappeared to during the attack, but he returned by night and pulled me from the heap of bodies. Out of nowhere, he produced a car and drove me and John to Nazareth, where the Franciscans took us into their hospice."

"What will you do now?"

"I don't know. The superior in Rome says we shouldn't go back there. Too much civic unrest. He said we must wait until he arranges transportation to America. That was six weeks ago. I haven't heard from him since. Things are very confused in Rome. There's no hint of it in the media, but I think there are struggles going on. Religious in several orders tell me the same story: communications are breaking down. We don't know what's happening."

"Can you return to the sisters?"

"Their own situation is precarious. The Latin Patriarch of Jerusalem is negotiating with the Israeli government for a promise of protection for the Christian orders, but it's the same everywhere—vagueness, delay, inaction."

"Father Prior, you are welcome to remain here."

"Thank you, Elijah, but I can see you have little food. How can you feed three on a diet that's barely adequate for one?"

"The Lord provides. I have a flock."

"A flock? One goat?"

"A little more than that. There is a village about two hours walk from here. I go every Sunday to say Mass. They make sure I have enough to eat and oil for the lamps."

"I didn't know there were any Catholics left in the region."

"There are perhaps forty families scattered throughout these hills."

"Is that all?"

"Most of them are Greeks, but they have had no sacraments since the Melkite Patriarch was arrested. Many of their priests have fled. A few pastors remain in Asia Minor, but they are in the cities, and it is difficult to find them. There are some Palestinians, of course. Also a group of Jewish converts. They are the most fervent of all."

"Even if there should be food for the three of us, of what use can I be? I don't think these arthritic hands could milk your goat."

"I need priests desperately."

"*You* need?" said the prior slowly.

Elijah went to an alcove at the back of the hut and drew aside a curtain, revealing a red vigil lamp and a small brass tabernacle set into the stones of the wall. He genuflected before the tabernacle, then picked up a ring from the ledge beneath it. He put the ring on his finger and seated himself across from the prior. The prior looked at it without speaking then went down on his knees and took Elijah's hand in his own. He kissed the ring.

Elijah helped him back to his seat.

"The Lord is full of humor", said the prior.

"Why do you say that?"

"Elijah, Elijah! Do you remember the time I was elected?"

"I remember it well. I voted for you."

"Did I ever tell you what happened to me the night before the election? No, I didn't. Well, now is the time, for the story has come full circle. You recall that it was fairly certain you would be elected. You were well loved; I wasn't. I was sure you would be our next prior, and I was very happy about that. To tell you the truth, I was relieved."

"And so, what is the Lord's little joke?"

"On the night before the election, I had a dream. It was a happy dream. I saw myself kneeling at your feet and kissing your ring; you had a shepherd's staff in your hand. The next day, when they made me the prior, I thought, 'Oh, no, a terrible mistake has been made!' I cried out to God. I decided to refuse the office. I knew that God had ordained you to shepherd our house."

"But it wasn't so", protested Elijah.

"Yes, now I know it. The council urged me to accept, because they said God speaks through the votes of the community. They told me that against this authority no dream has any weight. If I were to refuse, it would be a rejection of the will of God. I can't tell you how distressed I was. I accepted with agony in my heart. I knew my limitations all too well. I begged the Lord to let me off this cross, but He wouldn't. Now I see why."

They conversed in this fashion for another two hours. The small brother slept through it all and awoke only as the sun went down and the cool of the evening settled into the ravine. He was hungry and alert. He said little, contenting himself with accomplishing the simple tasks he begged from Elijah: washing dishes, milking the goat, gathering brushwood for the tin drum that served as a cookstove. From time to time, he cast beaming glances upon the host.

"Father," he ventured at last, "you have any trouble from the police?"

"No. My papers say I'm an archeologist, which of course I am.

I have been digging in the ruins of a Byzantine military camp near here. It was built during the campaign to throw out the Seljuk Turks in the eleventh century."

"You find any gold, Father?"

"I have unearthed a few coins, and the foundation stones of a street of tents. It will provide me with an excuse to be here for many years."

"Is it fun?"

"I am enjoying it. But I have found a very great treasure elsewhere."

"Treasure? What is it?"

"I will show you tomorrow."

* * *

They rose just before dawn, prayed matins, and celebrated Mass. After a simple breakfast of black coffee, boiled millet, and raisins, they set off by a footpath that zigzagged up the slope behind the hut. It traversed the mountain back and forth, up and down over hummocks in the land, becoming ever steeper as they climbed, gradually leading them into the dry scrub land of the hills. At the height of the ravine, they looked back toward the west where a vein of silver on the horizon revealed the sun reflecting on the sea. Ahead of them, they faced more climbing and rested for some minutes.

"What is it you are taking us to see, Elijah?" said the prior.

"A treasure that has remained hidden within the designs of God for almost two millennia."

"Gold!" joked Brother Ass.

"Yes, purest gold", replied Elijah, smiling.

The goat path ended after that, but a kind of trail continued on higher, a barely discernible, meandering line of broken branches and flattened dead grass, which Elijah's feet had made in his comings and goings to the scattered flock of the region. They reached a narrow plateau and paused again.

"Can't you give us a hint?" said the prior, gasping for breath.

"You will recognize it when you see it."

"Ah, still the mystic, aren't you? You like mysteries. And you make your friends suffer for it."

"It is much better for the soul."

The prior sighed, "Yes, yes, but I still prefer knowledge."

Elijah smiled at him. "Before this day is over you will be thanking me for your tired legs."

"You guarantee it?"

"Absolutely."

"All right, for now I will suspend my scholastic doubts. I will obey like a lamb."

"Me too!" said Brother Ass gleefully.

"You are a good flock!" said Elijah.

They mounted higher and went over a roll of earth into a trough that cut lengthwise along the flanks of the hill. The narrow depression, invisible from above and below, was just deep enough to hide anyone who walked in it.

"Where are we?"

"We are south of Ephesus. If we went higher and struck northeast for an hour, we would reach the town of Aya Solouk, above the ruined city. It is a stop on the railroad that runs between Smyrna and Aïdin."

"Don't tell me we're going back there?"

"No. We turn now and go along this trench for three kilometers."

"Three kilometers?" said the prior. "My old bones!"

"From here on our way is flat."

As they walked on the rubble-filled bottom, it became clear that this was the remains of an ancient road that had not been used for centuries. It was a natural defile, the origins of which were lost. Clearly, it had been improved by man in the distant past, for wherever the bank on the right became precipitous there were signs of low retaining walls, now collapsed.

"Is this Turkish?"

"No", said Elijah. "Much older."

"Does it lead to a crusaders' fort? Is that what you are going to show us?"

"Older still."

"Probably Byzantine."

"Older still."

"A remarkable state of preservation."

"It is from the Roman era."

"Surely, better routes run along the coast. Why would anyone take such trouble to build here?"

"There are passable roads above and below, some ancient, some modern. This is one that has fallen into anonymity. Its purpose is obscure."

"Built by shepherds perhaps?"

"Shepherds do not need such routes."

"Then what is it for?"

"Only a few miles long, it begins nowhere and seems to end nowhere. It offers no explanation at any point."

"Now you have intrigued me, Elijah."

They made their way slowly for another hour, stopping every so often to drink from the waterskin Brother Ass carried slung over his shoulder. Eventually, they came to an abutment in the hill, and the road ended abruptly.

"There is nothing here", said the prior.

"Nothing and everything."

"Where are we?"

Elijah pointed to the north. "A few kilometers in that direction we would come upon Ephesus."

"Why didn't we go by the road below, the way we came yesterday?"

"Because there is no longer any path up the mountains at this end."

"No longer?"

"There once was a trail from below, but rockslides have covered it. You see that heap of stones which tumbles down to the lower hills? The rest of the road is buried beneath it."

"And so? What have you brought us here to see, an amputated road that leads to nothing?"

"Not to nothing. Now look up above. Do you see the cleft in the rock?"

"I don't see anything unusual. Wait, you're right, there's a small gully. But it's impossible to reach."

"It's difficult but not impossible. We climb for a few dozen meters at the bottom end of the gorge. An earthquake blocked it long ago. When we go over that debris we will find what we are looking for."

With regret, the two visitors left the relative smoothness of the road, following Elijah uphill into a maze of bushes and chaotic stones. When they reached its top, they looked over the edge into a concave recession in the terrain, hidden on all sides by jumbled rock, and from above by an overhanging cliff.

They climbed down into the depression, six meters deep and about the same in width. At the bottom, Elijah pointed to a shadow in the rock. A circular stone lay there.

"A cave!" exclaimed the prior.

Elijah bent his head and went through the low entrance.

The prior and Brother Ass stayed outside peering in.

"Come inside. Don't be afraid."

When all three were seated on the dirt floor, Elijah struck a match and lit a kerosene lantern. The chamber was suddenly illuminated, and they gazed about them. Brother Ass was grinning and his one good eye was watering. The prior inspected the interior with studied interest.

"Ah, I understand now. This is the place where the scrolls were recently discovered."

"No. It isn't."

"Then what is it?"

"We are the only living men who know of this place."

"Father," said Brother Ass, "is this where the seven sleeping saints of Ephesus were buried?"

"No. That is another cave, farther to the north. There are many caves in the region, some of which haven't yet come to light."

"What makes this one so special?" said the prior.

"Soon you will know. We have not had an opportunity to be silent. We will rest here, and then after we have prayed, I will ask you what has been revealed to you."

The prior looked dubious; the brother seemed excited by the riddle.

The cave was about the height of a man, dry and cool. The walls were of stone, some of which had been enlarged by tools. At the far end was a hand-carved alcove in which there was a stone bench.

"Was this a refuge for priests during the persecutions? Surely, that's an altar."

"It may have been used for such, but that wasn't its original purpose."

"What then?"

"No more for now. We will rest. Pray. Sleep if you wish."

Brother Ass, gazing about him, lay his body down in the ground, and pillowed his head on an elbow. He closed his eye.

"You say we are the only ones who know. When did you first come here?"

"Shortly after my arrival. I was walking in the hills, returning from Mass at the Christian village. I had crossed the hidden road a number of times but had thought little about it—there are so many archeological sites in the area. One afternoon, I met a child on the hill above the goat path. Without any introduction or conversation, he came up to me and pointed down the road in this direction. He told me that I must find something, something important. He didn't explain. He answered none of my questions. He merely said, *Go to the end and up.*"

"Did he show you?"

"No. He left me and I never saw him again."

"How did you know where to find the cave?"

"I didn't. My feet seemed to know where to climb, my eyes where to look. The stone that lay across the mouth was itself covered with loose rubble. Were one to search for a thousand years among all these hills there would be no clue to distinguish this pile of rock from another. I just knew that I must remove *these* loose stones. Underneath, to my astonishment, I found the circular door-stone. It was obviously hand hewn. I rolled it away."

"There are tools here. You have been digging."

"Yes, I come as often as I can."

"Is there anything to indicate the archeological period?"

"I believe it is within the first century."

"Have you found artifacts?"

"Roman coins from the reigns of Nero and Vespasian. Jewish coins from the revolt that led to the destruction of Jerusalem in 70 A.D. This is good evidence that Christian Jews hid here after the destruction of the Temple. There are lamps of the kind once used in the Holy Land to burn olive oil. Some clay pots that are so small they must have been more decorative than useful. They may have held flowers. Ointment jars perhaps. The most significant object is a silver fish inscribed with the Greek letters $X\rho\iota\sigma\tau os$ —Christos. There are other inscriptions on the bench."

"Show me."

Roughly cut into the surface of the stone, at foot and head, were the Hebrew words *Daughter Zion, Firstborn of Woman.*

The inscription was repeated in Greek and Aramaic.

"Aramaic?" said the prior. "That's odd. Whoever wrote this was a long way from Galilee."

He sat back and pondered this. His brow furrowed, and it was obvious that conflicting thoughts were passing through his mind.

"You don't think . . . ?"

Elijah nodded.

At that point, Brother Ass cried out in sleep and half rose on his elbows.

"Thomas is not here!" he cried, "Has anyone sent for him? *It is too far, too far!* Hush, the angels will tell him. He will be here soon. *But he is beyond Persia. We cannot wait.* We must go ahead, though our hearts are cast down. *What will we do without the Mother?* She is with us, just as the Lamb is with us until the end of time. Do you not remember His word to us when He went up into the clouds. *When will He return, when will He return?* Lucanus, calm him. What will the women think? *Is the body ready?* Lydia has gone into the city for more herbs. The flowers in the garden are blooming. So many of them, out of season too. *Bring them. Bring them all.* Is the grotto prepared? *Andrew! Matthias!* All is ready. *Have the brothers in Damascus arrived? Will they come?* Macedonia and Galatia will come. They knew weeks ago she was failing. *Pray, brothers, pray that all will be able to come.*"

Elijah and the prior stared uncomprehendingly at Brother Ass. The small brother sat up and leaned against the wall. Tears were streaming from his good eye.

"Brother, wake up."

"I am awake, Father Elijah. *But she is gone, our little sister, our small mother.* How can we live now that she is no longer among us? *Is the light going out of the world?* Speak no more as if you do not have faith. The light is not fading. It is changing. She will do more good for us now. *Yes. I believe. I believe.* The women will soon complete preparations of the body. We must pray. *Our hearts are broken! How can we pray!* Do you not remember how we grieved when He was crucified. You remember how we fled. And then three days later what joy! Oh, my brothers, we must never lose heart. *John, tell us, tell us. Even our broken hearts obey your voice.* Be still my brothers, be still and rest on His heart. Be still and know the heartbeat of God."

Brother Ass's weeping gradually subsided. The two priests watched him without speaking, feeling only the pounding of their own hearts.

"Her hands were crossed over her breasts. The women cut off little locks of her hair for keepsakes. They laid bunches of herbs around her neck and throat. Peter and John approached the body in their mantles. John carried the vessel of oil with which Peter anointed her forehead, hands and feet with the sign of the cross. Then the women shrouded her in the winding sheet, leaving only her face exposed, restored to the beauty and freshness of its youth. *She is no longer old,* we said. They placed a wreath of flowers on her head and laid a veil over her face."

"Brother," said the prior, reaching forward, shaking Brother Ass by the arm, "wake up."

"I am awake."

Elijah gently pulled the prior's arm away and whispered, "Leave him. The Lord is showing us something."

"The body was so light. She was like a child in our arms. We heard her voice in our minds, *I sleep but my heart is awake. I sleep but my heart is awake.* Then we knew that though her body rested in the sleep of death, awaiting the Last Day, her soul was in Paradise. The body was laid in a box of white wood and the lid bound over it with leather straps. The men lifted it into a long straw basket shaped like a trough. On this litter, they carried her, six of the Gospel-Bearers, the ones who had walked with the Lord. They carried her in procession from the house, accompanied by the women. We all cried, but we sang in our tears. We did not wail as the pagans do. We praised the Father of All as we went up that hard road above the house. Along that path we walked the way of the cross which the mother had made for her prayers in remembrance of Jerusalem. At each place we stopped and kissed the crosses that John had scratched in the stones. The fall, the meeting, the place of Simon, the veil of Veronica, and the place of humiliation where they tore the garments from Jesus for all the world to see; then the nailing. Finally, at the memorial place of the Lord's death, we knelt. The Mother's body rested on the stones while we waited. Then Peter got up first and led us the rest of the way."

Brother Ass became silent, lost within the vision. The two other men offered no prompting.

"When we came to the grotto in the hills, four of the apostles carried the box inside the tomb and laid her on the stone bed. All of us went in, one by one, and knelt praying before the holy body, honoring it, taking leave of it for the last time. Then the stone was rolled over the entrance, and we departed.

"The following day Thomas came among us, accompanied by Jonathan Eliazar and a brown man from the lands beyond Persia. We gathered around them and told them. When Thomas heard that the Virgin was already buried, he wept with an astonishing abundance of tears and loud cries. He threw himself onto the floor beside the bed where she had died and could not seem to forgive himself for coming late. John consoled him. *It is in the Lord's plan*, he said, *none of this is outside of the will of the Father.* Then Thomas got up and knelt in front of the altar in Mary's bedchamber. After that, the elders took him up the hill in the dark, for he begged to see her face one last time. They bent the shrubs back and rolled away the stone. Thomas, John, Eliazar and the brown man went inside. They opened the lid of the coffin and behold it was empty.

"John cried out, *She is no longer here!* The rest of us ran in, saw, wept, prayed and lifted our arms to the heavens. *The Lord has raised her up, body and soul!* cried Lucanus. We gathered the grave linens and the coffin to keep as relics and returned to the house by the Holy Way, praying and singing psalms."

Brother Ass opened his eye. A smile of surpassing sweetness spread across his face, and he beamed at the two priests.

"She is very beautiful", he said.

"Elijah," whispered the prior, "we are in the tomb of the Virgin."

"She is so good", said Brother Ass, and lay down again. He closed his eye and fell asleep.

The prior looked at Elijah and exhaled. Then he too closed his eyes in a spirit of recollection. They remained without moving for a time beyond measure, resting in a seamless peace. Later, a beam of golden light slipped through the entrance and moved across the floor.

Elijah roused the others.

"The sun is setting. We must return to the house now."

They went out and returned to the hut in the gorge by the way they had come, none of them speaking, each of them held within a current of joy suffused with awe.

* * *

Elijah was awakened in the middle of the night by a sound of wind in the branches of the almond and terebinth. He got up and went outside to look at the stars. A large orange star passed to the east, falling slowly, fizzling out near the horizon, followed seconds later by a bright blue one, smaller and swifter.

He went back inside and knelt before the tabernacle. He remained motionless, praying hour after hour. He tried to recollect himself, but found it difficult to keep his thoughts focused. He was exhausted, of course, and this aggravated the distractions and weakened his will. The glow of the vision of the cave remained, but it was fading. Why was it no longer enough, when only hours ago it had seemed that nothing in this world or in the spiritual realms could tear it from him. The joy seemed to be seeping slowly out of some unknown fissure. Many thoughts coursed through his mind. He reminded himself of the sweet fire that leapt down to the hearts that would receive it. Once, nineteen hundred years ago, a group of men and women had believed in it. They had tasted it, and the world was changed forever.

Could it happen again? Yes. New life would be born, and new civilizations would rise. But would they not fall as all previous ones had fallen? And what was the cost in terms of human misery and lost souls? Why did God permit it? Was He powerless? Elijah flinched away from the thought as if from a devouring fire that had once burned him, not fatally, but leaving a scar that had only just healed.

Stripped before his eyes was the fundamental problem of his soul: he had been given everything and it did not suffice. He had been graced to see the actions of God as few men have seen them. The consolations poured out upon him and within him were extraordinary, and not the least of them was this day's miracle. And yet . . . and yet, the ancient scar of Adam within his nature dragged him inexorably back, again and again, to this desire for certainty. Not that he wished to force the Creator of the universe into a position of justifying His will, but he hungered for a trace of explanation.

He knew full well that if it were given he would soon need a larger one, and a still larger one after that, until in the end no explanation would fill the yawning abyss of his doubt. The illusion of understanding would only breed deeper confusion, more binding forms of inner protest against the violation of all that was beautiful. *Not-knowing* was the way to ultimate union with the Love whose embrace was the filling of every doubt, the binding up of all wounds. As a Carmelite, he knew the theology and spirituality of the mountain of faith, the way of nothingness — *nada* — the path that led by the straight route up the mountain of God. Why this relentless pull to the left and to the right, as if a path zigzagging through perilous ravines and precipitous heights were a better way. It was not a better way. He knew it, and yet the tug remained.

The question returned again and again, nagging, biting, seizing his attention whenever he sought to fix his mind on the Presence. Why did God permit it? Why? Were the little arrangements of man destined to fall ever short of the heavenly Jerusalem, endlessly repeating themselves until there came about some radical and comprehensive fall, some awful and majestic collapse into an ultimate evil, wiping away all delusions about the perfectibility of man?

Was this long lesson strung out through the course of history not a form of cruelty? Oh, yes, he knew all the replies, back and forth, up and down, inside out. Freedom. Human will. Man could not love if he were unable to *choose* love, and with this choice came the ability to choose love's opposite. Elijah could argue an atheist into silence, if one would listen, and he could go farther to implant the questions that could lead a soul in darkness to fairest hope. But beyond that there would loom the wider and more perilous questions still. His convert would have to face it eventually, for he, Elijah, was still facing it after all these years.

"Why do You permit evil to go so far? Would you let it devour everything?"

Not everything, said the quiet voice. *Not everything. And from a single seed comes forth entire forests, waiting to unseal their code, to cover the earth with life.*

He saw the many faces that, like seeds, had sunk into the dark soil of his memory. Ruth, the baby in her womb, Anna, Pawel, Mother, Father. So many had perished, consumed by the enemies of God. It was impossible to understand why God had permitted it. This question, the one that had haunted him from the moment of his parents' arrest when he was seventeen years old, had appeared and reappeared like a sharp stick probing the incurable wound. Yes, the consolation in the cave had refreshed him. Yes, he knew that God existed. Without such faith he would long ago have grown weary and stumbled, pleading with God to depart and to take with Him the pain of seeing. He was past that crisis, he knew. The despair of his youth was over and the losses that had followed were patiently borne, but beneath the scar tissue there remained an abscess—a question and the doubt.

He went back outside again, stepping over the sleeping companions in the dark. He sat on the edge of the well, watching the stars, asking for light.

The faces of those he had loved came to him with increased poignancy then, and he felt a sob within himself that could take no exterior form. They were gone. A fixed landscape of absence. Yes, he understood the message of the cave—that the small woman, the firstborn daughter of Zion, was a sign of the resurrection of the flesh on the Last Day. But now it had dwindled to a promise, a word he had once heard, an event that lay in some distant and possibly abstract future. He believed that God would draw the beloved faces after her into the sky, swirling up like birds of fire, up and up into a voluminous light that poured down to greet them. The vast panorama of man's history would become a memory, a simple tale told swiftly and soon over. All grief would slip away and all questions would be remembered as the uncomprehending wails of a newborn who did not grasp the meaning of his existence and hungered only for milk.

Within the box of time a drama had been enacted. The final scenes were approaching, but it might be that other births and deaths awaited this aging planet. Night and day. Seed time and harvest. Thrones rising and falling. The Word and the Antiword circling each other endlessly in a combat from which there was neither escape, nor relief nor truce. As long as man remained man, there would arise again and again the machinations of those who had no hope beyond the tactics of worldly power; always they would kill the gentle in their desperate efforts to rearrange the furniture on the stage. Metaphors collided in Elijah's mind, swarming, clashing, breaking apart into confused designs, like the shattered glass of an image that had once reflected the hidden face of God, and which now bore only the imprint of a boot.

He saw many scripts and many audiences. Palaces fell and the dwellings of the humble rose again from the ruins. He saw a world covered with the activities of the holy angels, and the songs of man feebly greeting them, as the morning star greets the dawn. But he also saw dragons coiling about cities and devouring wave upon wave of human souls who dwelt in them, as if the city of man were the city of eternal strength. Cities built by men who would not be born for another ten thousand years.

The ache and the futility of it hit him hard.

You see that time must have an end, said the voice.

"Can You give us more time?" he pleaded. "A little longer and we might yet make a place for love on this earth."

Evil cannot be permitted to devour the good indefinitely.

"I understand, my Lord, but is there not one more chance for us?"

Can you, My son, measure the full weight of time or track the seed of man in his course throughout the order of creation? Do you know the number of the stars and the number of the offspring of the flesh who would come into existence because of your pleading? Were I to grant another thousand years many souls would enter Paradise who might not have existed, and many others would throw themselves willingly into the pit of Hell.

He shrank from this knowledge.

"That is the explanation?"

The voice did not reply to this. For the briefest moment, Elijah felt the smile of his Creator, but this was a passing sense, and he wondered if it were only a sentiment. He turned to his intellect for help. He prepared a summation of his case.

"You are a fertile God. Many seeds are dropped into the soil. Many do not sprout. Yet beneath the appearance of waste nothing is wasted, nothing lost. Giant trees crash to the forest floor, decompose, and become the soil out of which the saplings arise. Similarly, in human affairs, movements are created, rise, do Your work in the world, decline, go back into the soil, and provide the rich humus out of which new life springs. Generations come and go. Sun and rain, winter and summer, seed time and harvest. Always Your Word remains constant. Your people are called over and over, generation after generation, back into this constancy, back to this mysterious fluid stability—the only security worth having. Can You not waste a little more time on us?"

Can you bear the weight of the souls who would despise this time of grace?

"If You give us time to warn and to protect!"

How much time I have already given. Two thousand years, and once again they fall into forgetfulness.

"Give us the voice to speak with authority."

If I were to make your voice shake the foundations of the earth like thunder, would they make themselves more deaf in order not to hear?

"O my Savior, You know our state, You know our weakness. How fragile is man! The mighty of the earth are moving toward absolute power to establish control over the chaos of the human condition."

They would make themselves divine in order to flee from God.

Elijah felt that he was debating with a Judge who was not only Mercy but Justice, the *Pantocrator,* the Lord of all creation, presiding at a trial in which the accused did not grasp the extent of their guilt. All heaven observed, and all hell. Unseen hosts were listening to the debate. Once, long ago, in the cold apartment of Pawel Tarnowski, during the worst days of the winter of 1943, he had found a book containing a poem about Heaven and Hell. He had read it to Pawel while all around them evil men were shooting the innocent.

> What in me is dark, illumine,
> What is low, raise and support;
> That to the height of this great Argument
> I may assert eternal providence,
> And justify the ways of God to men.

With what naïve joy he had read those words aloud. With what enthusiasm! He remembered the sound of his childish voice and the look in Pawel's eyes—his silence the only reply.

Now here he was, more than fifty years later, a man himself, moreover a man who had taken a shape the boy could not have foreseen. A man in a desert at the end of an age, seeking to justify the ways of man to God.

"O Father, may I argue our case with You?"

You may do so, Lawyer Elijah.

Anna had called him that. Anna who had died at the hands of evil men, just as Ruth and the baby and Pawel had died.

"I am a poor lawyer in the court of God. But, my Lord, is it so impossible that mankind may be restored? Nothing is impossible with You. Did not Mary's womb contain the impossible, the unthinkable? In that sacred little room of hers was nurtured the seed that would save the world from darkness. Encoded there, as if on a double helix, were the martyrs and mystics, the cathedrals and the statues, the Christian East and the West, the songs of the monks, the encyclicals, the poems, the millions of children who might not otherwise have been.

"Joseph too — small, hidden man from the least of villages — he contained the heart of a true father and made it possible for a new world to come into being. Joseph — fosterfather to a fatherless world, living icon of the Father. He remained open to messages and thus helped make it possible for You to come as man. His obedience protected Your very existence. His vigilance, his justice, his love, made it possible for You to grow as man. What a marvel this is — and what a scandal. Why all this weakness? Why the poverty, the smallness, the hiddenness? It does not make sense: You chose to be born in a cold time. Heaven came down to earth in a season of peril. The Savior of Israel revealed as powerlessness during the final ruin of the nation — for my people, my elders, it was the End. Therein lies the puzzle, the paradox, and the scandal: You came at the worst possible moment."

I came at the impossible moment, and the world, which was powerful and sick unto death, burning and dying in its sins, was born again.

"Where has that light gone? When did the hope that was born with Your birth depart? So much time has passed. It is hard to see in the dark. You must tell us again and again: Your strength is to be found in weakness. Nazareth of Galilee was the place where that small, clear, indestructible message was first lived. She taught us that, Your Mother. It is lived again and again in each generation, often in the face of overwhelming odds. Civilizations rise and fall. Saints and tyrants, kings and poor men are born, grow old, and die. Cultures, theories, opinions, fashions, theologies, movements, rise up and disappear again. That is why our faith can never be merely a system of religious thought, a set of ethics, or a beautiful culture. That is why miracles and visions can never be enough. When everything is stripped down to its essential form, our faith is a belief in One who loves us; in Jesus, true God and true Man, the only Christ, dwelling in the heart of His Church, He who was, who is, and who is to come. That is why our home is the universal Church, the throne on which You reign, a Church that is within time and yet outside of time. That is why her doors stand ever open to Anna and Severa and Smokrev and Billy and me and even to this possessed man who desires to rule the world. Do You intend to close the doors to mankind?"

You speak as if the sum of human souls is a single thing. Mankind is not an organism. Each soul is weighed as if he were the only one.

"Do you wish to end all of that? If You do, I will accept. I may even understand. But I see a thing I would litigate with You: the Church passes through eras in which she glories in the summer's triumph, and other periods when she goes down into the cold earth, apparently beaten. It may well be that her highest glory is to be found hidden beneath a stone, to all appearances dead, but very much alive, waiting for spring. I think often of our martyred Severa lying in the catacombs of Saint Callistus: *Sleep, little dove, without bitterness, and rest in the Holy Spirit.* Little girl, overcomer of lions! She will rise on the Last Day. We will see her face to face. We will chat with her, our small sister, our mother in the spirit. And my daughter who never came to birth, who never climbed the mountain or played in the wind. I see her child's drawings, her poems, her songs that never came to be. I see her smile. I see the seed time of Ramat Gan and the harvest that did not come. I see all that might have been. These frail letters inscribed on the surface of creation would have told a story larger than the sum of its parts. 'I am', they proclaim. 'I was here', they say. 'The world is beautiful. It makes me happy and I love it!'

"And at a deeper level they express the soul's awareness that, 'He who made the almond blossom made me.' She did not live long enough to tell You this."

I made her and she belongs to Me. She is happy. She tells Me this.

"Your words console, but in my boldness, I beg Your patience, for I must grow bolder still. Give us daughters and sons, and time, that You may have many children of the light. I cannot know the future, for I am a small man, and blind. You have anointed my hands with power to bring You to this earth so that we might feed upon Your very self. Yet will there be any flock to feed? The Church may yet go on to the third millennium and convert the world, or she may continue to shrink to a small remnant. Will there be any faith left on the earth when the Son of Man returns? We do not know. Only You know. But of this we can be sure: those whom You touch with Your fire will become what You wish them to become. Give us this fire, for we are dying of the cold."

How many are like you across this dark age? A few only. Elijah, My good and blind child, you are an almond tree flowering in dry ground.

"Let me then make the seed of a second spring, seed not of the flesh but of the spirit, bringing dead men to life again. For You have made me this way, and You have told us that we are wonderfully made. You have planted this longing within me. You have created this soul who pleads with You. Give us a while longer to speak the word that shatters lies. When the tyrants and the propagandists and the experimenters have all gone, when the hatred and hopelessness have exhausted themselves, the earth will grieve and be born again. Let it be this way, Father, let it be that Your

Bride the Church will remain. Let those who have sown in sorrow reap a harvest in joy."

But the Voice did not reply, and he was left alone with the stars. He went in, lay down on his mat, and slept.

* * *

On Sunday morning, Elijah hiked up the mountain with Brother Ass. They ascended the topmost heights and came to a barren flat land of scrub brush and untended fields. They crossed it and came to a dirt road that meandered east toward the Christian village. It was a two-hour walk, and he took the opportunity to ask the small brother about his experience in the cave.

"I was awake, Father. All the time I knew where I was, inside the cave with you and Father Prior. At the same time, it was like watching a film, but I was inside the film too."

"You spoke as if you were one of the apostles."

"I was beside them. I told you only what I heard them saying. I didn't understand it much. They didn't look like the apostles on the holy cards. They were a different kind of Christian from us. But they were the same as us too. The Holy Spirit took me there in my soul, and I saw it just as it happened. I heard it inside the ears in my heart. I saw it all. I cried when they cried. I was happy when they were happy. She was so beautiful. Her face . . ."

The brother's description faltered, and no amount of encouragement induced him to continue. He would only say: "I don't know how to tell you about it. You have to see it for yourself."

The small one whistled and skipped along like a child, occasionally lapsing into a reverie that clearly involved the vision he had seen. Whenever the young man's thoughts returned to it, his face glowed with a light that seemed more than natural.

A single telephone wire snaked out of the hills toward a dusty cluster of approximately twenty houses and shops. There was a decrepit petrol station and a post office, a food store, and a stuccoed Byzantine church, its windows smashed, its front doors boarded.

Elijah went into the food store. He was greeted by a shout of delight from a fat, white-haired woman in a greasy pink dress. This was Mrs. Cohen, the Jewish convert. She embraced him bustily and conducted him to a back room. For forty-five minutes, he heard confessions, then he robed in the Eastern Rite vestments someone had salvaged from the church. He offered the Divine Liturgy of Saint John Chrysostom for the gathering of a few dozen souls—farmers, shopkeepers, housewives, and children.

After Mass, Mrs. Cohen stuffed their backpacks with food.

"You've got a visitor eh? Here, you'll be needing more than usual. No arguments! Put that money back in your pocket! You don't want to get me cranky. Then I'd have to go to confession to you for getting mad at you. A fine pickle you'd put me in then, eh? Here, take this marzipan. It's Sunday. Enjoy it. Now what about the dried beans?"

And so forth.

At the end of her lecture, she removed two letters from her bosom and stuck them into the knapsack.

"My brother-in-law in Smyrna was here yesterday. Two letters for you."

Elijah did not open them until he and Brother Ass stopped for a rest at the halfway point on their return journey. He sat in the shade of a rock and read the envelope. The return address was a prison in Illinois. The stamp was postmarked Chicago.

Dear Buddy,

Don't worry, they can't trace this letter to wherever you are. I still have some friends. The touristy couple who are my couriers like to make pilgrimages to the mysterious East, and they promised to drop my immortal words into a mailbox in Istanbul, addressed to a certain Mr. Cohen of Smyrna. Wow! You do get around.

I recognized the handwriting, but I doubt if anyone else did on this side of the Atlantic. The alias gave me a chuckle.

Since when did you start calling yourself Davy? Oh well, I penetrated your disguise instantly. I read about your various crimes in the papers and recognized the scenario. Same as mine, right? Right! Nice people these new-world democrats. Home of the brave and land of the free. Looks like I'll be out in the year 2020, maybe sooner for good behavior.

I can't tell you how much your words meant to me. I've made my peace with being unjustly condemned. It does relieve a lot of tension. No more fundraising, no more torturous bingo nights, no more haggling with writers and committees—I never could stand all that ego-involvement. No more pride, no more rage. I work in the machine shop. I read the Scriptures. I spend a lot of time on the last book of the Bible, and I've got to say it looks more and more like a lens coming into focus. Maybe I got squashed under the big Apocalypse steamroller. So what! I finally get a cell of my own and plenty of time to pray. You'd be amazed at how many honest criminals there are in here. They're as guilty as sin and admit it, which is a better way of life than the folks outside who are guilty and think they're innocent. We're all criminals at heart, even those of us who are innocent, technically speaking. Cain and Abel—you know the story.

Some of the folks in here want ministering. I love it. Good old-fashioned priesthood. It's hard but at least it's honest. I worry a lot. It's still my biggest sin. I worry about the Church and I worry about you and I worry about my brothers' kids who have all jettisoned the Faith. Gertie died of a stroke. Thank God my parents died before all this happened.

They say the Holy Father is very ill. I guess there are a lot of people glad about it. What's going to happen to the Church with so many zombies walking around in her, spouting off in her? What comes next, Davy? Is there any hope for us? The Pope always talked about hope, and maybe that was his big grace. He taught us to hope when everything seems lost. I thought a lot about that last December during my trial. I always had a secret dislike of Advent, because it's such a crazy busy time of year for priests. But I really enjoyed it this year, if you can imagine anyone enjoying a liturgical season while he's being sent to jail for something he didn't do. Advent, placed so strategically at the dying of the year, is good, good training. We're not supposed to be like the ancient pagans who watched the coming of winter with a kind of terror-stricken obsession, mesmerized by the specter of death, enslaved to death, sacrificing their children to the insatiable appetite of death. Not supposed to be, but funny how the deathly vapors seep into your heart without you knowing it. During Advent, I learned to kick it out. I learned to gaze into the growing dark with spring in my eyes. Impossible? Yep! But Christians should always keep an icon of the impossible in their hearts. Right?

Well, it's Ordinary Time now, and back to the usual. Writing this has been good therapy—even better than baying under the moon. Thanks for listening. It's not often I get to rhapsodize. How many ferverinos do you hear out there in the desert? You did say desert. Where? Africa? Asia? Some European city? It's all desert now, isn't it?

I hope that somewhere, somehow, you've got a cell of your own.

Love,
Ed Smith

The second letter contained no salutation and no signature. It was typed, and like the first was addressed to "D. Pastore", care of Mr. Cohen of Smyrna. It had been mailed from Athens.

I received your message six weeks after posting. I am relieved to have news of you, and so is H.F., who sends you his blessing. Pray for him, for he is much maligned in every direction. Do not believe what you read about him, or about anything regarding our affairs. I hope to come to

you by late spring or early summer if the political situation improves. Our contact in Constantinople has been of great help. He will take me to Smyrna and from thence to persons who will connect me to your current location. I do not know where you are, but I feel assured that you are well. Feed the flock that has been given into your hands. I entrust you totally to the care of the Mother of God.
— *Fide,* C.D.F.

Elijah deciphered it easily. Constantinople was the office of the Patriarch of the Orthodox Church. *Fide* was Latin for Faith. C.D.F. meant the Congregation for the Doctrine of the Faith. The letter was from the prefect — *Dottrina,* Billy had called him.

The prior welcomed them back to the hut and set a meal of boiled lentils and onions on the table. For dessert they feasted on a patty of oat bread with sesame seeds and slices of sweet marzipan. Elijah told his companions about *Dottrina's* letter, and they were greatly encouraged by it.

"Think of it! A cardinal coming here!" said Brother Ass. "I've never met a cardinal before."

Elijah and the prior chuckled.

"Cardinals are just like you and me", said the prior.

"Oh, I don't believe that", said the small one. He jumped up and began to bustle about the hut straightening everything. He grabbed a broom and began to sweep the dirt floor.

"Sit down and enjoy your coffee. His Eminence may not arrive for months."

"I hope he comes soon, Father Elijah, then we'll have a regular monastery again. Four of us make a choir."

"We will elect you prior, brother."

"Never!" said the small one, shocked. "Never!"

"I think I shall be the chief theologian", said the prior, "and the cook!"

"We won't be the first to make a monastery here", said Elijah.

"These stones have fallen and risen more than once since the Incarnation. Behind the hut are the foundations of an ancient oratory."

"Who put this hut back together?"

"I did. It's only a beginning."

"You don't intend to reconstruct a whole monastery by hand!"

"Yes. One stone at a time."

After vespers, Elijah went outside and watched the stars as they appeared one by one above the ridge in the east. He was surprised to see the silhouette of a man standing against the deep blue of the dusk, looking down into the ravine, watching.

Elijah shouted a greeting, but it was doubtful that his voice carried that far. He waved, and the figure waved back.

He beckoned it down, but the figure remained without moving. Then it signaled that Elijah should climb to him.

Puzzled, he got up, dusted off his trousers, and ascended along the goat path.

As he neared the ridge, he recognized the figure. It was the boy who had showed him the cave several months before. He was an adolescent of about sixteen years, tall, sturdy, his bare feet planted firmly, dressed in white pants and shirt, his face flaming in the last light reflected off the western sea. Then Elijah realized that the sun had already set, and the burnished bronze of the boy's face was lit by an unknown source.

"Now you are to be shown a new thing", he said.

The boy turned and climbed higher, not looking back, confident in Elijah's obedience. Elijah followed him, going more by sense than by vision, for the dark fell swiftly and the pale dust of the track soon became invisible. He proceeded slowly, wondering, overcome with awe, guided only by the tower of the boy's back receding ahead of him.

XXII

Apokalypsis

As the darkness on the mountains increased, Elijah became anxious. The receding form grew dim, then invisible. He called to him, but there was no answer. He staggered along blindly for several meters until he tripped against a stone and fell. He sat and waited. The boy would soon notice and come back to find him.

The boy did not return. Elijah called again and again, but only insects and night birds answered. A fox barked in the distance. A ship out on the Aegean sounded its foghorn. Clouds rolled in from the west and blotted out the stars. He held his hand in front of his eyes but could not see it.

Eventually he began to wonder if the boy were a deceiving spirit. If he were an angel of the Most High, he would have returned by now. There was nothing he could do but wait for the dawn. If he tried to go forward into unknown terrain, he could stumble over the edge of any one of a thousand ravines and never be found. If he tried to retrace his steps, he would surely lose his way. He had spent many nights of his life listening in the dark. Always he had prayed, and always he had remembered to increase his prayer when the protests of his emotions struck their noisy chorus, their arguments, their vertigo, dragging him down into nightmare. During his life, he had hidden in sewers and attics, in barns and holes in the earth, in the bilges of ships and, deepest of all, in the spiritual night of Carmel. He was, therefore, accustomed to the assault upon the senses, the temptation to run somewhere, anywhere, in order to escape the eternal, relentless oppression; alternately, to attack the faceless dark with threats, sobs, and imprecations. He had learned the art of quieting his mind, then his emotions, and finally his spirit. Now he prayed, as he always did in such situations, the prayers of the will. He recited the Psalms aloud, slowly, employing each word deliberately, pushing back the shroud covering him in layers that grew heavier with each passing breath.

Recollection evaded him. Formal prayers fell from his tongue like lead. Eventually, he cried out, "O Lord, I need help. What did You lead me out here for? Was it You? Was it the enemy?"

The night did not respond; if anything, it thickened, pressing down upon his consciousness. Where had the voices gone? Why were they silent? The self-awareness that had come to him the night before now repeated itself: *Stripped before his eyes was the fundamental problem of his soul—he had been given everything and it did not suffice.* In the past the Lord had spoken to him through dreams, visions, interior locutions. He began to doubt them now. Was all of it the product of a tropical mythology planted within his subconscious? Was the dialogue merely an exchange between the hemispheres of the brain, the traffic between the bicameral mind? Was it intuition informing intellect, or the converse? Or was it pure imagination invested with a kind of magisterial authority by his beliefs? Was it no more than a set of ethics, a system of religious thought, a beautiful culture, blown away now by the winds of absolute reality? Was Smokrev right about castles and fairies? Maybe the only relief from a universe such as this was a choice between a deliberate leap into the abyss and a drive for power over what had not yet been sucked into it, sustaining for a time the illusion of freedom from the inexorable pull of gravity.

He no longer knew. And the unknowing increased his anxiety to the point that it began to rip through his chest, growing steadily worse until he wondered if the terror would reach pathological proportions. If it did not soon stop, psychotic fear would drive him to throw himself over the edge of a cliff long before his companions could search for him by daylight. He hoped that he was suffering a heart attack, and the possibility that he was dying cheered him for an instant, before the negations pressed in with renewed vigor.

He forced himself to think about everything he knew of the spiritual life, everything in his memory that gave evidence against the dark—but it was useless. Mysticism? Even to pretend to call this the dark night of the soul was an absurdity. To identify this abysmal nothingness, unrelieved by a flicker of consolation or certainty, or by the merest whiff of spiritual nobility, was so false a notion that to call it a parody of genuine spirituality was to be too kind. What was his name? Who was he: an Elijah without a raven; a David without a kingdom; a Professore Pastore scratching in the dirt of a thousand dead civilizations; a Dovidl spinning his dreydels on the parlor rug as the madman spins his fantasy with horrible logic; a bishop preaching his homilies to an empty cathedral—a hut constructed of stones that had fallen and risen, fallen and risen how many times, destroyed and recreated by the hands of man. Man? What was man? He was man, but what was this man-thing he pretended to call himself? A beggar, a hero-king, a sisyphus; a bird stuck on a thorn, its pierced heart palpitating in the cage of its ribs; a father potent with seed and self-inflicted sterility; a scribbler of plays with no beginning and no end, no hero and no villain—scribbling, scribbling as the train hauled him to the furnace; a painter, a poet, a huckster, a fool in the pigs' wallow of self-pity, a prodigal son spending the inheritance of his thousand kisses, running home to a father who did not exist? An angel, a satyr, a golem? None of these and all of them. He was man. Meaningless man. Meaningless, meaningless. Even the word *meaningless* was meaningless. He was nothing but a collation of mental and physical aches, a bag of foul memories that had managed to drag itself out of the fire of holocaust, surviving only by accident, leaving a smear of its egoism and its spiritual pride behind it like a snail's trail of putrefaction.

Ruth? Little one, my daughter? Anna? Severa? Pawel?

Empty words. Paper constructions, roaring up into the sky mixed with the oily smoke of burning human fat.

The ascent of Mount Carmel? This? He felt like vomiting at the thought of it. How could there be any life beyond the limitless expanse of corruption? To hope for life was to deepen the absurdity. Death, the permanent addiction. He longed to die, to escape the break-up of his mind. The heart attack was not happening quickly enough. But he lacked the courage to kill himself. If only he could get closer to a cliff, he might tip himself over into a freefall from which there was no return. Yes, he was capable of that at least—a sort of half-accident, half-suicide. A coward's self-obliteration. He tried to stand but his legs crumpled, and he fell back to the ground. He could no longer walk, but he could still crawl. Yes, he would drag his living corpse to the precipice and roll it over the edge as the final exercise of the logical illogic that had consumed his life.

He was a consciousness squashed beneath the flattened cosmos. But one dimension was left to him. He pulled his body along it. Through the compressed circles of a Hell that no longer existed, ring within ring, gyroscope within gyroscope, eternally trapped in the meaninglessness of the word *damned.*

He sought annihilation only. When he met it, he would gulp it down—no, he would throw himself into its mouth, and it would gulp him down.

Then he bumped his head against a rock and lost consciousness.

* * *

His broken head awoke him. There was gray light. There was smoke. There was dirt in his mouth and ash in his soul. At first he thought he was in Hell, for Hell might still exist if Heaven and Purgatory did not.

Beside his face there was a stone, and there was blood on it. He rolled over on his back and stared up at the ceiling of the universe, but it did not fall down to crush him.

He wondered why it did not.

He pulled his body upright and leaned against the stone. On the other side of it was a cliff falling a thousand feet toward the rocks by the sea.

The sea was still there, sighing.

A bird sang.

There were birds in the flattened universe.

Elijah spoke into the wind, for there was also wind in the flattened universe:

I have had enough.

God does not hear. He is silent.

The smoke of burning bodies goes up forever.

They stripped me naked and shaved the hair from my body and filmed me with cameras.

I fled from fear, and You led me into greater fear. But You were not there.

They were not content to kill the poetry, they threw the poet into the fire, and he too went up.

You were not there.

They were not content with killing men but tore a woman's body apart and cut out the living child. And they went up, mother and daughter, they went up into the place that does not exist.

Why were You not there?

Eli, Eli!

The fists rained down on old men who said their prayers and raised their hands to heaven.

And they too went up.

I could see them no more.

You were not there!

They tore the prayers of children from their little mouths. They ripped their limbs like dolls, and the last thing their screaming eyes saw as they were hurled into the pit were the laughing faces of strong men.

From the pit I cried to You, but You did not answer. You were not there!

They pierced our hands and our feet.

We were *rachmanim bnai rachmanim* — a compassionate people, the sons of compassionate people.

But You did not answer. And we did not go up.

Baruch dayan emet — God is the true Judge, we said.

The crime goes on without end, but the Judge and the trial are no more.

They numbered all our bones.

Out of the depths we cried to You.

They cast lots for our children's drawings and songs.

You did not answer. You have forsaken us.

We gave You our word and our life.

You let them humiliate our word. They took our life.

We grew to manhood searching the sky for signs.

But You sent no sign.

We pleaded and pleaded for You to come.

But You did not come.

The old man — the old, old man named Elijah — curled into a ball beside the rock.

"I am finished. I have had enough", he said to the rock. "You can kill me now. I am no better than my forefathers before me."

Then a hand touched his shoulder.

He did not believe in the hand.

It shook his shoulder.

"Get up."

He opened his eyes and uncurled his body. He rolled over onto his back. Across from him, standing beneath a broom tree, was the boy.

The sunrise shot through the mist swirling around him, mingling with the smoke of a cookfire. His clothes dazzling white. His face blazing with amber light.

"Arise and eat."

Elijah looked, and behold there was at his head a cake baked on hot stones and a jar of water.

And the boy said a second time, "Arise and eat, else the journey will be too long for you."

Elijah arose and ate and drank.

"Why did you leave me?" he croaked.

"I did not leave you."

"I was alone."

"You were not alone."

"I was afraid."

"You were in great fear where no fear was."

"Why did you not protect me?"

"The darkest place is where I will give a great light."

"You could have stopped it."

"If I had stopped it, there would be no harvest."

"I understand nothing."

"That is true. You understand nothing."

"Are you the Lord?"

"I am a servant like you."

"Who are you?"

"Who is like God? There is none like God!"

"Who are you?"

"Who is like God? There is none like God! — That is my name."

"I am finished. Leave me. I want to die."

"You are exhausted. Long ago, you accepted this labor and this burden. Have you forgotten?"

"I do not remember."

"Your soul remembers. Within your soul is the mark of your covenant."

"I know nothing."

"You know nothing, but you have obeyed."

"I want to die."

"Now we can begin."

* * *

The boy led him into the desert. A night and a day they walked, and as long as Elijah followed without questioning, he did not grow weary or hungry, though his heart was a dying thing within him, his mind emptiness, his flesh a vessel carrying an ember.

On the third morning, they came to a cave.

The boy pointed inside.

"Here you will rest. I will go away from your eyes, but I am with you, and your angel is with you also. Fear nothing. What has come upon you will bear fruit in many lives."

Elijah sat inside the mouth of the cave and closed his eyes.

When he opened them again, night had come and thunder boiled up out of the east. Rain fell. Lightning flashed but the voice of the Lord was not in it.

Fire burned wild in the valley below him, but the Lord was not in it.

A mighty wind tore up bushes and trees, but the Lord was not in it.

An earthquake shook the roots of the mountains, but the Lord was not in it.

On the thirty-seventh day, the boy returned and stayed with him.

He made the sign of the cross over the forehead of Elijah, and strength came into him.

"Your mission is near its end, but the greater part awaits you."

On the thirty-eighth day, the boy said to him, "The storm did not destroy you. Neither the fire nor the lightning nor the earthquake destroyed you."

On the thirty-ninth day, a gentle breeze blew from the south.

"Come out of the cave", said the boy.

Elijah went out of the cave saying nothing. He covered his face with his hands.

"Why do you cover your face?"

"Who can see God and live?"

The breeze blew gently upon him, and the Lord was in it.

"Look up."

He uncovered his eyes, and behold, the morning sky was suddenly blackness and the sign of the Son of Man was emblazoned upon it with light streaming from the holes of the wounds.

"This is a vision of what is not yet, but is soon to be. On that day, every human creature will see his soul stripped bare before his eyes. Then he must choose. You are to give witness for me against the Man of Sin who seeks to set himself in my house, to usurp the throne of God."

Then Elijah raised his arms and cried out, and the sky returned to normal. He looked around, and the boy was gone from his eyes. Then putting one foot after another, he walked back toward the place from which he had come.

*　*　*

On the morning after Elijah's disappearance, a boy had appeared at the door of the hut and informed the two others that Elijah would return in forty days. He instructed the prior to go to the Christian village to say Mass and to hear confessions during Elijah's absence. He departed without a word of explanation.

Too stunned to say anything, the prior and the brother stared at the empty doorway as if they had seen an apparition. They obeyed the instructions, and forty days later, Elijah returned.

Of his absence little can be said because little is known of it. Later, he would speak of it in vague terms, never able to articulate its true shape. The commerce of ordinary language had no equipment to convey what he had seen. Much of it had occurred in his soul, and could not be transferred to the mind of another. The language of mysticism and poetry approximated it, but fell short, pointing only in the general direction of the experience. Whenever a metaphor or a simile presented itself, he employed it in his attempts at explanation, but the prior and the small one could never quite grasp his meaning. The small one focused on the bare facts of the narrative, and the prior tended to abstract it into theology. In the end, they both misunderstood. They knew only that he had gone away into the desert and lived in a cave and had received something from God.

Now Elijah needed few hours of sleep each night. While the others snored, he rested, reading Scripture by the light of a lantern, pondering, praying, waiting.

Obedience, the angel had said.

Simplicity.

Unknowing.

These were his only wealth. These were the foundation. His mind was no longer preoccupied with questions, anxieties, intellectual deliberations. The physical tasks of sawing firewood, sweeping, laying the stones of the oratory one upon another were actions of great sweetness to him.

Not content with giving him visions, the Lord sent dreams. On the third night following his return, he dreamed of a gathering in a large modern city.

Many bishops of the world were celebrating a liturgy on a splendid altar, but the altar was not in a church; it was on a raised dais in the center of a congress hall. Hundreds of prelates were there, surrounded by countless priests and lay people. All were clothed in costly garments. The sacred vessels were richly ornamented. The main celebrant opened his mouth, and a star burst through the floor and went into him, and from out of his mouth, there issued a shining darkness. The crowd listened, and clapped, and rejoiced at the words coming from his mouth, and from their mouths there rose a tumult of praise for him. But among them, there were some who fell silent, for they did not approve of the words. They were a minority and could speak nothing against it.

The celebrant raised a black star above the crowd, and the crowd joined hands and danced in circles around it.

"We will build the city of Man," they sang, "and turn our night into day."

No, cried Elijah, *no!* He tried to tell them that they were deceived, but they could not hear him.

Those who had not approved of the shining darkness looked at him, straining to hear him, but they caught only a few of his words and looked back at the star, or at their feet, not knowing what to think.

"Look up!" he wailed. But they would not look up.

Then a hammering came upon the doors. Men dressed in black, wearing masks, bearing automatic weapons, came into the hall. They pointed their weapons at the prelates and fired. Bursts of flame tore into bishops and priests and laity, and they fell. Singing became screaming. People stampeded in all directions, but the doors were sealed. The gunmen sprayed the crowd until the room was a heap of silent bodies floating in blood. Then Elijah was taken away from that place, and he awoke.

On the following night, he dreamed of a violent storm. Like a shepherd, he was guiding a flock of children through a gloomy wasteland. He was disheartened by the enormity of his task.

Look up, said a voice.

He looked up and saw a distant city in the sky. It had twelve gates, and upon its battlements, ten thousand times ten thousand people were waving and cheering, urging him to enter. He was some distance from the main gate, moving toward it slowly, for the crowd of children was crying, confused, and frightened, and he was hard-pressed to keep them from scattering into the dark. He was forced to slow his pace so that the smallest of them would not fall behind and be lost. Behind was the world and a storm rising to a fury, the wind howling, boiling into black clouds, lightning flashing, and in it a red eye seeking the children to devour them. The slowness of their flight toward sanctuary was at first a torment, but an angel came out from the gates and flew around the little flock with a golden string, girding them and guiding them on. He awoke as they reached the gate.

On the following night, he saw a boy staggering around the blasted heaps of bombed ruins. He was naked, save for a *tallis* with which he wrapped his loins. He was weeping in agony for the loss of all that was true and beautiful and good in the world. *Everything is lost,* he cried, *everything.* He passed men and women who stopped and laughed at his nakedness.

"Repent!" he shouted at them.

"Repent of what?" they mocked.

"The fire is coming", he said.

"Look around", they answered. "There is no fire. We have defeated the fire."

"All is normal", said another.

"All is not normal", said the boy.

"Peace", they shouted. "Peace!"

"There is no peace!" said the boy.

They threw rocks at him, and he ran away. He fell and got up, fell again and crawled, cutting himself on broken glass. Through the ruins, he went on hands and knees until he came to the edge of a bomb crater. In the bottom of the crater was a priest, saying Mass on a cardboard box lit by stubs of candles. His chalice was a tin cup, and his paten was a broken plate. The priest was the Pope, assisted by three bishops. Thirty or forty lay people knelt around the altar, dressed in rags. They were worshipping the Host the Pope lifted up. Its light was dazzling, and it pushed back the darkness for the space of two hours, and another hour, and a half-hour. The people worshipped, but they were frightened. The Pope prayed, but his face streamed with tears.

Look up, said a voice.

The boy in the tallis looked up, and there in the sky, hovering just above the Pope, was the woman clothed with the sun, and upon her head was a crown of twelve stars. She looked down with great love upon the huddled group in the crater. And around her were the saints.

586

Among them, he recognized many who were beloved by him: John of Avila with his cross, David with his harp, Maximilian of Auschwitz with his two crowns, Beatus of Liébana with his quill and parchment, Maius with his puns and paint, Severa with her dove, and a strange old man carrying a raven. The old man glanced at the boy in the *tallis*, and smiled.

Behind the company of saints, he saw another choir of men and women singing and praising God, and among them was Billy and Matteo and an old woman with a string bag. Behind them stood yet another company of white-robed figures, and among them was a young woman cradling a little girl in her arms. The child raised her arms to him and smiled. Beside the woman was another, and in her hands she held a scale to weigh the judges of the earth. Beside her was a man who held an icon high above his head.

"Who are these people?" said the boy in the tallis.

You should know, said the voice.

"Where have they come from?"

These are the ones who have passed through the great trial. They have washed their robes and made them white in the blood of the Lamb.

Then the woman with the child, and the woman with the scales, and the man with the icon looked at him and smiled.

And he awoke.

* * *

On August fifteenth, Elijah went with Brother Ass to the village. After Mass, there was a wedding and baptism to perform. When everyone had gone home, Mrs. Cohen served them tea and a meal in her kitchen behind the store. Generous by nature, but jealous of her reputation as a curmudgeon, she could not resist the urge to extract payment of a kind: she nattered and gossiped and scolded them about their shoddy apparel. She turned on the radio while they ate and kept up a stream of commentary about the news.

"I don't know what all the hoopla's about", she grumbled. "So he's doing big things! So what! Anybody with millions of dollars can do big things. I don't trust him."

"Why not?" said Elijah.

"Just a feeling", she said towering over her stove like an autocrat. "Look at that! Finished already, Father? You men don't eat right, living out there in the desert. Here, have some more!"

Ignoring his protests, she dumped a heap of fried corn, rice, and chopped goat meat onto his plate. She did the same to Brother Ass's plate.

"I mean, all this nonsense about him being the only one who can pull the world together! I've heard it all before."

"You have?"

"Well, not from the horse's mouth, mind you. I was only six when we left Germany. We went on a ship and got to Istanbul just before the War broke out. I don't remember anything much about those years. But when we were growing up Mamma and Pappa told us a lot about Hitler, the way everybody thought he was going to save Europe. How could they be so stupid, I ask you?"

"It is easy to be wise by hindsight."

"I guess you're right. Still, he walked like a wolf, growled like a wolf, and in the end, he was a wolf. How come everybody was so surprised?"

"The President doesn't growl in public."

"Of course not. He's a nice man, isn't he. But just you watch, as soon as he's got everybody in his pocket, he's going to start growling."

She fussed over her pans moodily and then slapped her head.

"Oi! I forgot! There's a message for you. My brother-in-law's driving down from Smyrna this afternoon, and he's bringing a visitor. You mind waiting?"

Shortly after three o'clock, a rusting Chevrolet rumbled into the yard, raising clouds of dust. A short fat man got out of the driver's side and gave Mrs. Cohen a kiss. From the passenger side, a slender man got out and calmly surveyed the scene. He was dressed in the clothes of the working class of the region. His hair was white and his eyes thoughtful. When he saw Elijah coming out onto the front porch of the store he beamed and went up to him. The two men embraced.

"Eminence, I am very glad to see you."

"I am happy to see you also."

"Will you stay with us?"

"A day or two. Mr. Cohen will come back on Wednesday to pick me up. I will try to go on to Israel. I have messages for the Patriarch of Jerusalem."

"An arduous way to send a message."

"We are having trouble getting messages through by normal channels. The Holy Father has asked me to hand-deliver it."

"You couldn't fly?"

"Italy and Israel have been stalling us with paperwork. We can't wait any longer for a visa. Delays, endless delays. It's a ruse, of course. No one wants us in Israel when the President arrives next month."

"Eminence, it's a long trek to our house. Two hours over rough ground. Do you think you can do it?"

"I can do it", he said removing a large knapsack from the car. "Let's go."

After making their farewells with the Cohens, they went off in the direction of the hills.

Father Prior, Brother Ass, *Dottrina,* and Elijah talked far into the night. Elijah learned that Don Matteo had died of pneumonia during the winter. *Stato* was alive, but his heart was damaged, and he had accepted retirement. Cardinal Vettore came no more to the Vatican, but he was very active. He was back and forth across the world addressing national bishops' conferences, giving interviews that spoke of a new age for the national churches, publishing articles, making friends.

"I don't know how he does it?" said *Dottrina*. "All doors seem to open for him, but for us every door is shut."

"You mentioned a breakdown in communications", said Elijah.

"The ties between the See of Peter and the local churches are being severed one by one. The universal Church is in disarray. The press is full of news about the divisions. Bishops against bishops, cardinals against cardinals. Efforts to rally the faithful behind the Pope have had almost no success. Our people don't read; they don't think! The few Catholic journals that remain orthodox are isolated and dismissed as hidebound reactionaries. The security of mail and telephone is proving unreliable. The computer net is also compromised, and the Vatican has recently been denied a license renewal for its satellite channel."

"They are strangling us slowly", said the prior.

"Not so slowly", said *Dottrina*. "They are going as fast as they possibly can without making the public nervous."

"What are our adversaries trying to do?" said Elijah.

"They want the world to think that we say nothing because we have nothing left to say. We have short-wave radio, but there has been some jamming by unknown sources. Radio pirates, probably."

"You would think we are at war!" said the prior.

"We are at war", said Elijah.

"It's the strangest situation", said *Dottrina*. "All these outrageous things are being done to us, but not a hint of it gets into the media. Everyone thinks things are normal."

"What is the Holy Father going to do?"

"What can he do? He speaks and speaks, but even when some of his words reach the people, they hardly listen."

"How is his health?"

"Not so good as last year, but you know his indomitable spirit. I have tried to get him to consider some contingency plans in case there is an attack on Vatican City."

"Do you really think it would come to that?"

"Not for the present. The semblance of normality is essential to the plans of our adversary. He will strike in private and only when there are few left who support us."

"Who would strike the Pope?" said the prior. "Surely you don't mean physical violence?"

The cardinal raised his eyebrows. "Perhaps not. But we can no longer be sure of anything in the human scheme of things. They have already arrested some of our people on trumped-up charges, some for personal sins, some for political. I don't know who is next. A noose is slowly tightening around us, and I am sure the ultimate objective is the Vatican."

"If it comes to that, will you urge the Holy Father to go to a safe place?"

"I have suggested Switzerland. Possibly Australia, but like so many countries, the Church there is riddled with compromise, and I don't know of more than a handful of bishops who would welcome him."

"America?"

"That would seem more likely. However, the Church is bitterly deadlocked there, and the president of the United States is one of our enemy's strongest supporters. That is beside the point. The Holy Father will never leave Rome."

"Not even for the sake of preserving the chair of Peter?"

"He believes it would be best preserved by offering his life for it."

"Martyrdom?"

"He is convinced it is the path the Lord has chosen for him, and he refuses to avoid it."

"We have to pray for him!" piped up Brother Ass, speaking for the first time. The three priests looked at him. They saw what an effort it had cost him to open his mouth.

"You are right, Brother", said the cardinal.

They bowed their heads, and *Dottrina* led them in prayers for the safety of the Pope. When he was finished, he got up and cleared the table of its coffee cups, went over to a tub on a bench, and began to wash the dishes. Brother Ass started as if he were witnessing a shocking act.

"Please, your Eminent, I mean your Oliness, I mean cardinal—you can't do that!"

"Why can't I, Brother?"

"Because . . . because, it's *my* job!"

"You mean I took it without permission?"

"Yes—No! I didn't mean that!"

"Brother, would you please allow me to wash the dishes?"

"No, sir! I mean yes! Er . . . no!"

The prior suppressed his amusement, and the cardinal humbly turned over the washcloth to Brother Ass, who looked confused, wondering how to extricate himself from an impossible situation.

Elijah said, "Brother, can I borrow the cardinal for a moment? I would like to show him the oratory."

Brother Ass nodded emphatically and turned to the dishes with a red face.

Elijah and *Dottrina* went outside and around the end of the building, stepping over the low foundation wall into the oratory. It was open to the sky, illuminated by a full moon.

"I'm sorry. I didn't mean to embarrass him."

"He will recover quickly", said Elijah.

"Why did you want to speak with me alone?"

"I need your discernment about a problem. But first I must tell you of something the Lord did to me."

Using spare language, Elijah related what had happened during the forty days in the wilderness. When he was finished, the cardinal did not speak for a time.

"The experience is biblical", he said eventually.

"I don't know why it has happened, or what is going to happen next. At least not the details. I know only that the Lord has called me to Jerusalem to bear witness against the adversary."

"Then you must go."

"That much is clear. But how will I get there? What shall I say?"

"Your task is to obey. The words will be given to you."

"Should I go by myself? I fear to bring my two companions into danger."

"I'm not sure. Perhaps you could travel with me."

"Do you have the necessary papers to get across the frontiers?"

"Enough to take me as far as Jordan. From there, friends are going to obtain a permit for my passage into Israel."

"I might handicap you. I'm still a wanted man."

"We could go together as far as Amman, and from there you would have to play it by ear."

They left the matter unsettled, went in to the hut, and slept.

* * *

After breakfast they hiked up the mountain. The three companions would not tell the cardinal where they were taking him. Brother Ass especially delighted in the joke, and when they reached the ancient road, he could not stop himself from rushing on ahead, leaping from one pile of rubble to another. Every so often he would stop and wait for them to catch up. He abandoned every scrap of deference he had felt for the visiting dignitary on the previous day, calling, "Come on, Your Honor!" whenever they lagged behind.

"Slow down, Brother", retorted the prior. "Have a little mercy. We are old men!"

By the time they reached the entrance to the cave, the small one had already gone in. They found him sitting against the back wall, smiling ecstatically, tears running from his good eye.

"What is this place?" said the cardinal.

No one answered him.

He looked about the chamber, then slowly sank to his knees. He breathed a loud sigh.

"*Theotokos*", he said.

They remained in the cave for several hours. No words were spoken. Light filled them. Strength came into them. The four men raised their arms simultaneously and began to sing and praise God.

Their arms did not grow weary.

Joy came into them.

Song poured like a river from their mouths.

Tears like an oil of gladness streamed from their eyes.

When the beam of the setting sun crept into the entrance, Brother Ass lay down and fell asleep. The current of divine sweetness faded gently and then ceased, leaving the three priests enveloped in peace. Eventually the cardinal looked down at the sleeping form of the brother.

"You call him Brother Ass", he said. "A strange name. Does he like it?"

"As long as I have known him," said the prior, "that is the name he has wanted."

"What is his name in religion?"

"I can't remember for sure. I think on the day of his profession he was given the name Brother Enoch."

"Shouldn't we call him by his right name?" said the cardinal.

"If you think so, but he wouldn't like it."

"Perhaps", said the cardinal pensively.

At that point, the small one gave a sharp cry and sat up. He held a hand over his bad eye.

"What is the matter, Brother?" said Elijah.

"It's burning, it's burning!"

Elijah knelt beside him and pulled the hand away from the eye. The gnarled scar tissue, ordinarily white, was now inflamed.

Brother Ass grabbed Elijah's right hand and thrust the palm against his bad eye. Elijah tried to pull away, but the brother would not let him. The scar in his palm grew hot. He could feel its shape, the cross, like a burning.

594

"What is it? Is he all right?" said the prior.

"Leave them", said the cardinal.

Then the brother's grip loosened, and he lay back. Elijah's palm no longer hurt, though the mark of the burn was still livid upon it.

"Open your eyes", he said.

The brother opened both of his eyes. The bad one blinked and watered.

"I can see", he gasped. "With both my eyes. I can see!"

*   *   *

On a fine September morning, two men walked out of the wilderness of Moab, in the east, and crossed over the Jordan at the Hajalah ford. No one saw them, and on the Israeli side of the border, no one stopped to ask for their papers. From there, they struck south across the countryside until they came to a paved road. They turned west and walked throughout the remainder of the day, stopping only to drink from their water bottles and to eat a handful of figs and dates. Cars and transport trucks and vehicles of war passed by them, going in both directions.

In the early evening, they came to a junction where the road joined a highway along which heavy traffic was passing to and fro. An hour later, they came up over a rise and Jerusalem lay before them.

They stopped and unslung their packs. They raised their hands in the *orans* position. The elder, an old man with white hair, cried out:

We praise You, Lord God Almighty,
for You have brought us out of the wasteland.
We praise You, for You have hidden great things from the mighty,
and the lowly You have raised up.
Now do Your enemies make war upon Your servants,
and now do Your servants glorify You in the midst of great
    tribulation!

Upon the palm of his right hand was a cross, burning in the light of the red sky.

"Salvation and glory and honor belong to You alone, O Lord!" cried the younger one, in whose eyes was Jerusalem the golden.

> You are the Alpha and Omega,
> the First and Last,
> the Morning Star shining bright.
> The Spirit and the Bride say "Come!"
> Be with us now as we face our foe,
> that we might stand firm,
> and strengthen the things which remain.

Thus did Enoch and Elijah go down into the city, while above them, a jet banked and began its descent to the airport by the sea.

And I took the little scroll from the hand of the angel and ate it; it was sweet as honey in my mouth, but when I had eaten it my stomach was made bitter. And I was told, "You must again prophesy about many peoples and nations and tongues and kings."

Then I was given a measuring rod like a staff, and I was told: "Rise and measure the temple of God and the altar and those who worship there, but do not measure the court outside the temple; leave that out, for it is given over to the nations, and they will trample over the holy city for forty-two months. And I will grant my two witnesses power to prophesy for one thousand two hundred and sixty days, clothed in sackcloth."

These are the two olive trees and the two lampstands which stand before the Lord of the earth. And if any one would harm them, fire pours from their mouth and consumes their foes; if any one would harm them, thus he is doomed to be killed. They have power to shut the sky, that no rain may fall during the days of their prophesying, and they have power over the waters to turn them into blood, and to smite the earth with every plague, as often as they desire. And when they have finished their testimony, the beast that ascends from the bottomless pit will make war upon them and conquer them and kill them, and their dead bodies will lie in the street of the great city, which is allegorically called Sodom and Egypt, where their Lord was crucified. For three days and a half men from the peoples and tribes and tongues and nations gaze at their dead bodies and refuse to let them be placed in a tomb, and those who dwell on the earth will rejoice over them and make merry and exchange presents, because these two prophets had been a torment to those who dwell on the earth. But after the three and a half days a breath of life from God entered them and they stood up on their feet, and great fear fell on those who saw them. Then they heard a loud voice from heaven saying to them, "Come up hither!" And in the sight of their foes they went up to heaven in a cloud. And at that hour there was a great earthquake, and a tenth of the city fell; seven thousand people were killed in the earthquake, and the rest were terrified and gave glory to the God of heaven.

(Revelation 10:10–11:13)

597

Novels by Michael O'Brien in the series,
Children of the Last Days:

* *A Cry of Stone*
* *Strangers and Sojourners*
* *Plague Journal*
* *Eclipse of the Sun*
* *Sophia House*
Father Elijah

*Asterisk indicates book is not yet published, but forthcoming.

(35 lines × 10 = 350 WPP)
600 PP's
350 WPP
210,000 words